WILD AND FREE

A Wild Bluffs Novel

Emma Kate

PUBLISHING

Flirtation Point Publishing
Emma Kate
www.authoremmakate.com

Cover Design by Emily Wittig
Editing by Kelly Siskind
Copy Editing by Claudette Cruz, the Editing Sweetheart
Proofreading by Judy's Proofreading

Ebook ISBN: 979-8-9908678-5-7
Discreet Cover Paperback ISBN: 979-8-9908678-6-4

Contents

To all those who have experienced the loss of a loved one's memory, constantly mourning the pieces as they fade away, thankful each day the physical body hasn't decided to follow. And to the friends, family members, medical professionals, and caregivers who offer love, patience, and support throughout the journey.

***

Welcome back to Wild Bluffs.

Prologue

Carter

High School

"She's not my type," I mutter to my friend Jaxon. We're sitting at one of the booths in the back of the diner my mom works at, grabbing a quick dinner following baseball practice.

"Right, because hot, athletic, and smart is repulsive to all guys," Jaxon replies with a mock shiver. "Kelsey Harper? Ew."

"We grew up together. She's basically my sister," I say, ignoring his annoyingly sarcastic assessment.

I'm not lying. At one point in my life, Kelsey was just another one of the kids I've known since before I can remember. The one I'd been in classes with since I was five. It's how it works when you're in a small town and you've gone to school with the same fifty kids since preschool.

Until it wasn't.

I'm not exactly sure when it happened because, unlike in the movies, there was no fall, no big explosion that happened in my heart or mind. My feelings for her slowly changed. At first, I thought she was cute—that was around the time my adolescent brain stopped sending signals to my mouth whenever I tried to talk to her. It was about eighth grade when I realized Kelsey was really smart and surprisingly witty. Then, during our freshman year, I realized she was beautiful. But it has never been more than an innocent crush, a hint of feelings I will never act on. I won't be one of those people who gets held back by a teenage relationship—not after seeing what it did to my mom.

"Right." Jaxon shoots me a skeptical look at my blatant lie. "I lose my ability to talk around all my sisters too."

"You don't have any sisters," I remind him. "And anyway, I can talk around Kelsey. I do it all the time. We're in basically every class together."

Which is a bit of a problem because I spend more time watching Kelsey as she twirls that strand of hair from the back of her neck around her finger than I do focusing on what I'm supposed to be learning. Luckily, by May of senior year, everyone has given up on teaching us anything.

Jaxon, not one to be deterred, grins at me. He's chewing a mouthful of fries, not at all bothered by the ketchup on his cheek. "You should ask her out."

"No," I say gruffly. I can't say I haven't thought about it lately, but it doesn't make sense. Unlike Jaxon, who still has two years left in Wild Bluffs, Kelsey and I are both leaving soon. Graduation is in two weeks, and I'm finally out of here to chase my dreams of college and a career far, far away from this little town.

"Why not?" Jaxon presses.

"Even if I had feelings for her, which I'm not saying I do, everyone knows high school relationships don't work out. How many people do you know who "are going to be together forever" and then go to college, realize there are other fish in the sea, and then break up? Within months?"

"Doesn't mean that's what will happen to you. I've seen the way you stare at her practically every time she's around."

I feel warmth trying to spread to my cheeks. I can't deny it. Every time Kelsey walks into a room, there's a shift in the air. She's not just the smartest, hottest girl I know; she's got this strength about her that pulls you in whether you want it to or not. And as much as my body thinks it wants to, my brain is adamantly in the this-is-a-bad-idea camp. Kelsey and I both have too many things pulling us away from each other for it to ever work.

"Whatever," I say in response to Jaxon's claim. "I'm not asking Kelsey out."

Jaxon shrugs, tapping his fingers on the table like drumsticks. "Your loss."

Before I can respond, the door to the diner opens, and I don't need to look up to know who it is. The air turns electric around me.

Jaxon kicks my shin under the table, as if I might've missed the fact that Kelsey is part of the group who just walked in. I shoot Jaxon a glare as the girls take the booth farthest away from ours. Jaxon laughs, calling out a hello to Kelsey's sister Izzy—who also happens to be his best friend—when she spots us. She grins back, waving.

Kelsey walks up to the counter, a soft smile curling on her lips as she catches Jaxon's excited hello to her sister. The early-summer light hits her hair through the window, making it glow like a halo of white gold. Her eyes, always alight with an ice so cold it burns, scan the room, landing on me for just a split second, holding my gaze for all of a breath. My world shifts off-center.

She turns away, completely oblivious to the fact that I'm still staring at her.

Jaxon's shit-eating grin suggests he's very aware of it.

"Why don't you focus on your own Harper sister?" I tease.

"Dude. You know it's not like that. Iz is my best friend."

"Sure," I say, never quite positive if that's true or if it's just that neither of them wants to risk what they have for something more.

A group of men my mom's age come in, taking all five seats at the counter, talking loudly enough to suggest they must've hit up one of the bars in town as it opened before heading this way for their food.

I start giving Jaxon my scouting report on the first team we'll be playing at the baseball state championship tournament next weekend—making sure my catcher is ready for all the key hitters we're going to see. I lose myself in the analysis, no longer surprised by Jaxon's keen insights and ability to see hitters' weaknesses after watching one or two at bats.

Suddenly, I'm pulled away from our conversation by silence in the building. The kind of silence that suggests something major just happened. Jaxon and I share a glance, both uneasy by the shift in the room.

Kelsey's voice rises, but not in anger—just a calm authority that no eighteen-year-old should have.

I'm not sure when Kelsey went back up to the counter, but suddenly, she's there, leaning between my mom and one of the men.

"What did you just say to her?" she asks, her tone cool, her words sharp. "Do you know how disrespectful that term is?"

I start to stand, but Jaxon shakes his head, mouthing *bad idea*. I know he's right—if I go insert myself into the mess, the men are far more likely to do something we'll all regret.

Seeing my movement, my mom's eyes flash to me, warning me to stay away before she says something quietly to Kelsey and the man.

My mother, always the one to smile and nod through everything, is obviously trying to keep the peace. Kelsey, though? She doesn't back down. She stands there with a fire in her eyes, her shoulders squared, completely unafraid.

"It's not okay, Alice. Even if you did get the order wrong—which I highly doubt—he can't call you that." She turns and looks the man directly in the eye as she says it again. "That's not okay."

The man looks thrown off by a petite high school girl standing up to him. He stammers, trying to come up with some response, but Kelsey doesn't give him a chance. She keeps going, shutting him down with words that are pure steel.

I'm just sitting there, unable to tear my eyes away. Not because I'm surprised—because I'm not—but because I've never seen someone stand up for my mom like that. No one ever does. She's spent her whole life taking shit from people, thinking she deserved to be called names to her face and behind her back because she made one bad decision eighteen years ago. I've never really seen anyone else go to bat for her.

And Kelsey Harper? She just did. Without hesitation.

The guy doesn't know what to say. He stumbles out an apology and tosses some money to his friends before stumbling out of the restaurant.

My mom brings Kelsey a full cup of water, and Kelsey flashes a smile that's so effortlessly genuine, it makes my chest tighten.

"Are you okay, Alice?" Kelsey asks, her voice still the only one loud enough to hear across any room.

My mom nods, her lips pressed tight. "I'm fine, Kelsey. Thank you."

I watch Kelsey as she walks back to her table, her short track shorts pulling along the curve of her muscled thigh with each step. Her sisters and their friends immediately start talking the minute she sits down, and I can tell from across the room she's already annoyed with their questions.

"Not interested, huh?" Jaxon says, pulling me from my one-sided staring contest.

"No." *Yes. One thousand times yes.*

Jaxon snorts. "Sure. I definitely believe it now after watching you stare at her for two minutes without blinking."

"It doesn't matter if I like her or not, Jaxon. She managed to get into a military academy, and I got into my dream school with an ROTC scholarship. There is no possible outcome that ends with us together."

"Maybe someday," he offers, his smile gentle. Jaxon has always been a romantic at heart, setting up people in school he knows like each other and asking his prom date out with an elaborate song he wrote for her. He would believe there is some way Kelsey and I will magically end up together in the end. Unfortunately for him, I plan to leave this town and never look back—to live my life wild and free.

I shake my head. "Nah, man. There's no future for us."

CHAPTER ONE

Kelsey

Present Day: October

"This is only *the most* important contract of my life, but you're right, I'll try to have *fun* at the meeting. Thanks, Iz." I hang up on my sister and push through the doors leading into the commercial building on the east side of Denver. Hearing a footstep on the tiled floor behind me, I slow down, realizing my account manager is here with me.

"Sorry," I say to Lila. "I'm not used to bringing someone with me to these client meetings."

"That's okay. So you think we got the contract?" Lila asks for the fourth time since we left Wild Bluffs this morning.

I peer into the reception area of the meeting room rental company, taking note of the empty seats before giving her the same answer I gave her three times as we carpooled here. "Most people don't make you drive three hours just to let you know you didn't get the job. It'd be a pretty dick move. Though most people don't make you meet with them after the interviews, but before awarding you with the contract, either. So I guess I don't know. Our proposal was good regardless."

I walk up to the woman bent over her computer, forcing myself not to raise an eyebrow at the sight of her shoeless feet curled up under her on her office chair. When I realize she's not going to acknowledge my presence, I clear my throat.

"Excuse me, I'm Kelsey Harper, here for a meeting with SevenFour Entertainment."

She clicks a few buttons on her computer before saying, "Room 4. It's the one all the way to the end of the hall."

"Well, I guess that answers the question about whether Jaxon Steele will be here. No way a twenty-something female had that man walk past her within the last hour and isn't still hyperventilating," Lila observes as we walk down the hallway.

"You're a twenty-something female," I remind her.

"I know. That's why I said it with such confidence. I'm going to absolutely lose my shit the first time I see Jaxon Steele in the flesh. His music, his body, his—"

"Lila," I say, stopping us both in our tracks. "You cannot, *will not*, lose your shit when you see Jaxon Steele. You are here representing our company, and I will kick you to the curb—future relative or not—if you show one ounce of anything other than professionalism during these meetings. You are the most put-together twenty-four-year-old I know, *and* you're dating a professional golfer who most women react to in a similar manner. *And* your brother is a professional golfer. Get it together."

It's at that point I notice the corner of her mouth quivering, trying not to break into a smile.

"Was it Bryn or Izzy who put you up to this?" I ask.

"JT." Lila releases the hold on her smile, and it blossoms across her face. "He bet me I couldn't get you to threaten to fire me before the meeting. He thought you'd be too focused to throw around idle threats. And you know Bryn would be pissed at you for suggesting we're related when they aren't even engaged."

I shake my head as we continue down the hall toward the meeting space. We're almost thirty minutes early, but I didn't want to risk getting caught in traffic.

As we walk into the empty meeting room, I relax enough to smile back at Lila. "And do I even want to know what you won from the asshole who apparently has far too much faith in me?"

"Let's just say it'd definitely be classified as back-nine behavior."

"I hate that I know what that means," I say as I take a seat on the far side of the table. Seating arrangements are always harder to navigate when the person hosting the meeting isn't there first to establish where they want to be. Sitting at the head of the table would be too aggressive of a power move, but sitting in the middle makes me seem weak and indecisive. I opt for the seat to the left of the head of the table. Not only is it asserting myself as the second most important person in the room, but it also gives me the benefit of being able to see the door.

Lila sits down next to me, pulling out four copies of our proposal and a few KH Security pens from her bag. I grab a copy of the proposal and flip through it, though I likely have the entire thing memorized at this point.

"OH MY GOD!" A high-pitched scream comes from somewhere in the building.

"I guess Jaxon is coming," Lila deadpans, slowly perusing the proposal in front of her.

I shoot her a warning glare, which she pretends not to notice, though the corner of her mouth gives her away again.

The door to the meeting space is opened shortly after, and Lila and I both stand as two men walk into the room. Jaxon is tall, well over six feet, with chestnut-brown hair and equally dark eyes. The man with him is dwarfed in comparison, though the gray streaks in his hair give him an air of authority. Given that he's only forty-five, I have a theory that he adds them in to make himself seem more refined.

I walk around the table and meet them, extending my hand to Henry, Jaxon's manager, who I met during the interviews a few months ago.

"Hello, Kelsey," he says, shaking my hand.

"So good to see you again," I say with a smile. "Let me introduce you to Lila Walker, my lead project manager on this proposal."

I leave Lila to meet Henry and join Jaxon.

"Long time no see, Jax."

"Hey, Kelsey," he replies, pulling me into a friendly hug. "How's...everyone?"

I catch the slight hesitation in his question and know he considered asking about my sister Izzy, his once best friend, but if he's not going to bring her up, neither am I. "Good. Everyone's doing really well."

"That's great. I appreciate you taking the time to drive up here to meet with us. Henry felt we should have this conversation in person."

My stomach tightens at the statement, but I force a smile to my face and nod. I won't let a potential client see me looking concerned. Even if said client is a famous musician who once spent hours every weekend playing GuitarStar with my sister.

"Not a problem. It's an easy drive in from Wild Bluffs."

"Right."

Though I understand the value of small talk and forging interpersonal connections with clients or potential clients, I'd really like to see what this meeting is about. Hoping everyone will follow my lead, I head back to the table and sit down in my seat, now directly across from Jaxon.

"I know we're still a little early, but shall we begin?" I ask.

"We're waiting for a few more people," Henry replies as he takes the seat at the head of the table.

"Oh," I say, choosing not to ask who else is joining us.

We talk about the weather and a storm that passed through Jaxon's home in Nashville for a few minutes before finally, the door is opened again.

Two large men stalk through the door, their black polos pulling across their chests to show off the Mitchell Security logos on their left pecs. I know if I look in the parking lot, I'll find a matching black pickup with the white logo gleaming in the sun. The half brothers are opposites in every way except for the hulking frames they inherited from their asshole of a father.

My stomach churns at the arrival of the other security firm in Wild Bluffs, the twinge of unease from Jaxon's comment earlier growing into a full-blown case of heartburn.

"What a pleasant surprise," Trent Mitchell says as he takes in Lila and me standing to welcome them. "I wasn't aware we were going to be joined by anyone else today."

"Hi, Trent," I reply. "Carter." I nod my head toward the second man, the dark and broody to Trent's blond, used-car-salesman vibes.

Carter's dark eyes snap to mine, and he nods back, experience telling me that's all I'll get from the man. Even though we've known each other since preschool, I've always felt like I had to physically pull each and every syllable from his mouth.

We all shake hands, circling the table before finally taking our seats, Trent sitting next to Jaxon with Carter on his other side.

"Sorry for springing this joint meeting on you all," Henry says. "But after careful consideration of the proposals submitted and interviewing both of you this summer, Jaxon and I decided we'll use his six-week international leg of the Forever Starts Here Tour as a trial run."

Wait. Did he just say trial run? As in, competing for the real contract?

"We'd like both of your teams to provide security for Jaxon during the entirety of the tour. Now, as we covered in the request for proposal, this tour is going to be quick, with Jaxon playing almost every night for six weeks before we return to the States and Jaxon takes a much-needed break. So it'll be a seven-week commitment: one week in Vancouver for rehearsals and then six weeks with your teams traveling and working twenty-four seven."

Ugh. The last thing I want is to spend seven weeks working every minute with Trent Mitchell. I don't know if I can listen to him go on and on about how amazing he is or what expensive thing he just bought his new trophy wife without punching him in the face.

"Well—" Trent starts, but Henry cuts him off.

"I understand it's challenging to work with another company on things like this, but since you both specialize in different portions of the job, we need to understand which team performs better when working *with Jaxon* to make the final decision."

That...well, that sucks, but I can see why it would be challenging for them to pick between our two teams. Mitchell Security is known for its boots-on-the-ground security personnel, and KH Security excels at security logistics and using technology to pre-assess risks. When working with a large client like Jaxon, the security company manages all the protection officers and weeds out threats before they are even physically there, but comparing Mitchell and KH is like comparing apples to oranges—we're both fruit; which one you want depends on preferences and needs, not superiority.

Henry continues, "After the stalking incident during the US portion of the tour and the issues we had with his previous security team not responding the way we would've preferred, we feel it's vital to try out the firms before we commit to a three- or five-year security contract. But, because of coordination issues we've had in the past when we tried to contract with more than one team, we will be picking *just one* of your firms to work with moving forward."

Henry claps his hands together lightly, taking in everyone's faces before continuing, "So, in summary, you'll each get a seven-week contract with us. At the end of the seven weeks, Jaxon and his team will be selecting one—only one—company for his long-term security contract."

Shit. Shit, shit, shit.

I can't say no, even if the thought of working with Trent Mitchell for seven weeks makes me want to stick a fork in my eye. This is a huge deal for my team, and so many people have worked their tails off getting us to the point where we would even be competitive for this type of contract—though in this case, it's clear Jaxon is playing favorites with Wild Bluffs teams...even if it makes no sense. Last I knew, Jaxon hadn't set foot in town since he walked away from everything and everyone in Wild Bluffs the day he turned eighteen.

"Well, that sounds like quite the opportunity," I say. "While I'm confident in KH Security's ability to provide the highest-quality protection officers in the business, I have no doubt our team will be able to support the operations of Mitchell's CPOs while also focusing on threat assessment and security analysis."

Gross. I can almost taste the corporate bullshit lingering in my mouth.

Trent stares at me from across the table before looking at his brother, who is taking notes next to him. "I can't wait to have you as part of the team, Kelsey," he says with a malicious grin.

"I'm not part of your—" I start, but am cut off by Jaxon.

"Great," he says as he stands. "Then it's settled. We'll see you all in Vancouver in January. Henry will put you in contact with Gail, who will be your point of contact moving forward with the contracts."

Trent and I both shake Jaxon's hand.

"I'm glad to have people I can trust on board," he says before walking out the door.

"Gail will send the formal contracts later today so we can get the ball rolling," Henry says, quickly following Jaxon out.

There is a stunned silence as we all stand there. I look at Lila, but from the "what the hell?" look on her face, it's clear she's not sure what to make of the quick meeting either.

"Well...that was unexpected," Carter says gruffly.

"I'm not sure why we all had to drive into town for it," I say, almost to myself.

A deep, rumbling chuckle comes from Carter. "Trust issues will do that to you."

"Well," Trent says, interrupting his brother. "Kelsey, why don't you handle the advance-team work? Send me your plans once you have them, and I'll get back to you with which operatives of ours will be assigned to which roles. If you have questions about which of your coordinators will be best to place with our team, just shoot me an email. I guess we'll see you in Vancouver."

"Or at Wild Brews. Or the grocery store. Maybe even the movie theater," Lila jokes next to me.

"Sure," Trent says before picking up his briefcase. "It's always so nice to see you and your boyfriend."

"See you around," Carter grumbles, and less than ten minutes after the men arrived, it's just Lila and me in the room again.

"Well, shit," I say as I drop my head into my hands. "We've got to win that contract."

CHAPTER TWO

CARTER

Present Day: January

"Two pancakes and a side of bacon," my mom says, setting a plate down on the table next to mine. I try not to pay attention, instead focusing on the checklist I'm creating in my phone of things to pack when the team and I leave next week.

"Thanks, Alice," Janice says, digging into the pancakes I know she didn't order.

"Of course. And how is that pesky nephew of yours?" my mom asks.

According to my mom, Janice is the queen of Wild Bluffs gossip, and apparently, she spends most of her free time trying to set her nephew Matt up with any single woman in town. Which I can only imagine is as miserable as it sounds.

"Still refusing to date any of the women I set him up with. I really thought he and that Lila Walker were going to be a hit. Who knew professional golfers stealing the young women in town was a problem we'd have to worry about."

"Oh, but they make such a lovely couple," my mom gushes.

"Unfortunately. Now I have no idea who to set Matthew up with. That boy will be the death of me."

"I know the feeling," my mom jokes, sending a stern look in my direction.

I roll my eyes good-naturedly, knowing she gets a lot of enjoyment out of teasing me about my dating life—or lack thereof.

The two women continue to dissect poor Matt's love life before the sound of a bell dinging on the counter pulls my mom away.

As my mom heads into the kitchen, Bill, my mom's boss for the last thirty-two years, stops at Janice's table, quietly asking if she'd like the eggs she ordered instead of the pancakes.

Janice smiles before shaking her head. "No. Alice must've known I needed a pick-me-up today. The pancakes are delicious. Plus, this is what I get for not having a usual order."

Bill laughs and taps a finger on Janice's table before sitting down in front of me.

"How are you today, Carter?"

"Good." Or at least as good as I can be with the stress I'm currently under.

"She's going to be all right. I know you're worried about leaving now that her dementia has progressed, but she's going to be fine. Mildred and I will make sure she has everything she needs."

"I appreciate that," I say, though the fear still grips my stomach. My mom started showing signs of memory loss over three years ago, and after her diagnosis with Alzheimer's a year later, I left the Army and moved back to Wild Bluffs. After speaking with several memory specialists and spending countless hours down rabbit holes on the internet, I realized moving in with my mom after being gone for the last fifteen years might not be the best for her routine, so I moved into a small rental down the street, ensuring I would be nearby when she needs me. I've had dinner with her almost every night since then, and I'm worried about what changing her routine will do.

Unfortunately, I'm also worried about the mounting costs of her medication, the experimental treatments we have her on, and her increased need for care, so now is not the time to tell my boss I can't be the lead security agent on a six-week international tour—especially when my boss is my asshole half brother.

"How often does something like that happen?" I ask, tilting my head toward Janice and her plate of pancakes.

"Not often. We don't get a lot of people in from out of town, and most locals have usuals. She knows those like the back of her hand. But when someone orders something different? It happens about half the time. I've tried to get her to carry a notepad to write it down, but it's something new, so it doesn't stick too often."

"I can pay for the wasted meals."

"Honestly? You know how people in Wild Bluffs are. Everyone knows what she's going through, and unless someone has an allergy or an extreme dislike for something, they usually just go ahead and eat whatever they get."

"You'll let me know if it gets to be too much?"

"Sure," he says, his eyes focusing on a spot over my shoulder.

He won't. Even before his eyes gave him away, I knew the real answer. Bill and Mildred have been like grandparents to me since I was an infant playing behind the counter of their restaurant while my mom waited tables. Years later, I sat at that same counter doing my homework, getting help with math from Bill, and having Mildred proofread my essays. They saw my drive to get out of this town and never failed to provide me with the support I needed. Looking back, I see just how much they supported my mom during that time too.

"Thanks, Bill," I say. I'm not someone who likes to vocalize my feelings, but I owe a lot to Bill. So, for him, I'm willing to force the words out.

He takes a deep breath. "Don't thank me just yet. I do need to talk to you about something. It's not a big problem now, but when you get back, we're going to need to talk about cutting her afternoon hours." He holds up a hand. "Not because I don't want her here, but because she's starting to get tired in the afternoons. She'll be fine while you're gone, but once you're back, we need to consider it."

"She won't do well with the change."

"She doesn't do well when she's tired. She gets easily confused and is starting to get more visibly frustrated by little things."

"I'll tell Trent I can't go."

"I didn't realize you were in a position to lose your job," Bill shoots back.

The downside of sharing details about your life with people? They then know things about your life and can use them against you. Like the fact that I'm worried about money. The Army made sure I didn't have any school loans, despite attending one of the most prestigious colleges back east, but my mom's best option for treatment was a trial medicine outside of what her insurance would cover. Paying for everything over the last three years has drained almost every drop of savings either of us had. What she brings in from work barely covers her cost of living, so it's up to me to cover everything else.

"He'll listen to me," I say, though it's with little conviction.

"Didn't you already talk to him about it? And he insisted you be the one to go?"

"Yes. He doesn't want to leave Julie alone for that long." I sigh. "He already bought her a new car to make up for being gone a few days when he joins me on the road."

A smile flicks across Bill's worn face. "She sure does know how to get what she wants, that one."

I nod. Julie grabbed Trent by the balls the day they met almost a year and a half ago—not caring the man at the bar was almost ten years her senior—and hasn't let go since. They had the most ostentatious mountain wedding you've ever seen this past summer, inviting almost no one from our little town to come celebrate with them. I had the distinct displeasure of making the invite list, though my mom wasn't invited due to her strained relationship with Trent's and my shared DNA donor.

As both his half brother and his employee, I felt I had to attend. I regretted my decision the entire night as I was strangled by my black tie while trying my best to avoid Julie's sorority sisters.

"Well, I'm sure your mama will be out with your food soon," Bill says as he stands. "But don't worry about her while you're gone. Enjoy your time traveling around the world with that Harper girl. Which one is it again? I can never seem to keep them straight."

The gleam in his eye suggests otherwise, but I answer him anyway. "Kelsey."

"Right." The playful look in his eyes is now joined by a grin, and I've never been so pleased to see my mom as she pushes out of the back with a plate of food.

"Thanks again, Bill."

He nods, turning to leave as my mom slides my plate of food in front of me. My usual three scrambled eggs with avocado and toast on the side stare up at me from the beige oval plate.

"How are you feeling today, Mom?" I ask as I shovel a bite of eggs into my mouth.

"I'd feel much better if you didn't worry about me all the time," she grouses. "I managed to raise you by myself when I was only eighteen. I sure think I can handle a few lapses in memory at fifty-two."

I narrow my eyes at her but decide not to point out that it's more than a few lapses in memory at this point. I've taken over paying her bills after she forgot to pay for her electricity two months in a row. She would've had her power cut off if not for an old classmate of mine giving me a call to let me know what was going on. When she saw my sperm donor and his wife at the grocery store last week, she forgot the name of Trent's mom, despite their entwined histories of both being impregnated by the same boy from their class less than three months apart.

"Are you excited for your trip?" she asks, intentionally changing the subject.

It's one of the hardest parts about the disease, not knowing what she will remember at any given moment. I'm dreading the day she forgets my name, though I know it will be here before the end. She forgets a food order between the table and the counter but remembers I'm headed out on tour with Jaxon Steele, which I mentioned weeks ago. It'd be hard on anyone, and for someone like me who relies on knowing what to expect, it's an added layer of stress. Fortunately, I love routine and have found Mom's reliance on them to be just as beneficial for me as they are for her.

"I am. I haven't had the opportunity to travel much that wasn't on the Army's dime."

"You're saying you don't count your time in Afghanistan as a vacation?"

"It was better than others' time there."

My mom narrows her eyes at me. "Just because you could've had it worse doesn't mean you have to deny how hard it was."

"I know," I say. And I do. She's lectured me enough about it that sometimes that exact phrase plays in my mind on repeat while I'm working out. It makes for a long hour when that's constantly circling through my brain.

"It'll be nice for you to see Jaxon again," Mom says. "You two were good friends during your junior and senior years. I always felt bad for him."

"If it goes anything like the ten minutes we were together in Denver, I'm sure it'll be just fine."

"You should see if you can spend some time with him while you're there. You two always got along so well."

I grunt a reply, trying not to grimace or give extra attention to her repetition. We, as humans, repeat ourselves a lot. Most of the time, people don't pay any attention to it, but now I'm analyzing everything my mom says and does, and it's hard not to take a repeated phrase or a simple forgetful moment as a sign of something worse.

"I'm serious, Carter. You need a friend."

I shovel more food into my mouth before realizing she's going to make me answer. "I've got Bill."

"You need friends your age."

"I've got Wes and Vince," I say, naming my two buddies who served in the Rangers with me.

"Friends in Wild Bluffs."

"I went to that thing at Ken Harper's house."

"That was last summer!"

And I have absolutely no idea what I had been thinking. Jen Harper cornered me in the diner and invited me to their annual summer party. I tried to get out of it, but Bill heard and invited my mom—just my mom—over for dinner that night so I could go. I couldn't get out of it then, so I went. And it was...fine. I guess.

Except I had to double my time in the gym for the next month just to get the image of Kelsey Harper's lips wrapped around the tip of a longneck beer bottle out of my head.

No, *friends* is not what I need.

CHAPTER THREE

Kelsey

"We need another desk in here," I say as I look at my sister Bryn across the folding table where we're both working. "Remember the good old days when Lila's desk was free for us to use?"

"Or you could both go to your homes where you have offices," Izzy replies, leaning back in her nice office chair.

I wonder if I can convince her to give me her desk to work at today.

"No," Izzy says, as if reading my thoughts. "This is my office. Becca and I pay money for it. You can't have my desk."

Becca laughs from behind her screen, but I keep my gaze focused on Izzy.

"I'm not giving in to your mind-ninjaing," Izzy says sternly. "Buy your own damn desk if you want one in here."

"Why would I buy a desk for in here?" I reply. "This isn't my office. I have a perfectly good one at home. With far less company."

Izzy lifts an eyebrow. "Exactly *my* point. Go work at your house."

"I need to finalize things with Lila for when I leave next week."

"Then go work at her house."

"I pay for a desk for her here," I say.

"Which I'm at," Lila chimes in.

"See?" I ask.

My sister's long brown hair sways as she shakes her head. "No. What am I supposed to see? You do this on purpose just to fuck with me."

I can't keep a grip on my grin anymore, and I can tell Bryn, at least, notices, because she lets out a snicker.

"You know what?" Izzy asks, locking her computer as she stands up. "I need another coffee anyway."

As soon as she's out the door, I pick up my laptop and slide into her computer chair, moving her keyboard aside to make room.

"You're kinda a dick, you know that, right?" Bryn asks from across the room.

"Well aware," I reply. "But I'm a dick with a desk."

"Whose dick is as big as a desk?" JT Johnson asks as he and another hulking man push into the office, making the room go from full to overflowing.

"And I was told a *burrito* was too big for a dick," Bryn's boyfriend, Jameo, replies as he leans over my sister to kiss her cheek.

"Can we please stop talking about dicks?" I ask. "But before we do, there are a couple in this room, specifically the ones attached to annoying men, that could leave. You don't even go here."

"Come on, Kelsey." JT sends his bright blue, puppy dog eyes my way. "It's too cold to golf, and we already worked out. We're bored."

JT and Jameson are both professional golfers who've decided to call Wild Bluffs home recently. Even though I'd never admit it to Bryn, I'm glad my random birthday party at Wild Bluffs Country Club was the catalyst for my baby sister finding love.

"You should've thought of that before choosing such a boring career path," I joke. I'm not sure exactly how it happened, but somehow JT and his assistant, Sam, have become two of my closest friends in the six months since JT moved into Jameo's house and started dating Lila.

"Some people like professional athletes, Kels," JT says.

I roll my eyes at the nickname, knowing he'll just use it more if I say anything about it.

"Some people are idiots," I shoot back.

"Hey!" both Lila and Bryn say.

I look between them. "I didn't say you're idiots. Just that some people are. That's a fact."

"When do you leave again?" Bryn asks. It's her favorite joke these days.

"Not soon enough," I say, giving my usual answer.

"Lila says you finalized the advance-team-planning, top-secret security stuff with Mitchell Security," JT says.

I shoot my employee a glare for sharing work details with someone outside of work, but she just rolls her eyes.

"That's literally all I told him. No sensitive information left my lips," Lila says, defending herself.

"Do you want to murder Trent yet?" Bryn asks me from around Jameo's large body as he leans against the folding table. I question its ability to hold a man his size but decide it's not my problem.

"Surprisingly, no," I say. "He's responded quickly with good questions and suggestions."

"That's...odd," Bryn replies. "Didn't he basically flunk out of high school?"

I roll my eyes. "No. It's more or less impossible to flunk out of Wild Bluffs High School. The teachers would never let you fall through the cracks completely. Plus, they needed him eligible for sports. Though he wasn't the brightest bulb in the light store."

"Maybe he just didn't apply himself back then?" Becca chimes in for the first time since her office has been overrun by uninvited guests.

As I consider her question, I'm distracted by Becca's long blonde hair, the dark strands more prominent now that it's wintertime and she isn't getting any natural highlights.

"Maybe," I offer.

The truth is that I've been pleasantly surprised by the virtual version of Trent. I was worried about working together after he handed out assignments at the end of our meeting like I worked *for* him rather than *with* him, but that level of arrogance hasn't been there in our emails.

"I'm a little worried about my mental space right now because I'm starting to kinda like the guy. He's surprisingly witty in his emails."

Five sets of eyes all turn toward me, whatever flirting or work they were doing before completely forgotten.

"What?" I ask.

"You know he's married, right?" Bryn asks.

I roll my eyes. "I said he was witty, not that I wanted to steal him from his wife and have his babies."

"You probably wouldn't have to steal him from his wife to have his babies if he's anything like his dad," Bryn offers.

"Now who's being a dick, Bryn?" I ask.

"Um, Wilson Mitchell?" she asks like the smart-ass she is.

"Wait," JT says, tracking our conversation. "So Carter and Trent are...half brothers? Stepbrothers?"

"Half," Bryn and I reply at the same time.

"Their dad knocked up two women within a few months of each other their senior year of high school. Ended up marrying the first one—Trent's mom," Bryn explains. "Wilson never really claimed Carter and vice versa, but then in high school Carter legally changed his last name to Mitchell and was at least acknowledged by Wilson and the rest of the Mitchells."

"Damn. Did he know Wilson was his dad the whole time?" JT asks.

"This is Wild Bluffs, JT," I say. "What do you think?"

"So...he knew?"

"Carter and the rest of the town knew. It was never a secret," I say.

"But what is less clear is why he changed his last name," Bryn explains. "The working theory in town is that when Carter started high school sports and it was clear he was at least as good, if not better, at football and basketball than golden-boy Trent, Wilson wanted the Mitchell name on his back as well. Most people think Wilson increased child support or something like that to get him to do it. There has never been any love lost between Carter and his dad."

"Sperm donor," I say.

"What?" JT asks.

"I was in both brothers' class growing up. Carter always referred to Wilson as his sperm donor."

"And Carter is the one I met last summer at your parents' house, right?" JT asks. "The one with the huge crush on—"

"JT!" Lila cuts him off before he can finish, clearly trying to avoid the awkward conversation about Carter being interested in her.

Izzy—and the rest of the town, really—were trying to set Lila up with the single men they knew, and Carter happened to be the one Lila was supposed to meet at the party. Somehow, JT managed to worm his way into the game, and Lila ended up partnered with him rather than Carter. I'd like to say the rejection is what caused Carter to be so quiet during the game, but that's how he's always been. I'd guess he's not my biggest fan, but I honestly don't know what I could've done to make him dislike me.

"But, yes. Carter is the one you met," I reply to JT's initial question. "Trent is blond and has a twenty-four-year-old wife on his arm."

"And is there something particularly wrong with having a twenty-four-year-old wife?" JT asks with a raised eyebrow.

"Hey, you're not married. And you're not thirty-four."

"JT's cradle-robbing aside," Becca cuts in, earning a glare from both JT and Lila. "Long story short, Carter took the Mitchell name in high school before earning an ROTC scholarship to college, joining the Army Rangers, and never looking back...until his mom was diagnosed with Alzheimer's a couple years ago. He moved home and started working for Trent at the security firm Papa Mitchell handed off to his golden son about five years ago."

"And now you're about to go spend six weeks cozied up next to him at the hottest concert of the year," JT says.

"I don't think you understand what I do for a living."

JT shrugs. "Oh, I certainly don't, though Lila has tried to explain it to me multiple times. But I bet you could find some time for cozying if you really put your mind to it."

"I assure you there will be no cozying. It would be unprofessional on so many levels."

"What about with Jaxon Steele?" Jameo asks.

It's silent as we all stare at him.

"What? What did I miss?" he asks, looking from face to face.

I stare at him a bit longer, finally realizing he's not going to put it together himself. "One, he's my client, so no, I will not be cozying up to him. Two, with his history? No way. You couldn't pay me enough money to wade into that hornet's nest."

I don't share the fact that I've mixed business with pleasure once before, and it almost ended with me being cut out of my own business. Though from the look on my sister's face, she's thinking about my stupid ex and the indefensible decision I made a couple of years ago.

"Fine. Fine." Jameo holds up his hands in surrender. "You're going to have to explain it to me later," he whispers to my sister.

I glare at him again, just in case he thinks I'm getting soft, while silently promising myself this opportunity will be different. There will be no mistakes or anything that might make me or KH Security appear anything other than highly competent and extremely professional.

JT taps his chin, feigning deep thought. "Obviously Jaxon Steele is a bad idea, but I do think we're onto something here. Six weeks of traveling across the world? Plus a week in Vancouver? I think you need to live it up a little. Find someone to do some cozying up to. You're so single, it's painful—according to Sam! Not me!" he says defensively when my glare deepens.

I lift my eyebrow and set my jaw in a way I know has made at least one man cry before.

JT continues anyway. "So find someone else on the tour. Or find some random from the crowd. Or at a local bar. Hell, I hear golf courses are great places to meet someone. I'm sure they have at least one of those in every city you're in. Find someone. Have some fun."

"You're an idiot," I say, though my mind starts turning at his suggestions. Obviously, I'm not going to go around dating the people I'm working with. I'd never risk my company or my reputation that way, but I could go out a couple of nights when there aren't shows. Meet some new people. See what happens.

But then I'm reminded of how one moment of weakness, of how putting my trust in one wrong person, can make me lose everything I've worked so hard for, and I know I will spend the entire seven weeks focused on my business.

Chapter Four

CARTER

My knife thwacks against the cutting board as I imagine the potato I'm chopping is Trent's head. I know he's got a new wife at home, but I truly can't believe he won't leave her for seven weeks to oversee our largest ever contract. I told him as much when I asked him again to switch places with me so I don't have to leave my mother *with dementia* home alone.

He denied me, again.

So now I'm at my mom's house, following our nightly routine one last time before I climb on an airplane tomorrow.

My mom bustles quietly around the kitchen, adding vegetables and meat into the pan she's using to make the soup.

"We need those potatoes in here if you don't want them to be hard," she says, glancing over my shoulder to see how I'm doing.

"Sorry," I respond, quickly finishing the chopping and handing her the entire cutting board to dump into the pot.

It's a routine we've done a thousand times, even before her dementia and her need for consistency. My mom worked the evening shift when I was young so she could make sure she was here to get me up and ready for school. Then, when I got to middle school and started playing sports, she traded her dinner shift for breakfast so she could see my games. Since it's always been just the two of us, there hasn't been a time in my life when I wasn't helping her make our meals.

"What's on your mind?" she asks, the conversation so normal, I want to bottle it up and take it with me while I'm gone, just in case it's not here for me when I get back. I take note of her faded blue jeans and the navy sweater she wears tucked in just at the front. Her chocolate-brown hair, the same color gracing my head, stops just past her collarbone. As I look at her, I realize she has more gray streaks than I thought. That's the thing about seeing someone every day: you don't notice the small changes that somehow compound into something more—something major.

"Just running through my packing list for tomorrow's flight," I lie.

"Where are you going again?" she asks.

Fuck. My stomach drops. I'll quit my job. I'll find—

"I'm kidding, Carter. Jeesh. You should see your face."

I run a hand down said face, trying to calm my heart enough to respond without yelling at her.

"You can't joke about that."

"I've got to joke about it while I still know what a joke is," she says, a pleasant smile on her face.

"Mom!"

"You're no fun anymore. You used to be able to handle teasing far better than this." She raises her eyebrows. "See? I can remember that still, and it was *years* ago."

"I can handle teasing. Just not memory jokes. Hits a little too close to home, don't you think?"

She shrugs, moving around to stir the soup again.

I understand that for some people, my mother apparently one of them, joking about the loss of their memory is the only way they survive the fear of their gradual decline. It's something I read about early on in a few of the Alzheimer's support groups I found online. I just didn't realize how mad it would make me. I don't want my mom to joke about it. I want her to fight it.

She's fought everything that has come her way and won. I can't accept this will be any different, even though I know there isn't anything more that we can do than what we're already doing. I paid every dollar of savings I had to make sure of it, and I'd spend it all again in a heartbeat to have the reassurance I'm doing everything I possibly can for my mom. Exactly like she's done for me my whole life.

We work in companionable silence again, her finishing cooking dinner as I set the small dining table with placemats and bowls for two. Just like always.

As we sit down, I dig into my soup, enjoying the savory mix of the pork and potatoes. Regardless of my slow chopping, the potatoes are tender, cooked to perfection.

"That's a nice shirt," she says, pointing to my white button-up with her spoon.

I glance down. "I wear a shirt like this almost every day."

"Yes," she says, her eyes twinkling. "But this one doesn't have *Mitchell Security* embroidered on it."

I snort a laugh. My brother, like our sperm donor before him, is obsessed with seeing our last name everywhere possible. It's on my company pickup, on every black polo I own, and, for Trent and me, on numerous white button-downs to "set the leadership apart."

"This one is better," I agree. And I do. I never wanted to be a Mitchell, and I certainly never wanted to work for either my sperm donor or my half brother's company, but desperate times and all that.

"Maybe you should wear it when you're out and about," my mom says, pulling me from my thoughts. "Maybe when you ask Kelsey out on a date."

I choose not to respond, hoping my mom decides to leave it at that. Unfortunately, a peaceful dinner doesn't seem to be in the cards for me tonight.

"Are you ever going to ask that girl out?"

"Mom."

"Fine, woman. I still think of her as the feisty sixteen-year-old girl you almost got suspended for in high school."

"Mom!" I say again, though this time it comes out as almost a snarl. She knows we don't talk about that. Ever.

"I know, I know. It's a secret I shall take with me to the grave."

I continue eating, making sure to avoid eye contact.

"Your high school crush aside, I've seen the way you look at her when we happen to see her around town. If you're interested in her, I think you should pursue it."

"I don't have time for a relationship." It's the line I've used for years, but it's true now. My mom is the most important person in my life, and I'm not going to miss out on time with her just to go out with someone. Even if that someone is Kelsey Harper.

"That's a load of baloney, and you know it."

"I'm busy at work."

"So is everyone else."

"And I want to spend as much time with you as possible."

She looks at me, her dark eyes overflowing with sadness. "I know, honey, and I love I get to spend so much time with you. But you can't stop living your life. Take it from me, you never know when you're going to get news that changes everything. And I don't want you to be alone."

"You didn't need someone, why do I?"

"I had you."

"Are you suggesting I knock up a girl?" I joke, trying to lighten the mood.

"Is Kelsey an option?"

"Mom," I say in my best stern-parent voice.

Like a child, my mother rolls her eyes at me. "No, I don't want you to knock some girl up just to have a child to raise and keep you company. I want you to be happy. I want you to find someone to love you as much as I do."

"You were happy without someone, why are you trying to say I need a wife?" I ask again.

"You don't need a wife. I didn't need a husband either." She sighs. "But being by yourself, it can get lonely."

"I'm sorry I left you," I say, meaning it, even though I know I would've self-imploded if I hadn't left this town after high school. But I know what she means. I've felt the loneliness of being an only child, of not having any close family or friends in town these past few years. I feel the weight of every decision I have to make for my mom. I might be in a town full of people who know me and love my mom, but I've never felt as alone as I do as an adult back in Wild Bluffs.

"I'm not," she says. "I'm glad you left and found yourself outside of the shadow of my decisions."

"Mom," I say again, though softly this time.

"I would not change one thing about my life that brought you to me, even if it's not the life you deserved. But I wish I would've worked a little harder to live, rather than just survive, the last fifteen years. And I don't want you to look back fifteen years from now and think the same thing."

"That's a pretty low blow," I say, trying to lighten the mood.

"I'm not joking, Carter. Don't miss out on living your life."

"Okay, Mom. I'll try. Though maybe not with Kelsey Harper."

She raises her eyebrow. "And why not?"

"We're just not right for each other."

"Is that what you think or what she thinks?"

"Both." Probably. I've never asked her about it due to my inability to speak actual words in her presence. The fact that I didn't grow out of that particular trait while in the Army Rangers continues to shock and annoy me any time I'm in her vicinity. I can talk to anyone, though I'd prefer not to usually, but for some reason, Kelsey Harper has always made me question every thought I have.

I don't know what to say, so I just don't speak.

"I'm not sure I believe you."

I simply grunt in response.

The rest of the evening goes by without getting too deep, and as the final episode of *Ted Lasso* season two finishes, Mom turns off the TV before walking me to her front door. It's only seven, but we tend to end our nights early, since Mom has to get up before the sun to make it to her shift at the diner.

"Don't worry about me while you're gone. I'll be fine. I'll stick to my routine, and I'll reach out to Bill and Mildred if I need anything. You left me a huge sign on the fridge with the reminder of where you are and who to contact. I *will* be fine."

"I'm going to miss you," I say, pulling her petite frame into my large one. I wrap her up tight, telling myself I'm doing the right thing.

As I walk in the dark to my pickup, the one with *Mitchell Security* splashed across the side, I let myself give in to my mom's suggestion, just one time, for one minute, and live out the fantasy I've had since I can remember. The one where my forever is with Kelsey.

But just as quickly, I pull myself away, knowing it's a fantasy that will never happen. Because Kelsey Harper? She doesn't end up with a guy like me, especially when we're about to be competing for the same contract.

CHAPTER FIVE

KELSEY

"Bryn, go sit by your boyfriend," I say, shooing her out of the seat on my dad's right. "I'm left-handed. I'll bump elbows with everyone else if I don't sit there."

"I feel like you make that a bigger deal than it actually is."

"No, it's real. Plus, I don't want to sit between Tweedle Dee and Tweedle Dumber. Their hulking shoulders make me feel like I'm being suffocated."

My parents invited a group over for dinner on my last night in town for a small going-away party, and between my parents, my two sisters, Jameson, Lila, and JT, the table is full.

"You're clearly Tweedle Dumber," JT says to Jameson.

"That's the nicest thing Kelsey has ever said to me," Jameo says in response. "I mean, I'm pretty sure she complimented my shoulders. I've been working so hard on them lately."

JT flexes next to him. "We have been bulking up nicely."

Everyone at the table, including me, laughs as Lila reaches over and squeezes JT's shoulder, causing him to giggle.

"Why are you not somewhere golfing?" I ask the hulking brutes. I swear, for professional golfers who supposedly play in twenty to thirty tournaments per year, these men are always around.

"We start up again next week. We're in California, which isn't a bad place to be in early January."

"Are you going to see your folks while you're out there?" I ask JT. His relationship with his parents is rocky at best—likely because they are the worst humans on the planet—but he still wants to have them in his life no matter how many times I suggested he just cut them out completely.

"One dinner."

"I'm going to go with him," Jameo pipes in, shooting me a knowing look.

And, fine, he's right. I was going to tell JT not to go. JT has worked really hard to get himself to a better place in the last six months, and I'm worried seeing his parents will cause him to regress. I don't want him to put himself, or Lila, through that again. I'm sure he talked to his therapist about it before agreeing, so I should probably let the expert do his job, as much as I hate it.

Though, how much does his therapist actually know, anyway? Maybe I should run a background check on him and reach out to a couple of sources in the area. Just make sure he's as good as JT thinks he is.

"Not to worry, Kelsey. You won't have to miss us too much. We're still planning to see you in Sydney in a few weeks," JT says from across the table, pulling me back from my wandering thoughts.

"I still can't believe one of your tournaments lined up with a concert," I say.

"Have you asked about getting us tickets?" JT asks.

"No. And I'm not going to. I'm not going to use my position for favors before I've even started." I hold up my hand at the question on his face. "I'm not asking once I've started either. I don't like asking for favors. Plus, you two buffoons can afford a couple of tickets."

"But four tickets together are so hard to find!" JT exclaims. "Jaxon's concerts sold out months ago."

I glance at my other sister, Izzy, at the use of Jaxon's name. We, like most of the people in town, don't use it often, and especially not around Izzy. She seems to be okay, though, if not a bit quiet.

"So you two decided to tag along?" I ask Lila and Bryn.

"Yes," Lila responds. "And Bryn and I talked about meeting you in Melbourne and then reconnecting with the guys in Sydney. It'll give you and me time to connect about other clients, and you can show me the ins and outs of being the on-site head in case we get the full contract or another contract like this in the future. I want to be able to help you. I don't like that you have to do it all on your own."

I know it's smart to train someone else on my team to handle managing something as complicated as the security for an entire stadium concert, even if the venue supplies the majority of the actual manpower, but I also know myself, and there is no way I'm going to give up the reins for something as important as this.

"Sounds good," I reply anyway.

We talk about my upcoming trip for a few more minutes until my dad directs the conversation away from my impending departure, and

I let my mind wander, mentally double-checking the list of preparations I need to have done before tomorrow morning.

I shovel another forkful of spaghetti into my mouth as I try to decide whether I need two pairs of black tennis shoes or if the one I currently have packed will be enough. While I'll spend most of my days in blazers and dress pants with a pair of chunky-heeled boots on, I refuse to be in something I can't run in during the concerts. If something were to go wrong, I need to be able to jump in at a moment's notice, so black pants, a black polo, and black tennis shoes it will be. I don't miss much about the military; it was just a good way to pay for college and bulk up my résumé—a female officer in the Marines is impressive no matter what industry you're going into—but I did appreciate the simplicity of knowing what to wear to work every day.

I grab one last slice of homemade bread as my mom walks by, starting to clear the table. I slather butter on the slice as Izzy hops up to join her, grabbing the plates from in front of JT, Bryn, and Jameo. I follow her, still chewing the chunk of bread, with the rest of the plates. I deposit them in the sink for Izzy to wash. I tend to help Mom cook, and Izzy usually helps with the dishes. Bryn, like the youngest child she is, rarely helps with the cooking or the cleaning unless asked directly. At least when she's at my parents' house. When she was nomadic and living with me regularly, she did her own dishes, so she's likely not a lost cause.

"You're sure you don't want to join the whole crew in Australia?" I ask Izzy. I know she probably doesn't, but I want to make sure she knows she can come if she chooses to. It would be a lot for her to face her old best friend for the first time in a stadium with 83,000 other people. Or maybe that would make it better. She wouldn't even have to talk to him.

"I don't think so."

I wait, pretending to be very interested in one of the dark veins that runs through the white granite countertop. Izzy doesn't do well with long, awkward silences, so I like to use them to my advantage when I'm trying to get her to tell me something.

"It feels like a lot," she finally says when it's clear I'm not going anywhere.

"True," I say. "But you can handle a lot."

She rolls her eyes at me. "I don't need a speech about how I can do hard things."

"Apparently not. Seems like you already know it."

"You don't think it would be too much?" she asks. "For me to be there?"

"Not if you don't let it be."

"I'm not quite as good at being strong as you are."

I snort. "Well, I learned the hard way what showing weakness does."

"You seem to forget I was there when Lila first started her new job with you and was struggling with her new role. You gave her a whole speech about needing to ask for help and how it doesn't make you less of a person," Izzy says, scrubbing the pan I used to heat the spaghetti sauce.

"And I fully meant that," I say. "But it's different when you're the owner, the leader. You know that. Lila has *me* to help her. I have to know the answer. There isn't someone else I can turn to."

My sister's thick eyebrows pull together. "You have a lot of people in your life you can turn to."

"Totally," I agree. "They just don't know anything about security."

"Hey! I finally put a six-digit passcode on my phone," Izzy teases. "I think I could add a lot to a security conversation."

"Whatever you need to tell yourself," I say, grabbing a thin white towel out of the drawer to dry.

After a few moments of silence, Izzy turns to me and says, "I'll think about it."

From the uncertain look on her face, I know she means coming to a Jaxon Steele concert, so I offer a simple nod, continuing to dry the larger dishes as she washes them by hand.

Once Izzy starts rinsing the smaller dishes and loading them directly into the dishwasher as she goes, I leave her alone, heading toward the sound of the TV coming from the living room.

As I walk into my parents' living room, the one I grew up in, I look for a place to sit, annoyed to find couples subtly cuddling on both couches. Even my parents seem to have decided to join in, my mom snuggled up against my dad's side as he rests his arm over her shoulders. Bryn and Jameo are on the couch next to them, my sister's head leaning against Jameson's bicep, their hands intertwined on his jeans-clad thigh.

I sigh, focusing my attention on the other couch, the one JT is taking up the majority of.

"How is Denver already down by two touchdowns?" I ask, shoving JT's feet off the end of the couch.

He lifts his head from where it's resting in Lila's lap, a wildly inappropriate place for it to be in my parents' living room, giving me an annoyed look.

I shrug. Where else am I going to sit?

He leverages his large body into a sitting position, pulling Lila into his side. "Thompson threw a pick-six two minutes in," he responds to my question about the score as I curl up in the seat he vacated.

Less than two years ago, a send-off dinner would've just been me, my parents, and my sisters. I knew what spot at the table was mine, what seat on the couch would be left open for me.

I ignore the slight tightening in my chest at the sight of everyone in my life pairing up, moving on from the way things used to be. Change is good. And I'm about to cause the biggest change of all, leaving for seven weeks to undertake the most important contract of my entire life. The one that could finally put KH Security on the map. The one that would allow me to grow and expand into the company I've always wanted to lead—the one I was on the cusp of leading five years ago, before everything happened.

I focus my attention on the game, not interested in letting my thoughts dwell on the past. I learned from my mistakes. I started over in Wild Bluffs. Reflecting on it is not going to change anything.

CHAPTER SIX

CARTER

I PULL INTO KELSEY'S driveway the next morning, five minutes before I said I would pick her up to carpool to the airport together. Well, technically, she thinks Trent arranged for me to pick her up, but I'm not supposed to tell anyone I handle Trent's emails for him.

It's better for everyone this way. Not only is Trent shit at actually responding to emails on time, he also tends to give people incorrect information. Unfortunately, he's conceited enough to still want to be the primary contact for everything, so our compromise is that I monitor his email address and handle all the business that comes through it as if I'm him. Which is fine. I don't care if people think they're talking to me or him. I care that the company continues bringing in enough money to pay me my salary. The one I so desperately need these days. And we have a better chance of doing that if Trent gets nowhere near his email.

I put the car into park and unbuckle my seat belt to go knock on the door when I see light coming from the house, a sliver of warmth backlighting Kelsey's petite frame. She must turn the light off, though, because suddenly it's dark again, just my headlights illuminating the garage door in front of me.

I don't need more than the light from my vehicle to take in the mane of dirty-blonde hair flowing around her shoulders, the loose strands whipping around in the wind, or the outline of her strong thighs wrapped tightly in a pair of black leggings. She has on a black vest, the glowing red emblem indicating it's one of the heated ones. Her black tennis shoes complete the look. She makes a very basic part of me stir to attention. The same part of me I shove back down, down, down, to the place I've kept it since I moved home to care for my mom.

"Let me help you with that," I say, reaching a hand toward her suitcase as I meet her a few steps away from where I've parked.

I'm not surprised Kelsey packed everything she needs in a carry-on-sized suitcase. It seems her style. Plus, we're both traveling light, since our gear was sent in a truck last week. Two of my men are driving it to Vancouver, arriving this morning. From there, it will get broken into two identical storage containers, one for each of Jaxon's sets. While the first set is currently being built in Vancouver, the second will be sent to London as soon as our security equipment is added to it this afternoon. The first set will have one short day to make it across Canada to Toronto before being packed up and sent to Sweden. Luckily, besides making sure we have two sets of everything, the tour has its own logistics team who handle making sure the right things and people get where they're supposed to be.

"That's okay. I've got it," Kelsey says in response to my offer. She opens the back door of the pickup to throw her black suitcase in but stops. "Maybe we should take my car."

"Why?" I ask. I want to blame my confusion on the early morning, but the military teaches you to wake up quickly.

"I'm not sure I can be seen riding in a vehicle with that logo on the side," she jokes.

Or at least I think she's joking. In high school, the locker room talk frequently focused on dissecting something Kelsey said, trying to understand if she was insulting one of us or was flirting somehow. No one was ever sure, though Trent and his buddy Neil always seemed to think she was flirting with them. Unfortunately for all of us, I'm confident it was usually insults, though the fact that we never knew for sure was a clear sign of her superior intelligence.

"You get used to it," I say, pointing to my shirt and its matching logo.

I register the disbelief that flashes across her face, the same surprise I feel myself. That was an unexpectedly normal response from me.

"I can't believe I didn't wear my KH Security polo," Kelsey says, keeping the joke going.

"Missed marketing opportunity."

"Maybe I should just write it on my forehead. Do you have a permanent marker in here by any chance?"

A chuckle escapes me as she gives up her qualms about riding in my work truck and casually throws her bag into the backseat.

I climb into the driver's seat, though every bone in my body is screaming at me to walk around the truck and open her door for her. I know she won't appreciate the gesture—unless she's completely changed everything about herself since high school, I suppose.

As Kelsey opens her door and pulls herself up into the passenger seat, I turn on the radio, unsurprised to hear a Jaxon Steele song filling the cab. The title song from his album last year went multiplatinum, and with his tour starting soon, the world's appetite for his music has been reignited.

"I guess we're going to know all these songs a lot better by the time we're done with this," Kelsey says.

She twirls a thin ring around her middle finger, and I wonder if it's some sort of nervous tic or just a habit of hers. Nervous tics don't seem like a thing Kelsey would allow herself to have.

"I hope we aren't given a quiz or sing-along test when we arrive," she says. "I barely know any of his songs."

"Really?" I ask.

"You know how it is with him and Wild Bluffs."

"Not really," I say. "I was already gone when it all went down. So were you."

"I guess that's true. I only know because of Izzy."

I nod, unsure what to say. The silence between us grows, the weight of my uncertainty pushing down on me as I navigate town to reach the highway. A million thoughts race through my head: conversation starters, random trivia facts, anything. I know once we get started, I can hold my own, even in a conversation with Kelsey, but everything that pops into my head sounds too trivial, too mundane for her. I don't know how I was able to email her about work for the last few months— Work! That's it.

"So, are you ready for rehearsals this week?" I ask, my voice coming through gruffer than I intended.

Her eyes shoot to mine, the corners tightening as her body goes rigid.

Shit. That was not the response I was expecting.

"Yes, we're fully prepared. I don't know what Trent has shared with you, but we're ready to go. We completed and shared the advance-team reports for each location, just like Trent and I agreed." Her words are clipped, like she's impersonating a CEO from a movie. "Are you ready?" she asks, that same bite to her voice.

"I didn't mean to…" I trail off. "I was just trying to make conversation. I reviewed each of the sixteen location reports. They were remarkably thorough. Better than any I've seen before."

"Thank you," she says uncertainly.

"I mean it. I'm looking forward to working with you and your team on this. Logistics management isn't our strong suit, and I know there is a lot we can learn from you."

"That's because you stick your field people behind desks and expect them to be able to plan and coordinate security ops. It's not at all the same skill sets."

"And yet, you were planning to send your people from behind your computers out and expect them to succeed in the field," I say, knowing she wants to get this contract for herself just as much as we do.

"No. I was planning on hiring new people for it."

"Hiring…to expand. You're thinking expansion," I say, the weight of her words hitting me. If we win this contract long-term, it'll be a big get, but Trent has already declared we'll be filling the positions vacated by Kelsey's small team with internal people, mostly me. Kelsey's looking to grow her business—a move that, while unlikely, could be the downfall of Mitchell Security. There are only so many security jobs in the world, and if she's getting bigger, that slice of the market has to come from somewhere.

"Yes," she says simply. "Few respect a security firm unless you're able to provide big, buff guys like you to stand in front of a bullet or a camera. Even if all of those risky things can generally be avoided if you do the pre-work well enough." She picks at something on her pants. "Unfortunately, there is still a lot of bias in the industry."

My mind latches on to the words *big, buff guys like you*, and I barely catch the rest of what she says, a real dick move, but that's what happens when your dick pulls all the blood from your brain for its own purposes. I casually drop my right hand into my lap, hoping between it and the darkness, Kelsey won't notice the semi I'm now sporting.

"Sure," I grunt, mentally face-palming. Real intelligent response, asshole.

When it becomes clear I'm not going to say anything else, Kelsey props her elbow on the door, her head into her hand, staring out the window. The sun is rising behind us, washing the world in hues of green and yellow. The soft light hitting her blue eyes causes my chest to tighten, the sexual attraction from before morphing into something softer—sweeter. I want to pull her into my arms, to run my fingers through her long hair, and to press my lips against the smooth skin of her forehead.

I shake my head, forcing my mind away from those thoughts.

"Anything in particular you want to listen to?" I ask when the silence becomes too heavy again.

"Whatever is fine."

"We've got a long drive ahead of us. I'm happy to listen to a podcast or one of your playlists." I say it to be a good host, but the truth is, I would love to know what type of music Kelsey listens to, what type of podcast she likes.

"Okaay..." she says, tilting her head slightly to the side. "I'm actually really interested in this podcast about business acquisitions. They just released a new one yesterday on BulkCo—you know, the big warehouse stores. Supposedly, it's really good."

"Sounds good to me," I say, handing her the cord to plug her phone into the speakers. "And yes, I know what BulkCo is. Best steaks you can find."

She smiles at me, a real, genuine smile, and my heart stops beating for one glorious moment as I soak in the rare sight. Then the sound of the podcast host's voice blares from the speakers, and the moment is gone.

As I attempt to listen to the story of how BulkCo came to be, I can't help but think about the situation Jaxon put both of our companies in by forcing us to work together like this while competing with each other for the same long-term contract. I want Kelsey to do well, for her business to succeed, but I *need* Mitchell Security to do well. I can't afford to lose my job or have my pay cut if things go wrong. My mom's expenses are just going to keep going up, and if Bill is right, the meager income she already brings in is going to continue to decrease. I'm not sure how we're going to make it work if I don't help Trent win this contract and then leverage it to bring on a few more big clients.

As much as I hate to admit it, I need Kelsey to lose this contract. Unfortunately, based on the work I've seen so far, it's going to be a very tough battle to beat her.

Chapter Seven

Kelsey

"I HATE GETTING TO airports early," I say, dropping into the seat next to Carter in the waiting area. I wanted to go to the lounge area, but it's not in this terminal, so we opted to sit by our gate.

"We only have an hour until our flight boards," Carter says, his dark brows pinching together as he looks at the large smartwatch on his wrist.

"Exactly. We could've waited at least another thirty to forty-five minutes," I say as I prop my feet up on my suitcase, eyes scanning the seats around us.

His large frame shifts, turning to face me fully. "Are you joking?"

"No. I just don't see a need to be here earlier."

"So you don't miss your flight if something unexpected happens," he explains slowly.

"Ehh, it's not that hard to get another flight."

I pretend not to notice his wide eyes blinking as he takes in my statement.

"Kelsey, how many flights have you missed in your life?" he asks.

I shrug. "Not that many."

"But more than one?"

"Sure."

"How many more than one?"

"Maybe like four. Five? It's really not a big enough deal for me to keep count."

"This changes everything I've ever known about you."

I raise my eyebrow.

"Truly," he says. "You seem too...put together to be someone who misses flights." He leans forward as he says it, putting his elbows on his spread knees, his hands clasped in the middle.

"I just have better things to do with my time than sit in an airport. I travel enough that the time I lose during the *rare* occasion I miss my flight is more than made up for by the time I save all the other times."

"Huh."

I wait to see if my conversationalist travel buddy will say more. When it becomes clear he has nothing else to add on the subject, I pull out my phone, firing off emails to a few of my employees, confirming all the last-minute work we've been putting in for the start of rehearsals tomorrow.

I know my team has done everything we can to be prepared for this, I know we have. But also, have we? There is always something more that can be done, particularly when it comes to advance-team work.

I run through what we know about the woman Jaxon eventually filed a restraining order against last tour for stalking. Bennie Jensen learned the hard way there's a fine line between obsessed fan and stalker. Turns out, breaking into a famous musician's dressing room with a pair of scissors and nail clippers so you can take home "a few pieces of him" is so far over the line that you get a night in jail and a restraining order against you.

Street drugs were taken, prescription ones were not, and Bennie came to believe she needed a few toenails and pubes—I shudder at the thought—from Jaxon. Supposedly, someone named Dee told her she needed them for a love-potion. I'm a bit surprised Jaxon's lawyer didn't file more than a restraining order. Unfortunately, the forty-two-year-old hasn't been seen in the last six months. She stopped taking her medication again, and her older sister believes she might be living on the streets in San Francisco. I would've preferred to have confirmation of that before the tour begins, but in the end, Trent and I decided it would require too many resources, and even then, the odds of finding her would be depressingly low.

I email Lila again, confirming she has pictures of Bennie in the folders and asking about Dee, the infamous love-potion maker. There was nothing in the file about her, but I'm not sure if that's because the police didn't think she was real or because they couldn't find anything on her. My guess is the former, but I'd rather double-check some overworked cop's work than appear incompetent.

The truth is, Jaxon has over one hundred people that his former security firm identified as stalkers. There will be facial recognition at many of the stadium entrances specifically scanning for their faces, but for every hundred we know about, there has to be at least that many who haven't crossed our radar yet. Or haven't escalated from obsessed fan to just obsessive.

After finishing the work I can do from my phone and scrolling through my socials for what seems like a decade, I start people-watching. There is a hilarious kid, maybe seven or eight, who's just dancing along to her music. Since she has pink-and-purple headphones on, I can't tell what she's listening to, but she is getting after it with her headshaking. Dang—to be that carefree.

My attention is pulled away from the dancer as two women walk by in Denver College sweatshirts. They're young and excited, chatting animatedly about something. The one with her hair pulled into a messy bun does a double take as she passes Carter. At first, I think she must know him, but after her quick head-to-toe perusal and an elbow to her friend's ribs, I realize she's just checking him out. Not that I blame her.

Carter is inarguably attractive. He's roughly six feet tall with hair so brown, it's almost black, and dark-chocolate eyes. As terrible as the logo is on the black polo, I'll admit the shirt is doing good things for the man's chest and biceps. It doesn't hurt that it exposes his well-defined forearms either. Denver College should be sad she missed the show on the walk into the airport, though, because his dark-washed jeans were doing *great* things for his ass. Not that I was looking, of course.

Carter notices the woman's perusal and quickly averts his eyes, more focused on his phone than he has been the entire time.

I smirk but let them move out of earshot.

I point my chin at the woman's back as she sits on a black airport chair a few rows away from ours. "It looks like they're on our flight. I guess you'll have at least one option for fun tonight."

Carter doesn't follow my gaze to the girl, instead focusing on his phone. He shakes his head but chooses not to reply. Not the worst move on his part.

Unfortunately for him, I'm bored, so I'm not going to take his silence as an answer. I've been fairly successful at convincing the people in my life to reveal their deepest, darkest secrets to me lately, and now I crave the challenge of it.

"Are you the one man on earth who isn't interested in a fun night out with one"—I look back to the girl and her friend—"maybe two, college girls?"

Poking the bear is fun—as long as you're faster than it. And when it comes to intellectual speed, I'm always the fastest.

He rotates his head slowly to send me a glare that sends my heart racing. But then he looks back at his hands, acting as if I hadn't spoken. I let out a sigh, disappointed he's not going to take the bait.

"I think you do the male population a disservice with that comment," Carter says to his hands.

I force my Cheshire cat smile to stay hidden, the thrill of a verbal sparring match thrumming through my veins. And Carter is not just any sparring partner. He has the brainpower to be a worthy opponent for once. It's a rare find, and why I resort to arguing with my sisters and dad so often. I want the other person to at least have a chance.

"Or am I just an astute observer of human nature?" I ask sweetly.

"You're spending time around the wrong humans if that's what you're observing."

Why are smart men such a turn-on?

Not sure where that thought came from, I try to focus on a comeback rather than the way the muscle in his forearm is flexing and unflexing as he waits for my response.

"Or is there just an overabundance of men who would fuck any woman who looks like that, regardless of her age?" I don't swear nearly as much as my sisters, but that makes it an even better tactic for throwing people off.

Disgust. That's the only way to describe the look that crosses Carter's face, and since I do have to work with this man in a professional setting for the next seven weeks, I add, "As long as she's legal, of course."

Carter leans into me, his musky, clean scent hitting me as he nears.

How did I not notice that soul-stealing smell while sitting next to him all morning? And, more importantly, how am I going to make it through the next seven weeks knowing I could smell it again if I just get closer to him?

Normally. Like a normal person who should not and will not have weird thoughts about how good her coworker smells. That's how.

I force myself to pay attention to the words coming out of Carter's mouth, though focusing on his lips is clearly a mistake too.

"You don't even believe what you're saying, do you, Kelsey?" he says, his voice low.

Professional. Remain professional. Do not focus on the way he just said your name.

I take a deep breath and—bad idea. I force my eyes to stay open instead of closing like they want to at the scent.

"I do think it's true of some men."

"But not all of them?"

"No." *Ew. Why am I conceding that?*

He's still in my space, his shoulder pressed against mine as he leans close to me. Wait, is he getting into my space just to throw me off my game? I'm so impressed, I can't even pretend to be mad.

"Because you know most men—not boys—are after so much more than that. Most men, at the end of the day, want a partner—someone who challenges them, makes them better, and helps them become who they're meant to be. They want someone who shows them what it means to truly live, because with her, life is wild and free."

"No," I say, turning to look out the window. "I don't know that." I don't tell him that I know for a fact at least one man doesn't want me for a partner. No, he wanted me for an underling, for someone he could boss around. For someone to do all the work and take none of the credit.

"Well, it's what I want," Carter says, leaning back in his seat.

I'm sure that's what Lukas would've said five years ago, too. But it's easy to say you want a partner. Being a partner rather than in charge is where things get a bit more difficult. Lukas told me numerous times he wanted to be my partner, both in life and in business, and look how that turned out. When the opportunity came, he did everything he could to take control from me—at least with the business. So I took control of our life partnership and ended it faster than you can say *articles of dissolution.*

"What's that look for?" Carter asks.

"Nothing."

"You don't believe me?"

"I believe you believe it. I just don't think that, if given the opportunity, you wouldn't jump at a chance to move from partner to boss. It's why men—not just boys—like young women: they're easier to control."

I can tell from the shape of his mouth that he's not impressed by my comment, but that's too bad for him.

"Sometimes, Kelsey, letting go of a little control isn't such a bad thing."

"I haven't found that to be true."

"Then you've been spending time with the wrong men. Because trust me, I don't want some eighteen-year-old. When I take control, it's not taking away your power, it's giving you freedom. Because when you're with a real man, you learn being partners doesn't mean sharing power equally; it means letting it flow between you so each person gets exactly what they need. It's dominance and submission and unparalleled trust, all at the same time."

I hope he can't read the shock on my face because...what? How does Carter, the man who barely converses with anyone, say something like that out of the blue?

"You sound," I say, breathing like I just climbed a flight of stairs, "like you're talking about the bedroom."

His eyes gleam. "Maybe I am."

CHAPTER EIGHT

Kelsey

"Are you ready for the concert tomorrow?" I ask Lila as I pace the hallway outside the security staging room in Vancouver's stadium. The concrete floor beneath my feet is smooth, as if the millions of steps I've taken the last six days have worn it down to its glossy shine.

"We are. All the teams are ready to go. Everyone's familiar with their equipment. The team monitoring socials hasn't noticed any unusual activity," Lila replies.

I'm using my earbuds to talk to Lila so I can send a few last-minute messages on our team app before the meeting starts.

"We're good," Lila replies. "I mean, I had no doubt we'd be ready, but the whole partnership thing makes it a little less certain."

"I know. It's not a great situation. But we have to do it, and do it well, to make sure we win the long-term contract."

"Sabotage," Lila says, like it's a valid answer to anything we're talking about.

I laugh. "Right. I'll just put some itch powder in a few of their matching underwear sets, and we'll be good to go."

"Do they really have matching underwear? Do they have the logo embroidered on them? Do you think they're boxers or briefs?"

"It wouldn't surprise me if they did, but I hope they'd opt for screen printing rather than embroidery. Sounds scratchy on your junk."

Lila laughs. "In your mind, is the logo just right across the front?"

"You're thinking large across the ass?" I ask seriously. "It probably makes more sense. Larger that way."

"Well, once you get a look at Carter's undies, you let me know, okay?"

"I'm not going to see any Mitchell Security undies, least of all Carter's."

"Oh, please. That man is gorgeous, intelligent, and brooding. He has *Kelsey's type* written all over him. Plus, you know you wouldn't mess around with any of the guys who work for him or the contractors who work for you, so really, your options are limited."

I have done everything in my power to put Carter Mitchell and his bedroom-dominating ways out of my mind since we got on that plane in Denver. Every morning when I'm on my run around the city, each step reverberates through my head: *He. Is. Your. Coworker. Don't. Fuck. This. Up. He. Is. Your. Coworker. Don't. Fuck. This. Up.*

It's mostly working. Unless I happen to catch a glimpse of him as he's working out in the hotel gym. Or when he makes highly intelligent comments during our work meetings. But it doesn't matter. Because I'm not going to mess up this opportunity.

"You know there are hundreds of people who work on this tour, right?" I reply to Lila.

"I do. But I said what I said."

"Regardless, the Mitchell Security team has been remarkably easy to work with. We have our final run-through this afternoon with Jaxon's final rehearsal, but I have no doubt it's going to go well. Which is both excellent and makes it even harder to figure out how to ensure we come out on top."

I hear Lila moving around before a door shuts, street noises replacing the clatter of her office.

"Have you spent much time with Jaxon?" she asks.

"He made a short speech at the big dinner the first night, the one with everyone who will be traveling with the tour, but otherwise, he's been busy. Wait. Did you just leave the office to ask me that?"

I can almost hear her shrug through the phone, and I try not to be irritated. "Izzy's been weird this week."

I roll my eyes at the drama of it all. "She can handle hearing his name." I made sure she could before I started talking about the tour too much. "They were friends once. They aren't now. Who among us hasn't had a friend or two from high school we lost touch with?"

"I needed some fresh air anyway."

"You're a terrible liar. And stop coddling Iz. Convince her to come to Australia with you. It's the trip of a lifetime *and* the concert of a lifetime. Plus, it'd be good for her to rip the Band-Aid off," I say.

"I'll let you or Bryn handle that conversation," Lila replies.

"Scaredy-cat."

"Yes. Izzy is terrifying when she's mad. She's scarier than you are."

"That's not true." They just don't know to be scared of me. Izzy, on the other hand, is like a box of TNT that just accidentally got set on fire. It's a big explosion, scorching anything in its path. Then she feels terrible afterward. I, on the other hand, feel vindicated after my precision explosions take out my exact targets.

"If that's what you need to tell yourself," Lila says.

"Why do I employ you again?" I ask, mostly joking.

"Because you're a badass boss bitch who's about to have a huge contract with the most famous musician on the planet, and as much as it pains you to admit, you can't do it all by yourself."

"Huh. And here I was thinking it was because your brother is dating my sister."

"You're a jerk."

I laugh, turning toward the other end of the hallway as footsteps announce the first people arriving for the meeting. I nod at one of the men from Carter's team before wrapping up the call with Lila, making sure to let her know how much I've appreciated her work supporting me on this and managing some of the other admin work while I'm gone.

I make my way into the room set up for the final security debrief and pause. The normal room has doubled in size to make enough space, the old wall tucked away into a closet in the middle of the room. This is the meeting we'll have before the first concert at each venue. It's a big deal, as it's with the leadership from each of the different departments of the tour, plus the entire security team, including the gate and entryway security teams that the venue provides.

Carter and I planned the agenda two days ago, discussing how we wanted to handle everything. It was remarkably easy to work through who would share which pieces of information. Since my team covers the advance planning, I'll kick us off at each venue with the big picture, and Carter will bring it home with the specific team roles for his team and the venues' security teams.

As we near the start time, I interrupt Carter as he's talking to a couple of the men on his team, and we both make our way to the front of the room. The A/V team asked us if we wanted a microphone for these, but we're hoping we can be heard without one.

Jaxon enters with a minute to spare, finding an empty seat at one of the tables. You can tell the event security team is trying to play it cool, everyone focusing on their previous conversations or their phones, but having Jaxon Steele sit on the chair next to you is a pretty big fricken deal, and more than a few people are subtly sneaking glances his direction. I was told most performers opt out of these meetings.

I try to hide my smile, giving everyone an extra few seconds to come to terms with the star in their midst. To Jaxon's credit, he just smiles, his gaze focused on Carter and me at the front of the room, calmly waiting until everyone is ready.

I take two steps toward the center of the room but stop when the door opens again, this time letting in Trent Mitchell. His white Mitchell Security button-down, pair of dark slacks, and fancy loafers make me look like an amateur in my black tennis shoes and heat-up vest.

I glance toward Carter to see if he knew Trent was coming or if he's just as surprised as I am, but he's focused on the paper in his hand, not on either of us. I nod my head to Trent, hoping it's a cordial reaction to his unexpected appearance, and apparently, he takes it as a sign he should take over, because suddenly he's standing next to me, welcoming the group to the Forever Starts Here Tour.

How it's possible to speak for five minutes and say nothing, I'm not sure, but when Trent finally runs out of buzzwords and platitudes to say, he wraps up his motivational speech with a personal monologue about how he knew Jaxon growing up.

"And now, let me introduce you to Kelsey Harper, who works for us doing the security planning."

Is he kidding me? Anyone else and I might've let that slide as a universal us, but I've known Trent long enough to know he's using this little show of his as a way to make it seem like Mitchell Security is the one leading the charge here. The man hasn't been around the entire week, and suddenly, he's in here, making it seem like he's the one managing it all.

I force myself not to smile back at him when he shoots a smarmy grin my way, my face naturally wanting to respond in kind. Unfortunately, I'm off my game. My heart is racing from sheer frustration, and I'm mentally trying to cut the parts of my talk that Trent already covered. Sure, there isn't much overlap, but still. This has been planned for days, and now Mitchell Security just announced to Jaxon and all the other key leaders on the tour that they're in charge. And it's not like I can dispute it without it looking like I'm throwing a hissy fit.

Those are probably the words Trent would use, too. *Look at that small, blonde woman having a hissy fit because she thinks she's not being given enough credit.*

Then, all the men in the room would chuckle, adjusting themselves as they mentally move me from the professional column to the weak-woman one.

If Izzy were here, she'd suggest I hack into Trent's phone and change the autocorrect so every time he says "proposal" or "plan," it'd correct it to "dumb ideas" or "micropenis."

If only...

I finish my portion of the prep meeting and casually introduce Carter from Mitchell Security, our partner security firm. And fine, based on Carter's raised eyebrow, it's possible I overemphasized the word *partner*.

I stand silently next to Trent as Carter talks through team placement and rotation, ensuring everyone sees the image of Bennie he sent to their phones. Carter's team has been briefed on Bennie before, but a couple of the venue's security members have questions. They mostly want to know if she's dangerous or likely to be trying to hide her identity somehow. Based on her mental state the last time anyone saw her, it's unlikely.

When the meeting finishes, I stalk away from Trent, unable to bear the overpowering smell of his too-flowery cologne anymore.

"Kelsey!" I hear someone call me over the slight chaos of so many people leaving.

I turn, my eye catching on Jaxon waving at me from the front of the room, where he's now standing by the Mitchell brothers. It helps that he's almost six and a half feet tall, which is tall even in a room of big men.

I walk over, trying not to feel overwhelmed by the sheer size of the three large men standing in a circle before me.

"Everything ready for tomorrow?" Jaxon asks as Carter steps to the side to give me room.

"Ready," I reply.

"Great. I had my assistant Annie check over those few local fans' social accounts you sent over. She flagged two she's worried about."

"Okay. I can get a last-minute plan put together and send it out to the team tonight."

"I was actually about to head out to dinner at Biologica, a restaurant down by the harbor. Do you two want to join me?"

I look at Carter, still uncertain if I should be pissed at him or not for Trent's unexpected arrival. He matches my posture, arms crossing over his chest as he locks eyes with mine. A double eyebrow raise suggests it's my call. I can almost hear him saying "I'll follow your lead."

"Sounds good."

"Great. It's a date!" Jaxon says with a smile. A smile that makes me very much regret agreeing to dinner.

CHAPTER NINE

CARTER

"You what?" I say into my phone as I sit in the lobby of our hotel in downtown Vancouver. After leaving the stadium fifty minutes ago, Kelsey, Jaxon, and I agreed to meet here for dinner, since Jaxon insisted he change into something nicer before we left.

The Jaxon I knew twenty years ago didn't ever care too much about that sort of thing, but I suppose between time and fame, he's likely changed a lot from the sixteen-year-old I knew.

"I'm not going to be able to make it to dinner after all," Jaxon repeats. I can hear him pacing on his end of the line, though no muffled voices like I would expect to hear if the rest of his staff is there.

"Okay," I say.

"You and Kelsey should still go without me, though."

"That's all right, I'm sure we'll just grab something from the hotel restaurant." Though the idea of going out with Kelsey and taking in the city sparks something in me that I have to work very hard to snuff out.

"Andre will be heartbroken if you don't go. He worked really hard to get that reservation."

"I thought Annie handled all your meal scheduling." And as the most no-nonsense middle-aged woman I've ever met, I highly doubt Annie would care if we didn't take her reservation.

"Andre likes to help," Jaxon replies.

"What?" I ask.

"Don't worry about it. Just go, or Andre will be mad. Okay, have fun on your date!" The last sentence all runs together like he's in a rush to get it out, and then the line goes dead.

"That little liar," I say to myself, absentmindedly picking at a loose thread on my khakis.

"Who's a liar?" Kelsey asks, startling me with her nearness.

I give myself one full second to take her in—just one. I've learned the hard way that it's the only chance I have of pulling my eyes off her. A bulky black jacket covers her all-black outfit. It looks like one of those jumper things where the top is connected to the bottoms for unknown reasons. It's just tight enough to show off exactly how fit she is, her petite frame wrapped in long runner's muscles. With her thick, curly hair down for the first time since that morning we drove to Denver, she looks radiant.

Shit. I really thought the crush I had on her in high school was long gone. Turns out, it's a lot easier to pretend you've moved on from a crush when you aren't actively seeing and interacting with the woman.

Kelsey sticks her hands in her pockets, giving me a similar once-over. I dismiss the idea as quickly as it enters my head, knowing it's not *that* similar. I highly doubt she thinks I look radiant. Or debonair. Maybe attractive—I'm aware I'm decent-looking.

Regardless, I'm glad I went with a dark blue button-down *without* the Mitchell Security logo on it.

"Jaxon canceled on us."

"Oh." She looks around and then down at her outfit. "Shoot. I was really looking forward to eating at Biologica."

She doesn't sound like she's being sarcastic, but sometimes her delivery is so deadpan, it's hard to tell.

"You...were?" I ask.

"Yeah. It's one of the highest-rated restaurants in Vancouver. I have a list of the top three places I want to eat in each of the cities we're in, and it was on mine for here. I know there will be stops on the tour where I won't be able to make it to a single restaurant, let alone three, but I love traveling and eating, so..." She trails off, and I have to force myself to glance around the hotel rather than stare at her face.

"That...sounds like you." The understatement of the year for a display of the passion and intensity she has for things she cares about.

"Unlike my timing at the airport?"

I chuckle.

"Well, I'm glad you're interested, because apparently Andre will be devastated if we end up canceling the reservation he worked so hard on."

"Andre doesn't...ahh. Now I see who the little liar is. Are we thinking this might be like the time Jaxon tried to set up Bryn with Ethan Harris?"

"I don't think I know that story. I was thinking more about when he told both Shelby Richards and Pete Brown that he needed math help and then somehow never showed up at the diner—despite telling them both to order food."

Kelsey chuckles. "It's possible."

"Still up for it anyway?" I ask, my heart threatening to drop down into my stomach. It's a business dinner. That's all. I don't know why I'm so excited about the prospect of a meal.

She twirls one of her strands of hair around her finger as she considers the option, taking far longer than I would've liked.

"Yeah. Let's do it."

We decide to catch a rideshare, since a thirty-minute walk across Vancouver in the middle of January sounds anything but enjoyable. It's been dark for hours now, and it's snowed enough in the last week that everything is wet and cold. The black sedan pulls up in front of the hotel, and I grab the door first, holding it open for Kelsey. She slides all the way across the gray leather backseat, making room for me by my door, rather than having me go around like I intended.

I lower myself into the seat, resisting the urge to hold the hand she has resting on her leg closest to me. We ride in companionable silence to the restaurant; the man driving the car attempted to make conversation with us but quickly realized we wouldn't be that kind of ride. My mom would've happily answered every question he asked about where we were from and would likely have followed up with similar questions of her own. I suppose it's what makes her such a good waitress.

"How's your mom?" Kelsey asks, making conversation.

I've talked to my mom every day since we left, making sure to call her each night around the time I would've shown up for dinner—trying to keep some semblance of consistency even when I'm not there. I know it'll get harder once I'm no longer in a similar time zone, but I have a reminder in my phone every day so I'll at least be notified, regardless of if I can call her then or not.

"She's doing okay," I say, never sure how much detail someone really wants to know. It's why I don't go out in Wild Bluffs. People ask me about how she's doing all the time, and what am I supposed to say? "Bill, the owner of the diner, and his wife are helping my mom out while I'm gone."

I had a quick call with Bill yesterday to make sure there wasn't anything going on behind the scenes my mom wasn't telling me about or didn't remember. Despite telling me all was well, after some prying, Bill admitted my mom had a bad afternoon two days ago, getting confused about where her dad was—her dad who passed away three years after I was born. A death my mom always blamed herself for, claiming the stress of finding out she was pregnant in high school led to him having his heart attack.

Kelsey chuckles. "I know who Bill is. I'm glad you have someone who can help out. Let me know if they need backup; I'm sure my mom would be happy to stop by and say hello."

The vehicle pulls up in front of a white building with a wall of windows, large golden doors, and the word *Biologica* written in capital serif letters above the entrance.

The inside is just as swanky, the type of restaurant I've only been to once or twice in my life, and I'm suddenly grateful we're here to discuss business so that I can put the meal on Trent's business card. If the purple orchids filling the space didn't give away the price point, the full table settings with multiple wineglasses per spot sure would. It's a far cry from the Wild Bluffs Café.

"Did you know Trent was coming?" Kelsey asks as soon as the hostess leaves us sitting in our booth.

"No," I say, telling her the truth. Trent had given me no warning he would be joining us, and after Kelsey and Jaxon left the meeting, I'd asked him if he was planning on just showing up at random locations for the tour. He'd said "Yes." Just yes. No additional details. And when I'd pressed him on it, he'd told me he wanted me to be on my A game at all times, thinking he could show up at any moment. As if his presence is what makes me want to do my job well.

Kelsey squints at me, the disbelief evident.

"You didn't seem surprised by his appearance."

"I ran into him right before the meeting." I'd been headed into the equipment closet to get one of my guys a new shirt for tomorrow and had been truly surprised to find him there.

Disbelief is written across her face. "Why didn't you tell me he was here when we were both waiting?"

"I didn't think you'd care."

"And once he interjected himself into the meeting, wasted every-one's time, *and* made it sound like I work for him? Then did you think I'd care?" she asks.

"Honestly? No. I've learned to stop giving a shit what Trent says. I figured you had too."

"I don't like it when men treat me as if I'm beneath them."

"Just men?" I ask.

"Women are far less likely to try. Plus, I work in a very male-domi-nated industry, so I have to go out of my way to make men respect me. I start at a disadvantage because of my gender. Men look at me and see a petite woman with long blonde hair and automatically assume I'm not as good at my job as the meathead next to me." She holds up her hand before I can reply. "Look, I understand that my size is a disadvantage if it comes to being a human shield, but that is *such* a small part of the security industry. Even if you're providing personal security for someone, if you're doing your job right, you shouldn't have to step in front of the person to block them from anything but a long-range camera. You should've already done the work to make sure the area is clear before they ever enter it."

Kelsey, on an average day, is a sight to behold. She's power and fury and intelligence wrapped into a breath-stealing package. Kelsey, when she's passionate about something, is fire and brilliance—a force I can't look away from.

"I agree with you."

"Then you see why it *is* a big deal to have Trent come in and make it look like I'm not his equal?"

"I do. And I'm sorry it happened," I say. Because I am. Kelsey is everything a boss should be, and I wish I would've at least given her a heads-up about Trent, even if I had no idea he was going to insert himself into the meeting. Though, in hindsight, that is exactly the type of thing he'd do.

I stare in silence at the single candle burning between us. With the dark lighting these places love so much, it has a particularly romantic atmosphere.

"I can't believe that, even as an insanely famous musician about to kick off a world tour, Jaxon still has time to play matchmaker," I say, shaking my head.

I can only assume he has better things to do now than play matchmaker for me and a girl I may have had a crush on. Once. In high school. Not now, I remind myself. Because having a crush on the woman I have to beat for this contract is a bad idea.

Kelsey's fingers trace the stem of her wineglass. "I don't think a single one of his schemes ever worked. Do you think he does it just to mess with people? Or does he genuinely think the people need to be set up?"

"Oh, come on. Shelby and Pete dated for like two weeks. That's a successful high school relationship. And didn't that one girl in the class below us end up married to the guy Jaxon helped with that huge prom stunt? The one where he taped balloons over the entire school and each one had a note inside asking her to be his date for the dance?"

"Jaxon was involved with that?" Kelsey asks. "I didn't know."

We sit in silence for a beat before Kelsey shrugs. "Either way, I'm glad we got to eat here. I love eating at new places."

"I do, too," I offer.

"Oh yeah?"

"Yeah. Wherever I was stationed with the Rangers, I went out of my way to find the best local restaurants. When I was in northern Italy, a couple of buddies and I would go out at least a few nights a month, enjoying being off base and trying new foods."

Since coming home, my dining out has been limited to the diner and my mom's house. I don't even pop into Wild Brews for a coffee or stop by Wild Crusts or The Cattlemens for dinner. Even if I wanted to, the only people I spend time with these days are my mom and Bill.

"I enjoyed my time with the Marines," Kelsey says, taking another bite of her food. "I'm glad I served for a variety of reasons, but getting to travel on someone else's dime was the best part. Though I can't say I particularly enjoyed the food in Bahrain. I, unfortunately, didn't get a good food assignment like Italy or Japan. I did get to travel around Southeast Asia for six months on a ship, though. Made me glad I went Marines instead of staying Navy after my time at Annapolis."

"You just served back your five years and got out, didn't you?" I ask like I don't know the answer. Our assignments never overlapped, but my mom always made sure to keep me in the loop on what Kelsey was up to.

"Yup. I wanted to go to business school. Were you going to be a lifer if not for your mom?"

"That was the plan. I loved the Army—the Rangers especially."

The conversation eventually circles back to the reason we're here, the social profiles Kelsey's team has pinged as potential security risks. Even though she had Jaxon's assistant make the final call based on her knowledge of his social fans, these are also the two her team felt were most likely to be a credible threat.

After finalizing our message to the security team, Kelsey sets her knife down, her plate empty of the steak and potatoes that had once filled the entirety of it. I'd ordered the same thing, though I gave up on finishing it all a few minutes ago. The more time I spend with Kelsey, the more things I find to like about her.

"Here," I say, handing my business card to the waitress when she approaches our table with the bill.

"We can split it," Kelsey says, trying to hand her card over as well.

I wave her off. "That's okay. Trent's got it. It's the least he can do after today."

She chuckles but slips her card back into her pocket. No purse for Kelsey Harper.

"How are you liking Wild Bluffs?" she asks while we wait.

"Okay," I say, unsure what else to say without oversharing. I never wanted to be back there, but it's fine.

"Good. That's good."

"I'm sorry, Mr. Mitchell, but your card was declined," the waitress says, handing me back the credit card.

I feel my cheeks heat, and the waitress must notice, because she says, "It happens all the time to Americans up here. Some credit card companies make you call and let them know you'll be out of the country, especially before allowing charges this big. Smaller purchases like coffee or something like that don't always cause issues."

"Ahh," I say, trying to hide my embarrassment. "I'll make sure I call right away."

"Not a problem," Kelsey says. "I gave my company our travel infor-mation last week. I've got it."

"I'll talk to Trent," I tell Kelsey as soon as the waitress has left again. "I'm sure we can pay you back."

"It's really not a big deal, Carter."

"Well, I'll buy dinner at your top place in Toronto, then," I say, suddenly desperate to help her make it to all the places she has on her list.

"It's a date," she says, and even though I know she's making a joke about Jaxon setting us up, I find myself drawn to the idea of a real date.

Chapter Ten

Kelsey

"Jaxon! Jaxon! Jaxon!" the crowd chants as Jaxon switches his guitar before the final song of the set. They have two additional encore songs after this one, but the crowd knows the end is near, and the excitement in the place is palpable. Opening night of the Forever Starts Here Tour has been nothing short of phenomenal. Jaxon and the musicians are amazing, and the crowd is singing along at that perfect level of excitement that makes everything fun but not chaotic.

Our security teams have been on point, and from where I'm monitoring everything from the small room backstage, all is as calm as it can be. We had one fan rush the stage during the third song, but the venue security team knew exactly how to handle it in a calm, professional way. Carter's sitting next to me, his attention primarily focused on the security guard who's responsible for staying with Jaxon while he's on the catwalks moving around the stage to various new locations on the set. Kevin has been an integral part of rehearsals, and I'm impressed

Mitchell Security was able to find someone with the level of experience he has—he played the same role for Hailey Moore's tour last winter.

"Do you think that line is about Izzy?" Carter asks, pulling my attention from the screen where I'm monitoring the social media posts the team is sending my way. I sent security up to the third level an hour ago to pull a woman who once turned up at Jaxon's house with rope and a hammer to break in. It feels like if you're dumb enough to broadcast your location when you're not supposed to be there, then you should be kindly escorted out.

"What line?" I ask. Even though we've now heard Jaxon's setlist too many times to count, I'm embarrassed to admit I don't know many of his songs. I've been so focused on making sure our team is perfect that I didn't stop to really listen to any of his practice sets.

"We walked different roads, found love in the dark, but I always carried the light of your heart. I thought I moved on, thought I was fine, all the while imagining you by my side," Carter says, his deep voice not quite singing, but coming out in a lilting chant.

I listen to the song then, really listen to the words Jaxon is saying, and slowly shake my head.

"No. This song has a happy ending. It's the one a bunch of people use as their first dance song at their wedding. Unless Iz has been keeping a very major secret from me, those two never got their happy ending. I don't think either of them even realized there could've been a happy ending for them. They were friends—it never seemed to me like either of them felt more than that. Or maybe they felt it every once in a while, but they never wanted it. They were happy with what they had."

Jaxon reaches the end of the song, the last line, *forever starts here...with me and you* lingering in my head through the cacophony of cheers that erupt. I catch Carter staring at me from the corner of my eye and realize I've been staring at the screen showing the concert too long, a lone tear trickling down my face.

I wipe my cheek, pretending not to notice Carter's questioning stare. He doesn't need to know about my failed attempt at love or about how sometimes, just sometimes, I think this could be the start of something for him and me.

"Kelsey," he starts, and as I turn to look at him, I see a new account pop up on my monitor, this one live streaming someone walking backstage, sneaking through a storage room.

"Shit," I say as I see the message my agent sent along with the video: Security breach, room next to Jaxon's dressing room.

I swivel my screen toward Carter. "Breach in the room next to the dressing room."

"I'll call Weston," he says, raising his hand to his ear to touch the push-to-talk button on his earpiece. Weston is in charge of the close protection officers, or CPOs, who make up the backstage team.

"Weston, there is a breach."

Carter pauses.

"Weston, do you copy?"

Carter glances at me as he pushes the button in his earpiece again. "Amee, do you copy?" he asks, this time calling to the head of the stadium's security.

"Shit," he says as no voice comes through.

On my screen, a feminine hand starts knocking on a wall, as if trying to decide which parts are hollow.

"You're not coming through at all, boss," the man positioned by the door to the security room says, pointing to his own ear.

"Luke, you make the call. Weston. Now."

"Weston, you have a breach, do you copy?"

We all pause, straining to hear any return voice in his ear, as unlikely as it may be.

"Nothing, boss," Luke says with a shake of his head.

On the screen, the woman has pulled off her white tennis shoe. She points the camera at her face, showing a happy, if not slightly drunk, smile, before pulling a small saw out of a hole cut into the sole of her shoe.

"Cell phones," I say, standing quickly. "Call your team on their cell phones."

I take in Carter's white shirt and six-foot frame, realizing he can't be the one to make a mad dash across the stadium.

"I'll go," I say, grabbing my phone. "Luke, do not let them take Jaxon back until you get the all clear from Carter, understood? Head to door 102 where Jaxon will enter the walkways from the field. Get him inside but go no farther," I command.

I barely hear his "Roger" as I take off, sprinting down the hallways until I reach the public concourse that I have to traverse to get to Jaxon's dressing room. Luckily, almost no one is leaving this show early, so I have few people to navigate around as I run past the food and drink stands that have already closed for the night. It takes me less than three minutes to get where I need to be. A hundred yards to go. Then fifty. Ten.

I find one of the venue's security guards standing at the door to the back hallway. I flash my badge to him, confused about how the woman made it past him. "We've got a breach," I say to the security officer. "I need in now."

He opens the door, barely glancing at the badge I offer.

My phone vibrates in my hand, and I huff out a hello.

"We think she's still sawing," Carter says from my phone.

"Stay at the door!" I yell behind me when I hear his footsteps start to follow. The last thing we need is more unauthorized people getting back here because we left the fricken front door unguarded. "And don't let anyone out unless they show a badge!" I yell as an afterthought.

Carter starts again, giving me a progress report as I run, my lungs burning from the full-out sprint. "I'd say you have thirty seconds until she breaks through. Weston and his team are already waiting for Jaxon. They'll move him to location two. Luke is there now confirming that location is clear."

"'Kay," I get out between pants.

"There is no security camera in there, and she cut her feed. Your team has eyes on you in the hallway. Backup is on its way. Do not, I repeat, *do not* engage. Do not put yourself in danger."

"Need my hands," I say as I end the call, wishing I had brought my earbuds with me. Though they're usually worthless when you're using in-ear comms, it would be nice to be able to communicate hands-free with someone right about now.

I turn the next corner, spotting the guard stationed outside of Jaxon's dressing room. He's staring straight at me, hands by his taser holster as he monitors my loud approach. I halt, realizing I passed a door right before I turned—the door that must lead to the storage room.

"Comms are down," I say loudly to the security guard, the roar of the crowd drowning out most sound.

Recognition crosses his face as I approach, and he drops his arms behind his back into an at-ease stance.

"There is a breach. A woman, likely midtwenties, roughly my size, is currently sawing her way into the dressing room."

The flare of his eyes is the only outward sign of his shock.

"She's just about through, if not fully. I'll go in through the storage room to make sure she doesn't get out that way. You wait here for backup and confirm she doesn't get out this way."

He looks like he wants to argue but decides against it, giving me a slight nod to confirm my orders.

I run back around the corner, not wanting to put the agent at the door in harm's way if she decides to leave rather than wait in the dressing room.

Scanning the hall, I find it as empty as before. The crowd's roar has changed from the bellow of cheering to the noise of hundreds of thousands of feet walking—the concert is over. I grab the handle to the storage room with my left hand, my right shoulder pushing the door open. My right hand feels strangely empty, even though it has been almost ten years since I last practiced this maneuver with a weapon in my hand. Maybe I should start carrying a taser at these things too. It seemed unnecessary when I was just going to be coordinating things from the security room, but now I feel a bit naked without something to protect myself.

I slip into the room and silently shut the door. My biggest concern is that I can't remember if this room has another entrance or not. We have another concert here tomorrow, and if she gets away, who is to say she won't be back with a bigger saw next time? Or tell her friends how she got past our security, and we'll have a full mob of unstable fans in here sawing through walls.

Forgoing silence for speed, I hurry down the aisles of paint, wood, and other backup set pieces from various concerts. I catch a slight movement to my right and whirl just in time to see a shelf of paint cans crashing toward me.

Chapter Eleven
Carter

"Where is she?!" I bellow as I finally make my way into the hall with Jaxon's dressing room.

It has been utter chaos since that damn woman started live streaming her attempted break-in.

"The police took her to the precinct two minutes ago," one of the men guarding Jaxon's dressing room—I can't be fucked to remember his name right now—says.

"What?" I ask.

"The police on-site took her to the station," the man on the left side of the door tries, like maybe saying the same thing with slightly different words will make it clearer.

"Why would they take Kelsey to the police station?"

"Oh. No. She's in here," the man on the left—Nash, that's his name—says, his brows pulled together in confusion. My heartbeat is an erratic mess, the same way it's been since Kelsey ran out of the security room earlier, leaving me to handle the logistics while she physically confronted the intruder.

I know she can hold her own, but, goddamn it, I explicitly told her not to put herself in danger, and then she goes and apprehends the woman *on her own*.

My hand on the knob, I force myself to calm down before I enter the room. Finally, I push open the door to Jaxon's dressing room. My eyes find her instantly. She's sitting on the makeup chair, her eyes bright as she presses a white tissue of some kind to her head.

Her long blonde hair is starting to come out from the knot she has it captured in at the back of her head. Fiery blue eyes track my movement, a hint of pain flashing through them. It breaks my heart, which in turn brings my rage roaring back to life.

"What the fuck, Kelsey?" I snarl at her, crossing my arms across my chest in the hope of physically restraining myself from pulling her into my arms and inspecting her injury. My eyes can see clearly enough that she's fine, but my soul needs more reassurance. Reassurance that it is neither entitled to nor likely to get.

"I think the words you're looking for are *good job*," she says, as if we're having a fun chat while out at dinner. Not like she just put her life in danger while I sat in a fucking room and made phone calls, watching her sprint through the stadium as her team worked to keep eyes on her from the sky. The sheer dread I felt when the door to the storage room closed and I lost all sight of her will haunt me for a very long time.

"That was stupid. If you were anyone else right now, you'd be fired," I say from the spot I've taken up next to the door. I want to tell her to lie down on the couch, but I'm smart enough to know that will go over poorly.

"Excuse me?" she asks, her voice dripping with venom. "I did exactly what I should've. And I did it successfully, might I add."

"Successful? You call getting injured on the job successful?"

"I call taking down and apprehending an intruder who was attempting to break into our client's dressing room a success. Taking a paint can to the side of the head is a minor inconvenience. Plus, it's just a scratch," Kelsey says, pulling the tissue off her forehead to reveal a half-inch-long cut running parallel to her hairline.

It's not quite a scratch, but it's far better than the image Lila had sent through to me of her leaving the storage room minutes ago. Logically, I know head wounds bleed a lot, but knowing it and seeing blood dripping down her face in a grainy image are two different things.

"How did you even know I got hurt?" she asks after a pause.

"Lila sent me an image of you leaving the room."

"She's not even supposed to be working on this."

"Did you really think your team would keep this quiet—at least among themselves?" I ask.

She rolls her eyes, swiveling in her chair to look into the mirror behind her. I watch as she looks around for water and, finding none, spits on the tissue before scrubbing at the dried blood on her temple.

"I'll get you some water," I say. "You'll get an infection that way."

"I think I'll manage," she says. "Why don't you focus on something actually important, like what the fuck happened out there."

"She had a security badge," I tell her, summarizing what little we know. The woman, Juliet Osmond, had flashed a security badge to the stadium security officer to get back here. She came in before the show finished, so the full backstage team wasn't down here—just the few men guarding the important doors. It's unclear what she was after, other than the picture she claims she was trying to take in Jaxon's dressing room. Not even with Jaxon. Just in the room.

"Did you hear what she said when I asked her why?" Kelsey asks, the first she's interrupted since I started the debrief. Her eyes are filled with a mischief I feel is unwarranted at this specific moment.

"Something about losing a bet," I say, my eyes still scanning her for signs of any other injury.

"She told me she lost her fantasy football league, and this was her punishment."

"She's American?"

"Hard to say. I didn't notice an accent, but I imagine Canadians play fantasy football too. At least a few of them. It doesn't matter, though. It's clearly a bogus story."

"Why do you say that?" I ask as I mentally review everything I know about the break-in. "Fantasy punishments have gotten out of hand. Apparently, SAT proctors don't even blink an eye at middle-aged men showing up to take the test with a bunch of high schoolers anymore."

"Yeah, but the season doesn't end until next week."

"Maybe she's really bad?" I suggest.

Kelsey shrugs, using the toe of her right foot to spin herself side to side.

"I'm more worried about the comms," she says, her tone indeed carrying a hint of concern in it.

"Do you think Juliet had something to do with them going down, or do you think she just got exceptionally lucky?"

Her eyes shift away from my face before she says, "No. I think she got lucky. I think…"

I wait for her to finish, but she just starts twirling that piece of hair, a dark one that she's pulled from the back of her neck.

"What is it?" I ask.

"I'm…I'm worried my team did something wrong. The comms were our job. We checked them and doubled-checked them, but, no, I don't think it was her."

"It's an awfully big coincidence. Too big of one for my comfort. Plus, I was with you when you checked everything. We never had one outage the entire last week."

"Even if it was her, we clearly should've had a backup plan. It's my job to make sure we have a plan for every contingency, and I didn't even have one for the communication system with the guards going out."

An ache grows in my chest with her admission. I know she guards that vulnerable part of her as closely as her clients. I push my hands through my hair, forcing myself not to go to her. Instead, I drop onto the edge of the couch that takes up one wall of the room. My eyes drift over Kelsey's shoulder, staring at her highlighted profile in the mirror.

"You did have a plan, though," I say. "You gave the order to reach out by phone. You made sure Jaxon was nowhere near here. You handled an unfortunate situation like a pro. And we both know you can do as much advanced planning as you want, but unfortunate situations *are still going to happen*."

We're interrupted by a knock on the door, and a second later, it opens to reveal Jaxon, Henry, and, as luck would have it, Trent. Of course this would happen while he's here.

Jaxon's hair is still sweaty, his shirt damp from the workout he gets running all over the stage during his performance. He sits down next to me, one ankle crossed over the other knee, the arm away from me resting on the back of the couch. Henry stands against the wall near Kelsey in her chair. Trent stays in the middle of the room, spreading his feet and generally taking up the most space possible.

"Are you all right, Kelsey?" Henry asks.

"Fine," she says, quickly dropping the tissue into her lap. "Just a minor scratch from an errant paint can."

"Glad to hear it."

"What happened out there?" Jaxon asks from next to me.

"The comms went out," Kelsey says before giving a brief, professional recap of the events of the night.

"It never should've happened," Trent chimes in when Kelsey reaches the end. "Maybe we need to handle the comms portion of the contract. We've never had earpieces go out before."

"Well," Jaxon says. "Kelsey's team did handle the situation. She even took the woman down herself."

As much as it made me want to strangle her for it.

The admiration in Jaxon's eyes as he takes in Kelsey could be construed as platonic, but my gut doesn't get that memo and starts churning with something that feels a lot like jealousy. I dismiss it. It must be the spark of rivalry Jaxon has forced between us.

"Yes," Trent says, a fake mask of concern for Kelsey crossing his face. "A very valiant effort for sure. But the truth is, we should've never been in that situation. If the communications devices hadn't short-circuited, there never would've been an issue. Our *men*"—I want to punch his face in for the emphasis, as if Kelsey took a paint can to the head because she was a woman—"are equipped to handle apprehension. But they can't do that if they don't know about the breach."

"That's true," Kelsey says, looking past Trent to where Jaxon sits on the couch next to me. "I have no idea what caused the comms devices to go down, but I assure you I'll look into it and have a solution before tomorrow's show. This won't happen again."

Jaxon and his manager make eye contact, and it pains me to see Kelsey's mask of calm professionalism slip briefly. In that second, I swear I see every one of her doubts cross her face. I know she's questioning if she just lost the deal for her team.

I take a deep breath as if to say something, and Trent cuts me a look that clearly says "Stay the fuck out of this." It crushes a piece of my soul, just like working at Mitchell Security every day does, but for my mom, it's a sacrifice I'm willing to make. So I say nothing—I don't defend the fiercest, most intelligent woman I've ever met.

Rivals. That's all we are.

After an extended silent conversation between Jaxon and his manager, Jaxon finally says, "We're not changing anything up at this point. Kelsey, I trust you to get this handled before the show tomorrow."

"Of course," Kelsey says.

"This is just the first night, and mistakes are bound to happen."

I don't miss Kelsey's flinch at the word *mistake*.

"The concert went smoothly, and besides being taken to somewhere other than my dressing room—which no fans would've known about—the experience was exactly what it should've been. Henry will work with the PR team to get something released to the press to get ahead of the story, leaving out the part about the saw in her shoe."

"It was more like a serrated butter knife. Kinda like one of those little pumpkin-carving knives you get in the kits at Halloween. I don't think she could've injured anyone or anything but some flimsy drywall with it," Kelsey tells Jaxon. "She really didn't make it that far as it was," she says, pointing to the thin line running about two feet from top to bottom in the middle of the wall. "I was worried she was going to have a whole hole popped out by the time I got here."

"Regardless, let's not give people ideas," Henry chimes in.

We finish debriefing the incident, both Kelsey and I promising a full report by noon tomorrow. Finally, Jaxon and Henry leave, Trent going with them to "confirm Jaxon's personal guards are doing what they should be."

Kelsey lets out a long sigh before pushing to her feet.

"Want me to drive you back to the hotel?" I offer, watching her for signs of concussion, even though I know she allowed the on-site EMT to at least check her for that, even if she didn't let him bandage her head.

She scoffs. "No. I'll be spending my night checking earpieces."

"Want some company?"

Her weary eyes hold mine, searching for something—I don't know what.

"No. That's okay. It's going to be a long night. There is no way I'm going to lose this contract because of one tech issue."

That might not be the reason why, but I'm feeling more and more confident that Mitchell Security might actually stand a chance of winning this contract.

She stops in the doorway, holding on to it with one hand as she turns back to me. "What happened to 'You did have a plan'?" she asks, the bite in her voice cutting through me. "Didn't think that'd be something Jaxon would want to hear?"

"I..."

She raises her eyebrow, waiting for me to finish. But what can I say? No matter how I feel about Kelsey or her work, securing the long-term contract with Jaxon—making sure my mom is cared for—is the most important thing right now.

"Got it," she says before walking out the door.

CHAPTER TWELVE

Kelsey

"Great show tonight," Nash says to me as he hands in his earpiece before clocking out.

"Can you actually hear the lyrics from the dressing room?" I ask. "Or is it just crowd noise like in Vancouver?"

"Could hear every lyric. Mikayla bet me twenty bucks that I couldn't pick someone up tonight using just Jaxon Steele lyrics. They're going to be like putty in my hands."

"How did the ladies of Toronto get so lucky?" I joke.

He leans in close, his boyish enthusiasm lifting my spirits for the first time since the comms incident two days ago. "She doesn't know it yet, but by the end of this tour, she's going to be the one I have convinced to date me."

I cross my arms, giving him a stern look. "No fraternizing, Nash. You know Mitchell Security's contract is stricter than the tour's."

"I said by the end of the tour. I know the rules."

I laugh, considering how much trouble they could get in if they were caught hooking up while on the job. Though, maybe if I don't tell Carter, it'll look bad for Mitchell Secur— I shake my head, knowing that's not how I want to win this contract, even if it's possible the issue in Vancouver was caused by someone from Mitchell Security.

Instead, I make a mental note to have Carter separate the two of them during their shifts. Does it make me a jerk? Maybe. Am I willing to risk it after everything that has already happened? No. I'll just have to figure out a way to suggest it to Carter without getting Nash or Mikayla in trouble. Maybe I can suggest Mikayla for the security room detail when we reach London.

It's well after midnight when all the earpieces have been returned. The venue is finally empty of all the concert attendees. Jaxon left an hour ago for his hotel and was reported as safely tucked in bed about forty-five minutes after that. Apparently, the line of fans outside the hotel was huge but well behaved.

"Do you need some help?"

I turn, trying not to let the increased pace of my heart show. I'm not sure how Carter always manages to sneak up on me, but it's a bit worrisome for my ability to do my job...and my safety, I suppose.

The sight of him makes my breath catch, and I'm forced to question how I've known this man my entire life and yet, somehow, my traitorous hormones waited until the most inappropriate moment to decide he requires a response. Ugh. I'm even starting to think those damn Mitchell Security button-ups are attractive.

"I've got it," I say, carefully packing the earpiece back in the storage box. Lincoln, the tech expert on my team, determined the earpieces had been exposed to some kind of liquid, causing them to short-circuit. Not everyone's went down that night, but Carter's and mine both did, as well as the ones worn by the entirety of the team guarding Jaxon. It hypothetically makes sense—we store them based on teams, since they are preset to specific channels depending on which team or teams you may need to communicate with. It just doesn't feel right to me. I can't imagine someone spilling something in the cases and not mentioning it. And I know there wasn't any liquid in them when I handed them out the night of the concert. It's a loose thread that has kept me awake far longer than it should have both nights since.

"Right," Carter says as I continue to inspect each earpiece. I hope my dismissal will be the end of it, and he'll leave me alone to finish my work.

I should've known better than to think things between us were anything other than a workplace rivalry. Those are the exact words JT used when I told him about what happened yesterday morning. He called me, asking how things were going, and in a minor lapse of judgment, I told him about Carter not backing me in the meeting. JT had the gall to sound happy about it as he whispered, "Workplace rivalry. One of my favorites."

He's an idiot, but he's not wrong. Carter and I are rivals, and I'd be stupid to ignore the possibility that someone from Mitchell Security is behind the earpieces going out. I can't believe they'd stoop that low, but it is a competition, so I can't rule them out.

The door shuts behind me, and I sigh, thankful Carter decided to leave. I don't know when I started expecting more from him than the usual backstabbing bullshit I experienced with my ex, but for some reason his silence during the meeting felt louder than any criticism he could've thrown my way.

At the sound of footsteps behind me, I force myself to close my eyes and take a deep breath.

"I said I don't need help."

"I know you don't." His deep voice comes from a few feet behind me. "I'm not here to help. I'm just keeping you company."

"I don't need your company, Carter," I say quietly.

"I know."

The man is frustrating. If he knows these things, then why is he here?

"Then why are you here?"

"I'm sorry."

I snort. Classic patronizing. He likely doesn't even know what he's apologizing for. Lukas had that move on repeat when we were together.

"I am," he says, stopping next to me and looking over the equipment I have out on the table in front of us.

"No apology necessary," I say, shrugging. "I'm not even sure what you're apologizing for."

I can tell he's staring at me, but I keep my attention focused on my fingers as I quickly clean, test, and store another backup earpiece.

"It's considered common courtesy to look someone in the eye when they're apologizing to you."

"Society has a lot of norms I don't tend to agree with," I say. "And I don't need an apology."

He sighs. "I'm sorry I didn't stand up for you in Vancouver. The earpieces weren't your fault."

"They were. They were my responsibility, and they failed. That's on me."

"Sometimes, things are out of your control."

"Is that how you would've felt if you'd been in my position?" I ask.

He lets the silence in the room go on long enough that I don't think he's going to respond.

Tracing his finger along the side of the case in front of him, he says quietly, "When my mom first got diagnosed, I blamed myself."

Despite how dangerous I know it is, particularly to the structure of the wall I'm intentionally building between us, I turn to face him. His eyes are focused on the case, his mouth a grim line.

"You blamed yourself for her Alzheimer's?"

"Did you know less than ten percent of Alzheimer's cases occur before the age of sixty-five?"

I shake my head, leaning my hip against the table as I give him my full attention. I'm not sure why Carter is opening up to me about this right now, but there is a voice in the back of my mind telling me that whatever he says next is going to be a crucially important part of *him* that he doesn't share with many other people.

"My mom is fifty-two. Thirteen years younger than that." It's his turn to shake his head. "Anyway, they're not really sure what causes the disease, or to be more accurate, it's a number of factors."

His eyes are jumping, trying to find a safe space to land. He's clearly uncomfortable with the confession.

I turn back to my work, trying to give him the space to work through what he's saying.

"My brain focused on lifestyle factors that can contribute to it, like not sleeping well, social isolation, and lack of mental stimulation. Because do you know what having a kid when you're eighteen does? Especially when you're the *second* girl to get knocked up by the same asshole? You get all of those things in spades. My mom is the smartest person I know, but she didn't go to college. She became a social pariah in Wild Bluffs for a lot of years and never had any actual friends her age. She still doesn't. And having kids? It's basically a recipe to never sleep well."

He can't actually think his mom's dementia is his fault, can he?

"That's not—" I start, but he cuts me off.

"I understand now it's not my fault. Even if all those things are true, those are just a few of the many factors that cause early-onset Alzheimer's. And even if they were the only causes, they weren't decisions I made or had control over. So, yes, I understand wanting to blame yourself when something goes wrong. And when you're intelligent, it's even easier to make connections between your actions and the outcomes. But unless you spilled something on the earpieces and didn't tell anyone or do anything about it, it's not on you. You did everything you could."

"Not everything," I say reflexively, turning back toward him.

He lifts his eyebrow as he crosses his arms. My eyes track the curve of his left bicep as it presses against his body. The black polo he's worn the last two concerts is pulled tight across his arms and chest, directing my eyes to every bold inch of him. His time in the gym is clearly time well spent.

"Stop checking me out, Harper," he says, his voice gruff.

My cheeks warm at the callout, but I force my eyes to meet his. "Are we going by last names now, Mitchell?"

"God, no. I take it back."

I chuckle, turning back to finish the final earpiece, shutting the box with a resounding 'click.'

"I am sorry," he says after a few seconds in comfortable silence. "It wasn't your fault, and as much as I want to be the one to win this contract, that's not the way I want to win it." I can feel the guilt he's carrying with him, so I decide to let him off the hook.

"Thank you for the apology. It would've been nice, but it's not your job to stand up for me. I can stand up for myself."

"I know, but sometimes it's nice to have someone standing next to you."

His words hit a nerve somewhere near the bridge of my nose, and I turn away from him, making sure he doesn't see the tears that want to flood my eyes. I've never wanted someone to fight my battles for me, but the idea of having someone to fight by my side? To watch my back while I annihilate the enemies in front of me? That doesn't sound so bad.

"Come on," I say, keeping my back to him as I make my way to the door, the case with the earpieces for Mitchell Security's agents in my hand. "You can buy me a beer at the hotel bar to make up for it."

Chapter Thirteen

Kelsey

"I hate London," I say, staring across the Thames at the Tower of London jutting above the rooftops. Carter and I finished the pre-concert meeting an hour ago, and after dropping the box with the security earpieces off at my hotel room, we're heading to the top restaurant for the city.

After one beer turned into three last night, Carter and I have fallen into an easy friendship. We sat next to each other on the flight from Toronto this morning, occasionally tapping each other on the shoulder before sharing some inane thought or opinion.

The image of Carter, his headphones pulled off one ear as he leaned over to tell me he thought the movie version of *The Count of Monte Cristo* is superior to the book, will forever be stored as one of my favorite memories. His dark eyes were alight with joy, a rare smile taking up his entire face. It was Carter the happiest I'd ever seen him, and sharing that moment with him felt...special somehow.

Since we needed a full day to fly to London, Jaxon's concert here isn't until tomorrow night. Carter insisted we visit my top restaurant.

"I'm going to need more information than that," Carter replies. "You can't just drop the fact that you hate *London* of all cities and just expect me to go along with it."

I laugh, amazed we've somehow progressed to the point in our friendship where he says more than five words at a time to me. "It's a long story. Nothing was actually the city of London's fault, but it holds a lot of bad memories for me."

"I'm a good listener."

"Sometimes a bit too good of a listener. You could really say more."

"You scare the words out of me."

"That can't be true."

He looks me over, his dark eyes more contemplative than usual. "You make me question everything I might say. You're very intimidating."

"Thank you," I say, stepping behind Carter to allow a woman to pass by us.

"I wasn't trying to compliment you," Carter says, though my attention is fully focused on the man's ass in front of me. It has to be the pants. They do something magical that turns his normal butt into something I can't look away from.

"And yet you did anyway."

He slows his pace, forcing me to catch up with him before good-naturedly bumping his shoulder into mine. Or, technically, bumping his elbow into my shoulder due to our height difference.

"Apparently, I can't help myself," he says.

We walk a few steps before he asks, "So, are you going to tell me why you hate one of the most popular cities in the world?"

My stomach clenches at the thought of telling Carter about how badly I messed things up last time I was here. "It's not a story I tell many people."

He turns his head to look at me as we walk, his hands still buried deep in the pockets of his black coat. "Now I'm even more intrigued."

I should've known Carter wouldn't give up that easily. Twirling my ring around my finger, I consider if I should tell him about my fuckup with Lukas or not.

Fortunately, as I'm about to begin speaking, I see the sign for the restaurant up on our right. "Look," I say, nodding my head toward the building. "We're here."

The look on his face says he's not going to drop it, but I ignore him, leading the way to the small restaurant overlooking the Thames.

Once we're seated and I set down my menu, Carter says, "So you're really not going to tell me, huh?"

I drum my fingers on the top of the table, knowing he's not going to let this go. I don't know why I ever mentioned anything about hating London. Of course he was going to chase down that story; I would do the exact same thing.

On one hand, telling him about it feels far more vulnerable than I want to be on our fun night out, but he did share his story about his mom with me yesterday. It feels like a dick move to refuse to tell him about this. Even though, of all people, it feels like Carter would understand and not hold my lack of sharing against me.

"Only my family knows about it."

"I can keep a secret," Carter says.

And for some reason, I believe him.

"Well," I start, focusing my attention on the photograph of the London Eye on the wall across from me. "Five-ish years ago, I was dating this guy Lukas."

Carter snorts.

"What?"

"Sounds like a twat."

I roll my eyes, a chuckle escaping me at his use of the British word. "All you know about him is that his name is Lukas." I hadn't even told him it was Lukas with a *k*, which makes it more twat-y in my humble opinion.

"Fine. He's not a twat."

"Oh, no. He is. Just wait."

Carter folds his hands beneath his chin, exaggerating his focus on my story.

"Anyway," I start again. "Lukas and I met in grad school. We'd been dating for a year when we graduated. I always knew I wanted to own my own business, so after graduation, I stayed in California and started up a consulting business. I was contracting with some of the software companies, advising them on their cybersecurity systems and procedures. I had a lot of connections from my MBA class who went to work for the big tech companies, so it was easier than I expected to grow."

I bite my lip, thinking back to how full of myself I'd been back then. I felt like I was on top of the world and there wasn't anything anyone could do to stop me.

"My company exploded. I was bringing on clients so quickly, I needed help. Lukas had been in New York working in acquisitions before our grad program, and he hadn't found the right company to join, so I ended up hiring him to help me out, particularly with the finance side of the business."

"Did he embezzle from you?" Carter asks, his tone laced with disgust.

"No." I shake my head. "It would've been easier if he had."

Carter raises his eyebrow as he takes a sip of the dark red wine our waitress brought, both of us agreeing to just one glass.

With a sigh, I continue, "We decided it made sense to try to get investors, so we started taking meetings. I was so busy with all of the clients that adding in meetings with investors was becoming too much. I just couldn't do it all."

I take a deep breath, forcing myself to get to the meat of the story. "When an investor wanted to meet in London"—I nod toward the window and the city beyond—"I couldn't swing it. I had a bajillion client meetings and interviews to hire a new head of HR. So, when Lukas offered to go without me, I didn't put up much of a fight."

I pause, trying to think through how to share the rest of the story. It never gets easier admitting your mistakes, especially ones that cost you your business.

Carter's eyes bore into mine, and I track the dark edges around his chocolate irises. I expect him to balk at the silence and try to fill it, but he doesn't. He lets me process.

"He brought back this proposal that was great, but it stipulated that Lukas had to be a part owner with me. Lukas claimed it was because the investors were uncomfortable with investing in a security firm run by a woman. He told me 'They'd just feel more comfortable if there was also a man at the table.'"

Carter's mouth tightens, his anger on my behalf evident, but he doesn't say a word.

"It didn't sit right. Nothing about it did, but I couldn't figure out why. I thought about it a lot, but in the end, I thought Lukas and I were likely to end up married anyway, so why did the shares matter. Plus, I really needed the investment to cover all the upfront expenses of expanding my leadership team. We flew to London to sign the deal. Made a big PR stunt out of it to see if we could attract more investors with this investment."

I rush on, forcing out the words that I've only ever told my parents and sisters. "Then, in the bathroom of the investment firm, literally minutes before I was supposed to sign the agreement, I overheard two junior analysts talking. They were both irate on my behalf, wishing they wouldn't get in trouble if they told me that *my* CFO was out there getting himself a cut of *my* company behind my back. I thought I must be hearing it wrong at first, but then it all started to make sense—the discomfort I had felt but couldn't place, the completely misogynistic request from a well-established investment firm. I walked out of the bathroom and straight out of the office. Lukas saw me leave and ran after me. He finally caught up to me on the street, yelling at me about how unprofessional I was and how much work he had put into it. Once he finally took a breath, I fired him."

It's only because I'm staring at Carter's mouth rather than his eyes that I notice his lips twitch up in a grin.

"The investment firm ended up backing out of the deal—not that I wanted to work with them after everything that had happened anyway. It all went downhill from there. Lukas started his own company, taking about half of my staff with him. Because he was supposed to be doing me a favor when he started working for me, his employment contract was basically nonexistent. After about six months of hating every minute I was working, I sold the company to a competitor with the stipulation that I would not be sticking around to ease the transition, and I moved back to Wild Bluffs. KH Security is different enough from what I was doing before that I could start it right away without any issues."

Carter blinks once, then twice, before clearing his throat. "So he just tried to...steal your company?" Carter asks.

I shrug. "Something like that."

His eyes search mine, and I brace myself for the barrage of questions about to head my way. When I told my family, you would've thought I was being interrogated based on the rapid-fire questions my dad and Izzy shot my way. I know they meant well, but it's hard to answer questions about the hows and whys of the whole thing when it really just comes down to me trusting the wrong person and not putting in the work to confirm the information I was being given was correct.

And I clearly have shit taste in men. That fact can't be overlooked.

I catch myself twirling my hair and force my hands back into my lap.

Shrugging, I say, "So, anyway, that's why I hate London. I recognize it's not the city's fault that it holds some of my worst memories, but..."

"I'm sorry that happened to you."

"It was on me."

He raises his dark eyebrow. "There you go blaming yourself for things outside of your control again."

"I think giving someone the ability to negotiate away half of my company is within my control."

"It seems like a logical thing for a CFO to be in charge of."

"Oh, really?" I ask. "Would Trent let you have that much control over his company?"

Carter pauses before slowly chewing a bite of Turkish bread from the basket in the middle of the table. "I'm not the CFO," is all he says.

I shrug as our waitress brings out two large plates of food. Breathing in deeply, I inhale the glorious aroma of orange as it mingles with my salmon. Across the table, Carter has already cut into his black cod, dipping it into a sweet chili sauce before directing the fork to his mouth. I can't look away from the curve of his lips as he lets out a small groan of appreciation.

His eyes meet mine, the dark chocolate irises lost completely in the dark lighting of the room. I know I should look away, to break eye contact and stop focusing on the way that single bite sent waves of heat directly to my core, but I can't. Carter holds my attention, the air around us thinning, the world narrowing to a singular point—to us.

And then his phone rings, Trent's name flashing across the screen like the giant bucket of cold water it is. He declined the call, but it was enough to remind me: getting lost in Carter's eyes isn't an option—I can't, I *won't,* risk losing the company I built again.

CHAPTER FOURTEEN

CARTER

I'M PULLED FROM RELIVING my dinner with Kelsey last night by my phone ringing—it seems like someone is always trying to get ahold of me these days.

"Hi, Bill," I say, answering the call from the man helping my mom. I quickly do the mental calculations of how long I can talk to him before needing to leave for tonight's concert. Fortunately, we are essentially next door, so I have enough time to chat.

"How's Ireland?" he asks.

"You're a day off. We're in London tonight and will make the journey to Dublin bright and early tomorrow before his show tomorrow night."

"Ah, right," Bill says, the sound of paper shuffling coming through the line. "That is what your detailed schedule says."

"I just wanted to make sure you knew where you could find me in case Mom needed me for anything."

I cover the mouthpiece of my phone as Jaxon's assistant Annie asks me about moving Jaxon's leave time back five minutes.

"Is that Kelsey?" Bill asks once my attention is back on our conversation.

"Really? You too?"

"What?" he says innocently.

"You know what."

"She's a nice girl. You used to think she was more than nice. I don't see why you couldn't do that again."

Having feelings for the woman you're supposed to be competing against is a major inconvenience. Ten out of ten do not recommend.

It's similar to the number who would not recommend working with your asshole brother. Turns out, I'm shit at listening to the recommendations of others.

I'm still seething from my call with Trent last night. After learning I was out to dinner with Kelsey from one of the guys on our team, he called to make sure I knew what was at stake here. He went so far as to threaten that if we don't win this contract, he'll let me go and replace me with someone cheaper. He sounded serious enough that I'm treating it as a credible threat.

Fortunately, I'd stepped out onto the street after he called me two times in a row. Unfortunately, after assuring him nothing is going on between Kelsey and me for what felt like forever, my temper got the best of me, and I yelled, "I don't know why you're making this such a big deal. There's no way we're losing this contract to Kelsey!"

As fate would have it, Kelsey had apparently given up on waiting for me in the restaurant by that point, and when I turned back around, she was leaning against the door, watching me. In the same black jumpsuit as last time we went out to eat, her back was pressed against the brick wall of the building along with the sole of one of her black boots. As I quickly hung up with Trent, I kept my eyes trained on hers, looking for any sign of how she was feeling. I was greeted with nothing but cool indifference—the mask I finally thought I'd earned the chance to look behind.

That indifference hadn't thawed since.

"Carter?" Bill's voice comes through from the phone, pulling me back to the present.

"It was a teenage crush. That's not how it is now. It's"—I pause to think—"complicated."

Complicated is the understatement of the century. Spending time with Kelsey is torture in the most painfully enjoyable of ways. My brain screams at me that she is my competition, the one thing that could make me unable to be in Wild Bluffs *and* financially support my mom. My heart and my body, though, tend to break through the barrier my brain has erected, focusing on her twirling that small strand of hair at the back of her neck or the way she always smells crisp and warm.

Which aren't even smells!

"Everything I have that is worth anything started out complicated," Bill says.

"Aren't you supposed to say something about how when you find the right person, it isn't complicated, it's the easiest thing in the world?"

Bill snorts into the phone. "You've been watching too many movies, Carter. No one who has actually fallen in love with someone thinks love is easy. Love isn't like they show it in fairy tales; it's pulling your heart from your chest and handing the bloody flesh to someone else to see if they want to protect it or crush it. It exposes raw truths that leave you more vulnerable and *alive* than you've ever been before."

"Sounds terrible," I say, cringing at the image of ripping my own heart out just to hand it over to someone else. "I think I'll pass."

Bill snorts again. "The fact that you think you have an option in the matter is hilarious."

"How's my mom?" I ask, pulling the topic away from bloody body parts and back to the real reason I know Bill called.

The pause at the other end of the line tells me everything I need to know—it's bad. Between one heartbeat and the next, I've planned my flight back to Colorado, considered three get-rich-quick schemes to fund my mom's care once Trent fires me, and mentally sorted through every piece of information I've ever read about Alzheimer's progression.

"She had a pretty significant episode yesterday afternoon. She was tired, and a school bus with a high school basketball team traveling through stopped to eat."

I tense, not liking where this is going at all. Crowded places and overstimulation are both called out as things to avoid for people with dementia.

Bill continues, "She tried to help, though Milly and I both hustled out to take over from her. It was so busy. I didn't realize something was wrong until after they all had their food."

I'm not breathing. My mom. The only person I have in this world.

"Mildred found her in the back by the trash cans, rocking slightly as she covered her ears."

"I'm coming home," I cut in.

"You're not," Bill replies in a gruff voice. "Mildred talked to Alice, and she quickly came back to herself. I drove her to the hospital, and Dr. Pendleton shuffled her patients so she could get your mom in right away. It's not clear if she just became overstimulated or if it's a symptom of something else."

"Like what?" I ask, sensing he's holding information back from me.

"Doc is worried it might be depression, though that's just one possibility."

"I thought we'd made it through the point where most people develop depression." Then another possibility occurs to me, the one Bill might be trying to shelter me from. "Is it because I left? Is it because she's alone that the doctor thinks it might be depression?"

"No. After talking to your mom, we think overstimulation is the most likely answer, but Mildred and I came over for dinner at your normal time last night, and we'll keep that up until you're back. We can handle a routine just fine without you here, Carter."

"I can't believe you waited almost a full day to tell me this, Bill," I say, my voice betraying just how angry I am. Angry I wasn't called immediately. Angry I wasn't there to help. Angry my mom, who has already had to deal with so much shit in her life, also has to deal with losing her memory—by herself.

"It was the middle of the night over there when it happened. And there was nothing you could've done to help, Carter. Even if you'd been here, it might've happened, and there still wouldn't have been anything you could've done to help other than sit on your ass in the waiting room with me."

I push my fingertips into the corners where my eyebrows meet my nose, breathing deeply as I press along my eyebrows to work the tension out.

"I haven't talked to her in a few days," I say, the guilt growing in my stomach. Since Jaxon's concerts have started, I'm busy most of the day, and even with my mornings typically free, it's still the middle of the night there.

"Your mom can handle you being gone for a few weeks. Mildred and I are here, and we've got everything under control. I promise I'll call immediately if it's something you need to know about."

"No matter what time it is," I state, not even bothering to phrase it as a question.

"No matter what time it is. Now, you just stay focused on what's important over there."

"Making sure we win this contract."

"No, that's not—"

"I know, Bill. I know how important it is that I win this contract for Trent. He's already threatened to fire me if we don't." The energy is flowing through me, forcing me to pace, to *do* something. Bill's right.

I need this job, and I can't let anything get in my way of being able to provide for my mom.

"Carter, I know your job is important, but it's not ev—"

I cut him off. "I gotta go, Bill. Thanks for the update and all you're doing for my mom. Call me anytime."

I know just what I need to do to make sure we win Jaxon's long-term security contract.

Chapter Fifteen

Kelsey

"I can't believe I let you talk me into a virtual coffee date at seven forty-five in the morning," Sam says dramatically. Sam is JT Johnson's assistant and came into my life six months ago when we had to stage an intervention. It went spectacularly—his words, not mine. We somehow became friends, likely due to our shared disdain for the human population.

I glare at him, making sure to look directly into the camera at the top of my phone so he gets the full effect. "You're the one who suggested a coffee date."

"I didn't think about the time difference...or the fact that you only have mornings free," he says with a pout that makes me laugh loudly.

The woman across the lobby of my Dublin hotel looks at me, but she quickly breaks eye contact when I stare right back. Thank goodness I'm wearing earbuds; Sam cannot be trusted in public.

"Well, thank you for deigning to grace me with your presence anyway. I can't believe you, of all people, aren't joining JT and Jameo in Australia."

"Ew. You know I don't go to places with spiders that size."

"I don't think they're crawling around the stadium."

"One can never be too careful when it comes to spiders the size of dinner plates and snakes that drop from trees."

We both visually shiver at the thought.

"Plus," he continues, "it's my dad's sixty-fifth birthday, and my mom is throwing a huge party. I can't miss it."

We fall into a natural flow of conversation, and Sam tells me about the new guy he started dating. I fill him in on the tour so far, or at least the parts I can tell him about. Sam, like everyone else in the world, is a *huge* fan of Jaxon. I remain professionally neutral on the subject, though I have been pleasantly surprised at how good Jaxon is. Not as a musician, I already knew that, but as a human. When I took this assignment, I was worried I'd find out the kid I knew turned into your stereotypical rock star complete with the drugs, women, and temper tantrums. So far, I've seen no drugs or temper tantrums. The women, well, it would be a low to normal amount for any single, handsome musician out on tour. Unfortunately, I feel a slight twinge of awkwardness any time it comes through from his personal security detail that he's bringing a woman back to his room.

I, of course, tell Sam none of this, instead focusing on the information he could find online, like how many people are there, and describing the electric, emotionally charged atmosphere of the crowd each night.

"Okay, but we've been talking for thirty minutes now, and you haven't even mentioned Mr. Dark and Broody," Sam says, cutting me off midway through a story about a twelve-year-old girl bawling when Jaxon walked out on stage.

"I'm sorry, who?" I ask.

"No. We're not doing that. Lila told me about your little—or should I say big?—coworker over there, and I'm offended—*offended*, Kelsey—that you didn't tell me you were going to spend seven weeks cuddled up with a hunk of handsome man meat? And doing so while the most popular love songs are being crooned at you, live, by Jaxon Steele. Sigh." He follows up his verbal sigh with a real one, leaning his hoodie-clad elbow on the table and leaning his head on his hand.

"That's not how it is. We're just coworkers. We're actively in competition for the same job." I'm momentarily pulled back to the conversation I overheard between Carter and Trent in London. The hurt that flared through my chest and into my stomach when he said there was no way they were going to lose to me. The shield of icy calm I've kept in place since then. And, the worst part, when I purposefully walked past the empty seat next to Carter on the plane and sat next to Mikayla, I *still* turned midflight to tell him my opinion on the movie I was watching, only to realize it wasn't Carter.

"Oookay," Sam replies. "But what if—and just bear with me here—you said fuck that and fucked him instead?"

"Yeah, that's not going to happen."

"Why not? I know Lila didn't mislead me about how gorgeous that man is, because despite not being a professional hacker like some people I know—"

"I'm not a hacker," I cut in.

Sam ignores my interruption and says over me, "—I can cyberstalk with the best of them. So I know he is exactly as handsome as Lila claimed he is, potentially even more." He pauses. "His hair is perfectly styled, with the short waves on top. He's your ideal height. I don't care that Lila and JT are adorable together all big and small, too much over six feet is too tall for you. The man clearly works out, and he does *not* skip leg day. Or arm day. *Or chest day.* Actually, can you ask him for his chest routine, the pecs on that—no, I'm getting distracted. Where was I?"

I raise an eyebrow, refusing to engage in this line of rapid-fire...truths. Unwanted, but truths nonetheless.

Sam is, unsurprisingly, undeterred. "What is it about eyes that dark that makes me want to dive into them and never resurface?"

Choosing silence seems to be working, so I just stare at my phone.

"So, I expect a full report after you fuck him. And don't forget to ask him to send me his chest routine."

"I'm not doing that."

"Which part?" Sam asks.

"Both. Either."

"*Why?*" he gasps as if I just declined to save a kitten desperately hanging from a log in the middle of a river.

"You're being dramatic."

"If you don't tangle your hands in that man's hair as you kiss him passionately, I will fly over there and do it for you."

And damn it if that exact image doesn't burn itself into my brain, Sam's suggestion taking on a life of its own as suddenly my hands are no longer in Carter's hair, but skimming along the sides of his waist, the ridges of his stomach muscles under my thumbs exciting and sensual.

"You're welcome to—" I try to say, forcing myself to remember Carter isn't just a handsome man with the intellect to back up his strong jaw and Adonis physique. He's the guy I have to work with every day. He's the guy I'm trying to beat. I can't let my stupid fantasies get the best of me.

Now if only I could control my dreams.

"I've got to go or I'm going to be late for my spin class," Sam says, taking his phone with him as he heads toward the door in his apartment. "Sleep with the man. Send me all the deets. No." He holds up his hand as I start to speak. "I will accept zero excuses. I don't care that you work with him, and you can still destroy his company while letting him take you to Pound Town. People do it every day in New York. Don't deprive me of this."

And with that, Sam hangs up on me.

I drop my head into my hands, dragging my fingers over my forehead. Sam's wrong. Of course he is. Sleeping with Carter would be a terrible idea.

"Hey, Kelsey." Carter's voice comes from somewhere above me.

The timing couldn't be worse, considering Sam just reminded my body of every reason it's been pushing to see what Carter's hiding under that terrible shirt of his.

"Are you okay?" he asks, his brows rising in concern.

"Sure. Just praying for God to spare me from exasperating people."

"Ahh. Your sisters?" he guesses.

"I wish. They know not to be quite so annoying. Sam hasn't learned yet."

Carter's expression darkens so briefly, I almost missed it. *What's that about?*

"Who's Sam?"

"He's JT's assistant."

"Oh. I see," he says before clearing his throat.

"I was hoping he was going to join them all when they came to Australia, but I guess he isn't going to make it."

"Ah. That's a...shame."

I swivel my head to see what he's staring at so intently over my shoulder, but there isn't anything there but your standard hotel lobby photo of old cars at various locations I'm assuming are in Ireland.

"Do you have a minute to talk?" he asks once my gaze is back on him.

I check the time on my phone and nod. "Sure. What's up? Is everything okay for tonight?"

This is the first leg of the tour where we don't have a day between concerts to prepare in a new city. We arrived two hours ago, were handed our keys to our hotel rooms by the logistics staff, and we will leave for the security briefing in less than thirty minutes. It's hectic, to say the least.

Carter lowers his large frame into the small seat in front of me, our knees brushing under the small, circular table between us.

"No. Nothing like that. I think we're set."

"Okay," I say. "Then what's up?"

"I need to apologize for the other night."

I've played it so cool. Not a single person could look at the way I've handled hearing him say Mitchell Security was going to beat me and say I've been anything but professional. Anything but calm, cool, and collected. It doesn't matter if it was a shot of liquid fire to my gut, I masked it in a way that would make every woman who's ever worked in a man's profession proud. No over-the-top emotions here.

"Haven't we already done this?" I ask, looking him in the eyes—which is a mistake. No, I won't be distracted by those now.

"Not for the breach incident. For what you overheard me say the other night."

"No apology necessary. We both know we're competing. I plan on winning too."

"I still feel like I should apologize."

"Really not necessary. And, just so this doesn't become a habit, maybe stop doing things you need to apologize for," I say with a shrug like it isn't a big deal. I'm not fazed by him admitting his mistakes at all.

Carter bites his bottom lip, and the little glimpse of vulnerability does something to my heart, because I swear it stops beating for a second.

"Well, I'm sorry I said it was a done deal, us winning. I don't actually believe that. I think we're good, but you are too. The way I see it, it's anyone's game at this point."

"I appreciate the sentiment, but you'll excuse me if I don't value what you say to me in private when I know you'd never say it in front of other people."

His face flushes as his Adam's apple bobs. At least he has the decency to look ashamed of his duplicity.

"Well, I better go get changed," I say as I push to my feet, uninterested in continuing this conversation.

Carter's hand closes over mine on the table between us, the warmth of his palm sinking into my skin, shooting up my arms and directly into my core.

We both stare at the connection between us for a moment before Carter says, "Wait."

"Okay," I practically whisper as I sit back down, shocked by my body's reaction to our contact.

"Trent..."

I see the hesitation in Carter's eyes and am about to leave again when he continues, "This contract is more important to Trent than any other before."

"It's important to all of us," I say, yanking my hand out from under his to cross my arms.

"There is another contract on the line for us. And the musician has made it clear they're only going with us if Jaxon does. And Trent's made it clear I won't have a job if we don't win this, and I *cannot* lose my job right now. So, yeah, I'm doing and will continue to do everything in my power to make sure Mitchell Security comes out on top."

Fucking Trent. Of course he threatened Carter's job. Took that trick right out of his dad's playbook. As annoyed as I am with Carter right now, I can say with complete confidence he is excellent at his job. And even though our work together before the concert made me realize Trent isn't as big of an idiot as I always assumed he was, he has to be living under a rock if he thinks he could do this without Carter. Gosh, and with Carter's mom sick, he really does need the job. That's terrible, maybe I should let them— No! Nope. Never. No.

"Yeah, well, so am I," I say, trying to keep my conflicted feelings off my face. "I'm sorry your brother's a dick and is trying to motivate you with scare tactics, but that doesn't mean I'm going to take it easy on you or give up on winning this work with Jaxon. I've worked hard to build my business to what it is, and I have employees I have to think about too. Ones I would never threaten like that, for the record."

"I know you wouldn't. I've seen the way you work with your team. You're a great boss." He offers me a tentative smile.

"Thank you," I say. I'm not usually too affected by compliments—they tend to be more about the giver than the receiver—but Carter's seems so genuine that I can't help but feel a surge of pride.

"So...can we go back to being friends?" Carter asks, a pained smile on his face.

"Not if that"—I circle my finger in the direction of his grimace—"is how you feel about it."

He runs his hand down his face. "I just wasn't sure if you'd consider us friends."

"Do you?"

"Yes." The dichotomy between his uncertainty about my friendship and his certainty that I'm his friend melts the final holdout in my mind.

"Then we're friends," I say. "Friends who happen to be rivals."

Chapter Sixteen

Kelsey

"Thank you, Stockholm! You've been amazing!" Jaxon yells from the stage as he lifts his black cowboy hat into the air and bows. The other four musicians on stage join Jaxon, the group all bending at the waist in sync.

"Team Two in position for encore," Weston's voice comes across my earpiece.

"Go for encore," Carter repeats after using his computer to connect with Kevin near the stage.

Kevin waits for the confirmation from the show's logistics team and then nods, Jaxon picking up the signal. Since Jaxon refuses to let us talk to him through his in-ear monitor, we make do with physical signals.

Jaxon waves as he leaves the stage, the musicians following like a waddle of black ducklings. The crowd goes absolutely feral at his exit, and I scan the feed on my screens faster, my eyes trying to find any place the excitement has turned to destructive chaos. Fans can quickly become a mob if given the right catalyst.

I can feel Carter next to me, his eyes scanning the arena in front of us and the monitors, making sure each and every one of the security personnel is doing the same.

My team, on the other hand, is scanning every image our system is pulling off social media pages, using the combined power of our state-of-the-art technology with our highly trained team to help identify anything that could be getting out of hand. It's amazing how people's first reaction to something going wrong is to start filming it.

Despite the major mishap in Vancouver, the security team is running like a well-oiled machine. While the first few concerts required Carter and me to be intermediaries between the boots-on-the-ground team and those acting as the eyes in the sky, they're now working together, cutting us out of the loop to go directly to the person they need. It's how they would function if we were all one team, so I try not to be too upset about feeling redundant.

We go through the motions we've perfected over the last week, and with a final note, Jaxon closes down the sixth show of the tour.

"Steele is in the box," Nash says through my earpiece, and I lean back into my computer chair with a groan.

"I thought you were going to talk to him about that," I say to Carter.

"He thinks it's hilarious," he says, stretching his neck to one side and then the other.

"And...?"

"And Jaxon also thinks it's hilarious, so I'm letting it go."

"We practiced!" I yell in mock anger. "I spent forty minutes on the airplane listening to you rehearse how you'd tell him. I'll never get that time back. I could've sent *so many emails.*"

"I used it to talk to him about Mikayla instead."

"Did he cry?" I ask. "I can't believe you didn't wait until I could at least watch him get all flustered."

Nash is the sweet golden retriever puppy of the team. He's adorable, and everyone loves him, but he tends to chew up shoes if you don't keep an eye on him.

Carter chuckles. "No one wants to see that, Kels."

The nickname does something to my insides that I'm trying very hard not to think about. Carter and I are friends. Who are also rivals. For the most important contract of our lives. Nicknames fit into that...somewhere.

"I like making grown men cry, *Cart,*" I say.

"I think we need to workshop the nickname."

"What did your Army buddies call you?"

"I decline to answer," he says, turning away from me to pretend to do something on his computer. Well, maybe he's actually getting everything taken offline and put away for the night, but I'm not going to let something like a prompt cleanup distract me.

"Why do you do this to yourself?" I ask, sitting back in my chair and crossing my arms over my chest. "You know if you just said something like Mitchell, I'd give it a rest. *But you declined to answer.* Which means it's not just your last name."

"It's Mitchell. Obviously."

I hold up a finger. "One: you hate the name Mitchell, so I can only assume that's a lie, or they weren't actually your friends. Two: you would've told me if it was something normal."

Carter lifts one shoulder and drops it, *shrugging*. I ranted yesterday on the plane about shrugging. It's Izzy's go-to move, the shrug, and I can't stand it. It's the most annoying gesture someone can gesticulate. Either have the courage to flip me off or be ambivalent enough to simply ignore me. A shrug is a pity gesture. A *pity* gesture that I don't want.

So the shrug will be a no from me. I poke his shoulder, only taking one millisecond to appreciate the firm boulder my finger just ricocheted off. "Tell me."

"No."

"You're being a child." I jab my finger into his shoulder again, harder this time. "Tell me."

"*I'm* being the child?" he asks as I brandish my pointer finger like a weapon in front of me.

"Yes. We both agree on that account."

The computer in front of Carter dings, and he focuses his attention on the screen. I'm sure he's not going to answer me, but he says quietly, "Puffin."

"Puffin?" I let out a laugh. "Why?"

He shrugs again.

I try to tone down my eye roll, but it's harder than I anticipated. I snag the hair at the back of my neck, twirling it as I stare at him. He watches my finger, mesmerized by the movement, it seems. Maybe I can hypnotize people like this.

"It had to do with a tuxedo," he says, though the final syllable rises like he's asking a question.

"It's like you want me to call your bluff!" I say, laughing. The man is terrible at lying.

He shakes his head, a strand of hair dropping over his forehead. I reach out to push it out of his face, our eyes meeting.

I pull my hand back, shocked by my inappropriate behavior.

"Uh, sorry," I say quickly. "You just had...hair." I gesture to his general face region, not helping the situation at all.

"I appreciate the help."

Now it's my turn to use cleaning up as a distraction. We pack up the security room in silence, though not the awkward kind that it might've been a week or two ago. Carter and I move around the small room and each other in a flow so smooth, it might as well be choreographed.

"Why did you become a Mitchell?" I ask. "You don't seem that excited about it."

Carter sighs, and for a minute, I think he's going to decline to answer. But then he says, "I never wanted to be a Mitchell. I came into this world as an Anderson, and I wanted to stay that way. It was the name my mom gave me, the one I grew up with. When Wilson said he wanted me to legally take his last name, I said no. Or, to be honest, I screamed no, loudly, before stalking off like the surly fourteen-year-old I was. There was no possible way I was going to take the last name of the man who had ignored me my entire life. The man who married another woman when my mom was days away from giving birth to me."

I continue to clean, making sure he knows I'm listening but not prying. "But then?"

Another sigh. "But then my mom told me Wilson was offering to increase his child support by a thousand dollars a month if I changed my name. I still said no. Like the petulant child I was, I said no, claiming I would work all summer and earn as much money as he would pay us."

He coughs like his throat can't handle saying that many consecutive words at one time. "My mom's laughter turned into tears as she explained that working breakfast rather than dinner meant she was bringing in less money in tips, and for the first time, she wasn't sure where she was going to find the cash to pay our bills. I offered to quit football and get a job after school, but Mom wouldn't hear of it. She knew all about my plans to get out of Wild Bluffs, and part of that plan was an athletic scholarship if an academic one didn't pan out."

"I'm sorry, Carter. I..." *I what? Didn't know? We all assumed it was something like that.* "I shouldn't have pried."

"It's fine. But yeah, the day I formally became a Mitchell was one of the worst of my life."

It's silent as we both continue to pack our things.

"Are you headed up to check the comms devices?" Carter asks when we've both got our equipment packed and ready to be on a truck to Amsterdam in a few hours.

"I am."

"Want some company?"

I feel the slow smile pull on my face. Company in general? No. Carter's company?

"Sure," I say. "If you want to."

Shifting the backpack with my laptop and essential equipment onto my back, I mentally work through my checklist for tonight. The earpiece check should be the last thing I need to get done.

We're in Tokyo in a week, so the equipment we used in Dublin has already started its long journey there. Our gear from tonight will start the seventeen-hour drive south to the Netherlands bright and early tomorrow. It's a quick enough turnaround that I'm surprised we have a full travel day for it. We'll have almost twenty-four hours where only the executive protection team is working, and Carter plans to change them out fairly frequently to get everyone as much time off as possible.

It's that twenty-four-hour stretch that made the conversation with Nash about fraternizing with the other agents a requirement.

"So what did Nash say when you talked to him about Mikayla?" I ask.

"He assured me nothing was happening between them."

"But?"

"But he's interested in her, and as much as it pains me to admit it, I think she might be interested in him too." Carter runs a hand through his hair, the carefully groomed length on the top turning into valleys where his fingers pass through.

"Which means it's an issue; it's just not breaking the rules."

"Why couldn't he have fallen for one of your voices in his ear?" Carter asks. "There is no fraternization policy between teams."

"We don't actually have one at all."

"Really?" he asks, his eyebrows shooting up as he swivels his head to look at me, never missing a step.

"I considered it, but as we're rarely in person together, it's not really necessary. It's not like your team, where a relationship might cause Nash to pick protecting Mikayla over Jaxon."

"So you think I did the right thing?"

"You followed the rules of the company you work for. Is it up to you to decide what your fraternization policy is?" I ask, making the last turn to the security storage room.

"No."

"Then, there you go."

I stop a few feet away from the room, knowing there is a chance someone will be in there collecting earpieces for me. Nash, bless his heart, has been quite helpful when it comes to being another pair of hands for me, since I don't have anyone else physically here.

"But," I say, "I also think there are less aggressive answers. Like, couldn't you just make them disclose their relationship and then not have them be on the same detail? Or just turn a blind eye while they get it out of their system? Who is to say it's a long-term thing?"

He lets out a soft chuckle, his eyes darting to the door that Nash is most likely behind. He takes a step toward me, lowering his head to look into my eyes. "If they never would've said anything and just hooked up a time or two before it fizzled out, I would be happy to live in ignorance. Unfortunately, Nash felt the need to tell me there are real feelings there. Feelings that aren't going to go away."

"Give it time; that will change. Feelings don't tend to stick around too long."

He leans just a little closer, a sad grin tugging at his lips. "Some feelings don't just fade, no matter how long it's been."

That clean scent of his is back, his deodorant my new favorite fragrance. The air between us pulses as my eyes flash to meet his. There's sadness there, and something else I can't interpret.

"Hey, guys." Nash's voice comes from my right as the door to the security room opens.

I blink, and the moment with Carter is gone. He's stepped away so casually that I didn't even know it was happening, and now I'm questioning if it even happened. Was that a moment there? And if it was, what could it possibly mean?

"Nash," Carter replies, his voice friendly as he makes his way toward the room.

"I hear you got a talk about how *not* to spend your free time in Amsterdam," I say, smiling up at the large man as he hands me a case with the earpieces already tucked nicely into their spots.

"I told Grandpa over there that he didn't have to worry about me," Nash jokes, crossing his muscular arms across the black Mitchell Security shirt he has on.

He and Carter could almost be brothers with their large frames and dark hair. Though Nash's face is softer, his edges less defined. Carter gives a whole new meaning to strong square jaw.

"I think we both know that he very much *does* need to worry about you," I say, setting the black case down on the table in the room and beginning my inspection of every earpiece.

Nash shrugs. "Or he could just choose not to. It's not like I want to go out and experience all Amsterdam has to offer. I just want to take my coworker out for a nice dinner."

"I think you mean date," Carter chimes in, moving next to me at the table.

His arm bumps mine slightly, the warmth from the contact flowing through me as he reaches across me to grab the next earpiece in line. I shoot him a grateful smile, which he returns with a small one of his own.

"I thought only you were allowed to examine the equipment," Nash says to me.

I look over my shoulder, seeing the teasing behind the question on his face. He's not wrong. After Vancouver, relying on someone else to check the earpieces should be out of the question. I'm not sure why I'm so willing to let Carter help me, but I'm sure in a small room with two large men is not the correct time to try to figure it out.

"I just said that so you wouldn't feel bad that I didn't trust you manhandling them with those baseball mitts you call hands."

"Carter's hands are just as big as mine."

Do not look. Do not—shit. My eyes fall to Carter's hands where they gently grasp the small black device, turning it over as he examines it. I'm transfixed by the rough callus I can see on his thumb, imagining what it would feel like—nope!

Nash has a lopsided grin on his face when I finally drag my eyes back to him.

I narrow my eyes in response, but that just makes his grin widen.

"Well, I'm going to take my baseball mitts and leave this super important work to you two," Nash says after I turn my attention back to my work.

He leaves us to it, and we fall into a quiet rhythm, both focused on inspecting, cleaning, and turning off each of the earpieces.

As we work, something settles in my chest, something that makes me feel a little less alone.

CHAPTER SEVENTEEN

CARTER

"Did you just make a pot joke?" I ask my mom as she giggles on my phone's screen.

"Well, isn't that what Amsterdam is known for?"

"Yep. That's it," I say, hoping my mother doesn't know anything about their red-light district. There is only so much I can discuss with my mother, even if she'd be open to the conversation.

"Did you watch the *Ted Lasso* episode that takes place here yet?"

Watching the show together had been a fun part of our routine back home, and we decided to keep watching it independently while I was gone. Neither of us has enough going on in our lives to fill a whole conversation without the help of current events or a shared TV show.

"There's an episode in Tokyo?" Mom asks, making my heart clench, even as I force a smile onto my face.

"I'm still in Amsterdam," I say, trying to walk the fine line between correcting her and just letting it go.

"Oh, right. Of course you are. We were just talking about that!"

I can tell my mom's smile is forced, nothing like the broad smile she usually gives away so freely. As terrible as it is for me to watch my mom go through the stages of dementia, I know it is so much worse for her.

"Anyway, enough about Amsterdam. Tell me about your dinner with Kelsey tonight!" My mom's smile turns genuine as she asks.

This she remembers. I casually mentioned in a text that I needed to chat as early as possible tonight because Kelsey and I have plans to visit one of her restaurants, and my mom won't let it go. I even got a text from Bill about it.

Knowing I'm leading on my mom—and possibly my own heart—but unwilling to put a damper on my mom's joy, I tell her our plans, not bothering to correct her when she calls it a date and tells me to wear something nice.

I don't tell her that since I am living out of a carry-on suitcase, I only have one option. Since Kelsey's been in the same black outfit the other times we went to dinner, my guess is she's in the same boat. Not that I'm complaining. There's something about the contrast between the sleek, almost casual cut to her clothes and the wave of blonde hair that captures her entirety so well. It's like she's effortlessly put together, but there's this undeniable wildness behind those calm eyes—like she could take over the world—or tear it all down—on a whim.

Any denial I'd been living in about my crush on Kelsey fading with time has long since been debunked. That woman fully and completely has my attention, and it's the most confusing thing I've ever felt. Because even when I remind myself that she's my competition, that I *have* to win this contract instead of her, my heart doesn't seem to care. Every time I think I've got a handle on my feelings, that I've shoved them back down inside of me where they need to stay—at least until after this whole Jaxon Steele business is done with—she does something that throws me back on a collision course. A smile, an intelligent suggestion, something so small, yet it's like she holds the power to unravel every single plan I've made.

I've woken up every single night this week sweaty and breathing hard from dreams of her. Dreams I most certainly should not be thinking about while on the phone with my mom.

"Well," my mom says with a knowing smirk as I force my attention back to our conversation, "I'll let you go. Tell Kelsey hi for me."

"Love you, Mom," I say.

"Have so much fun out in Tokyo tonight, love. You deserve it."

***

"So, I had a weird conversation with Izzy today," Kelsey says as she sits across the small wooden table from me. We're at a farm-to-table restaurant that is in one side of a functional greenhouse. The tables are small and placed closely together, my large frame never feeling as out of place as it does now, sitting in a wicker chair that was made for men one hundred years ago, not giants like me. Thankfully, Kelsey offered to be the one to squeeze between our table and the one next to it to get to the bench seat.

She's not wearing the same black jumpsuit I had prepared myself for, and when she took off her coat to reveal a form-fitting navy-blue dress that ends midway down her thigh, I swear I almost swallowed my tongue. I'm pretty sure she didn't catch me staring, but I can't be sure.

"Oh yeah? How's Izzy doing?" I respond.

"I'm not sure. We didn't really talk about that."

Well, that's confusing, although I'm the first to admit I don't understand sibling relationships. I may work with Trent now, but we've never acted like brothers. We could barely tolerate each other growing up, and even now that I work for him, I don't really consider Trent to be anything but my boss I happen to share some DNA with. So I'm not sure how you have an entire conversation with someone and not know how they are doing.

Kelsey waves away my slight frown. "She's fine. I see now that the correct answer was 'she's fine.' Though, for the record, I never asked 'how are you doing?'"

The light is catching Kelsey's lip gloss, and I can't stop staring. Kelsey is naturally beautiful and rarely wears makeup, so I'm sure that's the reason I can't stop staring at her lips.

"Glad she's...fine," I say, pulling my gaze away from Kelsey's mouth. Not that looking at her eyes is any better. They're what I've heard my mom call gunmetal blue, but it's hard to say because there are so many colors when you start looking into them. A dark ring of sapphire lines the iris with streaks of a grayish green flowing into the moss-green color that circles her pupil. They're an ocean on a stormy day, and I feel like my boat just disappeared from under me, dropping me directly into their depths.

Kelsey tilts her head to the side, squishing her eyebrows together, but with a quick shake of her head, she continues. "Yeah, me too.

Anyway, she told me she was in the dealership getting her car looked at, and Trent came in. He was asking how much he could get if he sold back Julie's car."

"Why's that strange?" I ask. Since Trent started dating his trophy wife—his words, not mine—I've had the displeasure of hearing about the hot tub, car, and new kitchen he's bought her. It makes sense that he'd be upgrading her to a new model vehicle already. I'm sure he has the funds just lying around to buy whatever she wants, not that I'm bitter about it or anything.

The left corner of Kelsey's nose pulls up slightly as she looks at me with disbelief, and fuck if it isn't one of the cutest things I've seen in a long time. My cheeks heat, and despite my best efforts, a smile crosses my face. Kelsey returns it with one of her own, and it takes all of my willpower not to reach across the table and trace her grin with my thumb.

We do not caress our rivals. We do not caress our rivals. We do not—

"Do you not pay any attention to the town gossip?" Kelsey asks.

"No. I only see my mom and Bill, and they know I couldn't care less about what's going on in town."

"Hmm," she says, and there's something about her tone that suggests she disagrees with my decision not to know what's going on. Or maybe she's disappointed in it. I can't really tell.

"Are you going to tell me why anything about Trent is interesting?"

"You know," Kelsey says, "I would normally agree with you, and I still can't stand to be in the same room as the guy, but he's a lot smarter than I give him credit for. Or at least his emails make him sound interesting. Does he have an assistant who handles his emails?"

Of course Kelsey would be smart enough to figure out that Trent's IQ jumps about fifteen, maybe twenty, points in his written communication. Needing to avoid that conversation, I offer a noncommittal grunt before trying to pivot.

"Could be. But why is it interesting?" I ask.

"He just bought her the car. It was a whole thing because it's the second vehicle he's purchased for her since they've been married. The first one was a pale pink Mini Cooper, and then he bought this new electric one because she's worried about saving the Earth. To be clear, she kept the Mini, she just only drives it to the city—the men at coffee have had a field day with that one."

"So maybe she decided she doesn't actually care about the Earth," I say with a shrug. I've spent very little time around my brother's wife, and after what I witnessed at her wedding, I think I'd prefer to keep it that way.

"Yeah, maybe. Iz just said that Trent seemed weird about it. She used the term *shifty*."

"Well, Trent *is* shifty. He comes by it naturally. Have you met my sperm donor?"

"I suppose. Izzy just has a strangely good sense for other people's emotions, so I thought I'd mention it."

There's not much I can do about it from the Netherlands, and the last thing I want to do on our date—at our dinner—is talk about Trent. I don't really care why Julie doesn't want her car anymore. Maybe she's giving up driving or only taking gold-plated bikes from now on. Maybe they're getting a divorce—shit, I hope Trent has a prenup and the company isn't going to go down with their marriage. I add that to my mental list of things I *should* ask Trent about. Whatever it is, though, it's definitely not as interesting as the woman sitting across from me—nothing is.

Our conversation flows along with the red wine, which I've learned is Kelsey's favorite. She prefers drier ones but will drink just about any that's poured for her. My mom doesn't drink, and since moving home, I've limited myself to one a night, too depressed by the idea of drinking alone.

Kelsey has become more animated, her arms moving in larger arcs since we started in on our dessert. I'm not sure if it's the wine, the atmosphere, or the company, but my cheeks are physically hurting from smiling so much. It's the most fun I've had in...maybe forever, but definitely since I moved back home. I'm transfixed by the woman across from me, and it might be the wine talking, but there seems to be something between us. Something more than just the friendship we've casually fallen into.

As the waiter clears our dessert plates, I find myself reluctant for the evening to end. The restaurant has emptied around us, the other diners trickling out into the night, leaving behind a soft hush punctuated only by the clink of glasses and the muted conversations of the staff.

Kelsey's eyes sparkle in the flickering candlelight as she regales me with stories from her days in the Marines. Her hand gestures paint pictures in the air, and I'm captivated by the graceful dance of her fingers. The way she tucks a stray lock of her wild hair behind her ear, the curve of her smile, the natural cadence of her voice—every detail etches itself into my memory.

As she reaches the punchline of her tale, she leans forward, her hand falling on top of mine on the table, and every single nerve ending in my body fires at once. It's a heady rush of sensation, and it makes me want to lean across the table and press my mouth to hers.

She offers me a hopeful smile, one I've never seen on her face before, and as I stand, I grab her hand, fully intent on pulling her into me and taking what I've wanted since high school. The want that almost got me suspended all those years ago.

The ringing of her phone draws her attention from me, her eyes narrowing as she takes in the name of her number two, Lila Walker, flashing across her screen. Glancing at me once, she considers the phone again before reluctantly pulling her hand away from mine to answer.

Moving quickly, she walks toward the door, telling Lila to give her a minute until she can get outside. I trail after her, cursing myself for not kissing her when I had the chance.

"Hold on, Carter's right here," she says as I exit the door.

She waves me over, tapping the button on her screen to put Lila on speakerphone.

"What's up?" I ask as I move closer to Kelsey, our arms pressing together.

"An image from the hotel lobby just pinged. We think it might be Bennie and another woman."

My mind starts racing. A sighting of Jaxon's stalker in our hotel in Amsterdam is surprising, considering she was last thought to be living on the streets. I run through the schedule for the day in my head.

"Weston should be heading up—" I'm cut off by Lila.

"We've already contacted Weston. He confirmed Jaxon is safe in his room for the night. He sent a team to investigate, but the woman had already left by the time they arrived."

"Was it a positive identification?" Kelsey asks.

"Do we know where they went?" I ask at the same time.

"Nothing definitive. They arrived by taxi, ordered one drink, paid with cash, and left, also by taxi. We could expend the resources to try to track them, but between coordinating with the government and local businesses in the Netherlands, it feels like too large of an expenditure of resources without a positive identification. That said, it's why I'm calling. I want an official decision from Kelsey."

"Send through the images and security footage. We'll be back at the hotel in"—Kelsey pulls up a rideshare app on her phone—"ten minutes. We'll review the footage and make a final decision."

"Everything will be in your inbox when you get there."

Chapter Eighteen

Carter

"I'm leaving Nash here with the final vehicle to take you home," I say into my phone to Kelsey as I take in the windowed walls of the arena in Berlin from the backseat of the black SUV. Our hotel is over two miles away, and there is no way I'm leaving her here to get home by herself. The fact that she doesn't even argue but instead gives a tired "okay" before hanging up suggests she's even more exhausted than I am.

The last forty-eight hours have been some of the most stressful in my life, which is saying something, considering I've been deployed in active combat zones. The news about Bennie's possible reappearance in Amsterdam was like a bucket of cold water poured over us, and any lingering thoughts I had about where the night could go were instantly pushed aside to focus on the business at hand.

After reviewing each of the tapes, Kelsey and I were called to Jaxon's suite to loop him in. It was a brief meeting where we updated Jaxon and his team on our findings, Kelsey laying out her reasoning behind why she decided not to pursue the individual any further. I backed her fully and tried not to flinch when she sent a surprised look my way. Jaxon was quiet but considerate as we laid out his options, and ultimately went with our recommendation to limit his movements outside of his hotel suite and the concert venue.

Everyone was on high alert during the concert the next night, and even Jaxon seemed a bit tense during the show. The crowd in Amsterdam hadn't seemed to notice, though Kelsey and I both noted it during our time in the security booth. Kelsey's team had added an additional security camera at each of the entrances, and her computer screens had been full of the various feeds, her entire focus on being a second set of eyes. Fortunately, the venue in Amsterdam is one of the most intelligent arenas in the world, so plugging into their pre-existing systems made everything slightly easier.

The next morning, Kelsey climbed into one of the buses taking the crew to Berlin, offering me a small smile and wave that I interpreted to mean she was as unhappy about our time apart as I was. There's an air of unfinished business that, though shoved to the background for now, has been hovering between us since our date in Amsterdam.

No, not a date. Though maybe a date? Do you have to know it's a date ahead of time for it to be a date?

I stayed behind with Jaxon's security team, accompanying him to a TV interview before boarding the private jet for our flight to Berlin. We'd had ten minutes to drop off our bags at the hotel before heading over to the venue for the security meeting and sound check. Thank goodness for Gail and the logistics team handling check-in—all I had to do was grab my key from her.

Kelsey wasn't so lucky. The buses encountered icy roads on their drive, so they arrived two hours late, literally pulling up to the venue at the same time we did. Fortunately, the forty-five semitrucks with the sets and equipment had left the last venue immediately after the show was torn down, so they made it before the storm.

Since they arrived, everything has felt like a chaotic rush.

I let out an involuntary sigh, and Mikayla's eyes meet mine from where she's driving.

"I feel you. It's been a long fucking day."

"A long fucking few days," I respond, running my hands through my hair as I try to work away the headache forming at my temples.

Eddie grunts his agreement from the front seat as we turn off the road that runs along the Spree River, and I try not to be annoyed that he asked me to come back with him to discuss one of the agents on his team. Eddie leads the secondary CPO team for Jaxon—the counterpart to Weston's team. I'd wanted to put it off until tomorrow so I could stay with Kelsey, but he'd made it seem urgent, so here I am, heading back to our fancy hotel to discuss personnel while Nash makes sure the woman I can't stop thinking about makes it back safely.

When we arrive, Eddie and I grab a couple of seats at a small table in a secluded corner in the hotel's lobby. I try to push aside the thoughts of Kelsey and focus on Eddie's words. He explains that one of his protection officers, Leo, has been struggling with the crowds recently. He's either not in the right position or is too slow to move if someone is coming toward Jaxon. It hasn't escalated into anything major, but I can tell Eddie's concerned it will.

Leo has been with the team for almost as long as I have, but he's never been with as high-profile a client as Jaxon. None of us have, except Kevin. Though Hailey Moore's concerts didn't sell out as quickly as Jaxon's Forever Starts Here Tour did, so it might just be impossible to be as high-profile as Jaxon.

"I think he might do better on one of the other teams. One that spends less time guarding Jaxon in high-traffic situations," Eddie concludes.

It's a tough call. I've worked with Leo before, and he's solid, but I also know just how important it is that the entire Mitchell Security team is performing their best. We don't have room for any mistakes.

Maybe I should ask Kelsey what she thinks.

I squash the thought. Of course I can't ask Kelsey for advice. We may be friends now, or fuck, something more if I have a say in the matter, but *this* is the line I can't cross—at least until after one of us is awarded Jaxon's long-term security contract. So, even if Kelsey wasn't on her way back with Nash—

"Nash!" I say, startling Eddie with my outburst.

"What?"

"Leo can switch teams with Nash. It'll be good for Nash to get some different exposure, plus it resolves a possible situation we've got going on in their team."

Eddie raises an eyebrow, but I wave away his questioning look. I don't need one more person knowing about Nash's crush on his teammate.

"I'll talk to them about it tomorrow," I say. "Nash has been on pre-site duty rather than moving with Jaxon directly, so Leo will still have some exposure to Jaxon and the fans but won't be dealing with the same level of crowds."

Eddie nods his agreement, and we chat for a few more minutes about how things are going with his team and his family back home. He has two daughters in middle school, and I guess his wife is about to ship them both off to boarding school. For some reason I don't exactly understand, he finds the whole situation endlessly hilarious.

My gaze continually slips away from Eddie to the revolving door at the entrance, silently willing a woman with wild blonde hair to walk through.

When I realize I've yawned twice and completely lost the thread of the conversation, I say goodnight to Eddie and head to bed. I ride the elevator to the eleventh floor in silence, my mind fully on the woman who has somehow crept into every corner of my thoughts, turning even the hectic moments into ones filled with her.

It takes all my self-control not to text Nash to confirm all is well, but I know Kelsey would take it as an insult to her ability to take care of herself. I swipe into my room and head for the shower, fighting the urge to reach out and make sure she's safe, even though my heart keeps demanding it.

Between the stress and the constant thoughts of Kelsey, my body is on edge. As I step into the shower, the hot water cascades over my tense muscles, offering a momentary respite from the chaos of the day. But even as the steam rises around me, my thoughts drift inexorably to

Kelsey. Her intelligence, her quick wit, the way her eyes light up when she knows she's right—it all comes flooding in in vivid detail.

I close my eyes, letting the water run down my face, and I imagine her here with me, water droplets clinging to her curves, her lips parting as I pull her close. My hand moves lower, gripping myself as I picture running my fingers through her damp hair, tasting the water on her neck.

I stroke faster, lost in the fantasy of Kelsey's body pressed against mine. Giving my imagination free rein, I lift her up, pinning her to the shower wall as she wraps her legs around my waist. I can almost hear her breathy moans, feel her nails digging into my back.

I lean my forearm against the cool tile, my hand working faster as the fantasy intensifies. In my mind, Kelsey's lips crash against mine, hungry and insistent. I lift her higher, angling her hips just right as I slide into her warmth. The water pounds down around us as we move together, our bodies slick and urgent.

My breath comes in ragged gasps, echoing off the shower walls. I picture Kelsey's face, flushed with desire, her blue eyes locked on mine as she nears her peak. The imagined sound of her climax pushes me over the edge. I come with a muffled groan, my body shuddering as waves of pleasure wash over me.

As the last aftershocks fade, I let the hot water rinse away the evidence of my release. Guilt and longing war within me as I shut off the shower and step out, wrapping my towel around my waist. I start brushing my teeth, using the two minutes to look myself in the eye and remind my body of all the reasons it should stop fantasizing about Kelsey Harper. Or the one reason. The one and only reason: we both need to win this contract, and we can't both win. Though that's starting to seem like a flimsy excuse.

I pull open the door to the bathroom, a puff of steam escaping as I make my way to my bed. A beep to my right pulls my attention to the door, and I pause, unsure what to do as the door to my room opens, revealing a backlit figure.

"Um, this is—" I start to say, but the woman releases a yelp, automatically dropping her bag and taking up a fighting position.

A startled breath leaves me as I quickly assess the threat, but my thoughts falter when I meet the same blue eyes I was just fantasizing about. Kelsey.

The moment stretches between us, her eyes locking with mine, a mix of surprise and something deeper flickering there. It's all too much—the way my body reacts like it's been waiting for this. I blink, trying to determine whether this is real or some exhaustion-induced hallucination, but her presence is too solid, too real to deny.

My pulse races, my heart thumping in my chest as if it's trying to escape. This is her—the woman who has captured my attention and won't seem to let it go—and now she's standing in front of me, close enough to feel the heat of her breath.

The towel around my waist suddenly feels like it's not enough of a shield, or maybe is too much of one, as her eyes trace my chest, wandering along the grooves of my abs, up over my shoulders, before landing on my face. The surge of pride that flares inside of me at her perusal quickly flees as her brows pull together in confusion.

"Is this not..." she says as she steps back into the hall to look at the room number next to the door. "I think you're in my room."

"Bold statement from the woman who just walked in on me coming out of the shower in what is clearly *my* room."

Kelsey lets out a sigh of frustration, and without thinking, I close the foot of distance between us, wrapping her in an embrace that feels like it's been building for far too long. Her body stiffens, but then she lets out a soft breath, and I swear, it feels like the world settles for a moment.

"What are you—" she begins, but her voice falters, and she doesn't pull away. Instead, she leans into me just a fraction, like maybe she's testing the waters too.

"It's been a long fucking day, and I just need a hug," I admit.

Her breath hitches, and for a second, I think she's going to say something I don't want to hear—maybe pull herself away and tell me there's nothing between us. But she doesn't. She stays right there, her head against my chest, like she's listening to my heartbeat. I feel it—this rightness, like when you come back to your childhood home after you've been away, and everything is familiar and safe.

"Okay," she mutters, pulling back just enough to look me in the eyes. "I suppose I should call Gail and figure out how we got assigned to the same room."

Kelsey steps away from me completely and pulls out her phone. As she looks at the time on her lockscreen, she lets out another sigh, twirling the ring on her middle finger. It's already almost two in the morning. Her thumb hovers at the bottom of her screen as she glances past me to the king-sized bed in the middle of the room.

"Do you... It's just... I'm worried it's too late to..." Kelsey trails off.

Fuck. Is she actually considering staying here?

"It *is* really late," I say, doing my best to hide the excitement in my voice at the prospect of Kelsey spending the night here.

I'm not one to believe in divine intervention, but I might owe God, or at least Gail, a thank-you note for whatever this chance is they've given me.

"It's just one night," I say. "There's a king bed, and we're both adults. Plus, you look like you're about to pass out on the spot, and I'm too tired to track down Gail and move rooms at this point. Just stay here with me."

Kelsey looks at the bed again, indecision written all over her face.

"I can sleep on the floor," I offer.

She smirks, clearly amused by the offer. "On the floor? Really?"

"Yeah, if it'll make you more comfortable. It's not like I didn't sleep in worse places when I was in the Rangers," I reply, my tone light, trying to make a joke out of it. But even as I say it, my body rebels, begging for the opportunity to sleep next to her just once.

She bites her lip, looking at the king-sized bed like it might secretly be hiding the answers to the universe. Finally, she nods, and there is a softness in her eyes that wasn't there a second ago. "Okay, fine. No floor, though. You're just as tired as I am."

"Deal," I say, turning toward the bed so she doesn't see my smile. "I'll get changed out here if you want to have the bathroom."

"Thanks," Kelsey says as she grabs her suitcase and rolls it after her into the bathroom.

I hear the shower turn on, and I force my mind to focus on something—anything—other than the naked woman currently feet away from me. I fail miserably, though I do manage to get changed into a clean undershirt and a pair of black boxer briefs. I normally sleep naked, and as I've worn my workout clothes at least a couple of times each without washing them, this is going to have to do.

Minutes later, the shower turns off, and I hear her moving around, the sound of a zipper, and then her brushing her teeth. When the sink's water shuts off and I hear the door open, I realize I have no idea how to play this cool.

Not knowing what else to do, I slow my breathing so she at least won't know how hard I had to work not to join her in the shower. I stare at the wall, my back to her side of the bed. I want to flip over so I know what she wears to sleep in—if she's more of a silk nighty or oversized T-shirt kind of woman—but I force my eyes closed.

She pulls back the covers, her movements slow and deliberate as she climbs into the bed.

"Goodnight, Carter," she whispers, barely loud enough for me to hear.

"Goodnight, Kels," I whisper back, and it's like a weight lifts from me—like everything that's been building between us finally comes to rest. I can feel her presence beside me, steady and real, and for the first time in what feels like forever, I'm not thinking about my mom's Alzheimer's, or contracts, or the tour. I'm just thinking about the bundle of warmth in my bed and about how everything seems right in this tiny, perfect moment.

A moment I'll do everything in my power to make sure I have again because it's the first time in a long time I've felt like I'm exactly where I'm supposed to be.

Chapter Nineteen

Kelsey

The tingling feeling of my hand going numb pulls me from sleep. I stretch my back, pushing into the warmth behind me, only to encounter a hard wall. A wall with a...hard penis lining up with the center of my ass. Without thinking, I wiggle slightly, still asleep enough to enjoy the sensation without giving it more thought. Carter lets out a quiet groan, and I—oh, shit. Carter.

I stop moving, knowing I shouldn't keep going down this path with my unconscious colleague, but also *really* wanting to continue down this path. Maybe with a conscious Carter, though.

Suddenly, the conversation back in the office in Wild Bluffs comes back to me, JT reminding me that I'm so single, it's painful. The sexual tension between Carter and me the past two days has also been painful. Walking in on him in a towel last night did *nothing* to help that, at least on my part. The cold shower blessedly cooled me down enough to be able to fall asleep as soon as my head hit the pillow.

Moving slowly so I don't disturb Carter, I reach over to the bedside table, grabbing my phone to find out what time it is. Early. I still have an hour—two if I forgo my run today. That's enough time for a little fun...if that's what I want to do. No, I know I want to. The heat growing in my core at Carter's proximity is enough of a reminder of that. I just don't know if I *should*.

"Kels?" Carter's gravelly morning voice is soft against my back, and fuck if that nickname doesn't make up my mind for me.

I roll over slowly, my T-shirt and shorts bunching up as I turn within his arms.

"Morning," I whisper as I take in his bronze skin and the long, black eyelashes resting on his cheeks.

"Mmmm," he replies, pulling me tight against him.

Holy crap. The combination of his warmth, his clean scent, and his hard length pressing into my stomach makes me moan, an embarrassing noise I try to cover with a light cough.

"Shit. You've never made that noise before," Carter whispers, his eyes still closed.

I pause, staring at him. He's...does he think he's dreaming?

I'm glad his eyes are closed, because I am fully incapable of keeping the amused smile off my face, though it does present a bit of a conundrum for me. On one hand, I'm pleased to know I'm not the only one who's been having dirty dreams about us; on the other, I'm not sure how to turn this dream into reality without making it awkward. I bite my lip, taking a moment to nuzzle into his chest, when suddenly his arms go rigid around me.

I look up without moving from my new favorite location to find Carter's head angled down just enough that I can see his wide eyes past his jaw.

Offering a tentative smile, I say, "Morning" again before snuggling deeper into him.

He hesitates, his body still tense, before bringing his cheek down onto the top of my head.

A small sigh escapes me, and we stay like that for a minute, ignoring the world, the questions, and the morning wood that are trying to force themselves into our moment of peace.

"So, I have a proposition," I say when his cock twitches against my stomach and my body rebels, telling me it's had enough cuddling.

Carter chuckles, his warm breath moving the hairs on the top of my head. "A proposition, huh? So formal."

"Do you want to hear it or not?" I tease.

"Oh, there is nothing I'd like more."

How does one propose sex to the man who's currently wrapped around them? It feels like it should be easier. Do I use the word *fuck*? Do people still say *bang*? Do I just run my fingers along his dick and see what happens?

"I think we should hook up."

Carter goes still, only his heartbeat letting me know he's still alive. "You...you...what?" he asks.

"It can just be a one-time thing if that would make you more comfortable, but we're here. I mean, it's almost like the universe wants this to happen, and everything has just been so stressful lately, and I really enjoy hanging out with you...though maybe that's something that should go in the con column... Anyway, can you please just say something?"

What in the world was that? Since when do I ramble? I am not a rambler. Has my sister infected my mind with her constant rambling in uncomfortable situations?

The warmth of Carter's body presses into me as he uses his weight to roll me onto my back. Looking down into my eyes as if searching for something, Carter's hand comes to my face, his thumb stroking my cheek lightly. He leans in, lightly pressing a kiss to my lips, his eyes fluttering closed with the movement.

I let my eyes fall closed too as I lean up into the warmth of his kiss.

Wanting more—needing more—I pull him over me, lacing my hand through the soft strands of his hair. I flick my tongue along the seam of his mouth, silently requesting entry, but he pulls away, hovering over me.

"I'm not interested in a one-time thing," he says, and my heart curls in around itself, the pain of the rejection pulsing through my soul.

"Oh," I say, forcing myself to meet his eyes. "Okay. Sorry, I shouldn't have assumed..."

I trail off as I notice the slight smile tugging on his lips.

"Kels, I'm not interested in a *one*-time thing. Once I get a taste of you—of us—there is no way I'm going to be able to stop. So, if this is just a one-time hookup in your mind, I'm out, as physically painful as it'll be."

I bite my lip to hide my grin. However, I know I need to ask a follow-up question. "But we're not dating, right? Like, we aren't going to hold hands in front of the team or anything?"

"Is that what you want?" he asks, his eyes searching mine.

"I don't want people knowing my business. I don't want people congratulating you for hooking up with me while judging me for sleeping with you. And I especially don't want us sleeping together to somehow make it so neither of us gets the contract with Jaxon."

Carter's weight shifts, and he places a soft kiss on my cheek.

"I don't think Jaxon would do that."

"Are you willing to risk it?" I ask, daring him to make a bold choice for both of us.

His face is contemplative, his lower lip tucked beneath his teeth as he thinks. Finally, he says, "I'm willing to risk a lot of things for this—for you, Kels. But no, I can't risk losing my job when my mom is going to need me more than ever."

I can't help but smile at the admission, and a far less selfish part of me wonders if maybe I should call this off right now before it can turn into something that would ruin his life. Unfortunately for him, the selfish part of me is used to getting its way.

"So we won't do anything that would put either of our jobs at risk. We'll just keep doing what we've been doing, but maybe have a sleepover every so often," I suggest.

"Every night," he counters.

I snort a laugh. "Yeah, because none of our highly trained security personnel will pick up on that."

"We'll play it by ear."

"Okay." I nod like I'm conceding to him, when in reality, he's agreed to all my demands.

"Fuck, I love it when you smile like you're the smartest damn woman in the room," he says before dropping his mouth back to mine.

Keeping our mouths locked, I push into him, forcing him onto his back. If we're doing this, we're doing it my way. I've learned the hard way not to let the man take the lead, even if Carter's kisses suggest he knows what he's doing.

I straddle his hips, the length of him pressing into the heat between my legs. Sighing at the contact I've been dying for since I woke up with his morning wood pressed into me, I lift myself off him slightly so I can rub against him.

More. I need more.

Placing my hands on Carter's broad shoulders, I start to slowly rock back and forth, my hair covering my face and hiding me from sight.

"Hands up," Carter says, helping me sit up straight before pulling my black T-shirt off and throwing it across the room.

"Now it's—" I start before letting out a yelp as Carter flips me onto my back.

"I like to be on top," I say.

Taking my nipple into his mouth, Carter hums his response, making my entire body seize with pleasure. After tormenting the sensitive area, he lifts his head, offering me a smug smile.

"That doesn't surprise me. And you can be for round two. Come once on my fingers, and then I'll let you ride me until we both get what we want."

My body shudders at the dominance in his tone.

"Fine," I say, "but you need less clothing. Don't hide those pretty muscles you work so hard on."

Reaching behind his back to grab the neck of his white undershirt, Carter's arm muscles tense as he pulls the offending garment off. "Better?"

"Much," I say on a groan as he turns his attention to my other nipple.

His movements are soft, slow, as he brings his calloused fingers up to squeeze and stroke both of my breasts.

I wiggle, lifting my hips in the air in search of friction and the release he promised.

Carter moves down my body, kissing my stomach before sliding his hand to my waistband and pulling my sleep shorts and underwear off in one tug.

"Fuck," he whispers before slipping a hand between my thighs and splitting me open. I let out a soft moan as he presses a soft kiss to me before burying his face between my legs.

Pleasure pings through me at the contact, and my hips start moving, out of my control.

He places an arm across my body, pinning me in place as I continue to squirm beneath him.

"Fuck, you taste good," he mumbles against me, the vibrations of his words a torturous sensation.

"I need," I moan softly, not sure what comes next. "More."

Carter doesn't question the demand, pressing two fingers into me as his tongue moves against my clit. He curls his fingers once, then again, and my hips lift off the bed, his arm no longer holding me down. A groan slips from his lips before my hips drop back down, and he gently sucks my clit as he moves his fingers.

I shatter.

I come back into my body as Carter kisses the sensitive spot between my neck and shoulder. Holy shit. Did I just black out?

"Ready to be on top?" he asks, nuzzling the side of my face. "Or do you need a break?"

"Do I look like someone who leaves a job half finished?" I tease.

He scans me from head to toe, looking his fill. "I suppose not," he says when his eyes make it back to mine, and my heart flutters at the look of pure joy on his face.

"Damn right," I say as I grab the waistband of his black underwear, pulling them down as he watches me.

His dick juts up proudly, a drop of precum leaking from the tip. I swallow thickly as he grips his shaft, stroking slowly.

"Condom?" I ask.

His eyes widen, and he turns to search the floor. He hops off the bed, digging through his suitcase.

I sit up, enjoying the dance of his back muscles as he searches. Finding a black box, he stands up and tosses it to me.

I ignore the jolt of pleasure that flows through me as I realize it's brand new, completely unopened.

"Already went through your first box?" I joke.

He raises an eyebrow as if to say "What do you think?" before climbing back onto the bed and giving me another kiss. I pull off the plastic wrapping and successfully extract a condom from the box, shimmying in victory before throwing the pack back toward his suitcase.

I find him watching me from where he's lying on his side of the bed, his hands behind his head, his core flexed as he lifts up slightly to watch me. I crawl over to him on my knees, straddling the tops of his thighs. I press a kiss to his lips before turning my attention to his cock jutting up between us.

I lean over, lightly licking up the vein that runs along the underside of him. He convulses slightly as I reach the tip, tracing my tongue around his head. Grabbing his balls lightly, I give a gentle tug as I repeat the motion with my tongue.

Carter threads his hands in my hair, pulling just hard enough to make me stop.

"What?" I ask before licking right over the head of his cock.

"Fuuuuck," he moans. "You've got to—nope," he says as I lower my head to lick him again. "Ride me, Kels. I'm not going to last long, and I promised you round two this way."

A rush of power at his words flows through me, and I lean over to give him a quick kiss before tearing open the condom package with my teeth and pulling out the rubber.

As I roll the condom down, I realize he's bigger than the other men I've been with—not a surprise, since he's taller *and* broader than any man I've been with before, but still a bit daunting. Not that I will be telling him that. I'm sure I can handle it.

"Kels," he says, his voice a plea. "Please put me out of my misery."

"Well, since you asked nicely," I say, aligning the head of his cock with my entrance.

He watches, enraptured, as I lower myself onto him, inch by thick inch.

"You feel good," he says, swallowing thickly as he drops his head back, his throat arching. "So fucking good. Why are you so tight?"

He starts to move, pleasure blasting through me as he bottoms out with each thrust. I lean forward, finding the friction I need to come again.

Taking control of the tempo, I roll my hips. It takes only a minute for him to learn my tempo, and as he starts moving again, I take him impossibly deeper as he meets each roll with a thrust of his own.

My eyes roll to the back of my head as the sensations become almost too much, too soon after my initial breaking. But I keep moving, wanting him to feel just as good as I do.

Gripping my hips in his large hands, he helps lift me with each movement, slamming me back down onto his lap. With each movement, I can feel myself getting closer and closer to my climax again. Carter keeps up the rhythm, finding exactly the pace I need to slowly build. Finally, when I can't take it any longer, he slowly circles my clit with his thumb. It takes my breath away, and I clench around him, moments away from coming again.

Stars explode behind my closed eyes as I jerk on his lap, his fingers digging into my flesh as our movements become erratic. I've never felt this kind of pleasure with someone our first time together.

"Mmghh," he groans, his eyes fixed on the place where his body joins with mine as he finds his release.

I collapse on top of him, breathless and panting. After a moment, I shift my weight to roll off him, but his arm clutches me tighter to his chest.

"Not yet," he whispers into the top of my head, and I swear he smells my hair.

I lightly run my fingers through his smattering of chest hair as we lie there, our breathing evening out. Finally, I roll off him, heading to the bathroom.

When I walk out of the bathroom a minute later, I find Carter sitting on the edge of the bed, staring intently at his hands.

"Want to come on my run with me?" I offer, not sure how else to make it clear that we might not be dating, but I definitely want to do that again.

Carter's face morphs into the cocky smirk I've come to know so well. "Are you sure you can keep up?"

Chapter Twenty

CARTER

"Nope," I say as Nash drops his black backpack into the seat next to mine on the plane. No way am I spending this sixteen-hour flight to Tokyo with anyone but the woman who completely upended my world this morning. "Kelsey and I are using the flight to get some work done."

It's not a lie per se.

"It's okay, Nash," Kelsey says from behind him in the aisle. "You don't want to spend the whole flight listening to him whine about how sore he is, anyway."

Nash flashes a smile at Kelsey, and I flex my hand to resist punching him in his stupid face.

"I can't believe you convinced him to go on a six-mile run," Nash says as he moves farther down the aisle. "I tried to get him to go on a jog in Vancouver, and he didn't even answer—just shook his head as he walked away."

Kelsey's eyes sparkle with mischief as they catch mine.

"Turns out, Carter will do anything if you bet him he can't."

I grab Kelsey's black backpack and place it on the middle seat as she shoves her carry-on into the storage bin over her head.

"You know he's going to start betting me to do the most random shit now, right?" I ask Kelsey once she's sitting down.

"That was the goal," she says as she leans toward me to pull her laptop and headphones out of her backpack.

Do not kiss her. Do not kiss her.

"Wipe that look off your face, Carter Mitchell," Kelsey hisses at me so low, I can barely hear her.

"What look?" I ask, grabbing the safety card out of the back of the seat and focusing on the drawings.

Out of the corner of my eye, I can see Kelsey's narrowed eyes, but I continue my perusal of the features of our CloudBus C220 airplane.

Kelsey pulls out her phone, her fingers flying over the screen for a moment before a text pops up.

Kelsey

You look like you want to eat me.

Me

I do want to eat you.

You're fucking delicious.

Kelsey rolls her eyes.

I lean over and whisper, "I didn't peg you for a coward, Kels."

"I didn't peg you for an idiot, Cart."

She opens her laptop as she says it, clearly trying to indicate the conversation is over.

This has been, without a doubt, the best twelve hours of my life. January 28 will live on forever as the day I *finally* became more to Kelsey Harper than just some guy. The sex—the sex was fucking mind-blowing. But sleeping with Kelsey isn't what makes today worth remembering. No, it's that I'm finally able to drop the carefully constructed mask I've worn around her since high school. It's freeing to show just how interested I am in everything she has to say. Just how captivated I am by every move she makes.

Even if this stupid rivalry between our two companies is making it so she can't officially be mine, I will take any piece of Kelsey she's willing to give me—even the ones she's trying so hard to keep hidden.

And I will do anything to make it happen, anything except lose this contract.

Kelsey taps her fingers on the edge of her laptop, focused on whatever email or message she's working on. But I can feel the connection still humming between us—the energy lingering in the air like static.

I know she wants me to act like nothing happened, but I can't look away. Shit, maybe I should've let Nash sit next to me. At least then I wouldn't be spending the entire flight with a semi. And I wouldn't be obsessing over the fact that Kelsey's hair has every color in the spectrum, from almost silvery blonde to deep browns. Now that I really look at it, some people might even call her hair brunette rather than blonde—I might be overlaying her beach-blonde waves from high school over the darker shades that currently dance their way down her head and shoulders.

Forcing my gaze away from her, I place my headphones in my ears and pull up the "World War II meets zombies" movie I downloaded this morning after our run.

I don't care that she's pretending to be absorbed in her work. I know she's trying to rebuild the boundaries we upended this morning. Because if there's one thing I know about Kelsey, it's that she needs to be in control.

And right now, she's pretending we didn't just fully lose control this morning.

"So we're just going to pretend like we're both not thinking about this morning?" I ask, my voice low enough for only her to hear.

The crew turned the lights off about five minutes after we were airborne, knowing everyone is trying to get some sleep, so it feels less risky to talk to her.

Her fingers pause on her keyboard, and she bites her lip, clearly trying to figure out how to get the upper hand.

"I'm not thinking about it," she mutters, her eyes still glued to her screen.

"Liar," I tease.

"I have to work, Carter. You can flirt with me all you want, but I'm not going to play this game."

"Of course you are." I grin, leaning in closer. "I know you better than that. You love a challenge."

A small smirk forms on her lips. "Oh, really?"

"Yep." I pop the sound at the end just to annoy her. "What I don't know is if you're too scared to meet me in the bathroom in a minute. The one on the starboard side." I nod my head toward the back, where the last two rows of people are all in headphones, attempting to sleep.

"I'm not doing that."

I shrug like I don't care either way. "It's for the best, you probably wouldn't be able to be quiet with what I have planned for you anyway."

I hold her gaze as I stand up, waiting for her to put her things down so I can slip out of the aisle next to her.

As I pass by, I whisper into her ear, "This morning was real for me, and whether you join me in that bathroom or not, I *will* be tasting you again, very, very soon."

With that, I stride down the aisle and into the bathroom, which is much smaller than I remembered. Shit. How do people have sex in airplane bathrooms?

I check my watch for the fourth time in two and a half minutes, just about to give up, when there is a soft knock on the door.

I don't even try to hide my smile as I press my body against the wall, making room for both the folding door and Kelsey to push their way inside.

"You came," I whisper into her hair as I pull her tight against me, locking the door behind her.

"Did you think I would—"

I cut her off with my lips, my tongue diving into the warmth of her mouth. Her arm slides around my neck as her back presses into the sink. Grabbing her hips, I lift her up, her legs wrapped around my waist.

She lets out a soft moan as our centers press together, and I chuckle against her lips.

Turning us slightly so that she's above the toilet, I set her on the closed seat so she's standing before me.

"Pants off," I whisper as I pull down her black joggers. I kiss the exposed flesh at her hips before fully exposing her.

"Carter, I—" she starts, but her words change into a small squeak as I lightly nuzzle her clit with my nose.

"Quiet, Kels," I whisper, running my fingers along her strong, lean thighs, moving slowly up to the apex. Her hands fist my hair, tugging gently.

Knowing my time is limited, I begin feasting on Kelsey, my tongue and lips quickly finding a rhythm of licking and sucking that causes her hands to tighten, directing my motion. The memory of this morning is forever burned into my mind, so I add a finger, then two, curling them in time with my mouth.

Kelsey's movements against me become erratic, and she lets go of my hair with one hand. Seconds later, she breaks with a muffled moan.

Still in my slightly bent-over position, I look up into her eyes as I lick her from my lips before wiping a hand to clear her release off my face. Seeing the arm she still has pressed across her mouth, I chuckle, a wave of pride flowing through me at the image.

Standing up fully, I kiss her collarbone and then her cheek.

"I'll see you back out there," I whisper, checking my face in the mirror to ensure I'm presentable.

Her eyes widen. "Wait. What about you?" she asks softly, moving to sit down in front of me and my raging erection.

"I'll manage," I say, adjusting myself. "I needed to taste you again. Everything else can wait until we get to another hotel room."

She looks like she's about to argue with me, so I say, "Plus, I don't think we can be gone much longer without someone noticing."

I lean in and give her another kiss, this time a soft one on her lips. Fucking delicious.

"See you soon," I say before I slide out the door, thankful there isn't anyone waiting.

Once I'm back in my seat, I start my movie again, but I'm interrupted by a large man sitting down in Kelsey's seat.

"Oh, hey, Jaxon," I say, pulling my earbuds out. "Do you want to go over the security plans for Japan?"

"God, no," he says with a halfhearted wave, running a hand through his dark hair. He's clearly exhausted, and I can tell it's not just from the flight.

"You all right?" I ask, genuinely concerned.

"Just tired," Jaxon mutters, slouching back into the seat.

"Do you need me to..." I trail off. "I actually don't know how to help with that."

Jaxon laughs. "I just need someone to treat me like a normal person for five minutes."

"Well, as I've never considered you anything but a normal person, I think I can handle that."

As we exchange the usual banter, Kelsey walks past our row, her face illuminated by whatever she's typing on her phone. She pauses for a moment, eyeing us both. I notice the brief flicker of curiosity in her eyes, but she quickly masks it with a practiced smile.

Jaxon follows my gaze to Kelsey and makes to get up. "I can move."

While his attention is elsewhere, I subtly shake my head, answering her unspoken question about whether Jaxon's noticed anything strange between us. She seems to accept the answer, nodding in return.

"No need," Kelsey says to Jaxon with a friendly smile. "I need to chat with Annie about your interview schedule anyway."

Jaxon watches her go, and for a moment, there's a strange kind of quiet between us. The tension hangs there for a beat too long before Jaxon sighs, leaning back in his seat.

"Have you ever noticed how her smile is exactly like Izzy's?" Jaxon asks, almost to himself.

The question catches me off guard. I try to picture Kelsey's middle sister, but the image of Izzy is just a blur in my mind—tall, brunette. But Kelsey, she's something else entirely. Kelsey's smile is...magnetic. Unique. I can't imagine anyone else having that effect on me.

"Well, they are sisters," I mumble, unsure of what to say.

Jaxon doesn't answer right away, lost in thought. I can feel the weight of it, the unspoken history between him and Izzy, but I don't push. Jaxon's always been a master of keeping his cards close to his chest.

The silence lingers, and I'm about to retreat back into my movie when Jaxon suddenly speaks again, his voice more casual now. "So, how are things going with you and Kelsey?" Jaxon asks.

"She's been remarkably easy to work with," I say, trying to keep the conversation from going too far down that road.

"Yeah? That's good." He sighs, pressing two fingers into the space between his remarkably well-groomed eyebrows. He starts to say something but stops himself with a shake of his head.

"What?" I ask.

He raises an eyebrow. "Feel free not to answer this, but was it hard? Being around her again?"

He takes in my confused face. "You can't have forgotten that night after we lost the state semifinals baseball game, my sophomore year, when you told me all about how you were in love with Kelsey Harper. It was like a week after the whole restaurant incident where she stood up for your mom, and Kelsey Harper was all you could talk about." He glances toward the front of the plane to where Kelsey is sitting. "You said her full name like that too, 'Kelsey Harper.'"

I grimace. "I try to block out all confessions of love, actually."

Jaxon snorts a laugh. "Well, I've been curious to see if this trip would rekindle any flames," he says, amusement and something else flickering in his eyes.

"It wouldn't be very professional if it did," I say, hedging my words.

"Why?" His tone is genuine, his face showing nothing but casual interest.

"We've got a job to do. She's a colleague."

He nods his head like that makes sense. "But you *could*—hypothetically speaking, of course—be together and do your job, right? There isn't a fraternization clause in either of your contracts." He says it casually, but I can hear the undertone of something deliberate.

No. Even for a boy who loved to set people up, *that* is too ridiculous. A world-famous musician most certainly has more important things on his mind than playing matchmaker for two people he hasn't seen in almost two decades. And this would've taken a lot of time, planning, and honestly, paying attention to both Kelsey's and my lives, which I can't imagine he has done.

I look at the top of Kelsey's head, sorting through what I should say.

Before I can figure it out, Jaxon starts speaking again, "Anyway, it's none of my business, but if you feel anything like you did for her in high school, I think you should go for it."

"Why?" I ask.

He lifts one shoulder in a half-shrug, his gaze steady on a small tattoo on the inside of his forearm. "Second chances are rare—love's timing can be fleeting. If I were on the verge of missing my moment...well, I'd want someone to help me make sure I didn't."

"Is that a line from one of your songs?" I ask.

Jaxon's mouth lifts in a half-smile. "The first part is. And it was just as true when I wrote it as it is now."

"Damn, man. You should take that songwriting thing on the road," I joke.

Jaxon chuckles. "Ah, international tours are overrated."

"But what if they're called the Forever Starts Here Tour?" I ask, fighting to keep a serious face.

"Then you know the musician has a phenomenal marketing team…who also happens to give zero fucks what he thinks about the tour names."

We both laugh, causing most of the heads in our general vicinity to turn in our direction.

Once he stops laughing, Jaxon undoes his seat belt, clearly ready to get back to his awaiting assistants. "Anyway, Carter," he says as he stands. "I just wanted to make sure you and Kelsey knew that if something were to happen between the two of you, there wouldn't be anything wrong with it from my and my team's point of view." He takes a step into the aisle before turning back. "You'll let Kelsey know, right?"

I nod, trying my best to hide the smile that's threatening to overrun my face. Instead, I focus my attention back on my phone, tapping the Play button as I put my headphones back in.

Seconds later, Kelsey slides into the seat next to me. Holding out her hand, palm up, she asks, "What are we watching?"

I pull the earbud out of my ear closest to her, dropping it into her waiting palm.

"*Overlord.*"

There's a pause.

"What?" I ask, turning to face her. My nose is inches away from her. I want to kiss her.

"I didn't peg you for a zombie guy," she says, her warm breath caressing my cheeks.

"There's a lot you don't know about me, Kels, but you're going to get the chance to find it out. All of it."

Chapter Twenty-One

Kelsey

"Hello," I say, my voice gravelly with sleep.

"Kelsey?" My sister's voice comes through my phone. "Why is it so dark?"

Crap. I grab my phone and shove it into my pillow, confused about how I accidentally answered a video call without knowing it.

"Mmm," Carter groans from next to me, and I flip my phone back around, aggressively smashing the red button to end the call.

Carter's large body surges upright, his hand immediately reaching for the phone next to him. His eyes are intent as they meet mine. "What's wrong? Is everything okay with Jaxon?"

We had another potential Bennie sighting at the concert last night at the Tokyo Dome, and even though my team determined it was likely another false positive, everyone is back on high alert, especially since there are no cameras in the hallways of our Japanese hotel room.

Slowly scanning his bare chest, I take a second to appreciate his abs flexing above the crisp white sheet. I haven't gotten over how good he looks in the morning.

"All good," I say, leaning over to kiss him lightly. "It's Izzy. She video called me, and I accidentally answered it."

"Ashamed to be seen with me?" he teases as my phone starts ringing again.

"Just don't need more people in my business," I say, clicking the button on the side to stop the vibration. "Jaxon meddling in our lives is enough for me. Plus, once my sisters catch wind of something, they're going to continue to interfere until they get exactly what they want."

"And you're worried they're not going to like me?" he asks, concern flaring in his eyes.

I snort as I throw on one of my running outfits. "No. I'm more worried they're going to become best friends with your mom, and they'll have a wedding planned for us by the time we get home."

My phone starts vibrating in my hand again, and I stare down at it, unsure of what to do.

Carter stands up, pulling on a pair of black joggers and a T-shirt from his bag. Kissing my forehead, he grabs his key off the dresser and heads toward the door. "I'll go grab some coffees. You let them know I think red roses at weddings are cliché."

I laugh as I stare after him, impressed yet again by how firm his ass looks in all pants—especially those joggers that hug him just right, outlining every muscle as he moves. His legs, long and strong, seem to take up more of my mental space with each stride. Maybe I should start lifting with him in the mornings instead of making him come on runs with me.

The door shutting pulls my focus back to my phone, and I finally answer my sister's call.

"Hey, Iz," I say, pulling open the blinds to stare out at the roof of the Imperial Palace a few blocks over.

"Hey, Iz? That's how you're going to answer after hanging up on me and then ignoring my calls?"

"Would you have preferred 'What up'?" I joke.

"I, unfortunately, have to agree with Izzy on this one," my sister Bryn says, shoving her face into the screen next to Izzy's. With their straight brown hair, similar builds, and darker eyes, people used to get my sisters confused, even in a town as small as Wild Bluffs. The odd one out with blonde hair, blue eyes, and a petite frame compared to them, people tended to think I was sisters with Izzy's friend Becca instead of my actual sisters. When I moved to the East Coast for college at the United States Naval Academy, I realized I wasn't actually that small at five foot five, but I've never stopped feeling short. Carter doesn't do much to help with it, though at least he isn't a hulking behemoth like Bryn's boyfriend.

"Hey, Bryn," I say, forcing cheerfulness into my tone. "Any news on your house?"

"It's Jameo's house," she shoots back. "But it's coming along nicely."

I can't help but smirk at the annoyed look Izzy is sending Bryn's way.

"Don't let her distract you," my middle sister chides Bryn.

Noting the distinct windows of my sister's downtown office space, I ask, "Why are you all at the office on the weekend?"

"Lila said she had to come in to get some work done, so we thought we'd keep her company," Izzy says.

"Distract her is more likely," I tease.

"Hi, Kelsey!" Lila's voice carries through the phone from somewhere on their side of things. "I sent you a few messages, but nothing is pressing."

"I'll get back to you before I head to the venue for tonight's concert," I tell Lila, mentally calculating all the things I need to do before I leave for the Tokyo Dome at two. Luckily, today is the second concert at the same venue, so we don't have to have the larger security team meeting. This afternoon we'll just touch base with the team leads. I firmly shut Carter down when he asked me to stay over the first two nights in Japan, refusing to be distracted by this thing between us.

I'd tried to stay in my own room last night, but Carter had shown up, puppy dog eyes in full force, and said, "Okay, but hear me out, what if you stayed in my room for tonight? And tomorrow night too? Let's call it the next thirty to forty-five nights at minimum."

How am I supposed to resist that?

So, being the strong, independent woman I am, I said yes, but only for the night. There is no way I can do this job if I'm sleeping with him every night. Even if I actually believed I'd be sleeping, which, if last night is any indication, there isn't much rest happening.

"Sooo," drawls Bryn from my phone. "Who was that?"

I force my face into a puzzled expression. "What do you mean?"

"That very masculine voice that mumbled something when you answered the call earlier. The one when you were clearly in bed."

"I fell asleep with the TV on."

Both my sisters send looks of disbelief at me through the phone.

"It feels like she's lying to us," Bryn says to Izzy.

"Definitely lying. The real question is why."

"Do you think she's sleeping with one of her employees?" Bryn says, a smirk pulling up the side of her mouth.

"Technically"—Lila's voice cuts in, and both my sisters look away from the phone to listen to her—"there isn't anyone traveling with Kelsey who is her employee."

"Damn, so *everyone* is fair game?" Bryn asks. "Are you just sleeping your way through the Mitchell Security team?"

Their laughs twine together, a lighthearted sound that almost makes me want to join in. Almost.

"Yup," I deadpan. "Just waiting for Trent to show up again so I can complete the roster."

"Gross," Bryn says. "Thank fuck I know you're joking."

"She might not be," Izzy says, a contemplative look on her face. "She did say Trent wasn't as bad as she thought before she left. Maybe they're having an illicit affair."

"Is that why he was returning the trophy wife's car? Did you wreck their home?" Bryn asks. "Is this a Brad-and-Jennifer situation? Are you Angelina?" she gasps.

"You really spiraled there," I say.

"You're the one who brought Trent into the conversation."

Izzy's face lights up like she's just remembered something. "Speaking of Trent, I heard he was at the bank last weekend meeting with a loan officer. What do you think he's planning on buying the wife this time? A pool?"

Bryn laughs. "A pool? For the one week a year that you'd actually want to swim outdoors in eastern Colorado? If he's smart, he's buying a vacation house someplace nice...maybe Costa Rica."

"Did you two have something you actually wanted to talk to me about, or are you just bored because your famous golfer boyfriends are at a tournament?" I ask.

Izzy sticks her tongue out at me. "I don't have a golfer boyfriend."

"Cool flex, Iz," Bryn says, nudging Izzy with her shoulder.

Izzy rolls her eyes. "Can we not just be calling because we're your sisters, and we miss you?"

"It seems unlikely."

"Well, in addition to calling because we miss you, we also are calling because Mom has asked each of us about five times in the last three days if we've talked to you, and I think she's about to jump on an airplane and fly to Japan herself if you don't answer one of her calls or show some proof of life."

Crap. I've been meaning to call my mom back, but she calls at literally the worst possible times. It's like she doesn't understand the time difference. She called twice during the concert last night, but she left a message saying she was just calling to talk, so I didn't feel the need to return her call at two in the morning when I finally made it back to the hotel.

"I liked that picture of her coffee that she sent Friday," I say. "Does that not count as proof of life?"

"Honestly, it made us all wonder if someone stole your phone. I searched how to tell if someone was abducted," Izzy says, scrunching up her nose. "You're not a big liker of Mom's coffee photos."

"She sends the same one every Friday. It barely changes. It's a latte she makes at home with foamed milk on top."

"I like it," Izzy says. "They make me happy."

"I told her to take me off the text chain," Bryn replies.

"It's our family text chain!" Izzy exclaims.

"I said what I said."

"Fine," I say. "I'll call Mom."

"Wait!" Izzy yells. "Tell us who it was. It's Carter, isn't it? Oh my God, *please* tell me you're sleeping with Carter Mitchell. That man is the definition of brooding heartthrob."

"No comment," I say, and tap the button to hang up the call.

I call my mom back, making sure to show her the view out my window and tell her all about the drama between Mikayla and Nash. The surest way into the heart of Jen Harper is to tell her the elaborate backstory of two people she's never met before. She's immediately invested and will never forget their names or a detail about them. She'll probably inappropriately ask Nash about his crush on his colleague when she randomly runs into him in Denver, and suddenly she'll be his best friend, sending him care packages any time he's away on assignment.

My mom is annoyingly the best.

As I'm finishing up my call with her, Carter slips back into the room, juggling the two travel coffee cups he has so he can silently shut the door.

"Was that your mom?" he asks when I finally tell my mom goodbye.

"The woman herself."

"How are Jen and Ken?" he asks with a chuckle.

Everyone loves the fact that their names rhyme.

"They're good. My sisters are too. Though they're far more annoying than my parents."

He raises an eyebrow, taking a drink of my coffee. It's apparently our new thing. He was appalled our first morning in Japan to find out I never drink a whole cup of coffee, so now he just drinks half of mine in addition to his own. Bryn would undoubtedly be disgusted by the germ-sharing portion of it, but it doesn't bother me.

"They heard you this morning."

"Ah. And that's a bad thing, right?"

"Right...because we agreed we weren't dating."

"True. Though that was when we thought we'd get in trouble with Jaxon or his team."

I nod. "It's still probably best if we don't tell people. I mean, this is still really...new."

Carter clears his throat, his eyes darting over my shoulder.

"What?" I ask.

"I may have told my mom that we'd gone on a few dates. It's fine, though, I'm sure she won't remember it."

I start to chuckle and then realize that may not be the appropriate response to a memory joke about someone with Alzheimer's. I'm not

sure what to do with my face...or my body for that matter. "Did you...
Did you just make a memory joke about your mother...the one with
dementia?"

He chuckles. "Inappropriate?"

"I mean, I don't think I can tell you how to cope with your mom's
Alzheimer's, but...at least warn a girl if you're going to start going dark
humor about it."

A warm smile stretches across his face as he pulls me into a hug. "It
feels good to laugh about it for once."

"Did you talk to her while you were gone?" I ask, knowing Carter
tries to call her every day.

"Yeah." He sighs, dropping onto the edge of the bed. "I talked to
both my mom and Mildred, Bill's wife."

I sit down next to him, grabbing his large hand in my own.

"How is she?"

"It's hard to say because I don't think they'd tell me unless it was
really bad. It might just be talking to her over the phone or the change
in routine with me gone, but...it feels like she's getting worse."

CHAPTER TWENTY-TWO
CARTER

"WHAT ARE YOU DOING here?" Jaxon asks me when I join his team leaving the Dome the next night.

"Filling in for one of the guys," I respond. "Alan asked for some time off once the concert ended so he could call his daughter for her birthday."

Jaxon nods his understanding as we make our way quickly toward the SUV waiting to take us back to our hotel a few blocks away.

"Great show tonight," I say once we're all situated in the car, Weston at the wheel.

"There are few feelings in this world as great as having fifty thousand people singing your songs back at you."

"Do you write all your songs?" I ask.

"Every single one. I've been experimenting a bit with songs written by others lately, but I just can't seem to bring the same energy to them. There's something about knowing the feeling behind every word, every chord progression, that makes it feel real. Turns out, if I don't have that, I'm just a guy playing a guitar. Doesn't have the same impact."

"How do you have enough to say? You've got what? Six albums out with roughly twenty songs on each?"

"Seven albums. One hundred fifty-six songs. But I also write songs for other artists occasionally. I think I've written over two hundred and twenty songs that have been produced. There are at least a hundred more that I finished that have never seen the light of day."

"Why's that?" I ask, confused why someone would finish a song and not just work on it until it was what they wanted.

"It depends. Most of the time, it's just that my producers or I don't think it'll land right, or that it's such a 'quintessential Jaxon Steele' song—their words, not mine—that we can't sell it to someone else."

"I guess that makes sense."

We drive in silence for a few minutes, the bright lights of Tokyo flashing by in a blur of colorful streaks.

When we pull up in front of the hotel, Jaxon says, as if he's talking to himself, "There have been a couple I recorded that ended up being too personal, so I convinced my team to pull them from the final album."

I pause, my hand on the door to the car, and really look at Jaxon. He's still got on his dark jeans and black shirt he wears at basically every concert, his face still lightly coated in sweat. His black cowboy hat is back in the dressing room, ready to be packed up and shipped with the set to Australia, where the team will see this group of equipment next week. He looks tired, though it's the middle of the night, but it feels like more than just lack of sleep. The boy I knew in high school looks...weary now.

"Come on," I say. "Let's get you up to your room. I'm sure your team has your dinner waiting."

"Correct," Annie says, inserting herself into the conversation from the row of seats behind us.

"Want to join me?" he asks, and the small, hopeful smile makes me feel like a piece of shit for wanting to say no. I have a stubborn woman I need to convince to sleep with me, though I suppose I have a few hours until she'll be back at the hotel.

"Sure," I say, climbing out of the car and quickly moving around to meet Jaxon as he opens his door. An old pro at this, Jaxon is great about waiting until we're in position before moving.

"I'll get you some dinner sent up, Carter," Annie says, typing furiously on her phone as we walk toward the elevators.

Once we're all packed inside, Jaxon gives the order for Annie and the rest of his team to go to bed, assuring them anything they need can wait until tomorrow morning when they have their usual staff meeting.

Weston tells one of our officers to wait and get the food from the staff when it arrives but sends the rest of the team of close protection officers to bed. The CPOs stay in the two rooms next to Jaxon's and the one across the hall. Normally, Kelsey's team is monitoring the security footage at the hotel and coordinating with the CPOs to respond to anything that might come up while Jaxon is in his room. Unfortunately for us, there are a lot of hotels in Japan that don't have cameras in the hallways, and we're staying at one of them.

Once we enter Jaxon's suite, I do a quick security check, even though Weston's officers confirmed the room was clear before we entered.

"You're kind of a paranoid guy, you know?" Jaxon teases as he pours himself a glass of whiskey from the tumbler on the table. He lifts it my direction, silently asking if I'd like a drink.

I shake my head.

"A couple of tours in combat zones will do that to a guy," I say.

Jaxon's face turns serious, a common side effect of mentioning anything about my deployments. "I'm sorry."

"Don't be. I knew what I was signing up for, and overall, it was a good experience. Plus, I'm one of the lucky ones—the paranoia only hits when I'm working on security assignments. I know I'm safe at home, which is a lot more than many of the guys I served with."

Jaxon nods, leaning back on the sofa with a sigh.

"You want to talk about what's going on with you?" I ask, dropping into the chair across from him.

We're interrupted by a knock at the door, and I jump up to grab our food. I don't typically eat after the shows, but at the sight of the tuna nigiri on the plates, my stomach rumbles to life.

I deposit the food onto the black oval table between us, handing Jaxon a napkin with two chopsticks inside.

Jaxon seems uninterested in continuing the conversation, so I let it drop for the moment as we both dig into our plates of sushi.

"How are things going with you and Kelsey?" Jaxon asks.

I consider acting like I don't know what he's talking about, but the truth is I need someone to talk to about this. After our not-date dates and then that night together in Berlin, it felt like we were something, especially after Jaxon all but gave us his blessing. But then our plane touched down in Tokyo, and Kelsey went right back to being coworker Kelsey.

We still went out to dinner during our day off at the restaurant she'd picked out—a little restaurant hidden away in a back alley with only six seats in the entire place. We had a front-row seat as the chef prepared our four-course dinner on the flat, stainless-steel stove in front of us. It was delicious, though the image of the live lobster being placed directly onto the cooktop with a few ice cubes and then covered with a circular, domed lid will haunt me forever.

But we didn't hold hands as we walked there or back, and when we reached our hotel, Kelsey went back to her room, declaring she had too much work to do to come to mine when I'd asked. I'd been willing to chalk it up to tiredness on our first night in Tokyo, since we'd literally been on a plane the whole day, but I knew, when she'd turned me down the second night, that we're on two different pages.

It hadn't stopped me from trying again last night, unwilling to let this thing between us fizzle out. The relief I'd felt when she agreed to spend the night with me—I can't even begin to describe it, though I tried to show it to her with every kiss and every touch last night.

"It's confusing," I say, answering Jaxon's question honestly.

"Oh, yeah?" he asks, raising an eyebrow. "Why's that?"

"I think she likes me, but she also seems fine with just hooking up occasionally."

"And you're...not okay with hooking up?"

"I mean, I'm not complaining about that part, but I was pretty clear the first night that I wasn't okay with it being *just* about sex," I say.

"Ahh," is Jaxon's only reply.

Looking around the empty space, I realize we haven't heard many notifications of someone coming up to Jaxon's room with him lately.

"Speaking of just sex," I say. "Aren't you supposed to be a rock star? Why are you spending your night with me?"

Jaxon chuckles darkly. "Kelsey might be to blame for that too."

"Wha-what do you mean?" A blackness is rising in my chest, and it takes all my self-control not to let it out.

Jaxon's chuckle turns brighter as he glances at me. "You should see your face. Fuck, man. I obviously don't like Kelsey like that."

Dropping my head into my hands, I laugh at myself. "Right."

"She just reminds me of who I used to be, and apparently, that guy isn't interested in sleeping around."

"Oh, yeah?"

"Yeah, it's really fucking inconvenient. I used to have fun, Carter. *Fun.* Now it feels like I can barely remember what the word means if I'm not up on stage."

"And Kelsey is to blame for that?"

"Partially, I guess. I think you two being around just reminds me of Wild Bluffs."

I nod in understanding, pleased it's not actually about Kelsey herself, before realizing I don't actually understand. "Wait. Why does Wild Bluffs make it so you can't sleep around?"

"It's complicated," Jaxon says with a sigh.

"I'm pretty smart."

Clearly undecided on if he should tell me or not, Jaxon takes a long pull from his drink before saying, "I brought a woman back with me after the first show in Vancouver, ready to continue my normal pattern—the adrenaline from shows, it's fucking brutal—and as I was, well, helping her out of her clothes, I swear Izzy popped into the room with me. She was lounging in the chair in the corner of the room, her fucking legs draped over the padded arm as she gave her unfiltered opinion on my performance. Do you know how hard it is to fuck another woman when Izzy's laugh is flowing through your head?"

"No. Thank God."

"Yeah, well, I'd like it to go away, and it's happened every time I brought a woman back to my room this tour."

Thinking back to the beginning of our conversation and his comment about who he used to be, I ask, "And you think Izzy is the embodiment of past you? You don't think it's maybe about...her?"

"No." Jaxon cuts me off. "I think it has to be about her representing who I was when I first started playing music. I always swore to myself I wouldn't be the typical rock star, getting drunk or high or both all day every day, and sleeping with all the groupies."

"You don't do those things," I remind him.

"Tell that to Izzy."

I lean back against the cushion behind me. "Maybe you should tell that to Izzy. The imaginary one or the real one—dealer's choice."

Jaxon glares at me over the rim of his drink. "No. The stage of my life where I tell Izzy every little detail about my life is long gone. I just need her to leave me alone."

I shrug. "Okay." If he wants to continue to be haunted by the specter of his very much alive former best friend, that's his prerogative. "Though it might help. And I bet Izzy would like to hear from you."

I actually don't know that. I know things are weird between them since he jumped town all those years ago, but I can't imagine she wouldn't want to see the guy she was best friends with for so many years. And Kelsey likes Jaxon. If he'd done anything too terrible, she'd still hate him on her sister's behalf.

Jaxon shakes his head as if forcing some thought out. "Anyway, we were talking about you and Kelsey."

"I don't know what else to say," I respond. "I want her, and it's seeming more and more like she doesn't want me. At least, she doesn't want me for anything more than the occasional night here and there."

"But you're still going to take the occasional night because it's better than the alternative?" Jaxon asks, a knowing smile crossing his face.

"I'll take anything she's willing to give me."

And I would. I don't want to be just the guy she's sleeping around with when she needs a good lay, but I *will* be that guy if the alternative is going back to being nothing. I know I said I wouldn't, that I was only interested if it was something more than one night, but it turns out I was wrong. Now that I know what it feels like to be with Kelsey, I can't give her up. All of my eighteen-year-old fantasies are coming true, and it turns out reality is so much better.

"Not to be that guy, but why wouldn't she want to date you? Is she anti-marriage or something?"

I sigh. I've given this a lot of thought, and I'm sure it comes back to her ex. Even as a teenager, Kelsey was remarkably independent, never relying on anyone else for help, and after I heard about what happened with her first company, it makes sense that she would be slow to trust. Though the thought has slithered into my mind occasionally that it might just be me she doesn't trust, especially with Jaxon's long-term protection contract hanging in the balance.

"It's not my story to tell, but her ex was a dick, and so she doesn't trust many people. Or maybe she doesn't trust me. I did fuck up a couple of times and not have her back like I should've."

"Maybe. Or she doesn't trust herself," Jaxon offers.

I laugh. "Have you met Kelsey? She's the most confident person I know."

The look on Jaxon's face suggests he doesn't agree, but there is no way Kelsey doesn't know exactly how amazing she is. She's the smartest person in any room, she is fucking gorgeous, and if that's not enough, she actually gives a shit about the people in her life, including dumbasses like Nash. She's perfect.

"You've got it so fucking bad," Jaxon says, finishing off his drink. "I'm the last person you should be taking romance advice from, since I've never had a relationship that lasted longer than the length of time I was in a city for a show—and now I can't even get it up without picturing my old best friend's face—but if I were you, I'd get my shit together and figure out a way to convince Kelsey you're someone worth keeping around."

As I lie awake in bed that night, alone, staring at the ceiling of my room, I know he's right. I'm just not sure how I'm going to convince her I'm worth it. Especially with this rivalry inserting itself between us, giving her an easy out.

Chapter Twenty-Three

Kelsey

"You're an idiot," I tell Nash as he pauses midway through his story about the time he and his Army buddies decided to try heliskiing.

I'm only half listening, but any time Nash is this excited about a story, there's almost no doubt in my mind that calling him an idiot is the correct answer.

He laughs good-naturedly before diving back into his tale, not noticing he has almost none of my attention. Instead, I'm focused on the man across the aisle.

Carter didn't come up to my room last night. I stayed awake way longer than I should've, expecting every sound from the hallway to be him, every buzz of my phone to be a text asking to come join me, but nothing.

I don't know what to do with his silence. It's almost like he's back to the guy he was before this trip—the one who never had anything to say to me.

I run my fingers over my phone screen, considering texting him, but what would I even say? *Hey, why did you sit with Weston when the seat in my row was still open? Are you mad at me? Did I do something wrong?*

The worst part is, I can't help but feel like I did do something wrong. Like Carter expected something from me, and I didn't deliver. I hate being wrong, but I feel like I somehow let Carter down. And that feeling? It's worse.

I'm just not sure what it could be. We agreed we were keeping this casual. Spending every night together would be the opposite of casual. Plus, I can't keep up with my work if I'm spending every minute I'm not at the venue with him. I'm sure he needs the time too.

"Do you want to talk about it?" Nash asks, pulling me back. A smirk plays at the corner of his lips.

"Talk about what?" I ask.

"Why you keep staring over my shoulder? Or—and you're really going to be impressed by my powers of perception here—why, after sitting together on basically every flight so far, Carter left the seat next to you open."

Fucking Nash. Sometimes he's such a pain in my ass, I forget he's actually good at his job.

"I'm sure he had important things to talk to Weston about."

"Sure. Makes total sense," Nash says, taking a drink of the soda he ordered when the flight attendant came by a few minutes ago. "And it's not at all suspicious that you phrased it as 'I'm sure he had' rather than 'he had.' Makes it seem like you guys maybe haven't talked today."

I glare at him, but his smile just grows.

"Fine, Sherlock, what's your theory?" I ask, hating myself for asking, but also clearly needing someone else's perspective.

"Funny you should ask," he says, leaning forward slightly.

When I don't lean in as well, he crooks his finger a couple of times to beckon me.

I lean in with a sigh, and Nash smiles at his victory.

"Well, my working theory is that the two of you are fucking," he says, his tone light.

"Fucking? Really, Nash? No one calls it that."

"Yeah, they do, Kels."

"Don't call *me* that."

"Carter does," he says, the look in his eyes daring me to tell him Carter is different.

"Fine. Tell me this insightful theory about us 'fucking,' or I'm going to get some work done. It's only a couple more hours until we land in Seoul."

"You really take the fun out of things, you know?" Nash asks on a pout.

"I've been told."

"Fine, well, I think you two kids are fucking"—he gives me that shit-eating grin he wears so well—"but you're not on the same page."

"Wow, quite a theory," I deadpan, regretting letting myself get pulled into this conversation with Nash.

"I'm not done yet," he says. "I think Carter is ready to put a ring on it and start having your babies, but you're a big fan of your ice queen façade, so you pushed him away. Now, his little heart is broken, so he's gone into turtle-protection mode." He leans back with a smug smile like he just solved nuclear fission.

Well, this was a waste of time. I don't have an ice queen façade. And Carter doesn't want to have my babies—or for me to have his. *Fucking Nash.*

"Interesting theory," I say. "Just a few follow-up questions. You know females have babies, right? Not men? Two, how did you make it this far in life? And, finally, what the fuck is turtle-protection mode?"

"I see you're not disputing the accuracy of any pieces of it."

"Oh, I certainly am."

He holds up a finger. "One, yes. I'm just not sure who wears the pants in your relationship, so I figured I'd play it safe and assume you. Two"—another finger goes up—"I'm awesome." He lifts his third finger. "And finally, turtle-protection mode is pretty self-explanatory. You go into your shell to keep yourself safe."

"You're an idiot."

His smile falters, his face transforming into something serious. "Maybe, Kels, but I've known Carter since he started with Mitchell, and it's his go-to move. When he disagrees with something Trent is doing or when he gets bad news about his mom, he shuts down and avoids everyone. You don't have to confirm you two are together, though it's obvious to everyone who knows Carter. But if I were you, I'd figure out what I did to make him feel scared."

"Oh, please," I say. "Carter isn't scared of anything. He's been that way his whole life. He just doesn't talk to people he doesn't like. I respect that about him."

Nash shrugs, but his serious expression remains. "I don't think that's it. I think you put up your normal walls, and Carter took it as rejection. Let's say, just hypothetically of course, that you two were hanging out in a non-platonic way. He instigated you two 'hanging out'—and by hanging out I mean fucking, by the way—the first few times. Then you probably turned him down for a work call or to go on a run or something like that. He takes it as you not being interested, so he decides to be the bigger person and give you the space you so clearly want. Except, you don't actually want the space—as evidenced by the fact that you keep looking at the man instead of paying attention to me, even now, when I'm dropping real important knowledge on you."

His words hang in the air between us, and I feel a knot twist in my stomach. I glance over at Carter, who is still seated across the aisle, his eyes locked on his phone screen. Is he giving me space because it's what he wants? Or is it what he thinks I want?

"You're reading too much into things," I say, forcing myself to sound dismissive, even as I wonder how right he might be.

Nash gives me a knowing look. "I'm not, Kels, but hey, it's all hypothetical anyway, right?"

"Right, totally hypothetical," I say with a nod.

We both go back to our devices, my focus only partly on the emails I'm reading through from my team. Jaxon is in Seoul for one show tomorrow before we head to Singapore and then down to Australia.

By the time the airplane touches down in South Korea two hours later, Nash's comment has me fully in my head. I *did* instigate things that first morning, but I have let Carter take the lead from there. It's not that I haven't been interested, it's just that I've been unable to figure out how often is too often to be sleeping with my rival. Is that what caused him to turtle?

Only one way to find out, I suppose.

***

"Hey, Carter," I say as he walks into the hotel lobby that night after having a meeting with his team of CPOs.

He stops in front of me, his dark eyes intense as they scan me from head to foot.

"Hey," he says, his voice quieter than usual. "Did we have a meeting I'm late for?"

I shake my head, offering him a tight smile. "Nope, just…wanted to see if you want to grab dinner."

"Dinner?" he asks, his eyes soft but searching.

I hesitate, not wanting to get rejected, but also aware that I'm the one who needs to make the next move. "Yeah, like a date?" I say quietly. "I got a reservation for two at a place close by."

Carter's gaze doesn't leave mine as his right hand comes up and massages the back of his neck. His jaw tightens for a moment as he takes in the busy lobby around us, full of tour staff. Grabbing my hand, he pulls me into a secluded corner.

"Can I be honest with you?" he asks hesitantly.

I nod. "Always."

"I don't know how to do this, Kels," he admits, his voice almost too quiet for me to hear. "I hate being in situations where I don't know what to do, and I have no idea how to be casual with you."

I glance at him, my heart unexpectedly racing. "What do you mean?"

He runs a hand through his hair as he lets out a sigh. "You want the embarrassing truth? I liked you in high school and probably before that," he says, the words tumbling out in a rush. "But I never thought... I never thought you'd feel the same or that the timing would be right. And then you propositioned me as I held you in my arms, and I thought I was getting a chance—a real chance."

The words hit me harder than I expected. My throat tightens, and I blink rapidly, trying to process everything he just said. Carter Mitchell, the guy I've been spending all this time with, the guy I can't seem to stop thinking about, liked me all those years ago?

"But now," Carter continues, his voice low, vulnerable in a way I've never heard before, "I realize it means something more to me than it does to you."

I start to contradict him, but he shakes his head and keeps going.

"And that's okay. You were clear when we started that we weren't dating. I just didn't want to believe it."

I don't know what to say as I look into his dark eyes so full of emotion.

"I'm not good at this. At the whole...talking-about-feelings thing. But I need you to know that as much as I want to accept any little scrap of you you're willing to throw my way, I can't. Lying in bed last night, alone, willing myself not to reach out to you was one of the most painful things I've ever done. I can't do it for the rest of my life, let alone for the next three weeks, Kels. I'm not just looking for a fling or a few nights. I want something more. With you."

It's like the air is sucked out of my lungs. He wants more? My mind races, and I can't find the words to match the storm inside me.

"Carter—" I whisper, but he cuts me off before I can finish.

"You don't have to say anything," he adds quickly. "I know it's not what you're interested in. I just needed you to know why I can't do whatever this is anymore."

I stare at him, my mind working overtime. I don't know how we got here—how everything shifted so quickly between us. But letting go of Carter is not something I'm willing to do, even if I'm terrified of what it might mean.

"I want to have a chance with you," Carter says.

"And what if I don't know what I want yet?"

"Then we'll take it slow," Carter says immediately. "But are you sure it's that you don't know, or is it that you're afraid? Because I'm not him. I'm not your ex. I know it's hard to believe, but I need you to know—*I would never betray your trust.* I'm here for you, Kelsey. Whether you're my friend, my colleague, or something more, I've got you. No matter what happens, I've got your back."

I hesitate, searching his face for something—some hidden meaning or reassurance I guess I still need.

Carter wraps my small fingers in his large ones.

"I've never been good at trusting people," I whisper, hating the slight shake in my voice.

"That's okay. And I know I let you down at the beginning of the tour, which likely makes it harder. But I'm not asking you to trust me all at once. I'm asking you to trust me with today. And if you give me tomorrow, I'll earn a little more of your trust then. Slowly. But I'll earn it, Kels."

"Okay. Then...it is. What I'm interested in, I mean. Something more."

His eyes soften, and for a moment, it's just us. There's no competition, no pressure, just the quiet understanding that things are changing between us. And maybe, just maybe, that's exactly what we both need.

"You really don't make anything easy, do you?" he says, his smile returning, this time warmer, lighter.

"No," I say, shaking my head with a smirk. "But I promise I'll make it worth it."

His smile deepens, and I can feel the weight of everything unsaid between us, but for the first time, it doesn't feel like a burden. It feels like a promise.

I don't know what the future holds, but I know one thing for sure: whatever this is, I want to see where it goes.

CHAPTER TWENTY-FOUR

CARTER

"I KNOW YOU'RE ANGRY, Kels, but don't hurt the man!" I say, jogging after the petite blonde who captured my heart.

"I don't think you understand the magnitude of the situation, Carter," Kelsey shoots back as she continues her power walk along the tan tiles of the stadium.

The river comes into view outside the large glass windows that make up the walls of the building, and I narrowly miss the vendor packing up his snacks now that the concert is shut down.

"Kels, he's just fucking with you," I say, knowing it won't do any good.

"I'm going to make him wish he was never born."

I sprint a few steps, catching up with Kelsey just as she pulls open the door to the security staging room. After I slam my hand against the door to keep it shut, she turns the full force of her attention on me.

"Move, Carter."

"He's basically a puppy," I say, pleading Nash's case. "You can't blame him for chewing up a few shoes." I slide my body in front of her, holding the door in place with my back.

"I don't think you understand how dog training works," she says, an adorable crinkle forming between her brows as she pulls the handle with no success.

"True," I say, lifting my hand to cup her jaw. "I never had a dog."

"No fair using your power of seduction against me."

I lean down, lightly pressing a kiss against her lips. "Is it working?"

"Of course it's working," she huffs, though the tension in her body has faded away.

"You know he didn't post anything on your social media. He's just kidding."

"He better not have. I don't post shit on socials, *and he knows that.*"

My head drops back against the door as I laugh.

"Are you guys fucking against the door?" Nash's voice filters through from inside the room.

"Never mind," I say, stepping aside and opening the door for Kelsey. "He's all yours."

"Nathaniel Ashton Parker," Kelsey says, her tone deadly. "Where is my phone?"

I watch her stalk into the room, Nash backing up with a look of concern in his eye.

"Here. Right here. I was just joking. Just like you do."

"No, not just like I do," Kelsey says, crossing her arms over her small, perky breasts. "Because I'm funny. You. Are. Not."

"I was just teasing," Nash says, a puppy whine entering his voice.

"You're an idiot."

"Come on, Kels. You don't mean that."

She checks her phone quickly before flipping open the lid of the earpieces' container, pulling out one to check. "I most certainly do."

I join Kelsey on the other side of the table, pulling out another earpiece to examine.

"You can go now, Nash. We've got this," Kelsey says, gesturing toward the door with her hand. "Carter's mostly useful now."

"Thanks, babe," I say. "Quite the compliment."

Nash and Kelsey both look at me, eyebrows raised.

"What?" I ask.

"Did you just call her *babe*?"

Fuck.

"Nope. You must be hearing things."

"Kels, you definitely heard him call you babe, right?"

"I take back what I said before," Kelsey says, a smirk pulling on her lips as she keeps her eyes trained on the black earpiece in her fingers. "You're both idiots."

Nash laughs, a full, rich sound that bounces off the walls of the small room. "Sucks to suck, boss," he teases.

"Go away, Nash," I say.

"Oh, sure. Need some privacy. I totally get it." He walks to the door, pulling it open with one tug. "I'll just go see what Mikayla is up to!"

"Nash!" Kelsey and I both yell at the closing door.

Nash sticks his mouth into the small gap still open. "Just kidding, Mom. I'll keep everything on the up-and-up."

The door slams, and we both stare at it, not sure if he's coming back or not.

Kelsey looks at me with a raised eyebrow. "Did he just call you *Mom*?"

I chuckle at the confused look on her face. "No."

"It really sounded like it."

"He calls me *Dad*," I say, trying to match her seriousness.

Her eyes go comically wide for just the briefest second before she pulls her mask of neutrality back on. "You should fire him."

I can't contain the laughter that spills from me, and soon, Kelsey is chuckling along as well.

"I can't believe you called me babe. And said it in front of him." A hint of pink coats her cheeks at the statement.

"Is it a bad thing if Nash knows I use terms of endearment with you?" I ask, turning my full attention to her.

"No. I think Nash may have already been aware. I'm just not sure I'm much of a babe."

"*Sweetheart*?" I offer, but Kelsey only snorts.

"*Darling*?"

"Who are you? A shadow daddy?"

I cock my head to the side, not following the reference, but she just shakes her head.

"Lila's taken to giving me books to read."

"How about *angel*?" I joke, knowing she'll turn that one down.

In classic Kelsey fashion, she just glares at me.

I search my memory for another term of endearment, but *love* is the only other one I can think of besides *hot stuff*, and I feel both are likely inappropriate suggestions. Then it hits me.

"*Cupcake*? Final offer."

"Hard pass," Kelsey says on a laugh.

We work in silence for a couple of minutes before Kelsey pauses, looking up at me from beneath her eyebrows.

"Speaking of outrageous nicknames. Are you going to explain Puffin to me?"

Dang, this girl. She's got a memory like a steel trap.

"I did explain it," I hedge.

"I mean, you lied to me about why your Army buddies call you Puffin. But I thought now that you're throwing around terms like *babe*, you might tell me the truth." She flutters her eyelashes at me.

"God, you're cute," I say, leaning across the table to give her a light kiss on the lips.

Her hands reach up to cup my face, deepening the connection between us. We make out like a couple of teenagers before she finally pulls away a few minutes later.

"So, are you going to tell me?" she asks.

Her cheeks are rosy, her breath coming quicker than before. I can't help but stare at her lips, which are red from the friction of our kiss.

"I actually have a secret I think you'd like more," I offer.

"Oh, really?"

"Yep. But you have to promise it stays between us."

"Of course."

I pause, trying to build the drama. "I send all of Trent's emails."

A laugh bursts out of Kelsey. "What?!"

"I manage Trent's work email account. I respond to all his messages."

"So this fall…?" she asks.

"All me."

"That checks out," she says, her eyes twinkling with delight. "That was such a good secret. It all makes so much more sense now."

"You're taking this remarkably well."

"I started to think Trent was intelligent. I may have even admitted to liking the electronic version of him." I laugh again. "This is so much better."

"You like the virtual version of me? Ah, that might be the first time I've ever heard you give a compliment."

"What? No it isn't. I'm a nice person. I give compliments every time they're deserved."

"I said what I said," I respond.

Kelsey's mouth drops open. "For that, now you have to tell me about Puffin too."

"What? That's not the deal. I told you about the emails!"

"We never made a deal," she says, her smile wide. "You gave that information up freely. Now, tell me about Puffin."

No matter how stupid it makes me feel trying to explain myself to her, I know she deserves it.

"What do you know about puffins?" I ask, my gaze still on her lips.

"Um"—she twirls her finger around the hair at the nape of her neck—"they're birds?"

"Correct." I chuckle at her answer. "They also mate for life, spending most of their winters apart before coming back together each spring."

Kelsey cocks her head, thinking. "And you're...really loyal?"

I consider lying. I could spin this in a way that doesn't make me look like I've been pining after her since my voice first dropped, but I'm not sure that's what I want. If I'm going to have any chance of keeping Kelsey once we get back to Wild Bluffs, I need her to know that this isn't just some passing interest. I mentioned my crush on her in high school, but not how that somehow morphed into an infatuation that I've never been able to shake.

I walk around the table, my hand gently lifting her chin until her eyes meet mine. "One of the guys I was in the Rangers with was also my roommate freshman year of college. He knew about the girl I couldn't stop thinking about when we first got to college. The one I wished I had taken a chance on and asked out, especially after she stood up for my mom. The girl who never left my mind, no matter where I was, or what I was doing, even though I'd never dated her—even though she wasn't ever mine to come back to."

Her breath hitches slightly, and I see the realization flicker in her eyes. It's like a spark between us as my words finally sink in.

"My Army buddies would set me up with women, but they were never as beautiful or as interesting as you were—or at least the you in my head. So they got annoyed with me always coming back from dates unimpressed with the women and started calling me Puffin. And like all ridiculous nicknames, it stuck."

"How? You…we…you wouldn't even talk to me in high school," Kelsey says.

"Yeah. That's what happens when you have a crush on someone since middle school: your brain stops functioning around them." I brush my thumb lightly over her cheek. "But as for how, you know how small schools are: You know everything about everyone. You always fascinated me. And then, somehow, you burrowed your way into my heart and became the standard I compared all other women against. A standard that no other woman was able to meet. I realize it sounds ridiculous. Trust me, I've been told, and told myself, how ridiculous it was to compare every woman I met to you, someone I never even dated."

Her gaze locks on to mine, searching for something. And when she finally speaks, her voice is barely a whisper, but it's enough to send a shiver down my spine.

"I never knew."

"I know."

"Why didn't you tell me?"

I chuckle. "Tell you? When? In high school? I couldn't talk around you, and you were either dating seniors or seemed completely un-interested in any of the rest of us. But honestly? I never wanted to pursue anything. I knew it didn't matter. I wasn't planning on sticking around. We both had big dreams, and I wasn't going to risk holding either of us back. Honestly, high school me didn't think it was as big of a deal as my college and Army friends did. Turns out, not everyone had a crush on a girl their entire middle and high school years and never did anything about it."

"It is a big deal," she says.

I let out a low chuckle. "Are you saying I had a chance in high school?"

There's a twinkle in her gaze now. "I mean, no, probably not. But not because of you. I was so focused on getting out of town and making something of myself that I put zero thought into connecting with the people around me—even my sisters."

A weight lifts off my chest as she admits that, and for the first time, I understand why she always seemed so distant. Kelsey, always driven, always with her eyes set on something bigger. I can't help but marvel at how much she's changed—even though that drive in her is still the same.

"And now?" I ask softly, brushing my thumb along the curve of her cheek again. "Because I'm not going anywhere, Kels. Not this time."

She looks down at our hands, her fingers lightly curling around mine, then back up at me, her lips pressing together like she's holding something back.

"Why does this feel so...easy?" she finally asks, her voice barely audible.

"Because we've been waiting for this," I reply, my voice steady. "For a long time, and in different ways. We just didn't know it."

Her eyes soften at my words. "You really think we can make this work?" she asks. "Even once we're back in Wild Bluffs?"

"I *know* we can. You were the girl I compared every other one to for the last fifteen years, and now I know you're the woman no other can compare to. I tried to tell myself how irrational it was to have my baseline be a girl I was classmates with growing up, but it didn't work.

And now I know the real version of you is even better than the one my adolescent brain concocted. So giving up on us isn't an option. Not for me."

"Okay, Puff," Kelsey says with a smile. "Then it's not an option for me either."

And just like that, everything feels possible. Now, I just have to figure out how to break the news to Trent without losing my job.

CHAPTER TWENTY-FIVE
CARTER

KELSEY GLANCES AT ME, her hand brushing mine across the table. "You okay?" she asks.

I've been nervous since our plane touched down in Melbourne yesterday. Kelsey and I are sitting in the airport pickup line, waiting for her sister and Lila to arrive after dropping off their boyfriends in Sydney for their practice rounds. Despite knowing Izzy and, to some extent, Bryn—at least somewhat—my whole life, I'm still worried. I can't help but feel like I'm going to be under some unspoken scrutiny. What if Bryn disapproves of me dating her sister? What if everything I've been building with Kelsey crumbles under the weight of family expectations?

I smile, a little more forced than I'd like, but I don't want her to see the doubt clouding my mind. "Yeah, just...thinking."

"About what?" she presses, her thumb tracing the edge of my palm.

"About Bryn. And Lila too. I want them to like me. I want them to know that I'm serious about us. But mostly, I'm just...nervous about how they'll see this. Us."

After my confession following the Singapore concert, Kelsey and I stayed together in her room, spending the night talking about anything and everything—from favorite colors to the challenges of being left-handed. It was exactly the level of connection I needed after my declaration.

Yesterday, thankfully, was a travel day. I got to spend the entire seven-hour flight with her. We watched movies, shared half-finished thoughts, and casually chatted between sending emails and catching up on work. Even though it was essentially the same dynamic we had before—friendly and collegial—it felt different. Now, there's a thread of light connecting us, something subtle but undeniable, making everything we do together seem...more. Special.

I took her out to her top-rated Melbourne restaurant last night—an intimate spot that has the charm of a small-town diner but with food that could easily be mistaken for art. We laughed, ate, and talked about the future in a way that didn't feel rushed. There were no looming deadlines or questions about what's next. Just us, in the moment. And for the first time, I felt like maybe, just maybe, this could work.

Now, as we wait for Bryn and Lila to arrive, my nerves are back in full force. I have no idea how Bryn might react. The Harper sisters have always been close, and I'm worried I won't measure up in Bryn's eyes.

"You don't have to worry about them, Carter. They'll be excited for us. Honestly? They've essentially already figured out that something is going on between us. They seemed excited about the prospect of it being you when they heard your voice on that video call."

"I hope so."

"You don't have to be anything you're not. Not to my family. Just...be yourself."

I nod, feeling a surge of relief. It's just like Kelsey to cut through my worries with that calm, grounded reassurance.

I try to focus on the feeling of being seen, of being accepted, and let the anxiety about Bryn and Lila fade away. But all the insecurities I thought I'd overcome—the ones I'm realizing are directly linked to who I am in Wild Bluffs—are rearing their heads. And now is not the time for me to shut down, not when I need to make a good impression on the people important to Kelsey.

"They'll like you," Kelsey says, as if reading my thoughts. "And if they don't, well, who cares what they think? They're idiots anyway."

I chuckle, knowing Kelsey doesn't actually mean that. She's closer to her family than most people I know.

"Oh! Here they come," she says, sliding out of the passenger seat to go meet the women walking out of the sliding doors. "Oh my gosh! Is that Iz with them?"

I watch Kelsey walk toward her sisters, the familiar sway of her stride making my heart skip a beat. It's so easy to get lost in her, to forget everything else when she's near. But now, with not one but two Harper sisters finally in front of me, the nerves are back in full force.

Bryn and Izzy, both almost as tall as me, lead the way, their light brown hair catching the sunlight as they step into the Australian sun. Izzy's the one I've known the longest, since she was just two years behind us in school. She's also the one who I'm very surprised to see at a Jaxon Steele concert. I wonder if Jaxon knows she's here.

Lila follows behind, a black backpack like Kelsey's over her shoulder.

Izzy wraps her arms around Kelsey first, laughing as she picks Kels up in a tight, almost crushing hug. I can see the bond between them, the one I've never had with my half brother. Bryn does the same before Lila steps forward, offering a more casual hug.

Kelsey helps them load their bags in the back of the dark SUV we borrowed from Jaxon's fleet of rental cars. As the three travelers climb into the back, Bryn's eyes narrow, scanning me carefully. She's got that sharp, assessing look on her face, the kind of look that makes you feel like you're being sized up for a test you didn't study for.

Bryn's gaze flicks between Kelsey and me, a small smirk pulling at the corner of her lips. "Well, well, well. Carter Mitchell. It's almost like we called this."

Kelsey laughs, rolling her eyes. "It wasn't a secret, Bryn."

"And yet, you suggested you were going to hook up with Trent to try to convince us it wasn't Carter we heard," Izzy says, a teasing tone to her voice.

My head snaps to Kelsey, and she rolls her eyes as the three women in the back laugh.

"I'm obviously not hooking up with Trent."

I laugh too.

"Anyway," Lila says from the back row of the car. "I called you two getting together waaay before this trip even existed."

"What do you mean?" I ask.

"I could tell you were into Kelsey at that barbecue last summer at Jen and Ken's house."

Kelsey raises her eyebrow. "The one where Izzy was trying to get you to meet Carter...so you could date him?"

"Yup!" Lila says, the smile on her face only growing despite Kelsey's tone.

"Well, I'm glad you two kids figured it out," Izzy says as she leans forward to pat my shoulder from her seat behind me.

I chuckle nervously, glancing at Kelsey, who's watching me intently. "Yeah. Me too."

Kelsey's gaze softens, and for a moment, I'm lost in her eyes, forgetting that I'm driving a car full of people.

The car hums along, the chatter in the back growing louder with each passing minute.

"So, Izzy," Kelsey says, leaning back between the seats, her voice teasing but laced with curiosity. "What made you decide to show up last minute? I thought you were boycotting everything Jaxon Steele?"

Izzy shrugs nonchalantly, her gaze flickering toward the window as if considering her answer carefully. "I'm here for the girls' trip, not the Jaxon Steele concert. I wasn't going to let him ruin my chance to fly private to Australia for a vacation."

Everyone falls quiet for a moment, no one daring to push further. I glance at Kelsey, whose brow furrows slightly, but she doesn't ask anything more. Izzy's response seems to have satisfied her for now, even if it gave me just enough information to be curious. What exactly happened between Jaxon and Izzy?

Lila leans in from the back row, her smile wide. "And a hell of a trip it will be, too. I'm so glad you decided to come."

Izzy laughs. "Me too. I desperately needed to escape the bleakness of February in eastern Colorado."

Kelsey smiles, but there's still something in her expression that doesn't quite settle. She meets my eyes again, and I can see the flicker of concern in hers.

As we pull into the hotel parking lot, Kelsey hops out of the car in what I can only guess is older-sister mode. She hands out room keys and goes over the itinerary for the day.

"Iz, I obviously didn't get you a room, since you weirdly decided not to tell me you were coming…"

"Oh, shoot," Izzy says, turning around and walking backward to face Kelsey. "I forgot to yell *surprise* when I saw you."

"Anyway, you can have my room, and I'll bunk with Carter," she says with a wink in my direction.

"Wow, how magnanimous of you," Izzy says on a laugh.

"Thank you for acknowledging my sacrifice."

"What about me?" I ask, teasing. "Is it not a sacrifice on my part to share my room?"

All four women stop, their faces identical masks of skepticism.

"No," Bryn says, shaking her head. "You can send us a thank-you basket later."

"And you want…chocolate in that?" I ask.

"Chocolate is a good start," Bryn replies. "And then add in some sour gummy worms, a few romance novels, and"—she narrows her eyes at Izzy as if deciding what she needs—"a Jaxon Steele pincushion."

I snort a laugh as the door to the elevator opens in front of us.

As we ride to our rooms, the women make plans to meet for an early lunch before Kelsey, Lila, and I leave for the concert venue.

As soon as Kelsey and I are back in our room, she pulls out her phone, her fingers frantically moving over the screen.

"Everything okay?" I ask.

"Someone just called in sick for their shift tonight, so now I'm down a man. Their normal backup is on vacation, so I've got to find a replacement."

"Anything I can do to help?"

"No." She twirls her long blonde hair back into a knot at the back of her neck before letting it drop back over her shoulders. "I just need to make a couple of calls."

"Okay, well, I can head down to the lobby and work from there if you need the room," I offer.

"That's...actually, that would be great if you don't mind. I thought I was on top of things, but now, having two of my sisters just hanging out while Lila and I work...it's a little more stressful than just Bryn."

"Why?" I ask, not seeing the distinction between the two.

"Bryn travels all the time for work. I figured she would just hang out in the hotel with her laptop while we're at the stadium, and then she can hang out with Jameo or some of the WAGs she's gotten to know since starting to date Jameo. Izzy should actually get out and do things."

"I'm sure Izzy knew what she was in for. She seems pretty easygoing."

"She is. I just… I'm worried I'm going to let something slip if I get too busy—start thinking about too many things."

"Your sisters are adults. I'm sure they'll figure it out. But, if it'd help, I can put together an itinerary for them for while we're working, just in case."

"Could you? That would be great. I know they're grown-ass women, but if you leave travel planning up to the two of them, they'll just walk around downtown until it's time to eat. And even then, they'll just wander until they find something they think is interesting, or they get so hungry they just stop at the first place they see."

Even though Kelsey is more of a planner than I am, I can't fathom that level of uncertainty. "Well, we can't have that. Anything they do or don't like?" I ask, pulling up an app on my phone to take notes.

"Nope. That's part of the problem. They're remarkably indecisive."

"I'm on it," I say, grabbing my backpack with my laptop.

"Hey," Kelsey says, causing me to stop. "Thank you."

My response is cut off by her mouth pressing to mine. I lean into the kiss, reaching around to grab a handful of her strong ass before letting her go.

As I make my way toward the elevator, my phone buzzes with a notification.

It's from Trent.

Trent

> Can you meet me in the lobby? I need to talk to you.

Well, shit. I guess Trent is coming to Australia. I'm not getting sick and tired of him randomly popping up places. Not at all.

Trent

We have two potential clients on the line, but both are dragging their feet to see if we sign Jaxon first.

We need a game plan to win Jaxon so we can get these other two.

Chapter Twenty-Six

Kelsey

"Okay, but hear me out," Bryn says between bites of her brekky sando as we sit in the restaurant of our Sydney hotel. "What if you came to the golf tournament with us for a few hours? Just a few. And you got back before the concert even starts."

"Their tee times are too late," I object for the third time that morning. "I'd miss part of the full team meeting."

Having Lila and my sisters around has been a lot of fun, and even though Carter wasn't able to hang out with us as much as he wanted to, the last three days have gone smoothly. Both Melbourne concerts went off without a hitch, despite Trent's unexpected arrival and the disruption his presence and constant idiotic suggestions caused. Thank goodness he brought his wife and her gaggle of friends with him to whisk him off to the beaches that I won't get to set foot on during this trip.

"I know it would mean a lot to JT if you came," Lila says, offering the only argument that has any sway over me.

JT went through a lot last season, and I *do* want to be able to support him. I was so frustrated we weren't able to make it to Sydney in time for their first round yesterday. Fortunately, we'd been able to go out for dinner as a group. Unfortunately, Trent wanted to review staffing with Carter, so he hadn't been able to join.

I know everyone will love him, but I am a bit anxious to see how he'll mesh with everyone, including the guys who have quickly become part of the family.

I shake my head, feeling the weight of the expectations pressing down on me.

"I'm sure Jaxon won't mind," Lila offers.

"What won't I mind?" a voice asks from behind me.

I turn, catching Jaxon, Trent, and Carter as they follow behind a waitress on their way to a table. Jaxon stops in front of our table, and I quickly confirm the location of his security team by the front entrance.

"Hey, Bryn, Lila—" Jaxon's friendly greeting cuts off when his eyes land on the top of my middle sister's head.

Everyone's eyes dart to Izzy, who is practically hiding behind the drink menu. I look back at Jaxon in time to see him wrestle his shock under control. It's taken some coordination on my part, but I'm pretty pleased to say I've successfully been able to keep Jaxon and Izzy from running into each other while staying at the same hotel—until now, I guess.

"What...what can I help you with?" he asks, his eyes still glued to my sister.

"We're trying to convince Kelsey to come to watch JT and Jameson this afternoon," Lila says. "But she thinks she needs to be at the security meeting."

"We can handle the meeting," Trent offers, a smug smile on his face.

I want to punch him.

"We can, Kelsey," Carter agrees, his offer so much more sincere than his brother's.

"I'll think about it and get back to you," I offer.

"Are you all coming to the concert tonight?" Jaxon asks, looking around the table at the last second as if curious what Lila and Bryn are doing.

"Not tonight," Bryn says with a shrug. "The guys won't be done, but some of us will be there tomorrow."

"I'll be working it tonight," Lila adds.

"Did Kelsey hook you up with passes?" Jaxon asks, his gaze back on Izzy's menu.

"No," Bryn says with a pout. "She didn't want to abuse her power." She does little air quotes around the last three words, and I sigh.

"I'll make sure Annie leaves five backstage passes for you," Jaxon says, his eyes begging Izzy to look at him.

She doesn't, her face remaining hidden behind the menu. "Just four is fine. I don't listen to country music."

I swear Jaxon, the man who has energy and charisma shining from him at all times, deflates at her words.

"Well, I'll have her leave five, just in case." He offers a halfhearted smile. "And, Kelsey, you should go to the golf tournament. Carter and Trent can handle the meeting. It's essentially just rinse and repeat at this point, isn't it?"

Bryn and Lila both look at me with victory in their eyes, but it's the slight shudder I feel run through Izzy's leg that's touching mine that makes me agree.

"Yeah, I'm sure they'll do great," I say. "Carter, can we chat in the hall for a minute, then? Just to make sure we've got everything covered?"

"Of course," he says, nodding to his brother and Jaxon to continue on.

"Why didn't you guys ask me to grab breakfast?" I ask once we're out in the hall. It wasn't what I meant to ask first, but it just came out. I hate feeling like important meetings are happening without me.

Carter's face drops, clearly following my train of thought. "It's nothing like that, Kels. Trent asked if I wanted to grab breakfast after our meeting, and we ran into Jaxon in the elevator. It wasn't a premeditated thing."

I stare at his face, trying to find some sign that he might be lying, not that I have the best track record of spotting the signs of deceit on a man's face.

"I promise, Kels."

"Okay," I say slowly. "I believe you."

"Am I allowed to kiss you in front of all these people?" he asks, staring at my lips.

I look around, taking in all the people who would see us, and slowly shake my head. "Not here."

"Okay. Later, then." He winks at me, dispelling the cloud that had settled between us at my doubt.

"Are you sure you're okay to take the meeting today?" I ask.

"I'm happy to step up. Plus, with Trent here, we both know it's not likely going to go how either of us planned. It might as well just be me he's talking over."

"And you don't think it'll look bad if I'm not there?"

"No. Everyone who matters knows what an excellent job you and your team are doing. Honestly, it'll probably make you look even more important if you're too busy to come to a meeting."

I bite my lip, trying not to let the memory of Lukas taint everything I've come to know about Carter.

He is not Lukas.

"Okay," I say. "Thank you."

"Of course, Kels. I'd do anything for you. You know that," he says, sliding his hands into the pockets of his slacks.

Taking in his muscular frame, I'm once again annoyed by the fact that Trent pulled him from our bed this morning.

"Anything?" I ask, twirling a piece of hair around my finger like I just stepped out of a '90s rom-com.

Carter fights a battle against the smirk that wants to cross his face, ultimately losing. "Oh, definitely that. Whatever you're thinking, I'm more than happy to oblige."

"Amazing! I was hoping you'd go for a ten-mile run with me tomorrow," I tease.

"I would do anything…but I won't do that."

"Sure you would."

"Okay, I definitely would," he says before leaning closer to whisper, "But you'd have to help me forget about my sore muscles once we got back."

"All I'm hearing is excuses," I say as I turn to walk away.

Carter catches my arm, pulling me back into him. "You like being on top anyway. It's a win-win."

"I'm starting to see the benefits of changing it up," I concede, offering him a smile as I walk back to my table.

"Holy crap, Kelsey," Bryn says, coughing. "I can barely breathe with all the sexual chemistry floating around in here." She waves her hand like she's trying to fan away smoke before breaking out into a teasing grin.

Lila snickers beside her.

"Why do I hang out with you?" I ask.

"Because you love us," Izzy replies, her smile not quite meeting her eyes.

"You good?" I ask her.

"Yup."

"Just too many drink options?" I tease.

"So many choices. How am I supposed to decide if I don't thoroughly examine the menu?"

We finish our breakfast in a whirlwind of laughter, avocado toast, and good-natured jokes. After I finish, I quickly run back to the room I'm sharing with Carter to change into the golf outfit Lila brought for me to wear.

"On second thought," Carter says when I pass him in the hallway outside our room. "You should be at the meeting. I can't handle knowing you're walking around Australia like that."

"Jealous?" I tease.

"Yes. One hundred percent. And I'm confident enough to admit I'm also a tiny bit terrified that one of Jameson's pro-golfer friends is going to take one look at you and stop at nothing to make you his."

I laugh at the ridiculous notion, and Carter grabs me around the waist.

"I'm serious, Kels. They'd be idiots not to on a normal day, but with you in that little black skirt?" He bites his lip, and I feel his body go taut.

"It's a skort," I whisper in his ear, laughing when he realizes I didn't actually say anything sexy.

"I like a challenge," he says, lifting me over his shoulder and carrying me back to our room.

"I've got to go, Puff!" I say, slapping him on his ass as I hang over his shoulder.

"They can wait five minutes. I've got plans."

"Plans that only take five minutes?" I ask as he opens the door to our room.

"Well, that's mostly up to you, babe," Carter says as he sets me on the floor. "*I'm* not going to take the whole time."

"You've got five minutes," I say, dropping my hands to trace the outline of his bulge. "Don't let me down."

"You're so beautiful." Carter buries his nose in my hair. "I can't wait to show you just how much I want you."

He kisses his way from my neck down the front of my shirt before dropping his hands to the hem of my shirt.

"Not enough time," I say, shaking my head.

His eyes meet mine, a soft intensity filling them. "There is always enough time to make sure you get what you need."

With a conceding grin, I lift my arms over my head, my collared shirt quickly following. He leans in and licks a line from my collarbone down to my nonexistent cleavage. Goose bumps spill over me, my nipples hardening. Using his thumb, he pushes down one side of my bra, lightly licking my right nipple before sucking it—*hard*.

I moan, and he presses me against the mirror in the entryway, my back flat against the cold glass.

"Hurry," I manage to get out.

He glares at me as if I'm ridiculous for even suggesting he not take his time.

"Carter," I demand.

He pulls my black skort down in one swift movement, and I kick it off from around my ankles as his mouth devours mine. Sliding a hand around the back of my legs, he lifts me, notching my center directly against his bulge.

He lets out a hiss as I press myself against him.

"Less clothes," I say on a gasp.

He props my back against the mirror, holding me as he pulls his pants and boxer briefs down just enough for his cock to spring free. I grab the wallet out of his back pocket and extract the condom from there. I rip the package with my teeth and slowly wrap him.

Gripping my hips with enough pressure I know I'll have marks, he lifts me up, sliding my heat against his erection. Once. Twice. Three times.

"Touch yourself," he whispers in my ear. "My hands are full, and I need you to feel good."

I reach down, placing two fingers over my clit.

"Good girl."

With that, he lifts me again, slamming home inside me with a low moan.

My body begins to tremble as my orgasm builds inside me. The heels of my tennis shoes are digging into the back of his legs. I scrape my fingers along his broad back, a laugh escaping me as his hips spasm at the light pain.

I increase the speed of my fingers, matching his relentless pace. And it feels good. *So good*.

"Carter," I moan.

"That's right, Kels. Say my name. Let the whole floor know who's making you feel so good."

My back arches as I chant his name, unable to stop myself from giving him what he wants.

It's too much.

It's not enough.

Ohh— I break, all my senses fully giving in to the pure ecstasy that's flowing through me. Carter follows, hissing out my name as his hips jerk.

We stay like that, my back pressed into the mirror, his forehead against my shoulder, for a few breaths.

"I've got to go," I whisper, attempting to convince myself I shouldn't just stay here and do this all day.

Carter pulls away, gently setting me on the floor. He leans in and gives me a light kiss, his fingers stroking my arm gently.

I return the kiss before bending over to pick up my discarded clothes.

"Fuck, Kels. You can't bend over in front of a mirror like that." He runs his hand through his hair, his eyes staring intently at my reflection.

I wiggle my ass, laughing as he reaches down to stroke himself in a move I can only assume is unconscious.

"Are you sure you have to leave?" he asks.

"I'm sure," I say, pulling my underwear and skort on in one go.

Once I'm ready, I stand on my tiptoes to give him one final kiss. "Thanks for covering for me this afternoon."

"I've got you, Kels."

Chapter Twenty-Seven

Kelsey

I'M BACKSTAGE, A CLUSTER of voices buzzing in the air around me. The opening act is just finishing up, and I took a few minutes to dash out here to say hello to my family while I knew Jaxon was fully covered by his CPOs and my team monitoring the cameras. Yesterday's concert went off without a hitch despite my missing the pre-meeting, so I feel more confident sneaking out of the security booth for a few minutes today.

I try not to dwell on the fact that I might be unnecessary at this point.

Izzy's a few feet away, dressed in a thin-strapped tank top, her tight black jeans disappearing into the black cowboy boots she bought this morning.

"I'm so glad you decided to come, Iz," I say when I reach her.

"And miss out on backstage passes to the concert of the decade? Never," she teases, though her levity feels forced.

Her eyes keep darting around, and I'm not sure if she's excited or terrified to see her old best friend in all his Jaxon Steele glory.

"It really is a great concert," I say. "The crowd, the atmosphere? You're going to have a good time."

Bryn laughs, dipping out from under Jameson's arm to come say hello. "Great outfit, Kelsey."

I look down at my entirely black ensemble and then back at her. "It's my uniform."

"You could at least wear cowboy boots," she says, nodding at her own. I take in my youngest sister's outfit, noting she's gone full pretend cowgirl for the evening with her lightly faded jeans and a rust-orange tie-back tank top.

"Cowboy boots are not as easy to run in," I parry.

"As long as they let me stumble back to the hotel after a few beers, that's all I need," Izzy chimes in, opening one of the many beverages set out for the VIP guests.

I glance over at Jameo and JT, both looking much more relaxed than the rest of us, even though they just finished their golf tournament. Both men are standing near the opening of the stage, Jameo casually watching the band currently performing while JT takes a few selfies.

I wave hello, and both men come over to join our little group.

"How'd the tournament end up?" I ask, even though my sports app informed me of the results hours ago.

Jameo pulls Bryn under his arm, leaning on her. "It went all right. JT played like a man possessed," he says, a grin on his face. "His putt on eighteen was magical—seventeen feet out, he was on a different level than the pin, and he drained it. It was pretty."

Grinning at the compliment, JT says, "I had to do something to keep up with your drives. I'm still annoyed that I've spent the whole season training with you, and you still outdrive me every time."

I let out a laugh. "Wow, I didn't realize your bromance had progressed to this point. Do you need me to see about getting you a private room?"

"You're *so funny*, Kels," JT says. "Also, Sam says he *must* see a picture of us, so smile." He holds his phone up, sliding his arm around my shoulder and making an outrageous face before I can tell him no.

"You're an idiot."

I chat with everyone for a few more minutes, making sure they know where they can go to see the full concert if they don't want to be backstage the entire time.

Before I leave, I give Izzy one last hug. "You good?" I ask her quietly.

"Yup. It's just...a lot more emotions than I expected. I thought I was prepared, but..." Her words trail off as her attention catches on something behind me.

Pulling out of the hug, I see Jaxon walk by, his usual concert persona in place. He stalks toward the stage, a black guitar draped across his chest. With his all-black outfit, massive frame, and perfectly styled hair, it's clear why half the country is obsessed with the man.

The moment he notices Izzy, his steps falter. The two stand there, staring at each other, until almost everyone backstage has noticed and is gawking at the odd display. I don't know what it is, but there's something about the way she's looking at him that feels different. I want to say something, but it's not the right time.

I shoot Jaxon what I hope is a professional smile and pull Izzy away, herding her toward the door to get to their seats. The gossip will be raging by the end of the show, but luckily, Izzy's not close to any of the concert staff, so she likely won't hear any of it.

When I finally reach the security booth Lila, Carter, and I are managing for the night, I force myself to focus on my work.

"How's everything looking?" I ask.

"All set. It's so much more fun being here than doing this from our empty office at random hours," Lila says.

I settle in at my station, my mind already spinning through the checklists in my head.

As the concert starts, we all focus on our work, Lila and I both coordinating with various teams. After a small disruption between two drunk guests close to the stage is dealt with by the venue's security team, I focus my attention back on the various camera feeds.

All goes well, and I start to relax as Jaxon starts the final song of his encore.

That's when I notice it. A faint blinking light on one of the security monitors—just a small change, but it's enough to give me pause.

"Hey," I say to Lila. "What's going on with camera five? That thing on the wall wasn't blinking earlier."

"Not sure. Maybe it's just an alarm or something for the venue."

"That camera covers the hall to the stage entrance," I say, studying the diagram in front of me.

"Can you send someone to check it out?" I ask Carter.

"Already on it," he says, talking into his earpiece.

Relief washes through me when a voice answers, confirming the comms are at least still working. I watch the screen but don't see anyone moving.

The sense of unease increases when Carter's man calls back, saying there isn't a light on.

"Shit," I say, staring at Lila and Carter. "It's not the live feed. Carter, get a team as close to the stage as you can. Lila, get someone on this."

Lila grabs her phone, typing into our team's messaging system as she waits for someone to answer. "Hey, Lincoln, we've got a problem," Lila says, her voice sharp and urgent. "There's been a breach. We've got at least one camera playing a looped video." She leans over and looks at my screen. "Camera five."

With that, all twenty-four feeds on my screen go black.

"Vince, do you copy?" I ask, waiting for the head of the venue's security team to respond. As Jaxon's personal security team, we monitor the cameras that are important to the performer, but leave the other ten-to-a-hundred cameras to the venue's team. I don't want someone to steal from the concessions, but it isn't my job to focus on that.

"Copy."

"We lost connection to all of our cameras. Are yours out?"

"No, but...Kelsey, you've got a fan on the stage."

I stop dead in my tracks, my blood running cold. "What? *How?*"

I glance out the window that allows us to see the performance happening two levels below. Sure enough, there is a man with sandy-blond hair running around the stage, yelling something. He also appears to be...naked.

The band is still playing, though it's clear everyone is distracted by the man.

Carter is screaming into his comms, coordinating the extraction of the man. Finally, a team of five moves in from all sides, and an agent tackles the streaker.

A chant starts up in the crowd, something I can't quite make out, and Jaxon breaks from his normal choreography to chant along with them. Then I hear it, the "Action, Jaxon! Action, Jaxon!" that pulls me back to my youth, when I'd hear Izzy and Jaxon yelling that before he would do some dumb stunt in our backyard, or later when they were downstairs playing that guitar video game.

Finally, Jaxon starts singing again, the crisis seemingly forgotten by all but me and my team. But the panic inside me continues to build. *This is bad. This is really bad.*

The monitors in front of me are still black. The cameras that should've been providing security footage, the very cameras my team was responsible for, went down at just the wrong moment. I feel the weight of responsibility pressing down harder than it ever has before. We were supposed to be prepared for this. We were prepared. Why is this happening?

Carter is on his comms, barking orders. "Backup team, perimeter check, now. We've got no eyes. Weston, Eddie, I want both your teams moving with Jaxon."

I try to focus, but my mind is racing. The streaker is already gone, taken away by security, but the damage is done. The cameras were down, the equipment compromised, and it's on my team. My responsibility.

I glance over at Lila, who's still glued to her phone, sending messages, coordinating with the venue's team. Her face is tight, the urgency in her expression matching the way I feel inside. "What do you need me to do?" she asks, her voice clipped but focused.

"We need to figure out what happened," I say, my voice shaking a little. "Someone tampered with our equipment. It's the only explanation. We can't risk it happening again. I need to know exactly what happened."

Lila nods her agreement, and I look at Carter. "We'd better go check in with Jaxon. They'll have him back at his dressing room by now."

He gestures toward the door. "I'll follow you," he says, his voice calm, but there's an edge to it. I know he's pissed. I'm pissed.

We make our way backstage, moving quickly toward Jaxon's dressing room. As we approach, I hear raised voices inside—Jaxon, Henry, and several others I don't recognize are all speaking at once. My stomach sinks. This is exactly the kind of situation I've been trying to avoid: another failure on my team's part.

I knock before entering, trying to compose myself. The door opens, and the tension in the room hits me like a wall. Jaxon's standing in the middle, his brow furrowed. He's clearly pissed, but his eyes shift to me the moment I step inside. The room goes silent. Why does this feel so familiar?

Trent, whom I hadn't even noticed, speaks first, his voice clipped. "Kelsey, this should've been handled. My guys can't stop things they don't know are coming. That man didn't show up naked—how did you miss this?"

I want to pass off the blame. This wasn't our system. This wasn't my team, but until I have more information, I don't know that, not for certain. "Our system—all our cameras went offline. And at least one of them was playing looped footage before that. We'd just identified the issue when my team lost all visuals. It's...strange. The timing. I have a few theories, but nothing concrete."

"Is one of your theories that you're just not that good at your job? Because I assure you, this wouldn't have happened to my team."

Jaxon looks at Trent before he turns back to me. His expression softens slightly, but his frustration is still palpable. "I don't need to hear theories, Kelsey. I need answers. Your team is responsible for monitoring this."

I swallow hard, trying to steady my breathing. "I know," I mutter, frustration seeping into my voice. "It didn't pop up on any social media that we saw, and with the cameras out... I'm going to find out how this happened. But I need time. I need access to the logs, the systems—everything."

Jaxon's eyes narrow as he watches me, his face unreadable.

"This could've been a disaster. Luckily, *someone*"—he emphasizes the word, suggesting he's acutely aware of who it was—"started that chant and turned the whole thing into a funny little escapade, but people pay a lot of money to come to these concerts, and I'm responsible for making sure they get what they want out of it. Seeing some man's flaccid penis? No one wants that."

Carter snorts a laugh from where he's standing in the corner, but I refuse to break eye contact with Jaxon.

"I understand," I say quickly. "I'll get to the bottom of it."

We discuss the issue for a few more minutes before everyone shuffles out, Jaxon's team moving him back to the VIP area for a meet-and-greet. I wonder what he'll say to Izzy about her chant choice. If I weren't terrified I'm going to get fired, I might find it funny my sister likely just started an international trend.

But I can't shake the nagging feeling that's been tugging at the back of my mind since the moment the cameras first failed. This wasn't just random, and it wasn't equipment failure. It had to be someone inside. Someone who knew exactly what they were doing.

Suddenly, everything starts to feel much more sinister. This *isn't* just a glitch. This is intentional sabotage of me.

And who has the most to gain from my failure...? Mitchell Security.

CHAPTER TWENTY-EIGHT
CARTER

"Did you see her face?" Trent asks, slapping his hand down on the table between us the next morning. "I almost came in my pants. I've wanted to see Kelsey Harper have that look of confusion on her face for so long."

It's taking every ounce of self-control I have not to break his stupid nose because, as much as I want to, I don't need another incident like in high school. And sure, maybe I should've mentioned I was dating Kelsey when Trent, with Julie and her friends in tow, showed up unexpectedly again, but honestly, it didn't seem like his business. It also seemed like Kelsey wouldn't want him to know.

I shake my head, letting the disgust show on my face. "You're a dick."

"I know you've always been on Team Kelsey Harper, but come on, man, you have to admit how great this is for us."

I clear my throat. "I may be more on Team Kelsey now."

Trent looks at me, and instead of the anger I expected to see in his eyes, I see glee.

"No fucking way! You're banging Kelsey Harper?"

I take a deep breath, glad the little restaurant around the corner from the hotel is empty except for us. How did I end up working for this grade-A prick? And why the fuck does he say her last name every time he refers to her? Is that how I sounded growing up?

"We're dating."

He scoffs. "Sure. Does she know that?"

"What do you mean?"

"I mean, you two don't seem like you're dating. So it seems like maybe it's all in your head."

"We're just being professional. You should try it sometime."

"Oh, a little bit of heat from baby brother." Trent laughs.

"Don't call me that," I say, my voice low.

There is something about Trent's face that gives me pause. Trent's always been an asshole, but he's never been overtly evil, but there's something about him that makes the hairs on the back of my neck stand up.

"Anyway, tell me your plan for winning this contract. You do have a plan, right?" Trent demands, leaning his elbows on the table between us. "Because if we don't get it, we likely won't get the other contracts I've been working on, and I won't have any option but to start making cuts. And you're my most expensive employee."

I force myself to take a deep breath, reminding myself that killing him wouldn't help me. Then I'd just be working for his wife—or more likely, she'd sell the company off in pieces for the money, and I'd be out of a job. And now that I know about Kelsey's history, there's no way I could ask her to hire me.

"I think we're well positioned to win. Our team has been outstanding; no issues on our watch. Honestly, I think this most recent outage hurt us—"

"What do you mean?" Trent cuts in before I can finish my thought.

"Well, with the earpieces, that felt like it was likely a mistake that happened at a bad time. This thing? With the video feeds looping and then cutting off only for her team? That feels like sabotage."

"Or she's terrible at her job. I don't know why people keep skipping over that as an option. Her team's job is cybersecurity, and she can't even keep people from breaking into her own systems? Seems like a skill issue to me."

I rub my hands over my face, combating the headache that always seems to pop up when I'm around Trent. "Regardless, it doesn't change the fact that Jaxon and his team aren't idiots. And now it looks like someone is trying to make Kelsey look bad. And I can only assume they think it was us."

Trent's eyes go dark, and I'm forced to really consider if Trent could be behind this. He's never been the type to play that dirty before, but it is within the realm of possibility. Except he doesn't have the tech skills to pull something like this off. Not him, and not any of the guys on our team.

Noticing I've balled my hands into fists, I pop my knuckles to release some of the tension flowing through my body.

"Do you have something you need to tell me?" I ask, forcing a calm mask into place.

"Of course not," he says, though it feels a little too quick, the eye contact a little too forced.

"Good," I say. "Because not only are we above doing something as shitty as sabotaging our competition, but it's also a terrible plan."

The conversation swirls through my mind like a bad smell. I sit there with Trent, head aching from forcing myself to be calm while dealing with his shit. The idea of him being behind the equipment failures...it's a stretch, even if I'm now questioning if he'd be opposed to it morally—something I'm going to try not to think about, since I still have to work for the prick.

But why is the suspicion still there, burrowing deeper and deeper into my gut?

I shake my head, forcing myself to focus.

Trent continues to talk, oblivious to the fact that I'm barely listening. He's rattling on about winning the contract and then winning two others that we'll certainly get once they know we signed Jaxon. Occasionally, he throws in a sad smile as he laments about it being "too bad Kelsey's team couldn't play with the big boys." I can't help but tune him out.

I consider whether I should tell Kelsey about my suspicions, but I know she's already deep down the rabbit hole investigating the outage. If, somehow, it is Trent, her team will uncover it soon enough. It's exactly what they're trained for, and they're good at what they do.

She didn't come to bed last night, instead taking five minutes to say goodbye to her sisters before holing up in the security room at the stadium to work with her team to find the source of the issue. I'd left her to it, knowing Kelsey needed some time to deal with what she undoubtedly considers to be a major failure on her part. I texted her a few times, but her responses were understandably short.

I sigh, pushing back my chair, needing some space. "I've got everything covered," I tell Trent. "I'm going to head back to the hotel before the cars leave for the airport. Will you be joining us on the flight to Auckland?" I ask, realizing I have no idea when Trent plans to go back to Colorado.

I still can't believe he decided to fly his wife and her four best friends here for a couple of days on the beach. I need to ask for a raise if he can afford this spur-of-the-moment trip. The company's financials are something I've never been involved in, but maybe it's time I start.

As I walk back to our hotel, the sunny, seventy-something-degree weather is a nice change from the winter we've been battling in the Northern Hemisphere. Unfortunately, there's no chance of getting to enjoy it with Kelsey.

As I near the building, Bryn, Lila, JT, and Jameson exit the hotel, suitcases rolling along behind them.

Jameson notices me first, lifting a hand in greeting as he says something to the rest of the group that has them all turning my direction.

"Are you all headed out this morning?" I ask.

JT nods. "We've got a flight in a couple of hours. Jameo and I are headed straight to Palm Beach for the Classic next weekend."

"You guys' schedule is tough," I say, only knowing enough about the sport to guess at how frequently the two professional golfers must travel.

"Oh, yes, the poor things," Bryn offers with a sweet smile. "They fly around the world, only going to warm places, playing a game with their best friend. It's truly amazing they haven't simply perished."

Lila laughs, loud and clear, as Jameo sends a glare at his girlfriend.

"If it's so awesome, why don't you travel with me more?" Jameo asks.

"I'm at half, if not more, of your tournaments with you! Plus, I have my own travel for work."

Their conversation devolves into good-natured bickering as I focus my attention on Lila, noticing the dark circles under her eyes and the slight pale hue to her skin.

"Were you up all night with Kelsey?" I ask.

"Yeah. I just left her about thirty minutes ago to get ready for our flight."

"Did your team get anything figured out?"

"Not yet. We had a couple of false leads, and Kelsey told the team back home to clock out once she realized how late it had gotten there."

"You guys worked all night!" I reply, indignant on Kelsey's behalf.

"You know how Kelsey is. She's willing to run herself ragged but isn't willing to ask the same of her team. I can't decide if it makes her a good boss or a terrible one."

I'm about to rage at her for even thinking Kelsey could be a terrible boss when Lila laughs.

"God, you two are so cute together. Look at him, JT. Remember when you got that worked up about Jameo saying I wasn't good at card games."

"That was on the flight here," JT says. "So, yes, I still remember it, and now I'm annoyed with him again. Thanks a lot, Lila."

She winks at me. "He's more fun when he's a little riled up. But anyway, I know Kelsey is a great boss, but I'm not sure if that's a healthy trait of a leader or not."

Bryn's phone pings as a car pulls up to the curb, apparently their ride to the airport. I say goodbye, surprised when JT suggests I join him and Jameo for a round of golf when we're all back in Wild Bluffs.

It's a strange feeling, having plans with someone in Wild Bluffs who isn't over the age of fifty. I chuckle to myself, a small, genuine smile tugging at the corners of my mouth. Somehow, Kelsey's already changing the rhythm of my life back home, and we haven't even gotten there yet.

Chapter Twenty-Nine

Kelsey

"I grabbed your key from Gail," Carter says, sliding a pale-pink plastic keycard out of the small black envelope before handing it to me.

I raise my eyebrow. "*My* keycard?"

"Well, technically ours. Gail was pretty upset about how much all these rooms are costing, so I may have offered to bunk with you. Told her you're scared of riding in elevators alone, and she never suspected a thing."

"I'm sure one three-hundred-dollar room is really making a dent in the expenses of an international tour with hundreds of people on its payroll."

"My thought exactly! We'll likely be getting a thank-you card from Jaxon any day now."

"I don't think Jaxon or his team will be sending me a thank-you anytime soon," I say, my guilt returning to the forefront of my mind and bringing with it a deep throbbing in my lower belly.

Just as I was deplaning in New Zealand, the green grass and blue ocean visible out the plane windows, the news cycle in the US started pumping out stories about the concert. They started as can be expected—blurred pictures of a naked man and jokes about Action Jaxon—but it has quickly taken a turn to the blame game. In the most recent story, I'm the one being blamed.

After all the negative publicity my firm received when I backed out of the funding deal in London, I thought I'd be immune to having my name unfairly run through the mud. Apparently not.

"You know it's not your fault, Kels," Carter says as we both step into the elevator.

A hand catches the elevator door before it can close, and Jaxon's assistant Annie steps on. "Good morning, you two. Jaxon would like to see you in his suite immediately."

"Sure," we both reply, and I scan my key and hit the button for floor 21, knowing from the advance plan what floor Jaxon is on. He's normally on the top floor, but in this particular hotel, the top floor houses a rooftop bar, so none of their suites are located there.

I check my phone during the awkward silence of the ride, seeing yet another headline about the security breach. I quickly click into it, realizing this one has something none of the others did: information about the looping video and loss of camera connection before the streaker. I'm not sure why the American public finds this interesting, but there are already over 1,000 comments at the bottom. The first guy, Bob69_OhYeah, is calling for Jaxon to fire KH Security.

Fricken Bob.

As we step into Jaxon's suite, the tension in the air is palpable. His PR and legal team representatives are scattered around, some standing, others sitting, all looking grim. The room feels too small, crowded with their collective energy. There's an unspoken weight hanging over the meeting, the kind that feels like it's closing in on me. I try not to let my nerves show, but I can feel my pulse quicken.

Jaxon stands near the window, his back to us, staring out at the water or maybe the historic-looking building bathed in browns and golds just off to one side. He doesn't turn when we enter.

His assistant Andre closes the door behind us with a soft click, and the room falls silent save for the faint hum of the city below.

"Please, take a seat," Jaxon says, finally turning around to face us. His expression is unreadable, the usual glint in his eyes replaced by something colder, sharper.

I hesitate before sitting down, feeling the weight of the gaze from every person in the room. I try to remind myself that I'm just here to listen, but the sting of the public's scrutiny makes it hard to focus on anything else. I want to defend myself, to shout that I did nothing wrong, that I'm being sabotaged, but my team still can't figure it out—and maybe that alone means I don't deserve this contract. The headlines, the comments, the calls for my firing—all of it floods my mind, pushing everything else out.

Carter sits beside me, his presence a quiet anchor. He doesn't say anything, but his hand rests subtly on the back of my chair, a small but significant gesture of support. I draw strength from it, but it's not enough to calm the racing thoughts in my head.

Jaxon clears his throat, his eyes hard as they meet mine. "Kelsey, I've read the reports. The breach. The malfunctioning security footage. It's a mess. And somehow, the mess is coming with the type of publicity I typically try very hard to avoid."

I nod. Jaxon has never been the type of celebrity to believe all publicity is good publicity. He is very particular about what gets shared about him in the media, and he keeps a very tight grip on what the world knows about him. Even though the articles aren't focusing on him, I'm sure he hates not having control of the narrative.

Well, that makes two of us, buddy.

"Jaxon," one of his legal team members, a sharp-faced woman with dark hair pulled back in a tight bun, speaks up. "The media is already running wild with this. There's insider information that's been leaked—people are pointing fingers at Kelsey's team. If we don't act quickly, this will spiral."

I hear the word *insider* and feel a cold pang of fear shoot through me. As naive as it may sound, that single word forces me to consider, for the first time, that it could be someone on my team. Could this be sabotage from someone on my own payroll?

Jaxon nods, acknowledging the concern. "Right. We need to make a statement, and it needs to be soon. Does it make it better or worse if Kelsey makes a statement?"

"Better," Susan from the PR team suggests, but at the same time, one of the lawyers replies, "Worse."

"Great," Jaxon replies with a sigh. "So glad we're on the same page. What do you think, Kelsey?"

The room is tense.

"I'd prefer not to. I think it would make it look like I'm protesting my innocence too hard."

"Have you even said you're innocent?" the same PR woman asks. "For that matter, are you even innocent?"

Before I can speak, Carter does. His voice is firm, cutting through the room like a blade. "With all due respect, Susan, yes. The evidence is there that her team's equipment was tampered with." He stands, his posture straight, his eyes locked on Jaxon. The room falls silent, everyone taken aback by his sudden assertiveness.

"Kelsey shouldn't have to defend herself," Carter continues, his voice growing stronger. "You and your team should be doing it for her. You pay what I can only assume is millions of dollars a year to have a team to help deal with stories like these, and yet you've all waited until the narrative got out of control to do anything. You're able to help, and you've done nothing."

I turn to look at Carter, surprised by the fire in his voice. He's not one to speak in big groups. But I can see the determination in his eyes, and I know exactly what this is. It's Carter finding his voice. Not just for me, but for himself, too.

The room remains silent, and I can feel everyone's eyes on Carter, waiting for him to continue. But he doesn't. Instead, he turns slightly, his eyes meeting mine for just a moment, offering me the smallest nod of reassurance.

He's stepping up for me. For us. For everything I've worked for. He's making sure I'm not alone in this.

"Anything else you'd like to get off your chest, Carter?" Jaxon asks. His face is neutral, eyebrows slightly raised with the question, but I can catch a glimmer of amusement behind his eyes. He knows just as well as I do how unusual this type of outburst is for Carter.

"I'd be happy to make a statement on behalf of Mitchell Security," Carter says, his voice unwavering.

I blink, not quite believing what I'm hearing. Carter's not the kind of guy to make a PR statement, especially not without clearing it with Trent first. And I can guarantee Trent's not on board with this.

Jaxon takes a deep breath, looking between Carter and me. The tension in the room could snap at any second. Finally, he nods, a slight change in his posture. "All right," he says, his voice quieter now. "Kelsey, I need answers. I can't have someone on stage like that."

"I understand," I say, my voice steadier than I feel. "I'm doing everything I can to fix this. We'll get it sorted."

Jaxon's assistant Annie stands up from the couch, typing something into her phone. "Susan and her team will handle writing your official statement, Carter. She'll be by your room shortly to have you approve it and to collect any soundbites they might need."

As the meeting winds down, everyone begins to file out, their voices muted. Annie gives me a quick, sympathetic look as we're exiting, but everyone else seems to think this is on me.

We ride a crowded elevator down to our floor, and as we enter our room, the weight of everything hangs heavily on my shoulders

I drop the bag I've been lugging around with me on the floor and take a deep breath.

Carter's arms wrap around me from behind, his chin nuzzling into my trapezius muscle.

"Thank you," I say, turning in his arms. His eyes meet mine, and I can see the softness in them, the quiet pride he feels, but I can't help the flutter of worry that still lingers in my chest. This isn't over. The scrutiny isn't over. The investigation isn't over. It's all just one more thing I need to do and do right.

"I meant what I said," Carter replies, his voice low. "You're not in this alone, Kels. I know I've often resorted to silence as a shield, but this time, I'm not just part of the defense team. I'm in your corner, sword in hand, ready to fight your battles by your side."

"Thank you. It means so much to me to have you in my corner. And I'm sorry."

"For what?" he asks, his voice low.

"When you were talking earlier, about how people could help but do nothing? It felt personal to you. Like you were thinking of all the people who could help with your mom but who don't. I'm sorry I'm one of them."

He sighs, pressing a gentle kiss to my forehead. "I didn't mean you, Kels. I meant my sperm donor, the guy who has lived a life of luxury working a nice job while my mom is on her feet every day working in a diner because he knocked her up and then chose someone else. And then when she needs treatments and medication that she can't afford, he doesn't even offer to help out."

I pull him closer to me. "I'm sorry, Carter. I can't imagine how hard it is."

"I just once want him to offer to help her because he knows he should, not because he wants yet another thing from me."

"I know, Carter," I say, wrapping my arms around his neck and pulling him to me. "I know."

Chapter Thirty

CARTER

It's been four days since the security breach in Sydney, and its impact still hangs over us, even after an uneventful concert in New Zealand. Kelsey has been handling the fallout like a pro, but I can see the exhaustion etched into her face. The kind of exhaustion that's not just physical, but mental. She's been working nonstop trying to get everything back on track, and though she'll never admit it, I can tell the toll it's taking on her. The stress in her eyes, the tightness in her shoulders—it's all there, even if she tries to hide it.

Tonight, I'm determined to give her a break—and celebrate our first Valentine's Day together.

I'm in my nicest white button-down and gray slacks when I meet Kelsey in our hotel lobby. When she sees me, her eyes soften for a moment, a look of someone who just found a temporary shelter in the storm, even if she saw me briefly when she ran into our room to shower and change twenty minutes ago. If she's not out on long runs, she's in the hotel's business center, the small room now fully turned into her command post.

I give her a soft smile.

"Ready to escape for a bit?" I ask, holding out my arm for her to take.

She raises an eyebrow. "Escape? From what? Our job that we both most certainly still have to do while we're gone?"

I chuckle. "We're going to take one night off. You deserve it. No emails, no phone calls. Just dinner and me."

Her eyes soften again, this time in a way that makes my chest tighten. "I wish I could, Carter, but you know I can't do that. Can't we just agree to a dinner that's interrupted by texts and the occasional phone calls?"

"Normally, yes," I say, pulling her a little closer. "But tonight? No. Tonight, it's just us. No work. No distractions. And"—I cut her off as she starts to protest—"before you say no, know that I already made Jaxon promise not to leave his room, and I talked Lila into covering everything that would be going through you. Your team knows to route everything through her for the next four hours. Just four."

She sighs, but there's a slight twinkle in her eyes as she slides her arm through mine. "Well, as it appears you've thought of everything, I guess I'm in."

"Well, not everything—I may have realized about two minutes ago that men traditionally buy their girlfriends flowers on Valentine's Day...and I have none."

"Girlfriend, huh? Are we throwing around labels now?"

"Yes. You are, without a doubt, my girlfriend. I realize we haven't talked about it, but that's definitely what I want."

She offers me a wicked grin, one that makes sparks shoot up and down my body.

"Well, come on, then, boyfriend. Show me what you've got planned for tonight."

The car ride is short, but the city of Buenos Aires is alive with energy. Even on a Thursday night, it never sleeps. The streets are full of people walking, laughing, talking. Even in the backseat, I feel the vibrancy of the city pulsing around us.

We arrive at a classic Argentine steakhouse, the brick building tucked away on a cobblestone street. The moment we walk in, the smell of sizzling meat hits me, and my stomach growls in response. I hadn't realized how hungry I was.

We're led to a small corner table with a view of the grill, the flames licking up as the chefs work their magic. I can see Kelsey's shoulders relax just a little as she sits down, taking in the ambiance.

The waiter hands us the menus, and I notice Kelsey scanning the options, her eyes narrowing as she reads through them.

"So are you thinking steak...or steak?" I tease.

She rolls her eyes. "If I'm being honest, I could eat an entire cow right now."

"Don't tempt me." I grin. "We're here for the experience. Argentina is famous for its beef, so go ham—or go beef, I guess."

It's a terrible pun, but Kelsey chuckles anyway.

I study my menu but pull my eyes from the list of cuts of beef when I notice Kelsey stretching her neck. The tension is back in her face.

"It'll all still be there when you get back," I say.

Her eyes soften a little. "Yeah. I know. It's just hard to push the work stuff out of my head."

I nod, understanding what she means. I don't want to talk about it, though. Not tonight. We've dissected it every which way, and until her team gets a solid lead, there is only so much I can contribute.

Instead, I lean in a little closer. "You can do this—one night off. Just you, me, and some ridiculously good food. Deal?"

She hesitates for a moment but then smiles softly. "Deal."

I know it's not easy for her. Kelsey's the type who doesn't stop thinking about work, even when she needs to. But she deserves this moment. We both do. So I make a silent vow to keep the conversation light. I'll make sure tonight is about enjoying each other's company—nothing else.

We order the parrillada for two, a mix of different cuts of meat, grilled to perfection. The waiter brings over a bottle of Malbec, and Kelsey looks at me expectantly.

"What?" I ask.

"This is the part where you try to convince me you know everything about wine," she teases, setting her glass down.

I raise an eyebrow, giving her a mischievous grin. "I'm not going to pretend to be a wine expert, but I do know that a Malbec pairs perfectly with a good steak."

She laughs. "All right, fine. But just so you know, I think red wine pairs perfectly with just about anything."

"Ah, the side of Kelsey Harper I haven't yet gotten to experience—the casual adult one. I got to watch the version of you who excelled at everything through school, and now I know professional Kelsey, but I'm so looking forward to getting to know just normal, grown-up Kelsey."

She snorts but doesn't respond. I may have been teasing, but I mean every word of it. I *am* looking forward to getting to know the version of Kelsey who isn't in professional mode all hours of the day.

The food arrives shortly after, sizzling plates of meat that make my mouth water. Kelsey's eyes light up when the first bite of steak hits her tongue, and I can't help but laugh at the contented sigh she lets out.

"Oh my God," she says, taking another bite. "This is heaven. If there's one thing I can't complain about in this entire crazy tour, it's the food."

I smile, leaning back in my chair. "I'm glad you're enjoying it."

She meets my gaze, her eyes turning a bit hard. "I'm not sure if I've earned it, but it feels good to be able to relax for a bit."

We eat in companionable silence for a few moments, the clinking of silverware and the hum of the restaurant around us. Kelsey's focused on her food, and for the first time in days, she seems like she might actually be relaxed.

"So," I say, breaking the silence. "Tell me about something other than work. What do you miss most about home when we're on the road?"

She leans back in her chair, thoughtfully swirling her wineglass. "Hmm. I think I miss family dinners most of all. It's the routine and connection and just feeling like I'm back in a time when everything in my life was a bit simpler."

"How often do you have family dinners?" I ask, so intrigued by the idea of more than just two people sitting down to eat each night.

"We're not like some TV family with a set dinner every Sunday exactly at five, but we usually get together a few times a month. It used to be more based around Bryn's work schedule, but now my parents try to time it up when Tweedle Dee and Tweedle Dumb are in town."

I snort, wine threatening to come out my nose. "I can't believe you call two professional golfers and some of the most famous men in the country that."

"I don't know how I got so unlucky to be surrounded by famous people all the time."

"Ah, I'm starting to see my appeal now," I joke. "Common is now uncommon."

She snorts. "Don't play that game with me. You might not be as likely to have your face on a magazine cover, but in the right circles? The ones I happen to be a part of too? You've earned quite a name for yourself. I think military leadership all the way up to the White House wept when you decided to retire to come back to be with your mom."

"I never had dreams like that. I just wanted to do the best I could for the other guys in my squad," I say honestly. It's not something I've ever really let myself think about—the what-ifs, but I can't imagine anything else pushing me from the course I was on. I liked having a purpose. "Plus, I liked it. I was good at it."

"I'm sorry you had to give it up. Will you try to go back once everything is...figured out with your mom?"

Most people have that pause. The one where they're not sure what to say when they realize there isn't a way my mom gets better. Death is what will eventually set me free, and it's a freedom I don't want.

"I'm hoping it's a really long time from now. When I came back, I assumed it was forever. I thought I would have twenty or more years with my mom. Now, well, despite all the integrative care and other treatments we've had her in, it's looking like it might be possible for me to go back after all."

She squeezes my hand, her eyes meeting mine with an emotion I can't quite name, but it makes my chest tighten.

"Is that something you'd like to do?" she asks, more timid than Kelsey ever is, and suddenly I realize what she's asking: Is there a time limit on us?

"No. I think my path is elsewhere now," I say, hoping the look in my eyes can convey everything my words can't. I do want to stay, but if Trent fires me, I may not have an option. Harper Security has always been my backup plan—assuming I could learn to talk in Kelsey's presence—but now that I know about her history with her ex-boyfriend, I couldn't put her in the position of asking.

I smile, pulling myself from the questions and uncertainties. I'm here. With her. And for tonight, that's enough.

After dinner, we take a stroll along the river, hand in hand. The lights of the city reflect off the water, and Kelsey lets out a contented sigh, her head resting on my shoulder as we walk.

The moment is perfect. The city is buzzing around us, but in this small bubble, everything feels at peace. We stop occasionally to admire the view or simply to share a quiet moment. I feel the connection between us, the ease with which we now exist in each other's space.

I glance at Kelsey, her face illuminated by the streetlights, her smile brighter than I've seen in days. She looks like herself again—no work to distract her, no chaos swirling around us, just the two of us.

"Do you remember that Valentine's Day in seventh grade when you wore that bright red sweater?" I ask, breaking the quiet between us.

She chuckles softly. "No. Why do you?"

"I ran into you on my way out of the cafeteria line and spilled spaghetti sauce all over it. Instead of yelling at me or crying or something, you just stared at me like it was my last night on earth."

She laughs. "I do kinda remember that! I'm pretty sure you grunted once and walked away. You were always so gruff and aloof."

I laugh, shaking my head. "I was mortified that I spilled food on the girl I had a crush on!"

"Liar," she teases. "You wanted nothing to do with me."

We stop walking, standing side by side as we gaze out over the river. The sound of the water rippling is the perfect background for the peaceful moment we share. I can feel the weight of the world, just for tonight, lift from my shoulders.

"No. I just didn't know how to make words come out of my mouth when I was around you," I say quietly.

"If you say so," she says, her voice soft. "But either way, I'm glad we're here now."

I smile, my heart full as I squeeze her hand. "Me too."

The night stretches on, the city's heartbeat matching our own, and for the first time in a long time, I feel like we're exactly where we're supposed to be—together, in this moment, and I'll do anything to make sure we get more nights like these.

Chapter Thirty-One

Kelsey

THE SUN IS BARELY peeking over the skyline of Buenos Aires, casting a soft orange glow on the streets as we jog through the quiet morning. Carter's running beside me, effortlessly matching my pace even though he's not exactly a runner. I'm used to doing my 6-mile loop with only the steady rhythm of my feet and the sound of my breath for company. But I'm starting to get used to Carter tagging along, his presence a calming, steady force beside me.

I glance over at him as we near the end of the second mile. His face is flushed, but he's keeping up, looking like he's barely breaking a sweat. I'm impressed.

"You're doing good," I tell him, trying to catch my breath as we wait at an intersection. Turns out, I might actually enjoy the challenge of having someone running beside me, someone who's not only holding his own but looking completely unbothered.

"Yeah, well," Carter says with a teasing grin, "I didn't get into the Rangers on looks alone."

I laugh. "You're insane. I've been running for years, and when I take a few days off, it feels like I'm starting from zero."

"Well, I'm in this for the long haul now. Maybe I'll run a half-marathon when we get back."

We both laugh, knowing there is no way in hell Carter's training for a half unless I convince him to do one with me.

We keep going, both of us silently pushing through the last few miles. We slow to a walk as we get close to the hotel, and Carter lets out a dramatic sigh, his chest heaving as he tries to catch his breath.

"Okay, I'll admit it," he says, still walking beside me. "I could do more cardio in my daily life."

I chuckle. "I thought for a second I'd have to call an ambulance."

"Hey, it was your idea to drag me out here at seven in the morning. I offered a number of options to get your blood pumping, you know?" he grumbles, but there's a hint of affection in his voice. "Ones that would've been a lot more fun."

I smile, feeling that familiar warmth at how easy it is to be with him. The morning breeze rustles through the trees and the city slowly wakes up as we make our way back to the hotel. Carter stays at my side, still grinning like a dork, and I can't help but enjoy the simplicity of the moment. For once, there's no crisis, no tension. Just us, a run, and the quiet hum of Buenos Aires.

By the time we reach the hotel, the post-run endorphins are kicking in, and I feel lighter, almost ready to take on whatever the day throws at me. We head to the small restaurant in the lobby and sit down at a corner booth, the morning sunlight streaming through the windows and casting a golden hue over everything.

I order my usual: a kids' size coffee, fresh fruit, and some eggs. Carter orders a ridiculous amount of eggs and avocado.

As we sip our coffees, waiting for our food to arrive, Jaxon and his assistants Annie and Andre come in, his assistants taking a table in the far back corner of the room. Eddie takes a seat at the table between them and the door. Without thinking, I check the front entrance, ensuring the other two members of their team are in their positions. A month ago, I wouldn't have any idea where each member of Jaxon's personal security team should be, but now I think I've got it figured out.

"Good morning," Jaxon says, sliding in the booth next to me while Nash shoves in to sit next to Carter. "Fancy meeting you two here."

Carter harrumphs something into his coffee that has both Nash and Jaxon chuckling.

"I was promised people would kiss my ass when I became a super-star. Where's the ass-kissing, Carter?" Jaxon asks.

I laugh this time, and Carter rolls his eyes. "You hired the wrong security firm—hell, the wrong security firms—if you were hoping for ass-kissing."

"Turns out, I like straight shooters."

"We might be more equipped for that," I say.

"Anyway," Jaxon says, pulling us back to the real reason he joined our table. "I got news from the PR team that the public has been eating up Carter's statement. They're also patting themselves on the back for how well they've shut the story down, though I feel I owe you an apology, Kelsey, for not getting them working on it quicker."

"That's not their job," I say, taking another sip of my coffee for something to do with my hands. "I appreciate their help on the cleanup, though. Thank you."

Jaxon waves away my thanks and nods to Nash, indicating he's ready to go back to the table. Nash stands, and Jaxon follows, tapping a fist down on our table.

"I should've known that you'd defend Kelsey's honor again, Carter."

My eyes snap to Carter's as I take in the word *again*, and I'm quick enough to catch the look of shock that crosses his face before he schools it into neutrality.

Jaxon just walks away, apparently unaware that his parting words have left us both shaken.

"What did he mean, *again*?" I ask, my throat dry at the thought of Carter having to defend my honor on a regular basis. I can defend my own honor, damn it.

Maybe it was after the first issue with the comms—but no. He didn't say anything then.

The words hang in the air, unanswered, as I stare at Carter.

"What did he mean, *again*?" I repeat, my voice rough. My fingers grip the bright white coffee cup tighter, the cool porcelain against my hand doing little to steady me.

Carter's eyes dart to mine briefly before he looks down at his coffee, swirling it in his cup, his jaw tight. "I—" He pauses, taking a deep breath, clearly trying to find an answer other than the truth. "I don't know what he meant, Kels."

"That's a lie." Of course it is. I saw the look on his face. It wasn't even a good lie, though I'm starting to understand Carter just isn't a good liar.

I sit back in my seat, crossing my arms and raising my eyebrow. "It obviously can't be bad if it involves you defending my honor. Most people consider that to be a good thing."

He presses his lips together, clearly uncomfortable. "It's nothing," he mutters, his voice rough. "Who knows why Jaxon says half of what he says. He probably thought it sounded lyrical or some nonsense like that. It doesn't mean anything."

I consider letting him off the hook. I trust Carter—even if he's still my biggest rival—but I just know there's *so much more* to whatever he's trying to hide from me. Honestly, I even believe Jaxon didn't mean anything more by it, but somehow, it meant something to Carter, and I want to know what it is.

"Carter," I say softly, using the same voice I would to convince a small child to show me where they hid stolen cookies. "When have you defended my honor before this?"

Carter goes quiet for a long time, and I wonder if I'm going to have to wait and seduce it from him tonight, but then, finally, his gaze flicks up to meet mine, and I see something—maybe shame—in his eyes before he starts talking.

"This isn't a big deal, which is why I never told you about it," he says, his voice low and rough. "But, back in high school, there was this one time in the football locker room. And, well, a few guys in our class—Trent, for one—were claiming they'd slept with you."

I snort. The notion that I slept with any of the guys in our high school class, most of all Trent, is utterly absurd. I thought they were all idiots then, and only Carter seems to have made his way off that list even now.

"Anyway," he says, running his hand through his dark hair. "They were getting more and more detailed. You know how assholes are—just trying to one-up each other. It got...graphic."

I blink, stunned into silence for a moment. Those fucking assholes. I wouldn't touch one of them with a thirty-nine-and-a-half-foot pole, let alone let them do graphic things with me.

His voice hardens as he continues, as if the memory still angers him. "It pissed me off. We all fucking knew you wouldn't sleep with any of them, but I couldn't let them get away with saying things like that. So I stepped in. Told them to shut the fuck up. Punches may have been thrown."

Suddenly, a memory from high school resurfaces, a picture that was in the newspaper of Carter on the football field, a look of lethal determination on his face. I can only imagine what it must've looked like when he was mad enough to actually try to hurt someone.

"The coaches came in when they heard the yelling and broke things up. They were going to suspend Trent, Byron, and me, but my sperm donor came in and convinced them it was just a fight between brothers, nothing more than a little family squabble that Byron happened to be in the middle of, so nothing ended up on my permanent record."

Fucking Trent and Byron Linton. I mentally add both names to my list of people to make pay when I finally have the time. Izzy's always coming up with creative ways to make people's lives hell, like changing their autocorrect to make mundane words like *home* turn into *my mistress's house*. I'm sure she can come up with something good to make them pay for being complete dicks almost twenty years ago.

"How did I never hear about that?" I ask.

"I think everyone there was so ashamed they weren't the ones to make them stop that no one wanted to talk about it."

Unlikely. My experience with high school guys is that they rarely have that kind of self-awareness. Plus, that's the type of news that Wild Bluffs students would've spread like wildfire—Carter had a reputation for being an overachiever with a strict moral code and no need for friends. Which begs the question, why? Why would he have stood up for me back then?

"Why?" I ask. "Why would you risk everything you were working toward to stand up for someone who you probably said ten words to that entire year?"

He snorts, taking a bite of his eggs from the plate the waitress just set in front of him. "Honestly, I like to think I would've told them to stop if they'd been saying it about anyone. No one deserves to have lies told about them behind their back, especially as demeaning as those were."

I nod my head in understanding, realizing standing up against bullies aligned with everything I know about Carter.

He rolls his head to the side, considering. "But, if we're being honest, I doubt I would've actually fought them for anyone but you. I told you about my crush on you. It's probably why Trent even picked you. He was probably trying to see how far he could push me. It was one of his favorite pastimes—seeing if he could piss me off. Though looking back, I'm guessing it's because his dad would say shit to him about me being better in sports or school when he was trying to get him to work harder."

"Well, thank you," I say. "I can't believe you risked the future you were working so hard for on me, but I really appreciate having you in my corner, even if I didn't know it."

He shrugs. "Of course. Plus, you did the same thing for my mom."

"What do you mean?" I ask.

"There was a time, the end of senior year, when a few of the men in town were in the diner, and apparently one of them said something rude to my mom—I never learned exactly what they said, but I'm sure I could guess. Anyway, you stood up for my mom. Made the guy feel like shit. Honestly, I think it was that, seeing how effortlessly badass yet kind you were, that made it so I could never get over what I thought was just an innocent little crush in high school."

"Oh. I do remember that. It wasn't a big deal. It was a totally inappropriate thing to say to anyone, let alone your sweet mom," I reply.

"Well, thanks anyway."

"And thanks for having my back with this most recent incident," I say. "I...as much as I hate that we are, at the end of the day, still competing for a contract we both really need...I'm really glad you're here."

The noise of the restaurant fades, and I realize I mean it. Every word of it. I wouldn't trade this time with Carter for anything, even the final contract with Jaxon—and I'm not sure if that is heartening or absolutely terrifying.

Chapter Thirty-Two

Carter

"We're here in Rio for two days, then three shows in New York, and then we're home," I say to my mom as I chat with her before I head to the stadium. Being back on the same side of the globe has made catching up far easier, but I'm so busy these days with the tour about to wrap up that I still haven't been able to talk to her as much as I'd like.

I'm sitting at the small table in the corner of the hotel room I'm sharing with Kelsey, the steady hum of the air-conditioning working overtime the only noise besides my voice. Kelsey left a few minutes ago, saying her team finally found a lead.

"That's great, Carter. I'm so glad you're enjoying your time in the Army. I always knew you'd make a great soldier."

I consider telling her again where I am and what I'm doing, but right now, I need to learn more about her most recent visit with her neurologist. Based on the timing of her appointment with the specialist in Denver, she should be about halfway back. Bill went with her and is likely driving.

"How did your appointment go with Doctor Roman?" I ask.

"What appointment?"

I rub my forehead, trying to suppress the frustration...and devastation...rising within me. I hate hearing her sound so disconnected, even if I know her appointments always do this to her. They take her out of her routine, and they cause her stress, two major influences on my mom's ability to remember.

"The one you had today," I say, my voice quiet. "The one with Doctor Roman." I try to keep calm, but I can feel the weight of my mother's memory loss pressing down on me, threatening to overwhelm me.

She goes silent for a moment. I can hear her breathing, slow and measured, before she clearly holds the phone away from her and says, "Bill, did I see Doctor Roman today?"

"You sure did, Alice," Bill replies, his voice upbeat despite the situation, which, more than anything, suggests how bad the news must've been.

"I sure did, Carter," my mom says, her voice mimicking Bill's cheerfulness.

"Here, Alice, let me say hello to our boy for a minute." Bill's voice is more difficult to hear, but after a brief pause, the phone is passed over.

"Hey, Carter," he says, his voice thick with concern.

The image of the seventy-six-year-old man talking on the phone and driving is enough to send me to my feet in concern. "Hey, if you need to focus on driving, I can call you back later," I offer, pacing back and forth—two steps in one direction, two steps in the other.

"No, that's all right. I pulled off on the highway so I could talk to you. Your mom did great during the appointment today, but, well, he said we will likely need to keep a closer eye on her soon. He's recommending we start looking at lining up some full-time support."

I hear Bill's voice crack, and I know it's because of the guilt he carries. He's so much older than my mom, yet he's still sharp, still has his mind intact. He told me when my mom was first diagnosed that he always assumed it would be my mom taking care of him and Mildred when they got older. That she'd be the one running the restaurant when they couldn't do it themselves. Now, he's taking care of her.

"Okay," I say. "I'll start looking into it."

Bill coughs, clearing his throat. "I'd offer that Mildred and I can move in, but I just don't think we can handle the diner and care."

I can tell he's censoring himself, trying to make it feel like we aren't talking about my mom when she's sitting right next to him.

"I'm sorry," he says gruffly, as if he's letting me down.

"Bill, don't," I cut him off. "I know you're doing everything you can, and I appreciate it more than I could ever express. I will figure out care that isn't you. I can move in with her and then find an in-home nurse for when I'm at work or see if I can transition to working from home more."

My brain is spinning, spiraling out of control as I try to process the news. It's clear the doctor's diagnosis wasn't good. Last time we went in for a full checkup, he was thinking at least two years until we would need my mom to be under some sort of care.

"Carter, you need to think long and hard about if that's the right decision for you. You've got a lot of exciting things happening in your life right now. You can't take the full weight of this on your shoulders."

I know he has more to say on the subject, but he's holding himself back to make sure he doesn't upset my mom.

"Did he say anything about her medication or any other treatment options we could at least try?" I ask, my voice quieter now, as if asking the question will somehow change the answer. The weight of it all presses down on me, the responsibility, the helplessness. Every word feels like it's dragging me further into an abyss.

Bill's voice is steady, but I can hear the weariness in his tone. "The doctor says her medication is still helping a little. But, Carter, it's not going to stop the inevitable."

I know that. Logically, I do. It's the hard truth you have to face every day when someone you love is diagnosed with an incurable disease. You can treat the symptoms, maybe slow the progression, but from the time it's diagnosed—shit, from the time the symptoms hit hard enough to warrant a diagnosis—life will never be the same. There is no getting past it, just through it.

I nod, even though Bill can't see me. I've been dreading this conversation, dreading the moment when I'd have to face the truth—and I thought I had more time than this.

"Okay," I say softly, trying to gather my thoughts. "I'll look into options in Wild Bluffs and the surrounding towns. It's not great timing for me, but I'll make sure we're prepared."

Bill is silent for a moment, and I know he's thinking the same thing I am. How do you prepare for something like this? How do you wrap your mind around the idea of losing someone slowly, piece by piece, when there's nothing you can do to stop it?

"You've got a lot on your plate right now, Carter," Bill says finally, his voice softer. "With the tour and everything going on... I just want you to make sure you don't lose yourself in all this. You've been carrying a lot already, and I don't want you burning out. I want you to have a life outside of this."

I don't respond right away. I just stand there, looking out the hotel window, watching the harsh midday light filter through the curtains. His words hit hard. Even with everything going on, this last month has been almost a vacation. Yes, I'm working basically every day, but it's fun. I come back to the hotel at night and curl up next to the woman I'm crazy about, and I don't have to worry about money or bills or medication or if my mom's still going to remember me. And while I was gone, living this life, my mom's been getting worse. Suffering. Maybe if I'd been home, if I'd— No. I shake my head. I can't let myself go down that road.

"I don't have a choice, Bill," I say, my voice breaking slightly. "I can't just walk away from this. From her."

"I know," Bill replies, his voice steady but full of empathy. "But you don't have to do it alone, Carter. Mildred and I can help you make sure you get the help you're going to need—whatever it ends up looking like."

"I know," I repeat, but the words feel hollow.

The conversation lingers in the air for a moment longer, but it's clear there's nothing more to say right now. There's no easy fix for this. No magic words that will make it go away. Just the hard reality that we're—I'm—going to have to make some tough choices.

"Thanks, Bill," I finally say, my voice rough. "I appreciate you being there. For both of us."

"We're happy to help, Carter," Bill says quietly. "I'll call you tomorrow around this time, and we can debrief the entire appointment."

"What appointment?" I hear my mom ask in the background, and I can't stop the tear that trickles down my face at the question.

I hang up the phone, but the silence that follows feels heavy. The noise of the city outside the window does nothing to fill the void that has replaced my lungs. I run a hand through my hair, trying to push away the tightness in my chest. My mom's diagnosis, the thought of losing her, is too much.

The door to the hotel room opens, and Kelsey steps in, her energy instantly filling the space. She gives me a quick smile as she sets down her bag, but when she sees the look on my face, her expression falters.

"What happened?" she asks, walking over to me. "Bad news from the doctor?"

I hesitate, debating whether I should tell her. It's so hard to talk about, and I've never wanted to spend the time I have with Kelsey focusing on anything but the light and joy she brings to my life. But I need someone—I need Kelsey—for support.

"She's not getting better," I say quietly, my voice barely above a whisper. "The Alzheimer's...it's getting worse. The doctor said we need to start looking at care for her. Soon."

Kelsey's face softens with understanding, and she steps closer, her hand gently squeezing my arm. "Carter..." Her voice trails off as she searches for the right words. "I'm so sorry."

I look at her, the weight of everything finally crashing down. "I can't... I don't know how to help. I don't know what to do. Why is this happening? She's *so* young. It's not...it's not fair."

She steps forward and wraps her arms around me, pulling me into a hug. I rest my head on the top of hers, the warmth of her embrace grounding me. She doesn't say anything, just holds me as I let out a shaky breath.

"It's not fair," she agrees. "It's not fair for your mom, and it's not fair for you—"

"I don't care about me," I interrupt.

"I know you don't," she says, stroking her fingers down my back. "But I do. And I care about you enough for the both of us."

I close my eyes, feeling the tension in my shoulders ease slightly. I still don't know how I'm going to make it through everything—the tour, my mom, the contract—but I don't feel so alone. It's as if, for the first time since this all started, I have someone who can help me carry the weight of it.

CHAPTER THIRTY-THREE

KELSEY

"WHAT TIME IS IT?" Carter asks groggily as I unzip my suitcase, searching for my black running shorts. So much for being quiet and letting him sleep in before our flight out of Rio later this morning.

Carter's conversation with his mom two days ago really threw him off his game, and part of me wonders if he shouldn't just go home now instead of to New York with the rest of us. I know it would only get him home three days sooner, but I can tell how much he needs to see his mom and reassure himself that she's okay—that even if things are getting worse, she's still his mom.

The other part of me is terrified of what it means for this tour to be over. Carter's mom needs him, and I'm not sure how I fit into that. I'm not the caretaker type, so I'm sure I'll just be in the way if I try to help.

The fact that we head home in four days didn't hit me until this morning. The last week has been a mad rush to not only work with my team to figure out what happened in Sydney but to also ensure everything is ready for the concerts each night. We're so close to figuring out who it was that sabotaged the system. Unfortunately, they clearly know what they're doing, because they've been leading my team on a virtual wild goose chase around the globe.

"Five forty-five," I respond, stepping into my running shorts.

"Why are you up so early?" he asks, rubbing one of his strong hands over his eyes.

"I couldn't sleep. I didn't mean to wake you up. You should go back to sleep."

"*You* should come back to bed. We got back from the concert four hours ago."

I haven't been sleeping well, getting pulled from my dreams each morning with something niggling in the back of my mind—something I can't seem to grasp. I'm not even sure if it's about the breach, Jaxon's security, or something else entirely.

I'm going to be pissed if I finally put together what it is and it's something stupid like I forgot one of my socks at the last hotel.

Carter climbs out of bed, and I slowly take in the hard planes of his chest, the grooves of his abs, before sliding lower to the prominent bulge in his black boxer briefs.

My perusal finally ends back at his face, where his lips are pulled in a sleepy smirk.

"Good morning," he says, his voice still raspy.

"Good morning," I reply, unable to keep the smile off my face. There's something about waking up with Carter and seeing this cuddly version of him that melts my insides in a way I've never experienced before.

Carter steps toward me, the heat of his body seeping through my lightweight running clothes. Cradling my head in his hands, he lowers his lips very slowly toward mine. His hands are tender as he holds my face. His lips brush mine, slowly sweeping back and forth, barely touching. He's everywhere, driving me mad with longing, yet never quite settling his mouth on mine.

Catching his face, I still it, rising up on my toes to capture his lips, taking control. My tongue sweeps between his lips, and I close my eyes, savoring his taste. He shifts, a subtle move that brings me more completely against him, as he deepens the kiss. His hands move to wrap around me, enfolding me in his arms.

"Tell me what you want," Carter commands.

"You. I want you." It comes out as a whisper, a plea.

He lowers his head, his lips brushing over my neck, just below my ear. His tongue licks, soothing the places his teeth scrape. My nerve endings are in overdrive   or in shock. I'm hot and hungry and desperate.

"You've got me. For as long as you'll have me."

His body is radiating heat, and I squeeze my legs together, unable to find the friction I need.

I pull away and reach up to trace his lips, following the warm, firm curves.

"Do I? Is this really going to work once we're back?"

"Yes," he says, the absolute conviction in his tone mixing with something softer in his eyes—something that feels terrifyingly close to love. "I know what it feels like to only get small pieces of you from afar. When it was all I thought I'd ever get, it was enough, but now I know what it's like to be with you? Now I know what it's like to have access to your brilliant mind and beautiful body? There's no way I'm giving it up—giving you up. You're stuck with me."

"What if you get the contract and Trent sends you to live with Jaxon?" I ask. It's one of the many questions that have plagued my waking and sleeping hours.

"I'm not leaving Wild Bluffs indefinitely like that, but, before you ask, if you get the contract and have to go live with Jaxon, then we'll do long-distance. I will take whatever version of you you're willing to give me."

His confidence in us, in our future, does something to my body, and I can't think of anything else but having him buried deep inside me.

Carter's mouth finds mine again, his hands working quickly to relieve me of my tank top and shorts. Our tongues dance between desperate kisses as we devour one another.

Carter shifts, throwing me on the bed before prowling forward on his hands and knees to hover over me.

"You're so beautiful," he says, gently moving a strand of hair from my face and tucking it behind my ear.

His attention shifts lower, pulling up my sports bra to access my nipple.

My head falls back as his mouth moves, slowly sucking, biting, teasing. He changes the angle of his body, and suddenly his thick erection is pressed tight against my thigh. I bite back a moan, my eyes drifting shut as pleasure flows through me. His mouth is rough and sensuous on me, and his other hand teases the other breast, pulling at my nipple and cupping my small mound possessively.

Unable to stop myself, I squirm against his leg, and he releases my nipple, a dark chuckle escaping.

"Needy this morning, huh, Kels?" he teases, pressing too-gentle kisses to my stomach.

"I'm going to take care of it myself if you don't hurry," I chastise, though the effect is likely lost with the breathiness of my tone.

"Liar," Carter whispers in my ear before reaching for his wallet on the bedside table and grabbing a condom. He quickly tears open the package and wraps himself, his eyes never leaving mine as he does it.

I watch, entranced, as Carter pulls my panties to the side and lines himself up with my entrance. He slowly pushes in, my core tightening with each centimeter gained. His mouth finds mine again, his kisses scorching as our bodies seek the rhythm we're both looking for. Finding it, the fire inside me starts to build, my nerve endings roaring their pleasure to the world. Carter lifts himself higher, his right arm locking behind my knee to pull it toward my shoulder, changing the angle. I thrash my head side to side as Carter's relentless pounding brings me right to the edge. I'm chanting his name, begging for the release my body so desperately needs.

His thumb finds my clit, the tight bundle of nerves firing in excitement at the attention. One, two, three circles of his rough thumb is all it takes, and I explode, my walls gripping tightly as Carter follows me into oblivion.

"Ugh," I groan, my body limp as Carter climbs off the bed to take care of the condom. "Now I'm going to be sore the entire run."

Carter's dark eyes smolder as he takes me in, lying on the bed in my underwear and a bra shoved up around the top of my chest. Signs of just how hot and fast our coupling had been—just how much we both needed the release.

"You know," Carter says, his right hand reaching down to stroke himself, "if you skip your run, I'll let you be on top this time."

"Pshh," I say, my eyes tracking his hand as his cock slowly rises back to attention. "As if you *let* me do anything. Don't kid yourself into thinking you're the one in control here."

Carter lowers himself onto the bed next to me, his fingers lightly tracing my inner thighs. "I'll fuck you however you want me to, Kels. I don't care if I'm on the top, bottom, or upside down on the moon, as long as I'm the man getting to worship your body."

"I love you," I say, the words slipping out.

Shit. Shit. Shit. SHIT. What in the world? Where did that come from? I have never once been the first to admit anything in a relationship—how did I blow my freaking love load early like that?

Carter looks at me, his wide smile turning gentle as he watches me freak out internally.

"You can take it back if you want," he says, his expression becoming distant as he gives me the out.

I take in the hard lines of his face, the shadow of his dark stubble accentuating his strong chin. The way the very corners of his lips curl up, even when he's not smiling. The two lines that run between his eyebrows, the ones I always want to smooth out with my fingers, just to show him he doesn't have to be worried about others all the time.

I open my mouth to take it back, to blame it on the sex-induced endorphins, and it's almost as if I can see Carter start to build a wall between us. A wall intended to either keep me out or to keep in the hurt that's currently playing across his features.

"No. No, thank you," I say instead. "I meant it."

He raises his eyebrow, clearly questioning if I'm being honest, and I can't help but think about how truly unromantic this whole exchange is. I can't ever let my sisters hear this story. Or JT. God forbid Sam hear it. He would have *so many* thoughts on how fucked up I am as a person.

"To be fair, I don't think I realized it until just now, but I do. I love you. And I totally understand if this is too soon. I'm not expecting you to say it back, I—"

Carter cuts me off by placing his mouth gently over mine.

"Of course I love you. I couldn't stop thinking about you when we were in eighth grade and you always had blue rubber bands on your braces so they'd match your eyes. I thought I was in love with you when we were eighteen and you were so kind and yet so strong when standing up for my mom. And I know I love you now that I've gotten to know the real you—the one you keep hidden from everyone else but me."

He kisses the tear that snuck out of my eye.

"There is no too soon for me. No amount of commitment is too far, and there is sure as hell no possible future that I don't plan on having you in. You're not in my future—you *are* my future. If you're not at the center of it, then it can't be my future, because everything that I am—everything that I will be—revolves solely around you."

"I... That's..." I say, wiping the tears that are now flowing freely down my face. "That's the most amazing... I..." I trail off, unable to express the depth of my love for him.

He kisses me gently.

"I love you," I say after I pull away from the sweet kiss. "And you're my future too."

Chapter Thirty-Four

Carter

One more day.

As much as I've enjoyed this whirlwind international tour, I need to get back to Wild Bluffs. I've connected with the nursing home in town, and even though I don't think my mom or I am ready for that level of care yet, I feel like I need to be there in person so I can talk to potential caregivers and see the places where my mom might be stuck living for decades.

If I'm lucky.

I have meetings set up with two different women who might be able to stay with my mom while I'm working once she has to stop her shifts at the diner, but again, I can't really move anything forward until I can meet with them.

I feel like everything with my mom is in a parallel universe. I know she's going to need care, but she doesn't need it today. I need to be prepared for it, but I can't *do* anything about it at this time. It's frustrating, and I feel overwhelmed by the need for action when there is nothing I can do.

I'm sitting at a small table in the lobby, writing down a to-do list, generally feeling overwhelmed. I'm also drinking my third coffee of the morning, which may be contributing to my anxiety levels, but I need the caffeine to get through this last day of the tour.

The team is on high alert after the location of our hotel went viral, and my eyes are locked on the line of people outside waiting to get in. The crowd is two people deep leading up to the entrance, where a doorman and one of our security guys are making everyone show either a room key or a confirmation number before they're allowed in the building.

I must be getting old because there's a part of me that wants to go out there and yell at everyone to get off my grass, but I don't think it'd have the desired effect.

I glance at my phone to check the time—almost ten now. With tonight's show being the last one Jaxon has scheduled for the foreseeable future, the crowds are going to be extra chaotic. Kelsey and her team have already alerted me that six different big-name actors and actresses will be in attendance tonight, and her team is working on coordination plans as needed. I'm sure there will be more who decide to join last minute—especially with the ticket prices for this show reaching well over two grand.

Recognizing there's nothing else I can do for my mom until I get back to Wild Bluffs, I head back to our hotel room. Kelsey is frantically typing on her laptop when I walk in, her fingers moving a million miles an hour as usual.

Sitting on the edge of the bed, I run my hands through my hair, forcing myself to focus on the work that's in my control, not the people hundreds of miles away in Colorado.

"I moved up our flight home tomorrow," Kelsey says without looking up or pausing her typing. "Weston and Eddie will take care of packing everything up and will work with the logistics team to make sure all our equipment ends up in Wild Bluffs."

"Thank you," I say, breathing a sigh of relief. "You can stick around too if you need to."

She stops typing, looking over her right shoulder just long enough to shoot me a "yeah, right" glare.

"What?" I ask. "What if Jaxon decides he needs to meet with you tomorrow to give you the long-term contract?"

"So you've finally accepted that I'll be winning it?" Kelsey teases.

And, damn it, I know she's saying it just to get my mind off my mom. Kelsey has all but given up on the competition after Sydney. She still works hard and does an outstanding job, but she doesn't comment on it anymore. I bring it up occasionally just to see if she'll fight with me about it, and she still will, but I can tell the spark is gone. She thinks she's lost.

"You know you still have just as good of a chance at winning this thing as we do, right?" I say, though the truth is, I don't know if I believe it. I know she *should* have just as good of a chance.

And maybe, just maybe, if she and her team had found the person behind the attack on the camera system in Sydney, they'd be back in the running, but it'd be hard to justify the choice.

"Sure," she says, rolling her shoulders as if one is bothering her.

"You okay?" I ask, moving behind her to give her a shoulder rub.

When my mom was working all the time when I was in high school, I used to do this for her regularly. She claimed my large hands were only good for one thing: shoulder massages.

"That feels good," Kelsey says, her tone so close to a moan that my dick perks his head up in attention.

Not now, I silently reprimand my blood flow.

"Why are you so stressed?" I ask.

I get the over-the-shoulder look again. "Really?"

"Yeah, talk to me about it."

"It's the same reason I was stressed yesterday, and the day before that, and the day before that."

"Well, tell me about it again. Maybe talking it through will help."

"Okay, but you have to keep rubbing my shoulders," she says.

"Deal."

"Tampering with our cameras doesn't make sense."

"Why?" I ask, prompting her to keep going with her train of thought.

She taps her fingers on the table in front of her laptop. "Because there is no reason to have done it."

"I mean, the security cameras cover the entire venue. And there are a lot of people and money in there on a concert night," I say, playing devil's advocate.

"Yes," Kelsey says slowly, though I can tell her mind is moving much quicker. "But that would only make sense if they'd targeted the venue's monitoring system too."

"So what does it tell us that they didn't?" I ask.

"Well, the only reason to have targeted *our* system and not the entire venue's is to get to Jaxon."

"Which someone did," I add.

"Which someone did," she repeats, clearly thinking. "But it was just a streaker. I mean, between our two teams, we stop multiple people a night from getting up on the stage with Jaxon. If my team is watching looped videos for long enough, one of the crazies is bound to make it through." She pauses, considering. "Plus, the hack was impressive. Why would someone spend that kind of time and money just to have a possibility at streaking onstage? And we both saw the tape of the streaker's interview—that guy had no idea about the cameras being out."

We both sit in silence as my thumbs continue to dig into the tight knots in her shoulders.

"It can't be about the streaker," she says finally. "That has to be a coincidence. Right place, right time."

"Then what's it about?" I ask.

"Well, if we take the streaker out of the equation, then it looks like...then it looks like a penetration test."

"You think someone was trying to penetrate you?" I tease. "Am I going to have to kick someone's ass?"

Kelsey doesn't laugh. She's thinking so hard, I can almost feel the genius pushing through.

She whirls around to face me, her mane of curly blonde hair whacking me in the stomach as she turns. "What if the earpieces going out wasn't just an accident? What if it was sabotage too?"

"But who would want to sabotage you?"

Her face tells me she thinks I'm an idiot for asking the question.

"Okay," I concede. "But you know I'm not doing it."

"You do have a half brother who has far more to gain from this than you do."

"Don't love that you didn't acknowledge that you know it's not me…" I pause.

She rolls her eyes. "Fine. I know it's not you."

"Ahh, thanks, babe. Your confidence means so much to me," I tease.

"It could be Trent," she says, staying focused on the discussion at hand.

"I've thought about it," I admit. And I have. Everything that has happened has made Kelsey's team—just Kelsey's team—seem like they're dropping the ball. Of course I've considered Trent, the person with the most to gain from Kelsey looking bad.

"I just feel like sabotage isn't Trent's style. He's far more likely to try to convince Jaxon with golf trips or drinks at some fancy club, or to try to piss you off when you're in the same room as Jaxon. Then there's the tech side of things. The man can't respond to his own emails. The earpieces—it's not likely, but he could handle spilling water on something. But with the video? I just can't imagine he'd be able to handle the tech side of the infiltration. We don't have anyone on our team who could."

"If it's not him, though, who could it be?" she asks, not even attempting to mask her frustration. "Why would someone try to make me look bad?"

CHAPTER THIRTY-FIVE

CARTER

I CAN'T STOP THINKING about Kelsey's question as we load up the vehicles and head to Regency Circle Garden for one final concert. Or, more accurately, I can't stop thinking about the only answer that makes any sense—Trent needs this contract.

I still believe sabotage isn't his style, but he has been talking more and more about the other two contracts we're certain to get once we land Jaxon. These last few weeks, it's almost all he talks about when he checks in with me, but then again, he's always been focused on the business development and shmoozing. He likes that kind of thing.

Trent couldn't do the hacking portion by himself...but who's to say he didn't outsource the work to someone not on our team?

When we arrive at the arena, I tell everyone else to head inside, pointing to my phone when Nash starts to hang back from the crowd.

Questioning if I want to have someone dig into my half brother's life, I hover my finger over the contact information for Julian, an old college buddy of mine—one who dropped out midway through our junior year. I'm 99 percent sure he's a hacker, but I've never wanted the moral burden of knowing for certain and not doing anything about it.

I watch Kelsey walk into the arena, and the sight of her makes my decision for me. I tap the call button.

"Hey, Carter," Julian says when he answers.

"Hey, Julian. You got a minute?" I ask.

"For the guy who got me through American Literature 101? I've got at least five."

I snort, remembering how much Julian had hated that class. The final essay had to be handwritten in class and was based on a topic the teacher randomly decided at the beginning of the finals period. Julian almost cried when he realized there was no way he could use his considerable computer skills to help himself.

"But first," Julian continues, "tell me how you came to be providing security on Jaxon Steele's tour."

"How do you even know about that?" I ask with a laugh.

"Dude. Did you really think I wouldn't keep tabs on you? I get notified any time your name pops up online. I was impressed by your statement about the security breach on the tour. Very buddy-buddy with KH Security, though. I did a little poking around on their website. Their owner looks like the real deal."

"She is," I say, unable to keep the admiration I feel for her out of my voice.

"Oh, shit." Julian laughs. "You fell in love with the competition? Rookie mistake, my guy!"

"Yeah. It's working out okay for me, though."

"I'm glad you're happy, then...and getting to do cool shit like go on tour with the hottest musician in the world."

"Thanks, man."

"Of course. Now, why don't you tell me why you called," Julian says, turning our focus back to the purpose of my call.

"Let's say, hypothetically, a guy needed to find out the financial situation of someone they work for," I say tentatively, feeling him out. "Is that something you'd be able to help with?"

"You know," he says, the pitter-patter of his keyboard filling the background. "People always seem to call me about hypothetical situations...or 'their friends' who need help."

"And I'm sure most of them offer to pay you a consulting fee for your time..."

"They sure do. However, most of them didn't play video games with me every day for an entire semester or buy pizzas to split with me when my parents cut me off. I'd say, with interest, one consulting job would likely make us even."

"You sure, man? I know people pay well for this kind of thing."

"Unless you happened to hit the lottery and didn't tell me about it, I'm not sure you can afford me without a steep discount," Julian replies, and I'm not sure if he's joking or not.

"No lottery, I'm afraid," I reply.

"Ah, well, in that case, consider this one on the house."

"Thanks," I say, meaning it. I'm not sure I was ever in a financial situation where I could afford Julian's help, but I know I'm not in one now.

"Tell me about this hypothetical boss of yours."

So I do. I tell him what's going on, giving him all Trent's information I know and talking for over the allotted five minutes as I tell him everything I can about Trent's personal life, business accounts, and where he may be keeping his money. I even know his social security number, since we were born at the same hospital just months apart—they're the same but his ends with a two and mine ends with a nine.

"I'm finishing up a job for another client now," Julian says when he has everything he needs. "But I'll look into this as soon as I can."

I run a hand through my hair. If it's just Trent trying to make Kelsey look bad, he's already accomplished it, but if it was someone testing our systems, then they may be planning to use this last concert as a chance to escalate things. Plus, I just need to know. Now that I'm considering Trent, I'm not going to be able to relax until I know one way or the other.

"Any chance you can look into it now?" I ask.

There is silence on the other end, and I'm worried I asked for too much, when Julian finally says, "It's that important?"

"It is. I wouldn't be asking if it weren't."

"Okay. I'll get right on it, then. I have a friend who owes me a favor, so I'll reach out to her and see if she can jump in too."

I thank him, promising another night of pizza and video games next time I see him before hanging up the call and heading inside.

The crowds haven't been let in yet, but the rest of the employees are there, everyone pumped about the final night of the Forever Starts Here Tour. The arena is buzzing with energy in the lead-up to the final concert, but my mind is elsewhere, still swirling with thoughts of my mom and concerns over Trent.

As I make my way through the backstage area, I can't shake the feeling I'm missing something. Maybe I'm just making problems where there aren't any, but I can't ignore the churning in my gut.

I find Kelsey on her way to the security meeting and pull her aside, just for a moment. I know how important it is to Kelsey that we keep our relationship low-key and very professional at work, but I need the comfort of having her around me right now.

"You good?" she asks, pulling her long, blonde hair into a tight bun at the nape of her neck.

"You look like such a Marine when you do that," I say, forcing my hands to stay by my sides rather than reaching out and tugging a strand loose. Her hair was made to be wild and free, not pulled back tight.

"This is at least better than that bob they made all the women get when we started at the Naval Academy."

She scrunches up her nose in distaste as she says it.

I smile, imagining Kelsey's hair cut short and making a mental note to ask her mom for pictures when we get back to Wild Bluffs. "I bet you were cute with a bob."

She purses her lips. "I was. That was the problem. I hate being cute."

A chuckle slips out of me, causing a small smile to grace her lips as well. "But you're just such a petite little thing. How can people not think you're cute?"

"Have you seen this face?" she asks, pulling the iciest scowl in her arsenal.

I pretend to shiver. "Terrifying. Please, put it away."

"You're an ass."

"But like, a cute ass, right?"

"You're an idiot," she says, turning as if she's going to walk away.

I grab her wrist lightly, pulling her closer to me, though not all the way into my arms like I want. "You all set for tonight?" I ask, trying to force my mind onto the task at hand. We didn't bust our asses for twenty-three concerts just to lose our concentration and drop the ball on the final one.

She gives me a quick nod, though I can see the worry has crept back into her eyes. "Yeah, just a few last-minute details. You?"

"Same. Just a little...distracted."

"Your mom?" she asks.

"Yeah," I say. "I'm also still thinking about our conversation from before. What if it was Trent?" I ask, knowing I'm going to feel guilty if I don't tell her I'm at least considering it could be him.

"It could be. I've accepted that possibility this whole time."

I drop my head but lift it again when I feel her small hand on my shoulder.

"It doesn't change the fact that I didn't do my job," she says softly. "Yeah, it's a lot harder to protect someone when there is a mole inside, but my team should be able to ferret him out, even if it's Trent. Hell, especially if it's Trent. He's such an idiot."

A laugh bursts out of me, and as I take in Kelsey's face, I can't stop the ache in my chest, the one I know is my love for her exploding through me. The fact that she can make me laugh even with so many things weighing down on me blows my mind. She's my lighthouse, showing me the way through any storm and rocky patch of water.

"All we can do is our best at this point," Kelsey says with a shrug.

"When did you get so wise?" I tease.

"I've always been wise, Puff. You've just never been smart enough to see it."

"Nah, I always knew how amazing you were. I just never had the opportunity to tell you."

"We're going to be late," Kelsey says.

"Let's do this, then," I say before pulling open the door to the room for our last security meeting of the tour.

Chapter Thirty-Six

Kelsey

"Did you just see that?" I ask Carter as we stand in the security room together during the final sound check.

We finished up the final team meeting about an hour ago, and everyone's nerves are fried. Tonight is a big deal, and we can't let anything go wrong. We're also coordinating with four separate security teams here with their A-list clients tonight.

"See what?" Carter asks, his eyes scanning the four screens in front of us.

"I swear the camera to Jaxon's dressing room just flickered."

Without pausing, Carter presses the button on his comms. "Weston, do you have eyes on Steele?"

I appreciate the faith he has in me, not even questioning whether I may be seeing something or if I'm overreacting—he just takes the necessary steps to confirm the client is safe.

"Weston? Confirm Steele is in his dressing room," Carter says again after a second passes with no response.

"Confirmed." Weston's voice comes through the device in my ear.

"Well, that was terrifying for a second there," I admit, my eyes focused on the monitors in front of me, watching as the crowd filters in past each of the security checkpoints.

"Having flashbacks, Kels?" Carter teases, lightly banging my shoulder with his.

"Not the time for jokes."

"We've got this," he says with more confidence than I'm feeling.

I'm on edge, and I can't figure out why. The team is ready. We've got our full team tonight, even bringing in an additional coordinator to work with the personal security teams who will be with celebrities around the venue tonight. We know what we're doing at this point in the tour, and even if we haven't figured out the source of the last breach, we feel fairly confident we can have the system up and running again in less than thirty seconds should it go down.

It's not perfect, but it's the best we can do.

A message from Lila pops up on my computer screen.

Lila: *Possible Bennie sighting at C. Fourth line.*

Attached is a picture of a woman wearing a large cowboy hat, jean jacket, and boots. It's hard from the picture to tell if it's her or not. It definitely could be, but it could also be almost any woman at this concert.

Me: *I'll get one of Mitchell's floaters on it.*

Lila: *Already asked. Eddie is trying to find her.*

"Carter," I say, pointing to my screen to keep him in the loop.

"Just what we need," Carter says. "How many possible stalker sightings are we going to get today?"

"It's the last day. My team is being extra vigilant. Plus, the sighting from earlier ended up being a false alarm. Maybe this one will be too."

We sit in silence, watching as the opening act performs their first two songs. Being on tour with Jaxon has given this group a lot of confidence, particularly the lead singer. She has an amazing voice, and the crowds have been coming in earlier each concert to see them play rather than waiting until it's almost time for Jaxon to start like they did in the beginning.

My eyes continue scanning the screens, continually going back to the one showing Eddie searching the concourse.

"What's Eddie doing?" I ask Carter when I can't wait any longer for an update.

"Fuck if I know," he says, raising his hand to his ear to ask him.

"Eddie, we need a status report on the potential Bennie sighting."

He tilts his head, listening to the response. Eddie isn't on the same channel as I am, so I don't get to be a part of the conversation.

"He says he can't find her," Carter relays.

"Not acceptable. Is he working with my team to spot her from above?"

"They can't find her either. She turned a corner and got lost in the crowd. There are about ten thousand hats just like hers out there, and that's assuming she even still has the damn thing on."

Me: *Need the seat info for the Bennie potential.*

Lila: *Already sent to Eddie. He's headed there now.*

"He's headed to check her seat," Carter says at the same time Lila's message comes through. As frustrated as I am that we can't seem to find this woman, I'm impressed with how well Lila is anticipating every move I'm going to make and even beating me to it. Plus, she and Eddie are coordinating well without Carter and me having to be the middlemen. It's seamless and so different from when we first started six weeks ago.

I'm about to have Carter check in with Eddie again when a sudden crackle of static fills my ear.

It's gone just as quickly as it came.

"Did you hear that?" I ask Carter, my heart rate quickening.

"Someone may have just hit their mic by accident," he says, looking at the open comms app on his desktop like it might've malfunctioned.

The static comes again, lasting longer this time before cutting off, replaced by the eerie silence of nothing.

"Weston?" Carter says. "Report."

Silence.

Our eyes meet, and I see the same look of annoyance and fear that I know is on my face.

Carter breaks eye contact and tries again. "Weston? Report. Weston!" Carter is practically shouting now as he touches his finger to his comms device a third time.

"It's not coming through to me," I say. "Call him," I demand, pointing to his phone.

He nods and pulls up Weston's contact information when suddenly, every single image on my screen goes dark.

I freeze, my breath catching in my throat as my phone vibrates in my hand.

Lila

We're on it. Lincoln says to give him 30 seconds.

I flash my phone to Carter, who nods, still clicking Weston's name to call him.

The cameras on my screen flicker on and off, but it's not enough. The comms system crackles again, and this time, a voice comes through, saying something I can't make out.

"Weston, report. Now," Carter says as soon as a voice comes through the line.

That's when it hits me—the cold rush of dread spreading through my veins.

It wasn't just a flicker on the screen. It wasn't a random glitch. This is planned. They tested our systems, and now they—whoever they are—are putting it to use. Our equipment is all failing at once, and there is no doubt in my mind that it's on purpose.

Carter's eyes meet mine, and I know something is wrong. Everything about him is tense, from his shoulders to his hands as they grip the phone too tightly.

"Shit," I mutter, grabbing my phone and calling Lila.

It was bound to happen. I knew—*I knew*—it couldn't have been for nothing. No one puts in that much effort so a streaker can get on stage. How was I unprepared for this?

What? I mouth, but he just holds up a finger.

"We're working on comms and video," Lila says when she answers.

"Good," I say. "But I think there's more. Hold on."

"We'll be right there, keep knocking, but wait for us," Carter says before hanging up. "Jaxon's door is locked, and he's not answering."

"What?" I ask, my mind running through a million different scenarios. Like Bennie kidnapping him and cutting off all his toes.

"Don't go there," Carter says. "Maybe he locked the door and fell asleep. The room is huge, so maybe he didn't hear the knocking. There's a bathroom attached too, maybe he's in there. Or maybe he just doesn't want to be bothered by all the people constantly around him anymore. I know it would drive me insane."

Carter starts locking down his computers, clearly believing the drivel he's spouting about Jaxon falling asleep this close to his show about as much as I do—not at all.

"My gut says this is serious, but how could it be?" I ask Carter, trying to shake the feeling of unease flowing through my stomach as I follow him out of the room at a pace that is purposeful but not so fast as to draw attention to ourselves. "He's in his dressing room surrounded by security personnel how could anyone get to him? Plus, shouldn't his prep team be in there with him?"

Carter's hand runs through his hair, his jaw tightening. I can see the wheels turning in his head. He's piecing together the same things I am. The cameras going down at the same time as the comms, and *then* Jaxon doesn't answer? It doesn't seem like a coincidence.

His phone rings again, and Carter answers, listening to someone give an update. "Do we have confirmation of that?" Carter asks whoever he's on the phone with now. "He's not with any CPOs? He's not in the bathroom somewhere? He's not down at the concessions stand wearing dark sunglasses?"

The hand he runs aggressively through his hair is all the answer I need.

I put my phone back to my ear. "Lila, Jaxon's missing," I say, summarizing the information for her. "Or maybe locked in his dressing room—it's unclear."

The line is silent for a moment.

"How? Where could he have gone?" she asks, putting voice to the same questions we're all thinking.

"I don't know. That's what I need you to tell me. We had eyes on the hallway," I say quickly, my thoughts racing as I try to match Carter's pace down the long hallway. "Mitchell Security has multiple CPOs stationed around the dressing room. Find out where he went." I pause before hanging up. "Oh! and I need a key to open that door. Get someone from the venue down there now, but don't say why. And message Jaxon's team to update their standard rider—his security needs the key to his door every place, every time."

Carter and I continue to navigate the hallways full of people. Jaxon takes the stage in a little more than thirty minutes, so the majority of the crowd is on their way to their seats now.

My adrenaline is flooding my veins, my feet wanting to run when my mind knows we can't create a scene.

"The stadium team is bringing the key to the dressing room. They'll be there in five," Lila says.

"Don't forget about Bennie, Lila. My gut tells me she's involved somehow."

Chapter Thirty-Seven

CARTER

Kelsey and I turn the corner to the hallway leading to Jaxon's dressing room when her phone rings again. She puts a headphone in her left ear, the one without the comms in.

"We're just about to the room. What have you got?" Kelsey says as she answers, her strides never faltering.

She mouths *Lila* to me as she listens to the answer.

"Are you sure?" she asks.

Her face tightens slightly.

"They think Bennie is in there with Jaxon," she says to me, her pace increasing.

"What?" I ask. "How is that possible?"

"Don't know yet. But that's their best guess at this point," she answers me before returning to her conversation with Lila. "What, Lila? Okay. Well, we're here. Stay on with me."

Kelsey and I stop a few paces from the door to the dressing room where Weston and Nash stand with a short woman with frizzy brown hair wearing a polo with the arena's logo.

"Any update?" I ask Weston quietly.

"No movement," Weston answers, his eyes betraying the regret and embarrassment he must feel for this happening on his watch. It's the same look I've seen in Kelsey's eyes since Australia.

"Well, let's get this door open," I say to the lady with a smile. "I'll take the key."

"I'm supposed to keep it on me at all times," she says hesitantly.

Kelsey offers her a winning smile. "Not to worry, Deidra. We have permission from Nick to keep it until after the show. I promise I'll meet up with you as soon as Jaxon is back in his room tonight."

"I don't..." the woman, whose name is apparently Deidra—though I have no idea how Kelsey knew that—starts, but I can tell Kelsey casually dropping her name and Nick's—the head of operations for the arena—has shaken what little confidence she had to begin with.

"Thank you," Kelsey says, holding out her hand, the smile still firmly on her face.

Deidra tentatively hands over the key and, after an awkward moment with everyone staring at her, turns and walks quickly down the hallway.

"We'll go in on three," Weston says to Nash.

"No," Kelsey says, her voice quiet and her fist wrapped around the key. "Carter and me only. There's a chance no one is even in there, but if it is Bennie, we can't risk sending in a bunch of men."

"What?" Nash asks, voicing the confusion I'm feeling.

"Did none of you read her file?" Kelsey asks quietly again, her eyebrows pinched and her frustration evident.

"Never mind," I say, mimicking her quiet tone. "You can tell us your reasoning later. If Kelsey says she needs to go instead of you two, then we do it her way."

I mean it, I really do. But a huge piece of me, the one that wants to protect the people I love, hates letting her put herself in danger. Even if it's her job. Even if she's smart and capable.

Nash looks ready to protest again, but Kelsey anticipates it.

"Just Carter and I go in," Kelsey says to Weston and Nash. "If it is Bennie, she doesn't do well with men. You two stay here and guard the rear. Do not come in unless called or you hear gunfire, understood?"

"Gunfire?" Nash asks, his face draining of color slightly.

"It seems very unlikely," Kelsey says. "So don't come in."

Weston and Nash both nod their agreement, though I can tell they're even more apprehensive about the decision now than they were before Kelsey's statement.

"You cover me," Kelsey whispers, handing me the key so I can unlock the door and push it open while she slips in.

"I'd feel better covering you if I had a gun," I respond with equal quiet as I slip into position. Letting her go in first has my heart squeezing, my anxiety ratcheting up. I won't be able to shield her from whatever is inside. Hell, I won't even know what's inside until after it's already a threat to Kelsey.

"Well, you don't. Welcome to the other side of security." With that, she nods her head, indicating it's time.

I slide the key into the lock as quietly as possible, not wanting to alert anyone inside. With a nod, I pull down on the handle, pushing the door open just enough for Kelsey to fit.

Kelsey slips into the dressing room, and I follow directly behind her, leaving the door open as I slide through. She's calm as her eyes sweep the room. Everything is exactly as it's outlined in Jaxon's rider for dressing room requirements. The extra-long couch, large enough to fit his frame in case he needs a nap, is stretched out against one wall. An empty hanging rack stands opposite, suggesting Jaxon has already changed into his concert outfit. A wall of mirrors surrounded by lights reflect images of Kelsey and me, but no one else.

Jaxon's not here.

Kelsey nods her head toward the bathroom, where light is streaming from under the closed door.

We silently move toward it, Kelsey nodding at the handle to indicate we utilize the same maneuver as before.

She holds up a finger, then two, and as she lifts the third, I push down on the handle—only to find the door locked.

Shaking my head, I mouth *locked*.

Key? she responds.

We both look at the lock, realizing this is one that just uses a pin key, rather than the regular jagged keys you find on most doorknobs.

Kelsey squints one eye, thinking, before raising her hand and knocking on the door.

"Jaxon?" she says, her tone pleasant, like an assistant making sure their boss isn't dying of food poisoning or something. Which, for all we know, Jaxon might be.

The dream of this being an intestinal parasite–caused incident is quickly crushed when a quiet, feminine murmur reaches us. The voice isn't loud enough to know what's being said, but it's clear Jaxon's not in there alone. Unfortunately for the part of me that wants this to be something mundane like a last-minute backstage hookup, it seems unlikely with all the tech problems, plus I know he wouldn't want to risk invoking the ghost of Izzy so close to a performance.

Kelsey pulls a bobby pin from her hair, using her teeth to pull the little plastic drops at the end off.

"I'm a bit busy," Jaxon's voice says, his tone neutral.

"Oh," Kelsey says, straightening the bobby pin and pulling another from her hair. "Well, it's about time for you to go on."

She hands me the pin, indicating I should use it to unlock the door. I nod my agreement, impressed by her quick thinking.

She counts again, but this time, she starts talking to Jaxon as she holds up two fingers. "What are you up to?"

"Getting a haircut—"

I push open the door, and Kelsey slips inside. Following on her heels, I shove my way in, my heart leaping when the woman, Bennie, whirls around, throwing something large and metal directly toward Kelsey's heart.

No. No, no, no. I'm moving before I can truly think about what's happening, time slowing down as I reach out to drag Kelsey behind my back.

I just found Kelsey. She's the joy I didn't know I needed, the love I didn't know I was missing, and the support I never knew could feel this strong. We're not just a love story—we're the endgame.

As I pull her arm, Kelsey turns, her body rotating so the object is heading toward her side rather than her heart. She lets out an *oof* and grips a spot on her upper arm.

"Ow," she says, her tone annoyed. "Did you just throw scissors at me?"

A tsunami of relief rushes through me at her words and tone. *Scissors. Not a knife.* At most a cut, based on how calm she sounds.

Bennie faces us, the dark hair from the picture earlier now a deep red, a wig slightly crooked on her head. She's standing directly behind Jaxon as he sits in his makeup chair, but as far as I can see, her scissors were the only weapon she had.

"Bennie, isn't it?" Kelsey asks, offering the woman a smile as she subtly kicks the scissors toward the door. "What are you two do-ing...alone...in the bathroom...of Jaxon's dressing room?" Kelsey asks.

She turns her head slightly toward me, and as I spot the white headphone sticking out of her ear, I realize she's telling Lila what she needs to know to pass along information to our team and the police.

Bennie's smile is loving as she looks down at Jaxon, meeting his reflection in the mirror.

I use her distraction to step away from Kelsey so I'm in a better position to incapacitate her.

Kelsey flashes three fingers behind her back, and I nod my under-standing. We move in three.

"I'm just giving Jaxon a haircut," Bennie says, her eyes still on him. "He said I could keep *all* the hair I trim to use in my love-potions! Dee thinks we need pubes, but Jaxon says they aren't as potent, since love comes from your brain, not your dick. Isn't he just the greatest?"

Kelsey's third finger joins her other two just as Bennie finishes her sentence.

I move, my body reacting on instinct, relying on the hand-to-hand combat training I received in the military. My body slams into Bennie's, driving her to the ground inches from the toilet before she can grab hold of Jaxon. She grunts, struggling as I put my knee in her back and pull her arms behind her.

Kelsey is there, a zip tie in hand.

"Wow. That is *super* nice of Jaxon," Kelsey replies. *Wait. Why is she still playing this game with Bennie?* I send her a questioning glance as I hold Bennie's wrists together while Kelsey loops the tie over them and pulls tight.

Kelsey shrugs before saying, "I'd love to have a little chat before things get too busy tonight, Bennie. But Jaxon has to get ready, or he'll miss his show. You don't want that, do you?"

"I don't know, Kelsey," Bennie says with a giggle, her head turned to the side. "I know you and Jaxon grew up together. Are you two in love? Childhood sweethearts? I'm not interested in meeting his side piece. Now that I'm back in his life, he won't have time for you, I'm afraid. Plus, I don't like talking to men without Jaxon there—I don't want him getting jealous, you know," Bennie says, her eyes on Jaxon as he stands from the makeup chair.

"Oh. You don't have to worry about Carter or me," Kelsey says, forcing out a giggle at the end to match Bennie's. "We're very much in love with each other. Jaxon knows that. We're not a threat to your love *at all.*"

"They're my friends, Bennie. Don't you want to get to know them too?" Jaxon asks, moving toward the door.

"I don't know. What do you think, Dee?" Bennie asks, looking toward the corner just past the toilet. The very empty corner.

My knee still in Bennie's back, I look toward Jaxon to see if he understands what's happening. He responds with a slight shrug that I take to mean this isn't the first time Bennie has talked to the invisible Dee.

"Okay, well, if you think so," Bennie says to Jaxon. "Friends are *very important*. It was my new friend who helped me get to see you. He's such a nice guy. He paid for my ticket to fly here all the way from California. I could get the money, but my mom taught me never to steal. It's not nice to steal."

"What friend?" I ask. Based on the looks of displeasure both Kelsey and Bennie send my way, I can only assume it was the wrong question to ask.

Jaxon takes that moment to slip out of the room with a nod that I'm sure means he'll find his guards.

"This guy," Kelsey says, like I'm the unreasonable one in the room. "Just ignore him. I would love to hear how you got in here. You must really love Jaxon to figure out how to get past all those big lugs outside."

"Did you know the Ancient Romans used a system called a hypocaust to heat public baths and houses?" Bennie asks, singing softly under her breath as she rubs her cheek against the tile floor inches from the toilet.

"I did not know that," Kelsey responds. "Did you know the first modern air conditioner was invented in 1902?"

Bennie nods her head like that's the only appropriate response, and I keep my eyes on her, trying to figure out why we're talking about the Ancient Romans.

"I didn't realize a person could fit in the vents," Kelsey says. "Or that you could navigate them without getting lost. Did your new friend help you with the map?"

"No, silly," Bennie giggles. "Can you hand me a couple of pieces of hair? I need it for my potion. And I want to smell it. Jaxon smells so good. Can you believe he smells so good? The potion I'm going to make is going to make him mine forever. It's all about pheromones. Don't you think that developing a pheromone cocktail using Jaxon's own pheromones to find their compatible ones makes the most sense, Kelsey?"

I can feel the grimace that takes over my face at her comment. It's clear Bennie is smart, even if she's not firmly grounded in reality.

"I'd have to research it more before I could say for sure," Kelsey hedges. "But, hey, Bennie, you said your friend didn't help you get in here. Can you tell me more about that?"

"I said he didn't give me a map."

"Ah," Kelsey says, and I can see her trying to figure out what question to ask next.

Bennie giggles. "I changed the plan."

"Oh?"

"Can you keep a secret, Kelsey?" Bennie asks, her face totally serious now.

"Of course. I'm very good at keeping secrets."

"Dee didn't trust Trent."

Chapter Thirty-Eight

Carter

"I'M GOING TO KILL him," I snarl as I pace away from Kelsey, back in the control room.

The police showed up seconds after Bennie dropped her Trent-shaped bomb, and because there was an active restraining order in place, they took her back to the station quickly and quietly. Eddie followed the police to the station to give the initial statement, Lila on speakerphone with him to provide any updates necessary from the KH Security team as they continue to review tapes and put everything together.

Jaxon, Kelsey, and I promised we'd give our statements tomorrow morning, since Jaxon is due on stage in less than thirty minutes.

Jaxon is backstage now with his team, all of them extra vigilant after letting Bennie slip through the literal cracks in the building.

"Take a breath, Carter," Kelsey says, grabbing my forearm to stop my pacing.

My face is pure wrath as I look at her, but she takes it, a lone rock in the storm that is my life.

"Take. A. Breath."

The air I force through my nostrils and down into my lungs stings, the stale taste of the small space flooding my senses.

"We don't know it's Trent," Kelsey says in a low tone.

"How the fuck not?" I whisper-hiss back.

"First and foremost, because Bennie only said the name Trent one time. And she continues to talk about this plan being between her and her imaginary pal, Dee."

"It can't be a coincidence that she used Trent's name!" I say, my frustration getting the best of me.

"True, but she used my name too. That doesn't mean it was me. She might've researched us after the publicity last week."

"So what do we do?" I ask.

"We ask him about it," she responds calmly, like it's the most obvious answer in the world. "Text him. Tell him we need his help with a situation in the security room. He loves to feel important, so I'm sure he'll be here in no time."

I tap a few buttons on my phone, sending the message to my asshole of a half brother.

Me

We have a situation. Need you in the security room.

"Nice," Kelsey says, reading over my shoulder before moving her eyes back to the screen to monitor the show.

Five minutes later, Trent swaggers into the office. I see Kelsey send a quick message to her team, telling them she's out for the next five minutes.

"Where are they?" Trent asks, searching the small space like he might have missed them.

"Bad news, Trent," Kelsey says, making a little click with her tongue. "Your accomplice gave you up."

"Excuse me?" he asks.

"You know, your girl Bennie?"

His eyes widen at the name, and I know Kelsey caught the movement too with the way her smile turns feline.

My body isn't so sure a smile is in order. It feels like my world just dropped out from beneath me. It goes rigid, my hands balling into fists of their own accord.

Fuck. The guy I tied my wagon to just drove us into a wall and then lit our supplies on fire.

My phone dings with an incoming text message, and, when I see it's from Julian, I open it quickly.

The fraying piece of hope I was holding on to that Trent might actually be telling the truth snaps.

"Really?" I ask my half brother, the coldness in my tone startling everyone. "Because I just got a text from a friend of mine who says there is a money trail from you to Bennie. It looks like you wired a thousand dollars to one Bennie Jensen at the beginning of this month…"

I trail off, my eyes scanning the second message that just came through, the pieces of the puzzle coming together quickly.

"The same woman who, as it turns out, was weeks away from completing a degree in computer engineering at MIT before she dropped out and was barely ever heard from again."

"I did the job you two couldn't do. I found her. And she was living on the streets. I felt bad for her, so I gave her some money, that's it," Trent says, his face a mask of annoyance.

I shake my head. "I don't think so. You're not the kind of guy who would spend time searching the camps and shelters in San Francisco yourself when it's not something we're being paid for. And even if you were, you expect us to believe it's a coincidence you paid her and a week later Kelsey's systems were hacked in Australia?"

"Coincidence," Trent replies.

I was mad before, but now I'm livid. He's lying, and we both know it, but instead of confessing, he's doubling down.

"Are you sure about that? Because guess what? My friend found something else interesting in your financials…you're drowning in debt."

At that final statement, Trent's bravado breaks. He drops into a chair, cradling his head in his hands. He looks so much smaller than he actually is.

"I couldn't lose this contract. The company would go under. I can't mortgage anything else, and I can't tell Julie no—she thinks I fucking walk on water because I buy her anything she wants. It's the only reason she's even with me."

"Are you kidding me, Trent?" Kelsey asks, voicing my thoughts. "You took advantage of a woman who clearly needs help and put Jaxon's life in real danger because you can't have a real conversation with your wife about money? You know how ridiculous that is, right?"

Trent shakes his head adamantly. "What do you mean? His life was never in danger."

"You helped his *stalker* get into his dressing room!" Kelsey rises to her feet, pacing a few steps as she talks. "How is that not dangerous?"

His eyes go wide. "I didn't. I swear I didn't. Is Jaxon okay? She was just supposed to mess with your equipment. Make you look bad. Make it seem like your team didn't know what they were doing."

"And that's not putting his life in danger? He needs us for a reason. Bennie isn't his only stalker. The man has fanatics around him at all times. All times," I say, choosing to make Trent wait to find out if Jaxon was hurt or not.

"Did she hurt him?" Trent asks again.

Kelsey sighs. "He's sporting a new haircut—which honestly looked surprisingly good—and will likely have nightmares for the rest of his life after his stalker crawled through the vents to get a few pieces of hair for her fucking love-potion, but yeah, mostly fine. At least he talked her out of needing pubes."

Trent's eyes widen. "The vents? She went off script."

"No way," I say, unable to keep the sarcasm from my voice. "The woman with significant mental health issues and an imaginary friend didn't follow your plan? How strange."

"She was just supposed to take down a couple of cameras. Just continue what I did with the earpieces...I mean, what happened with the earpieces. Damn it. It was just supposed to be little things like the earpieces."

"Someone almost broke into his dressing room when the earpieces were down!" Kelsey says, venom dripping from her voice.

Trent looks at the ceiling. "Yeah, I may have underestimated that woman. She was very intoxicated, and I may have casually given her a badge and told her when it would be a good time to try to get backstage, but I swore her to secrecy. She seemed harmless. Who knew she came so well prepared?"

Kelsey's face is a mask of disbelief at his statement, but she quickly focuses her attention.

"And then, after that was so successful, you decided to find Bennie and pay her to upskill your sabotage?" Kelsey asks. "How did you even know she could hack like that? It's not in any of the information we had on her."

"I didn't know. I was in San Francisco for a meeting, trying to get a loan, and when I saw a shelter, it hit me—I could use Bennie to make sure I won the contract. She was the reason the last team lost their contract with him. It seemed like an easy solution. But I was just going to fly her out here, put her in a wig, and help sneak her backstage after the show. Then just blame Kelsey's team loudly as one last failure to make sure Jaxon left the tour with a clear understanding that we are the team he needed. Then once we landed Jaxon, we'd get the contracts for the Holton tour and with the comedian. I'd have enough money to at least keep up with all my payments." Trent massages his eyes with his hands. "When I talked to her, she offered her hacking abilities up without me even asking. I suggested she do a couple of trial runs, telling her she needed to test your systems to make sure Jaxon was safe."

"So how did she end up giving Jaxon a haircut in his dressing room today?"

"I don't know. She hasn't responded to my messages in a few days. I figured she just disappeared."

"How are you such an idiot?" Kelsey asks, her hands on her hips as she stares at Trent with a look of disgust on her face.

"I don't fucking know," he admits, his posture one of defeat. "It just...spiraled. It's not like I masterminded some evil plan. Things just kept...happening. I was in the supply closet and accidentally spilled my drink next to the box with the earpieces. And I just thought...but what if I spilled *on them*? And then Kelsey's team looked bad, so I thought, why not do it again?"

The room is silent as Kelsey and I absorb his confession.

"What are you going to do?" Trent asks. "If you tell Jaxon, Mitchell Security will be ruined. I'll be ruined." He looks at Kelsey. "Carter will be ruined too."

Kelsey's eyes meet mine, and I can see the war taking place inside her.

Luckily, I don't have the same issue. I know exactly what I need to do.

Taking out my phone, my fingers fly furiously over the screen as I do what needs to be done.

"What are you doing?" Trent asks, his tone curious.

I hold up a finger, asking for a second, and smirk as Kelsey raises her eyebrow.

"Almost done," I say, typing out the last few words.

"What are you doing?" Trent asks again. This time, his tone has changed from curiosity to confusion.

"Check your email."

Both Kelsey and Trent pull out their phones, and Kelsey audibly sucks in a breath as she reads.

"Are you fucking kidding, Carter?" Trent growls. "You just destroyed our business!"

"*I* didn't destroy it. Didn't you read the email *you* sent out to our employees and current contracts—the one from *your* email? *You* destroyed the business. *You* put our client at risk. *You* put our entire team at risk. *You* did this. Not *me*."

"That's a risky move," Kelsey says, her voice softer than normal.

It pulls me up short. Shit. It was risky. And impulsive. And I'm never impulsive. I'm just so frustrated and angry at Trent for putting Jaxon and our team in danger. For putting Kelsey in a spot where she had to choose between what was right and what would protect me, damn it.

I didn't think about it. I just did what needed to be done to ensure she was going to be okay. To make sure she didn't have to sacrifice her principles, her morals, to protect me.

"It's done," I say, shrugging my shoulders.

"Are you fucking kidding me?" Trent says, his voice cracking. "What am I going to do? What am I supposed to do now, Carter?"

"I'd suggest getting a job. Probably having a conversation with your wife about her getting a job as well."

I feel no joy at the statement, just bone-weary defeat. Trent is an asshole, but I never wanted to screw him over. He gave me a job when I needed one. We got along...fine. But then he put so many people at risk just to protect himself. Even if I hadn't felt compelled to expose his mistakes to save Kelsey from choosing between her morals and protecting me, Mitchell Security—and especially my time there—would have been through.

Now I just have to figure out what's next.

Chapter Thirty-Nine
Carter

I SLOWLY PUSH OPEN the door to my mom's house, knocking once to let her know I'm there. It's only been seven weeks since I left, but it feels like a lifetime, and I'm not sure what to expect.

"Hi, honey!" my mom gushes, racing from the kitchen to throw her arms around me.

She looks the same: dark hair pulled back into a ponytail, dark eyes bright with joy.

I don't know why I thought she'd look different, but with the news from Bill, I just expected a frail old woman. Logically, I know that's not how my mom's disease works, but logic and fear so rarely function together.

"Ready for dinner?" I ask, holding up a bag of groceries I brought with me.

Her smile is large, the energy in the room bubbly and light. There truly is nothing better than coming home.

"Yes! You must be exhausted. Sit down and tell me everything! I'll get to work on the food."

I *am* exhausted. After confronting Trent and impulsively sending that email, we still had a concert left to work. Despite everything he'd been through that day, Jaxon did not disappoint with his final show. I thought the crowd was going to bring down the whole place with their chanting. Ignoring his security and logistics teams' requests, Jaxon even played one additional encore song, his very first song ever released, solo with just him and his guitar. It sent the place into an absolute frenzy.

This morning, the NYPD came to Jaxon's hotel room to take statements from everyone involved in the Bennie incident, so Kelsey and I were forced to move our flights back to this afternoon. Jaxon didn't make any announcements about his long-term contract, and since I'm unsure of Mitchell Security's ability to pay anyone's wages, I offered to escort him to his plane myself. Kelsey, of course, decided to tag along. Jaxon told us on our drive to the airport that his lawyers are pressuring him to file civil charges against both Bennie and Trent. I didn't ask him if he was going to, and he didn't offer the information, but he did make it clear he was aware no one else from the Mitchell Security team was involved.

Jaxon's assistant Annie informed me Jaxon has a small security team for his house on staff and assured me they were prepped to pick up Jaxon and guard him until a final decision is made about the long-term security contract.

Saying goodbye to Jaxon felt like closing a door on a possible friendship and time in my life that I wasn't ready to say goodbye to, but we made some tentative plans to get together next time I'm in Tennessee, whenever that may be.

It all went smoothly, and with the time change, I was still able to make it home in time to drop Kelsey off at her house, grab some groceries, and make it to my mom's in time for dinner.

Ignoring Mom's request to sit down, I grab a slightly wilted head of lettuce plus two peppers and start washing the salad ingredients while my mom pulls out the large pan to brown the meat for the spaghetti sauce.

"How was the tour?" my mom asks, and it's amazing how one simple question can make my heart happy.

I tell her about all the places we went, the dinners Kelsey and I went to, and the chaos that is life as a famous musician.

"Poor Jaxon. I always liked that boy so much. It's such a shame."

I chuckle. "You know he's the most famous musician in the world, right? I don't think you need to feel sorry for him."

My mom waves her hand like that couldn't possibly matter. "If I've learned nothing else in my life, it's that being successful and being happy have almost nothing to do with each other. Oh, and speaking of the Harper sisters—"

"We weren't speaking of the Harper sisters," I say.

My mom smirks. "Well then, now that you bring them up, how is Kelsey? When does she get back? When are you going to invite her over for dinner?"

I can't stop the smile that spreads across my face at the thought, and my mom's eyes light up like a dog who's seen a bone.

"Please tell me you're dating that girl."

"I'm dating that girl," I say, keeping my eyes trained on the vegetables I'm cutting up.

"Yes!" my mom screams, fist-pumping as she races around the kitchen. She's laughing as she skips behind me, whacking my ass with the dishtowel over her arm.

"You're being way too much right now," I tell her, even though I secretly want to do the same thing every time I realize how lucky I am.

Finally, my mom stops her nonsense, pretending to be winded as she leans over and pants loudly.

I shake my head at her, enjoying the ease of spending time with my mom. It feels like old times, before everything was too complicated, and that's exactly what I need right now.

The timer dings, signaling the noodles are ready, so I carry the rest of the food out to the table. My mom joins me a minute later with a bowl of steaming noodles.

"It's not Italy, but it'll do," my mom teases.

"Nowhere else I'd rather be," I say. As the words leave my mouth, I realize it's the truth. Sometime in the last two months, while I was out seeing the world, I realized Wild Bluffs is my home—not just the town I grew up in or the place I'm living while I take care of my mom.

Mom and I fall back into our natural rhythm of conversation—her pestering me with questions until I've given complete-enough answers for her to be satisfied. I know we need to talk about real things like her work and care, and how we're going to afford it when I'm out of a job now that I know Trent is drowning in debt and Mitchell Security is no longer an option. But I don't want to.

My mom is having a good day, rarely repeating herself and tracking the conversation, even the parts about where I was and what I was doing. I'm not going to waste this gift on talk of in-home care, cutting hours, or anything else.

Finally, though, my mom takes the decision out of my hands. "I assume Bill told you I'm going to have to cut my work hours?"

I pause, my fork halfway to my mouth, and look at her. The reality of the conversation I've been avoiding settles in. I slowly set my fork down.

"Yeah," I say, my voice betraying my concern. "He mentioned it. How are you feeling about it?"

My mom's expression softens. "Well, honey, we both knew it was coming. The doctors say I can keep working for now, since I'm so familiar with the diner and with Bill and Mildred, but I can't keep up the same pace. I'm not my best self when I get tired."

I nod, though my chest feels heavy. My mom has been amazing through this entire diagnosis, never letting it get to her, and I feel like I have to be as strong as she is.

"I've been looking into some of the options. Maybe...maybe we should look into hiring someone to help around the house while you cut back on hours?"

What I actually mean is someone to be around to help make sure she doesn't get confused or overwhelmed when she's home alone, but helping around the house sounds nicer.

Alice Anderson is not buying it, though.

Mom waves her hand dismissively. "I don't want to be a burden. I'm not ready for that yet. Just..." She sighs, looking out the window for a moment as if gathering her thoughts. "Just make sure you don't get so focused on taking care of me that you forget to take care of yourself too."

I feel a lump rise in my throat, but I push it back down. "Oh, you mean like you did for the first eighteen years of my life?"

She smiles, her eyes filled with love. "It was the best way I could possibly spend my life."

Tears pool in my eyes, and I blink, trying to force them back. "Then why won't you let me make the same decision for you?"

"Because you have someone else to focus on now. Don't let your love for me keep you from loving her. She's where your future lies."

The words hit me hard. I think of Kelsey, of everything we've been through, and how right it feels when I think about focusing all my love on her. No, I'll never stop loving or caring for my mom, but she's right, I can't let it consume me—I have other things worth living for now.

"I just hope you don't wait too long so I can remember your wedding," my mom says, a smug smile pulling at the corners of her lips.

"Mom!" I chastise. "You can't say things like that."

Though, now that she's brought it up, I can picture it. A small wedding backed up against the sand bluffs that surround the town. Just a small group of people, Kelsey's family and mine, watching as Kelsey walks toward me in a white dress with a loving smile on her face. I know with everything in my heart that it's a glimpse into my future, but my mom's right—there's a chance she'll have progressed to a point where she won't remember it.

She laughs, and I can't help but chuckle too. "I can joke about it if I want. But, just a heads-up, if you don't bring Kelsey by soon, I might just forget you aren't married and insist on calling her your wife all night."

"You know, for someone who never decided to get married, you sure are pushing it hard," I say.

"I just want you to be happy," she says, reaching out to pat my hand. "And since you were a boy, Kelsey Harper has made you happy. I'd just hate to see anything get in the way of that—including your dumbass half brother. What is going to happen to Mitchell Security?"

"I don't know," I answer truthfully, not at all surprised that the news of Trent's poor decisions has already made its way through the Wild Bluffs gossip mill. "I can't get a hold of Trent, but I know he leveraged everything to support his new lifestyle, including the firm. So I can only assume it's so underwater, we'll be lucky if we can pay employees their last paychecks, let alone keep running the company."

"Do you think you'll go back to the Rangers?" Mom asks.

When I left the Army to come back to Wild Bluffs, there was nothing I wanted more than to get back in. I enjoyed the life, the men and women I worked with, and the constant challenge. Now? Now I have too much for me here. The freedom and opportunity of military service just doesn't call to me anymore.

"No," I answer. "I'll find something else I can do in the area. I have no idea what it'll be, but it's not like I'm unemployable."

My mom laughs. "Not unemployable at all. In fact, some might think the other security company in town would want to hire you."

I sigh. I've put a lot of thought into working for Kelsey. It would make the most sense, but after her experience with her ex, I don't want to force her into that position again.

"Kelsey and I work well together, but I don't know if it makes sense right now based on our relationship."

"Really? Lots of people in town work with their spouses."

"It's different when you're dating," I reply. "Less permanent. Greater chance for awkwardness." It's the truth but not the whole truth.

"You could make it permanent," my mom suggests.

"Maybe I can work at one of the banks or something," I say, ignoring her comment.

My mom raises her dark eyebrow. "The bank? Really?"

"It's a good job!" I protest.

"You'd hate sitting in a bank all day."

She's not wrong, but it's one of the best-paying jobs in our small town. "I'll figure something out."

"I know you will," my mom says, her confidence in me evident on her face. "Just make sure it's what you *want* to do, not what you think you need to do for me."

"What if what I want to do is whatever is best for you?" I question.

"Then you're a good man. But a good man who will quickly realize why *work* is a four-letter word. You'll find a way to do something you enjoy. I know you will."

The evening continues, lighthearted and filled with the comfort of normalcy. But in the back of my mind, I know things are shifting. Changes are coming, and I'm not sure how I'm going to face them all.

Chapter Forty

Kelsey

"Come in," I yell, jumping out of the burrito I've rolled myself into as I watch TV in my bed. It's just so good to be home.

I hustle to intercept whichever one of my sisters decided to come over after just seeing me at our parents' house for dinner. As much as I enjoyed seeing them after my time away, we don't need to get back into the habit of them showing up whenever they want and eating all my food.

"Hey!" Carter's voice reaches me, and I speed up, slipping a little in my socks as I round the corner. I right myself just in time to see him shutting the door behind him.

"I hope it's okay that I invited myself over," Carter says, his eyes betraying his concern. "I was going to call first, but..."

"I'm so glad you came! I wasn't sure if you were done with dinner with your mom, so I was waiting until after nine to text you. Not like a booty call, I just... I know you've got your shows to watch. Which one did you two decide to start?" I ask, hoping Carter missed my unfiltered-nonsense spewing.

"What are you questioning, Kels?" he asks, pulling me into a hug.

"I'm not questioning anything."

"You've rambled about two times in the thirty years I've known you, and it's only ever been about relationship things."

"I'm not sure how we work now that we're back," I admit. We were all but living together for the last month, but now we have two houses, two work schedules, two separate lives. It crossed my mind to invite Carter to dinner with my family, or to offer to go with him, but I knew Carter wanted time with his mom, and it felt awkward to ask if I could come along for his welcome-home dinner. Not because I didn't want to be there—it wasn't about that. I'm excited to see his mom and get to know her better. But now we're back to our normal lives, and I'm not sure who we are. Are we the type of couple who spend every minute together like we were on tour? Do we have a standing Friday-night date night? Do we text during the week? Do we have shows we watch together?

"We work the same as we did before," Carter says, pulling the end of my ponytail to get me to tilt my face toward his.

"That's not true," I say. "We're not going to be spending every minute together. We both have houses, jobs, families."

"Well, I'm going to have to move out of my house, and I highly doubt I have a job anymore," Carter says, his tone light like he's trying to make a joke, but I know how much it must hurt to admit those things. "So I guess I'll just follow you around. I can carry a speaker and play Jaxon's songs all day if it'd make you feel more comfortable."

I shake my head, stepping back. "You're ridiculous."

Carter looks around us, cataloging my slate-gray floors and white countertops before shifting his attention to my dining room table. "Your house is really nice."

"Thanks," I say, realizing he's never been inside before. I look around, trying to see the space through his eyes. I've lived here for almost six years now, and I've done a few DIY projects with the help of my dad to fix it up. I like the clean lines and open spaces it offers. "Want the tour?"

"Of course," Carter says, looking at the spot under my hallway table like he's considering whether or not to take off his shoes.

I'm glad to see I'm not the only one questioning how this night is going to go.

"I don't mind people wearing shoes in my house," I offer before deciding to just put my cards on the table. "But if you're going to stay the night, this is the best place to keep them."

"You're sure you're okay if I stay?" he asks, his tone betraying his uncertainty.

"I'm not sure I can sleep without you anymore," I say in jest, but like all good jokes, there's a kernel of truth in it. I probably could sleep without him, but I don't want to.

At my admission, Carter takes off his shoes, placing them nicely under the table where they're out of the way. "And why would you want to?" he says, offering me a wink.

"You're moving in with your mom?" I ask, mentally working through what it means to date a man whose room is next door to his mom's as I lead him up the stairs to show him my guest rooms.

"I don't have another option. Cash flow is going to get tight, and that's the easiest way to get an extra thousand dollars a month. I don't think it's either my mom's or my first choice, but it is what it is."

"Hmm." I'm not sure what to say, as "luckily, I have my own house, so we can bang here" seems a bit uncouth.

I continue the tour, Carter making the appropriate noises of interest as I show him each room until we make our way back to the kitchen.

"I think you missed the most important part of the house," Carter says, his face bright with mischief. "Where's your bedroom?"

"Oh, a lady never tells," I say, fluttering my eyelashes at him like a woman from a regency movie.

Carter chuckles before scooping me up and over his shoulder, my head inches from his ass.

"Hey!" I yell, lightly slapping the firm muscle in front of me. "Put me down, you oaf."

"Process of elimination would suggest your bedroom is behind that door," he says, and I lift my body enough to see that he's pointing to the white door that's tucked away at the back of my dining room.

The door to my bedroom. Stupid smart men.

Without waiting for me to answer, he hauls me to the door, a pleased vibration flowing through his body when he pushes it open and finds my king-sized bed, the white comforter bunched up on one side, pillows strewn everywhere.

"Nice bed, Kels," he says before tossing me onto it on my back. "I can't wait to fuck you in it."

"Then what are you waiting for?" I ask, holding his gaze as I slip out of my clothes.

He pushes down his jeans and kicks them away before crawling over me, finding my mouth and fusing our lips together in a demanding kiss.

"You. I didn't know it, but I think I might've been waiting for you for most of my life."

He kisses his way down my neck, then my breasts, before draping my legs over his broad shoulders.

"I'm yours," I breathe.

He smiles at me, a wicked tilt of his lips that promises pleasure like I've never felt before. Lowering his head, he nibbles the inside of my upper right thigh, and my breath fully vacates my lungs.

He strokes his fingers over me, and I shudder. The movement causes him to pause, his blazing eyes meeting my own. I can't take my eyes off his face, off the lust and love moving together like the dancing sparks of a raging fire.

Slowly sinking a finger into me, his eyes darken as mine fall closed at the overwhelming sensation.

His thumb flicks my clit, and I moan, my hips moving upward of their own accord, trying to find relief. Dropping his gaze from my face, his focus turns fully to my center, and he replaces his thumb with his hot, wet mouth. In a long, lazy stroke, he licks up the full length of me as if he has all the time in the world.

A timeframe my burning body very much disagrees with.

My core tightens, my thighs gripping the sides of his face, and the vibrations from his responding chuckle almost send me over the edge.

"Carter," I moan as my hips rise, asking for more.

"On your knees," he orders, and I rush to follow his command. As I do, I realize this only happens with Carter. Only with Carter am I okay with giving up this kind of control. Because I know it's not giving up my independence or power but sharing it with the man I love.

Carter's warm hand traces up my spine as he moves behind me. I turn my head to the side, watching as he aligns the head of his thick cock with my entrance. He pushes in, just the tip, and catches my hips as I try to take control and press back onto him.

"I'm going to fuck you hard and fast, Kels," he whispers, planting kisses up my spine. "I can't help myself. I want to love you slowly, but I just..."

"Do it." My low, rasping voice is a plea.

"Condom?" Carter asks.

"I'm on birth control," I say, knowing the smart answer is to wear a condom anyway, but wanting the feel of him bare inside me too much. And the idea of an unplanned pregnancy is somehow a little less scary now than it's ever been—I know I'm with the man I want to build my life with.

"I'm...fuck, I'm clean, but...are you sure?" It's a quiet question that suggests he knows the offer means more than just increased pleasure for us both.

"Yes. Please."

Carter obliges, slamming home until he's fully seated, his cock hitting against my cervix.

"Oh," I whimper. My eyes fall closed as the ripples of pleasure course through my body.

I move against him, letting him control the pace as he continues to pump into me.

I'm at the edge, seconds away from falling, and judging by the erratic pace Carter is moving, he is too.

I drop to my elbows and snake my left hand between our legs, lightly squeezing his soft sac.

"Fuck." His groan is barely audible, and he quickly pushes my hand away, reaching around to find my clit again.

One firm circle of his fingers is all it takes, and I break, my walls squeezing him as he finds his own release.

We stay like that, neither of us strong enough to do anything for a few long seconds, before I finally collapse.

Using my arms as a pillow, I lie on my stomach, catching my breath as Carter pulls the covers over us both.

It's peaceful.

"Tell me about your dinner with your mom," I say.

He does, and I'm so glad he was able to have a good night with her. He worried so much about her while we were gone; I know he wasn't sure what it would be like when he returned home.

"But I don't know what I'm going to do," Carter concludes, kissing his way along my ribs. "I'm going to move back in with my mom. It's not ideal for her memory or for me, but it will mean more money and fewer hours I'll need to hire care for her down the road."

"What if you moved in with me?" I offer. I know people would say it's too soon, but I also know this thing I have with Carter isn't going to go away. And if being able to call my house home base would help him with his mom, I'm all for it. Actually, after what we just did, I'd be all for having access to that every night for the rest of my life, even if he didn't need a place to live.

"That's..." He trails off, and a wave of uncertainty washes over me.

"No pressure," I say, closing my eyes like I'm about to go to sleep. "I just thought I'd offer."

"I just don't want you to feel obligated to ask me," Carter says, his hand sneaking into my maze of limbs to find one of my fingers to hold. "When we move in together, I want it to be because we can't stand being apart from each other, so we need to cohabitate."

I chuckle, peeking out at him from behind my eyelashes. "Well, if the last five hours were any indication, I don't like being apart from you. There is also something to be said for being practical. I have a house that's big enough for a family of five, and I live in it by myself. You need a house. We love each other. Move in."

"People will talk," Carter tries again, and this time, I realize it's not that he's opposed to the idea; he's worried about me.

"So? People will talk no matter what we do, so we should do what we want."

"And your parents?" he asks, but I can tell he's about to agree to it. I didn't realize I wanted him to move in so badly, but now I'm arguing it, I want him to live with me. And not just because I want to win the argument—though I do love to win. Living together makes sense. And I'm excited to start our life together.

"My parents will respect my decision. As will my sisters. That's what family does."

"Okay. Then, when my lease comes up at the end of the month, I'll move in," he says. "That gives you a week to change your mind."

"Not going to happen."

"And I'll figure out what I can pay you for rent," he says quickly. "I'm not sure what it'll be right now, but I'll pay something."

"Carter, Bryn lived with me off and on for over three years and never paid me a dime. Plus, that defeats the purpose of you saving money."

"It doesn't feel right to make you pay for everything," he says, his voice low.

"How about this? We'll split utilities, and you're in charge of doing the dishes *and* the laundry. And we'll call it even."

He's quiet, and I know he's thinking through it all. Trying to decide if it's an arrangement he feels okay about.

"Okay. Thank you. I love you, Kels," Carter says, placing a light kiss on my cheek.

"I love you too, Puffin," I say, and he nips playfully at me at the nickname. I know he secretly loves it, though.

I was worried I'd be bored once I was back in Wild Bluffs, but now I know that won't be the case. Carter's living situation is solved, and I get my favorite person as my roommate. Not bad for my first night home.

Plus, I have a plan for Carter's job, I just need to call Jaxon Reid—I mean Steele—first.

CHAPTER FORTY-ONE

CARTER

"YOU KNOW, I ALWAYS expect you two doofuses to be stronger, considering you're professional athletes," Kelsey says, bringing a large wooden bowl filled with salad to the table.

"We don't carry boxes around for a living, Kelsey," JT replies, snagging one of the dinner rolls off the pile in front of him. "And you weren't complaining when we were helping the Lindens move Carter's couch and recliner out."

"They were small," Kelsey shoots back. "I could've moved them with only Izzy to help."

"Hey!" Izzy cries. "Why am I your choice for weakest member of the family?"

The table breaks out into arguing over the best way to measure strength, and I lean forward to share a soft smile with my mom, who's sitting on the other side of Izzy.

It's been like this all day. The Harper sisters chatting or arguing or making fun of Jameson and JT. I was surprised when Lila and JT pulled up in jeans and sweatshirts this morning to help move me into Kelsey's, but when I asked Kelsey about it, she said they were essentially part of the family now. JT even goes with her dad, Ken, to the old-man coffee group sometimes.

My mom came this morning to help finish packing up a few of my boxes of dishes and kitchen gadgets, but the exertion and new faces were hard on her. I took her home before lunch and told her we could decide later if she felt up to dinner tonight at Ken and Jen's house.

She'd insisted she wanted to come. I considered telling her not to, just to protect her from the chaos, but Kelsey reminded me my mom is still capable of making her own decisions for now, so I should let her do what she wants while she still can.

Kelsey's mom, Jen, has been great, chatting with my mom about what I was like in high school as my mom sat at their island, watching as Jen and Kelsey finished making dinner. I was surprised when my mom sat next to Jen at the table instead of me.

"I think you're overly discounting the local workout class *and* the benefit I have by being five inches taller than you," Izzy says, still arguing with Kelsey about how strong she is.

Kelsey turns an exasperated look my way, but I just shake my head, smart enough to know I don't want to be in the middle of that.

Bryn catches the look and snorts. "You think Carter is going to save you? He's said five words total since you two got back."

"Was it the conversation on relative-versus-absolute strength you wanted me to weigh in on, or your intellectual discussion earlier about which of the 'Jo Bros' ended up being the best one to marry?" I ask, keeping my focus on the pale green iceberg lettuce I'm shoveling into my mouth.

"I see your point," Bryn says. "Your input isn't useful. You don't understand the finer points of either argument."

Jameson throws his arm around Bryn's shoulder from his spot next to her, pulling her toward him to kiss her hair. "Don't bully Carter, B. Not everyone grew up with annoying little sisters to prepare them for this chaos."

"I was not the annoying one of the two of us," Lila chimes in from the other side of Bryn. "Teenage boys are bad enough, but ones who think they're going to be professional athletes? It was excruciating."

"I didn't *think* I was going to be a professional, I *was* going to be one. I *am* one," Jameson replies, leaning around his girlfriend to see his little sister.

"We know you are, sweetie," Bryn says, patting his arm like she's consoling a small boy who just found out he can't be a dinosaur when he grows up.

"Why did we come home this weekend?" Jameson asks JT. "We could've been playing golf in Florida."

"You're the one who convinced me to take a break before the big tournament next weekend," JT says, his mouth full of food. "Plus, it's fun when Bryn makes you cry."

"I need new friends," Jameson says. "Carter, any chance you're available to fly to Florida for The Players with me next weekend? I promise it'll be a good time, and we'll leave all the women here so no one will make you cry."

"He's only offering to leave us behind because he knows I have to be in New York for a couple of meetings," Bryn says, pointing at me with her fork.

I know he's joking, but it's nice to feel like I might have friends around town to do things with, even if they're professional golfers who spend most of their time on the road. It's something I've missed since leaving the Army.

"I'll have to take a rain check," I say. "I finally got access to all of Trent's books and financial information for Mitchell Security, and I have to spend the next few weeks closing everything down and seeing what I can do to get the guys paid for their latest jobs."

Trent has completely jumped ship. He and Julie listed their house, packed up a trailer, and moved to Ohio so Trent could work for her dad's used-car dealership. I have no doubt in my mind he'll be great at it. Unfortunately, he hasn't done one thing to try to get Mitchell Security figured out before he left. I feel I owe it to the employees and our current clients to end things as well as possible.

"Let me know if you need any help, Carter," Izzy offers. "Becca and I don't tend to work with people going under—so hard to get them to pay us—but we're pretty good at finances, and not to speak for Becca, but I'm sure we'd both be happy to help."

Holding back my surprise, I send her what I hope is a gracious smile and nod. "Thanks."

"Do you know what you're going to do once you're done cleaning up Trent's mess?" Ken asks from the head of the table.

"I'm still trying to figure it out," I confess. "I've talked to a few people who work at the banks to see if they're hiring, but nothing is open right now."

"Have you considered anything else?" Ken asks. "I could talk to some of the guys at coffee and see if they know anyone hiring."

I clear my throat, hating the turn this conversation took. I appreciate that they care, it's just...embarrassing. Especially for a meet-the-parents dinner. "I'm pretty open to anything, really," I say. "I figure if all else fails, I can join one of the construction crews in the area for a while until I find something that uses a bit more of my skill set."

"My cousin owns one of the construction companies," Jen says, joining the conversation for the first time. "Let me know if you want me to introduce you."

"Thanks. I'm not there yet, but I'll let you know."

I glance at Kelsey and realize she's annoyed, though trying to hide it. "What?" I ask in a whisper, nudging her gently with my shoulder.

She turns her head, stopping her lips inches from my ear. "Those are both terrible options."

I open my mouth to respond, but she turns her face away, smiling at her family. A second later, I feel her hand grab mine under the table, squeezing once as if to indicate we'll talk about it later once we're home.

Home.

That first morning I stayed at Kelsey's last week was like a dream. The sunlight streamed in, waking me up far later than normal, and I could only lie there and feel pure contentment—absolute satisfaction.

Kelsey's bed was soft and warm, its owner draped over my side, her soft breasts pressed against my ribs. She let out a soft sound as she moved, and I knew I would do everything in my power to wake up like that for the rest of my life.

I didn't think our relationship could get any better, but this week proved me wrong. Kelsey joined me for dinner with my mom most nights, only skipping Friday to join her sisters, Lila, and Becca for pizza at Wild Crusts.

There was a small part of me that worried Kelsey and I were going to have less in common now that we aren't working together every day, but that hasn't been the case. We're starting to build routines, both together and separately, which make me realize how fulfilling it can be to share your life with someone, although I'm not sure it would ever feel this way with anyone but Kelsey.

"I can't believe you're both going to be living with your boyfriends," Izzy says to her sisters. "It makes me feel so old."

"Like half of the people we grew up with are already married," Kelsey replies, frowning slightly. "We're too old for this to be so shocking to you."

Izzy takes a bite of her food and raises one shoulder. "I'm just glad I still have Becca. Hopefully we can just grow old together and be those old ladies who cause havoc around town, flirting with younger men and conning the old ones out of their retirement funds."

"Oh, Izzy," Jen says. "You don't mean that. You'll find someone." It's a very motherly comment, and all three of her daughters have looks of exasperation on their faces.

"Not everyone needs a man to be happy, Mom," Izzy shoots back.

"No, but having a partner is special. It's the chocolate kiss on the top of a peanut butter cookie—it's not necessary, but it sure does make it taste better."

"Great, now I want a peanut butter blossom," JT groans. "Any chance that's what's for dessert?" He looks eagerly toward the kitchen, scanning the counter for any sign of the cookies.

I join in the laughter at the table, knowing I would've agreed with Izzy just a few months ago. But now that I've gotten a taste of life with the extra chocolate, I know there's no way I'm ever going back.

"I'm inclined to agree with Jen," my mom says, and I can see the look of regret flash across Jen's face.

I know she didn't mean anything insulting with her comment, but it's easy to forget my mom ended up single her entire life. Jen's life—marrying Ken in her twenties, having three kids, two cars, and one house—didn't match my mom's experience with love and partnership.

"It's not about needing someone—I'm proof of that," my mom continues, patting Izzy's hand. "It's about choosing to share your life with someone who gives you the love and support to be your happiest, best self. I never found that, but if I had, I would've grabbed on to it and never let go."

Izzy nods, her smile softening. "I get it. I'm just not in a rush to find that person."

"And in the meantime, you can make all the mischief you want with Becca," Jen jokes. "Though that's hard to do when you're in bed by nine every night."

"I get sleepy, okay?!"

That causes chuckles around the table, and for a moment, the conversation turns lighter again. It's funny how family can dance around difficult subjects, confronting them while still keeping everything in balance. It's something I've never really experienced with just my mom and me.

I watch them all, the easy flow of conversation, and I feel this pull in my chest. It's something I never expected to feel—the ache of knowing that, in some ways, I'm more at peace now than I've ever been, but that peace comes with a price. It's not just chocolate and peanut butter that makes life better. It's love, connection, and finding someone who fits into your world, someone who knows the pieces of you that you thought you'd never share with anyone else and somehow loves those pieces the most.

And maybe that's what Jen was trying to say: It's not about the chocolate kiss or the peanut butter cookie—it's about the new treat they become that's still peanut butter and still chocolate, and yet, somehow, something so much more.

"All right, enough of this talk," Jen says, shifting the conversation to a new topic, eager to keep the vibe light. "Let's focus on what matters now—dessert! Unfortunately, no cookies, but who wants brownies?" She stands, grinning at the chorus of requests.

After we're all full to the point of exploding, I take my mom home, hugging her a little longer than usual as I drop her off.

"What's that for?" she asks.

"For putting aside your quest for love to love me instead."

"There was always space in my heart for all the love I could find. I just wasn't one of the lucky ones who found my chocolate kiss." She strokes her thumb over my cheek. "But I'm so glad you are."

Chapter Forty-Two

Kelsey

"Where is he?" I ask Lila, pacing in front of her desk.

"Why couldn't you do this at your house?" Izzy asks, typing furiously on her computer. "This isn't your office, you know."

"I don't like mixing work and pleasure."

Her fingers freeze on the keys, a look of pure disbelief on her face. "Didn't you sleep with the guy you were competing against *while working*?"

I consider it. "That's not how I'd describe it, no."

"But it's what happened, right? We can all agree on that?"

Ignoring her, I turn back to Lila. "He said he just had to finish up a meeting with one of the potential helpers for his mom at Wild Brews, and then he'd be here."

"Does Alice really need full-time care already?" Lila asks. "She seemed fine this weekend when we were all at your parents' house."

"I don't think they're ready to hire someone right now, but Carter being Carter, he wants to make sure he's prepared. Then, when the time comes, he doesn't have to start the whole process." I pace in the other direction. "Also, I don't think he knows what to do with his time, even if he's spending most of it getting Mitchell Security closed down."

Lila nods in understanding, biting the end of her pen as she sits at her desk. "I've met Alice a few times at the café, so it's not like I know her well, but I wouldn't have been able to tell that she has dementia if I hadn't been told ahead of time."

"I don't know her well either, but from what I've picked up in the last week, it comes and goes. Her Alzheimer's hasn't progressed to the point where she's confused more often than not, but even then, she'll have moments of clarity. It's one of the challenges of the disease; you never know what you're going to get. You can't prepare yourself."

"That's so hard," Lila says, her face a mask of sympathy.

"Ugh," I groan. "Where is he?"

Izzy pokes her head out from around her computer and stares at me.

"What?"

She bites her lip, tapping her fingers on her keyboard without actually typing. "I'm going to ask something, and I don't want you to get mad."

"Then don't ask me stupid things."

Her pursed lips give away just how unamused by my answer she is. But what does she expect? I can't promise I won't get mad.

"Are you sure you want to do this?"

"Yes," I say without hesitation.

"But you know what happened last time—"

"Yeah," I cut her off. "Of course I do. I was there."

"I just want to make sure you've thought it through and aren't just trying to help Carter. I mean, you already asked him to move in with you. Isn't that enough? You've been dating for all of one minute."

"When did you become so cynical?" I ask, truly looking at my sister for the first time since I've been home. There are little bags under her eyes, and her face is paler than usual.

"I'm not cynical. I'm a realist."

"You're sad," I say, stating the truth on her face.

"No," she retorts, her voice strong. "I'm mad. And there's a fucking difference."

The door to the office pushes open, and Carter enters, holding two to-go cups of coffee.

"When they realized the small coffee I ordered was for you, they gave me a kids' cup," he says, handing me the little coffee and leaning in to kiss my cheek.

"Well," says Lila, standing quickly, her phone in hand. "I'm going to go get some coffee myself."

"Sorry, Lila. I should've brought you one. That was rude of me. Do you want mine?" Carter asks, offering his cup to her.

"No, that's all right, but thank you. Izzy and I were planning to go grab one and some food for lunch anyway."

"We were?" Izzy asks. Then her face changes to one of understanding. "I mean, *we were*. See you later, alligators." She grabs her phone and bustles out the door, throwing a peace sign up over her shoulder as she leaves.

Now that the office is empty, the magnitude of what I'm about to do hits me. But instead of feeling trepidation or uncertainty, I feel calm. Certain.

Carter settles himself against the corner of Lila's desk, his dark jeans and gray sweater making him look more academic than he did in his Mitchell Security shirts. "What's up?" he asks with a smile.

"I...have a proposition for you."

He leans in close to me, his nose centimeters from my ear. "Those windows are pretty visible from Main Street for another one of your propositions, Kels." His tongue flicks out, briefly touching my earlobe. "But I'm game if you are."

I squeeze my eyes shut, forcing the image out of my mind. "Not that kind of proposition," I say as I pull back and focus on his face. "Though good to know you're game."

A light chuckle rumbles in his chest, and he reaches out to grab my hand.

"What's your proposition, love?"

My heart does one of those hand-on-the-head, exaggerated faints at the casual way he's started dropping his love for me into every conversation.

"I am going to expand KH to include personal security," I say, my fingers finding a strand of hair at the back of my neck and starting to twirl it.

"That's great. Now's the time to do it for sure!" His eyes brighten like he's figured something out. "Oh! Yeah, I can get you contact information for the guys who were with Mitchell. Of course you should pick them up. It'd help you and them."

Carter *would* assume I'm asking him for the phone numbers of his former employees.

Shaking my head, I say, "That's not my proposition either."

"Oh. Well, regardless of what happened with Trent, our team was solid. You really should reach out to them and see who you can bring over."

"I was thinking *you* could reach out," I say.

"Me?" He thinks about it. "Sure. I could do that. A few of them have asked me if I know of anyone hiring."

I purse my lips to keep from laughing. "What if you understood what I'm offering, Carter?"

"What if you said what you're offering, Kelsey?"

"I'm offering you the position of head of the personal security division of KH Security."

"You're...what? I don't know if that's a...you've already done so—"

I cut him off. "I'm not offering this to you because we're dating. Even if you'd still been with Trent, I would've tried to poach you after seeing how invaluable you were during the tour."

"You're sure you're not just offering it to me because you know I need a job?"

"I'm offering it to you at a ridiculously low salary because I know you need a job," I say with a wink, hoping he knows I'm teasing. I had Lila put together a very competitive offer.

"Then yes," he says, scooping me up in his arms and pressing a kiss to my lips.

"You should really look at the offer and take some time to think it over. It's not an ownership position," I say, wanting to make sure I'm clear. "You'll just be a department head."

Carter looks at me, his arms still tight around my waist. "I don't need my name next to yours on the wall of the office. As long as it's my last name you're using in the future, that's all that matters to me."

I scrunch up my nose. "I'm not planning on changing my last name."

His laughter shakes us both. "Of course. As long as you promise your name will be next to mine on the marriage certificate someday, I'll take it." He kisses me, long and hard. "Plus, Mitchell is a shit last name anyway. Maybe I'll just take your last name. We can become the Harpers."

"It's a deal," I say, extending my hand.

Carter searches Lila's desk and finally comes up with a pen and the back of an envelope. "I'll plan to start next week once I get things wrapped up with Mitchell Security. I'll also make sure I let our top guys know they have a spot here. How many CPOs do you think we'll need? I know it's hard to estimate, since we're just starting and don't have any jobs."

"About that..." I say.

Dark, round eyes meet mine. "You already have a client? How?"

"I told Jaxon I was going to hire you, and he gave us the contract on the spot."

His eyebrows almost reach the dark hair hanging over his forehead. "He did? After we let him get his hair cut by his stalker?"

"Well, we got there before any real damage was done, didn't we?"

"I mean, after we flew his stalker out to his concert."

"Hey, I was in no way involved with Mitchell Security. Don't put that on me."

"I can't believe Jaxon would trust us—okay, me—like that," he says, using his palm to shove the strand of hair back. "I figured we'd have no chance of getting his contract, and you got it on the first try. Damn, you've got a way with people."

I cross my arms, fighting the grin threatening to take over my face. "What can I say? I'm persuasive. Plus, it helps when he's secretly in love with love. And with my sister."

"I think that last part might still be a secret to him," Carter says.

An image of Izzy's face as she watched Jaxon prepare for the concert flashes through my mind. "Somehow, I think the only people it's a secret for are Jaxon and Izzy."

Carter picks up the envelope again, jotting down a few quick notes. "I'll start reaching out to the guys from the tour who might want to pick back up with Jaxon now that he's at home. We can have two shifts of two men on a rotating four-days-on, four-days-off schedule, and then we'll add more if Jaxon has any events." Carter pauses, considering. "Can I use Lila to help me coordinate with his team?"

I nod in agreement, making a mental note to tell Lila.

Carter leans back in his chair, his fingers tapping against the back of the envelope. "All right. I'm in. This is going to be...amazing."

A laugh tumbles out of me, wild and free, as I take in the joy on his face.

We both stand at the same time, the weight of what's ahead settling in, but with the realization that this—whatever comes next—is exactly where we're meant to be.

Chapter Forty-Three
Epilogue

Carter

"Who would've thought, of all of us, Carter and Kelsey would be the first getting married," JT says, sipping a glass of whiskey while we wait for the wedding coordinator to tell us it's time to take our places.

JT and Jameson are both here, as well as Kelsey's dad, Ken, and two of my Army buddies who flew in for the long weekend. We're all dressed in our black suits, and we've been instructed to wait. So we're doing that—talking, laughing, and drinking the finest whiskey two pro golfers could find.

The air in the room feels light, almost electric, with the nervous excitement that can only come before a wedding. I glance around at the guys, each of us fidgeting in our own way. Ken is smoothing down his tie for the fourth time, and Jameson is stretching his neck like he's about to go to war. JT, of course, is already on his second glass of whiskey, taking it like he's preparing for some kind of emotional speech...which he might be.

We're in the groom's room in the back corner of a big red barn a few miles outside of Wild Bluffs. Calling it a wedding venue would be a bit insulting to places that host weddings every weekend, but it's beautiful and rustic and was available at a month's notice.

"It'd be romantic if they weren't so practical about their shotgun wedding," Jameson says.

I breathe in, stifling my eye roll. "It's not a shotgun wedding. She isn't pregnant."

"So you both keep saying," JT jokes.

I feel the weight of the words hanging in the air for a moment, the tone playful but edged with something deeper—something real. It's been a whirlwind these last few months between moving in together and building out the personal security side of the business. Fast, yes. But it feels like everything is finally clicking into place.

Deciding to get married four months after we started dating wasn't a decision Kelsey or I took lightly, but when my mom's memory reached the place a month ago that I decided I needed to bring in someone to stay with her during the day, I just kept thinking that she might not remember my wedding.

That night, when we were lying next to each other in bed, I told Kelsey about it. Her response? "Let's get married, then."

I shrug, turning toward JT. "I know it's fast, but it was important to me that my mom still be my mom at my wedding. She's the only family I have."

"Don't let these assholes make you feel bad," Ken says. "When you know, you know. Waiting months or years to figure it out doesn't mean you're any more likely to be happy together. It just means you've wasted more of your life not being with the woman you love."

JT and Jameson share a look, and if I didn't know any better, I'd guess Ken just won the local jewelry store a few new customers.

"Plus," Ken continues, "Kelsey's always known her mind. When she decided to share her home and her business with you, it was essentially the same thing as her proposing—she's been in it this whole time."

"So have I," I say. Kelsey is the other half of my soul, the one I come back to again and again, no matter how long we're apart—she's my puffin. My mind may not have known it when we were in high school, but it turns out my heart sure as hell did.

"Did you know before the speeches that a baby puffin is called a puffling, Puff?" Wes, my buddy from my time in the Rangers, asks. "I almost shot my beer out my nose when Izzy included that in her speech yesterday. I sent it out in the WhatsApp group, and all the guys got a kick out of it."

Damn Izzy and her fun facts. It's a fucking adorable name for a baby animal, and now all I want to do is have a puffling of my own. Something I've never cared about before.

Ken winks at me. "There's plenty of time before you start popping out pufflings. Though—"

Before Ken can finish his thought, the door swings open, and the wedding coordinator pokes her head in, looking at us with a knowing smile. "Gentlemen, it's time."

We all stand at once, and for a brief moment, I feel a weight settle in my chest. It's a good weight. It's the kind that comes with finally stepping into a life you're meant to have. The nervous tension is gone, replaced by a calm certainty that this moment is exactly where I'm supposed to be.

I glance at my reflection in the mirror, adjusting my dark blue-and-green tie before walking out to the ceremony area.

It's beautiful in a rustic way, with tall cottonwood trees and a slight green tinge to the light-brown grass. The seats are old church pews that the guys and I moved outside this morning. They were way heavier than anticipated, so I counted it as my workout for the day. At the front is a simple metal arch with twigs and early spring flowers wrapped around the side. It's understated yet beautiful, simple yet bold—just like Kelsey.

My mom is waiting for me outside the door for me to escort her to her seat.

"Ready?" she asks, giving me a knowing look.

I nod, my hands steady. "I think I might've been waiting for this moment since high school. I'm just annoyed it took me so long to figure it out."

I walk my mom to her seat next to Bill and Mildred and then step in front of Wes at the head of the line of groomsmen.

The music starts, and Lila exits the barn, smiling in a dress of darkest green, followed by Kelsey's friend Sam in a dark green suit. Izzy and Bryn come out together, Kelsey unwilling to pick either one of them to be her maid of honor. She said it was because she didn't want to spend the rest of her life listening to the other one bitch about it, but I know it's because she couldn't possibly choose between her two favorite people in the world.

Finally, the music changes, and everyone stands as the door to the barn opens again, Kelsey stepping out in a chic white jumpsuit. The deep V-neckline draws my eyes down her strong silhouette, past the delicate lace that covers her stomach and hips before hitting the wide-leg pants that flow gracefully to the floor. Her hair is a riot of soft waves floating behind her. She looks perfect—elegant and modern and just so her. I know she was a bit nervous when she decided against the traditional wedding dress her mom so badly wanted her to wear, but I can't imagine a more perfect picture than the one in front of me.

Her steps are slow, purposeful, like she's savoring every moment of this walk, this declaration of love.

As she and her dad make their way toward me, her blue eyes brighter today in the warm sunshine of eastern Colorado, I know I'm exactly where I'm supposed to be.

When I came back to Wild Bluffs to care for my mom, I felt caged in by the dreams I was putting aside and leaving behind. But fate had other plans—it turns out, coming home set me *free* to live my wildest dreams.

Bonus: Want a sneak peek into Kelsey and Carter's HEA? Use the QR code below or this link to download their bonus scene!

***

Ready to return to Wild Bluffs?

Don't miss Izzy's story coming Fall of 2025!

And keep reading for an excerpt from Bryn and Jameson's story,
Forever Wild!

Follow me on Instagram @authoremmakate or join my newsletter at www.authoremmakate.com to stay up to date on all the latest Wild Bluffs news!

***

Thank you for reading *Wild and Free*. Carter and Kelsey's story means the world to me, and I hope it gave you a few laughs, some swoony moments, and a happily ever after you love.

Awkward author ask: If you enjoyed this book, it would mean SO MUCH if you left a review. Reviews are like gold in the book world—they help readers find my books, and they honestly make my day (okay, week). Whether it's a couple of lines or a heartfelt essay, your thoughts matter.

Hit up <u>Amazon</u> or <u>Goodreads</u> (or whatever platforms the cool kids are leaving reviews on these days) and let the world know what you thought!

Thank you for being here.

Happy Reading, EK

Acknowledgements

Unsurprisingly, Kelsey demanded her story be told. It wasn't a request, and she didn't stop glaring at me until I had the entire thing written. Carter found her pushiness a whole lot more endearing than I did.

As with all things Kelsey does, it didn't disappoint. I feel this book is my best yet. I love the story. I love Kelsey and Carter, and I love the side characters old and new.

I was terrified when I started writing and publishing the Wild Bluffs series that the people close to me would judge me—either silently or to my face—for choosing to write romance novels. I couldn't have been more wrong! I have some of the most supportive friends and community members. Thank you for your constant support of me and my books.

To Emily, Kelly, Claudette, and Judy—thank you for putting the sparkle on my stories. Through your genius, my tales become more than I ever thought possible. Thank you for caring about my books as if they're your own.

To C, A, and M—thank you for always being willing to read my stories when they're still in the messy middle. You give me the confidence to push through.

To my biggest fan (you know who you are)—thank you for always asking me how my book is coming along and for listening to me talk for hours about book marketing, design, or outlining. I love sharing my passion with you.

To my family—your support means everything. Thank you for being some of my biggest cheerleaders and for always being first in line when I release a new book.

To my kiddos—you're pretty awesome. Thanks for entertaining yourselves when I'm on a self-imposed deadline, for asking me awkward questions about the stories I write, and for always being a source of creativity and joy. I love you more than you could ever know. (Now stop drawing on my outlining whiteboard, you naughty pufflings.)

To my husband—I'd never have gotten here without you. You are my courage when I'm insecure, my voice of reason when I'm overwhelmed, and my source of inspiration when my creativity runs dry.

And finally, to you, the reader—books are just dead trees until someone decides to pick them up and experience the worlds within. Thank you for visiting Wild Bluffs.

See you back here for Izzy's story.

Also by Emma

Wild Bluffs

(Small Town Romance)

Forever Wild

Wildly Inappropriate

Wild and Free

About the Author

Emma Kate is an author of rom-coms and contemporary romances. She lives in a small Colorado town with her rancher husband, three kids, a dog, and a whole lot of cows. When she's not writing or reading, she can be found chasing after her kids, eating ice cream and cookies, or binge-watching sitcoms.

PREVIEW: FOREVER WILD

Keep reading for a sneak peek of Emma Kate's *Forever Wild*, available now!

Bryn

"Take any longer and our balls are going to turn blue," my sister Kelsey yells from the next tee box, where she and her friends are waiting for me. I heft the golf bag onto my shoulders, and the straps immediately dig into my skin. Relishing the warm sun on my face, I make my way over to the group. The course looks exactly the same as when I used to caddie here as a teen. Luckily, today I'm carrying my own bag rather than schlepping around someone else's.

Developed in an old cow pasture, Wild Bluffs Country Club was built on the sand dunes that surround Wild Bluffs, Colorado. With its golf holes enveloped by a natural grass rough, you have a hard time finding golf balls if your shot isn't straight down the fairway.

I spent many an hour searching for members' lost balls, working to get a better tip as a teen. Even at that age, I knew college wasn't going to pay for itself.

Today is different, though. We're here for the 32nd birthday party of my oldest sister, Kelsey. The music is blaring—spurred by our mutual friend Becca's recent breakup—and our group is the only one still out on the course. The rest of Kelsey's friends, along with a couple of groups of golfers who flew in for a weekend of fun, gave up after nine holes and headed to the bar for food and drinks.

"When you see my face, hope it gives you hell," I sing along under my breath, loving that Becca is fueling her angst with 2000s pop.

I adjust my stance and take a few practice swings before putting down my Titleist 4 golf ball on the tee. Closing my eyes, I inhale deeply and then launch the ball through the air. It soars but slices right into the rough between our hole and the one next to it.

I swear under my breath. The sun is too bright to follow the ball. It's definitely somewhere between the second or third yucca clump, right?

Why did I let Kels talk me into a bottle of wine each last night? It wasn't even her birthday yet.

Making my way through the sandhills, I search for my ball with my 7-iron, hoping to get out of the weeds before finding any rattlesnakes. Spotting a Titleist approximately where mine landed, I quickly hit it back into the fairway where the other girls had all managed to find their tee-shots.

As I follow its trajectory, I suddenly hear the thud of a bag being set down and somehow know it wasn't my ball that just flew off.

Oops.

Turning around, I see a dark-haired man standing there, looking in disbelief at the ground. I slowly approach him and see my Titleist 4 golf ball lying next to his feet, complete with the small penis Izzy drew on it this morning.

"So you know how to mark a ball, you just don't know how to *use* the mark to identify your ball?"

Looking into his face, I can't help but cringe a bit at the bitterness in his voice, despite being pleasantly surprised by the fact that I am actually looking up at a man for a change, a rarity at five feet, ten inches.

"Oh. Shoot. I'm playing a Titleist 4 too, and I wasn't paying enough attention, I guess. Yours was right over there." Recognizing how ridiculous I look pointing at the spot he had clearly just seen me hitting from, I quickly lower my arm and glance at his face again.

In addition to being tall, this man is all kinds of eye candy. He clearly hits the gym on a regular basis, if how tight his white, collared shirt is pulling across his chest is any indication. His dark brown hair matches a thick beard.

Don't I know him from somewhere? I'm usually pretty good at matching faces with names, and there is something about his dark green eyes that seems familiar. Maybe the facial hair is throwing me off.

Would it be inappropriate to ask if he has a beard all the time?

He crosses his arms, the movement drawing my attention to his defined biceps. "Sure, well, a lot of good that does me. It's still a stroke. Maybe pay more attention next time you and your sorority sisters decide to use Daddy's golf membership, okay?"

Definitely an inappropriate time to ask about the beard, then.

"Excuse me?" I feel my eyebrows shoot up under my baseball cap. "First, you've got to be joking about it being a stroke. You are out here"—I look around—"alone? You get to decide what number you write on your scorecard. Second, fuck you. This is my sister's membership, you arrogant prick."

I turn to point at Izzy, an almost six-foot-tall brunette decked out in Wild Bluffs Country Club attire, nicely proving my point.

The fact that she decided to curtsy with her hot-pink golf skort after her shot does not help my case, but, in her defense, it was a pretty damn good shot.

He pulls his baseball cap off and runs his hand through his hair, a gesture I find irritatingly handsome. "Ahh, yes. A real credit to the sport of golf, that one."

"Again, fuck you. Just play my ball. It will be easy for everyone to identify as yours."

Arms crossed warily across his chest, he shoots me a confused look.

"...because you're such a dick?"

Continuing to search his face to figure out who this man is, I'm surprised when I see an almost smile pulling at the corner of his mouth.

"Original. I've never been called a dick before."

Despite his gruff attitude, I feel a pull to keep talking to this man. Okay, yes. By *pull*, I mean a purely physical attraction that is entirely due to his large frame and handsome smile now on display.

"Well, welcome to Wild Bluffs. Home of the honest."

"Wow. What a tagline. I'm surprised they've managed to keep its existence a secret from the world for as long as they have."

I laugh, my annoyance morphing into something else. He's got a sense of humor and can at least keep up with me in a verbal sparring session.

"Oh, the town hired the same PR team that helps keep Atlantis's location a mystery. It's a bit pricey but clearly worth every penny."

He chuckles, leaning casually on his golf club while we banter back and forth.

"Do you think they'd let me in on the secret?"

"Not a chance. It's not for the likes of you."

"Oh really? And just how is that decided?" he asks.

"Multiple rounds of interviews, an IQ test, and an intense psychological evaluation. Unfortunately, I don't think you're going to make the cut," I tease.

"How will I ever recover?"

"I'd suggest therapy, which you can clearly pay for if you're a member here, but I'm not sure it will help. If you can't pass the test, you can't pass the test."

"Of course you'd go there. Whatever." His face changes abruptly, his eyebrows pulling together into a deep crease. He swings his bag onto his shoulders, making me realize again how tall he is. I watch him stomp away, leaving me and my penis ball behind to recover from that emotional roller coaster of a conversation.

***

The back nine flies by in a flurry of stories and laughter. By the time we reach the eighteenth hole, the sun is starting to set, staining the sky with its own watercolor painting of pink and purple.

Becca leads us back toward the clubhouse, talking excitedly about her new plan to stay single for a while.

"Taking a couple months off from the dating scene will allow me to find my sshpecial sshomeone," she slurs slightly at the end, clearly in need of some hydration and likely some food to soak up the booze from today. "You agree, don't you, Bryn? It's working for you, right?"

Before I can answer, Kelsey grins over at us, clearly ready for some mind ninjaing, a side effect of her days with the Marines and now at her cybersecurity firm.

"I don't know if three years can actually be considered 'a couple months,' Becca."

Becca looks at me, her warm green eyes widening at the revelation.

"You haven't had sex in YEARS?" she practically yells.

I grab her elbow as she loses her footing and her bag starts to tip her backward.

"Jesus, Becca, could you say it a little louder? I don't think all the old men in the locker room heard you," I angrily whisper back.

"One"—Becca holds up her finger—"you know most of those men are not that old and would totally be doable at this point. You're twenty-eight. Also, three years is a long, long time to go without...ya know...*companionship*."

I sigh deeply, hoping she'll get distracted if I just stay silent.

"Bryn." She grabs my face so I have to look at her.

I spot Izzy and Kelsey over her right shoulder, waving to the rest of the birthday party already encircling the firepit but clearly planning to stay and enjoy the show.

Just great. The last thing I want is for my sisters to start thinking they need to meddle in my love life. Like I don't get enough of that from my mom, and apparently now Becca.

"Peter was a dick," she continues at a more reasonable volume. "It wasn't fair that he put all the blame on you when you guys broke it off. Relationships are two-sided. He expected a lot from you he wasn't willing to give in return."

Goodness, I'm tearing up a little bit, which I most definitely do not want to do.

Unluckily for me, Becca isn't done. "It's not a good enough reason to go without S. E. X. for"—she drops her voice to a whisper—"three whole years."

"I promise it has nothing to do with asshole Peter. Have you met the men who are on dating apps these days? None of them have been worth a second date, let alone actually sleeping with. Plus, there is no need to worry, Beccs. I can take care of myself, if you know what I mean?" I say with a wink, hoping I can get out of sharing that it has been a hell of a lot longer than three years—twenty-eight, to be exact.

True to Becca form, she turns bright red and starts giggling. She's been this way forever. She so badly does not want to be a prude, but she most definitely is, at least at heart.

Not that I have a leg to stand on, of course.

Becca turns and starts toward the fire, muttering something about needing some damn s'mores in her life if she isn't going to be getting any action, and I can't help but roll my eyes.

My sister Izzy hangs back, the only one who knows about my un-popped cherry. "You could tell them, you know. I don't think they'd make you being a twenty-eight-year-old virgin into as big of a deal as you seem to think they would."

"But they would make it into *a* deal. Which is the exact opposite of what I want. You know I don't care about being a virgin. If I did, I wouldn't be one. It just hasn't happened. And it's not like I'm lying to them."

Izzy gives my shoulder a squeeze, prompting me to continue before she offers me sympathy I most certainly do not want. "They've literally never asked me if I've had sex with someone. Plus, all the men I've gone out with in the last three years have been complete skeazeballs. I wouldn't have slept with them even if it weren't my first time."

"While it was pretty obvious from the fact that you were best friends with all the guys in high school that you were a virgin then, we all assumed you and Peter had sex. You dated for *three years* and never once complained that *he* was the one holding out."

"Meh. The effort of fighting him on a decree from his mother did not seem to be worth the reward."

She grimaces. "It's like he gets worse every time I hear about him."

"You know, he wasn't a bad guy. He was actually a good boyfriend the majority of the time. He just had mommy issues."

"And, apparently, performance issues."

"I want to deny it, but in hindsight, it does feel like there could've been a bit more spark."

"A lot more spark, Sis. A lot more spark," Izzy says as we make our way after our friends.

***

Jameson

After I finish the back nine, I head to the weight room for my second workout of the day.

Yes, I may have gained a few too many pounds in the last year. Yes, it may have been equally due to stress eating chocolate chip cookies and sad beer drinking.

After a month of two-a-days in the gym and walking at least thirty-six holes a day, I'm finally back in shape. Okay, fine, it probably doesn't hurt that I've also cut back to a few beers a week rather than the few beers an hour I was consuming before.

But it's mostly the extra workouts.

I finish the final set of my core round, wishing I were back home in my gym with extra fans and air-conditioning rather than sweating my ass off in this little one the course keeps open for nonlocals like me who stay the night in their guesthouses and hotel rooms.

As I start the short trip back to my hotel room in the building just next to the putting green, I notice a group of women sitting around the fire. They're cute, but as one catches my eye, I quickly turn my face away, hoping she doesn't recognize me.

The girl from this afternoon wasn't with them. Maybe she went home? Why do I feel a little sad about that? I mentally shake my head. I've learned my lesson about getting involved with women like her.

After closing the door to my room behind me, I lie down on my bed, letting the air-conditioning cool my sweat. The extra endorphins from my workout didn't even last all two minutes of my walk back, and the scorecard sitting on my desk sapped what little joy remained in me as I walked in.

I bury my face in my pillow and let out a deep sigh.

Ugh. I suck at golf.

My phone rings, and I barely register it's Erica, the head of the public relations team handling my downhill spiral, before I answer it.

"Hi, Erica."

"Just calling to check in on my favorite golfer."

"I can't possibly be your favorite golfer, Erica. Tell me what's really up."

"I just wanted to let you know that my team has been in contact with all your current sponsors, and things are starting to settle down now that you're out of the spotlight. I think we're going to be able to keep them all."

Thank God. While I wouldn't be hard up for cash or anything like that if I lost those deals, I'm not sure my ego can handle any more losses this year. I've always been the go-to golfer for sponsorship deals and ad campaigns, and the fact that I've lost that status hurts far more than I ever expected it to.

"Thanks, Erica. That's great news. Any news of the couple of new ones you were chasing?"

"Nothing yet, Jameo," she says, underemphasizing the "O" in my nickname so it comes out as "Jame-ah" instead of "Jame-oh," like it does for everyone else. "Just focus on your game. Don't get drunk. Don't hit on random women. You know what? Let's just say no women whatsoever."

"Of course. I haven't done anything but golf and exercise since I got here."

"That's what I like to hear."

We make small talk for another minute before Erica has to go. As I hang up my phone, I think about how stupid I've been the last year. Sure, I was hurting, but I made some bad decisions that almost cost me the profession I love and a lot of money in winnings and sponsorships.

But I'm totally focused now. I've barely looked at a woman since arriving at Wild Bluffs until today, and she only serves to remind me what terrible taste I have in women.

With that thought, I roll off the side of the bed and make my way slowly toward the shower, legs burning from the extra eighteen I got in today after the first two rounds ended poorly.

The water pounds down on me like a hundred tiny punches but doesn't put a dent in the feeling of defeat that has settled into my bones. I stand in the shower, my six-foot-four frame slumped as I let the hot water run over me, trying to wash away the disappointment of failing to score more than five under par yet again during my third round.

The round started out fine. And then it had been rough—the trudging through cacti and yuccas to find my balls in the, well, *rough*. That is the essence of golf: the more time you spend in the rough, the rougher the round becomes.

And the hot-as-hell girl who stole my ball and called me a dick before casually mentioning I'm rich? Why is it that women can't help but focus on my money?

Been there, done that. It is the one mistake I'm not interested in making again.

As soon as a woman mentions me being rich, I'm out.

Not that my dick seems to remember the last part.

"Damn it, Jameo," I mutter to myself as I lean against the tiled wall. "Get your head in the game." But the image of her smirking at me from under the brim of her cap refuses to leave. If it weren't for my self-imposed celibacy and her clear interest in me being "rich," she'd be my usual kryptonite, all tanned legs and a fiery mouth.

Just what I need to screw up my already precarious career.

Unfortunately, my brain and my anatomy down south don't seem to agree on what our focus is in Wild Bluffs.

Knowing my head is unlikely to win this battle, I let my mind wander back to the girl from this afternoon. Down her long legs and back up to her adorable smirk, my hand and thoughts wandering into carnal territory. I'm just about to give in to the urge—it's been a hot second since that specific club of mine has gotten any play—when the sound of an incoming text pierces the steamy air.

That, of course, will be Lila, my younger sister and—jeez, I'm lame—my best friend. Unfortunately, and unbeknown to her, she has always had a disturbing habit of interrupting my most private moments. And getting a text while thinking about getting myself off in the shower is actually very low on the list of embarrassing moments she's intruded on.

In high school, as I was losing my virginity, I heard my sister's pipsqueak friends *giggling* about Lila playing seven minutes in Heaven...as I was about to come inside a girl for the first time.

Needless to say, it was not my best showing, and no one had a happy ending, least of all Bryan Godsey, the sixteen-year-old I found behind a tree with my thirteen-year-old sister. He was so scared, he may have left with a bit of pee running down his leg. He should feel lucky it was me rather than my dad who heard her friends.

It wasn't until college that I met Sarah, who fortunately hadn't heard the story of me leaving my date unsatisfied in a field. Unfortunately, Lila called halfway through, and my phone played the "Cheetah Girls, Cheetah Sisters" song she had picked out as her ringtone until I finally found the Decline button through my horny haze. Luckily, Sarah was willing to try again after I figured out how to silence my phone.

I have, thankfully, gotten better since then, although my sister's bad timing remains the same.

Knowing the moment is gone—shit, how pathetic am I that I can't even romance myself these days?—I sigh and turn off the water.

I grab one of the white, fluffy towels from the rack, sling it around my waist, and sit on the edge of my room's extra bed.

Lila

> **Hey, Jameo, how's the golf thing going?**

I can't help but smile at her nonchalant way of referring to my career.

Me

> Could be better.

> How's grad school treating you? Need more cash for textbooks or late-night pizza?

Lila

> **Haha. I asked for pizza ONE TIME. And I was drunk and very hungry, in my defense.**

> **Plus, you've paid for enough. I told you my internship should be enough to cover tuition this semester.**

My heart tightens at the memory of the first time she had to ask me for help with her tuition and how embarrassed she had been. If I hadn't been such a self-centered ass, I would've known the small college fund our parents had saved wouldn't be enough to cover all four years of an engineering degree plus a master's degree. Especially with no sports scholarship like I had.

Me

I'm happy to help you. You get paid shit at your internship, and you should be having fun.

Lila

Like you're having fun right now? When was the last time you saw any of your friends?

Me

You know being seen with me right now is a black mark on someone's image, right?

Lila

That's what private clubs are for. I thought that's why you were out in the middle of nowhere at the only fancy golf course on the planet where you might accidentally step in cow shit.

Plus, JT reached out to me. You've ignored all his texts and calls. FOR A MONTH.

Me

How did he get your number? I swear to God, if he was hitting on you, I'll shove my driver so far up his ass, it tees up his eyes.

I'm actually very certain Lila and JT haven't been talking about anything other than how pathetic I am. They actively hate each other with a passion so strong, I can rarely be in the same area as both my favorite people at once. My parents set up two tables at Thanksgiving, supposedly because there are so many of us, but really so JT can come without having to fight with Lila the entire time. Still, it's nice to remind her every once in a while that she's too good for every man ever.

Lila

> Super gross, oddly specific visual, bud. Plus, who I text is not your concern.

> You avoiding the world for the last month, on the other hand, is my concern. I know you haven't seen your BEST friend. Have you talked to anyone?

Me

> I would gladly endure the required brain bleach to even know you'd had a one-night stand at this point.

I sigh, running a hand through my wet hair.

Me

> I talked to a hot girl just this afternoon, in fact.

Not *not* true.

Lila

Ooh. Tell me everything.

Actually, on second thought, don't. Go find her. Kiss her. Hold her hand. TALK TO HER. And then never tell me what happens.

Me

Lila

UGH. You are so infuriating. You need a rebound. It has been a year since you broke up with she-who-will-not-be-named. YOU NEED TO GET LAID. I have it on good authority it has been A YEAR. That's too long for anyone, including yours truly.

Me

Jesus, Lila, TMI.

Lila may be twenty-four and completing her master's in engineering next spring, but I do not need to think about her getting laid. And as much as I want to deny it, I also know she's right. It has been a long time since I've felt any interest in anyone—until that infuriating girl today.

Fuck. No, not the girl today. That zing I felt in my chest was pure anger at her comment, nothing else. No sparks.

Me

And just who is this "good authority"?? Stop talking to JT!

"All right, Sis," I say out loud, grabbing my keys and wallet. "You win. I'll go to the bar tonight and see what happens."

Let's just hope the woman from today isn't there. I'm not sure how long my body will let me stay away from her, even knowing she is just after my money.

***

Keep reading *Forever Wild* to find out what happens next!
Find it on Amazon now!

www.ingramcontent.com/pod-product-compliance
Lightning Source LLC
Chambersburg PA
CBHW070310310726
48976CB00005B/1655